THE

COLD
ONE

Also by Christopher Pike

The Listeners
Sati
The Season of Passage

THE

COLD
ONE

CHRISTOPHER PIKE

TOR

A TOM DOHERTY ASSOCIATES BOOK
NEW YORK

THE COLD ONE

Copyright © 1995 by Christopher Pike

This book is printed on acid-free paper.

A Tor Book
Published by Tom Doherty Associates, Inc.
175 Fifth Avenue
New York, N.Y. 10010

Tor ® is a registered trademark of Tom Doherty Associates, Inc.

Library of Congress Cataloging-in-Publication Data

Pike, Christopher
    The cold one / Christopher Pike.
        p.   cm.
    ISBN 0-312-85117-0
    I. Title.
    PS3566.I486C65   1995
    813'.54—dc20   94-37835
                                                            CIP

First edition: January 1995

Printed in the United States of America

0 9 8 7 6 5 4 3 2 1

For Tom Doherty

 THE

COLD
ONE

PROLOGUE I

❋

THERE ARE LOGICAL REASONS. There are strange coincidences. When the power failed at Kabriel Clinic in southeast Iowa during a thunderstorm, and the backup generators also failed, Penny Hampton didn't know if God was playing a joke on her or if she was simply unlucky. Not until later did she think of a third possible reason. When the crazy man with the knife came to visit.

But that was not until much later.

Penny was a thirty-year-old physical therapist with great hands. Kabriel Clinic was an intensive care facility with forty beds. Penny had worked part time at Kabriel for two years with mixed feelings. The money was OK, she received ten bucks for each patient she stretched and massaged. Since she could do three an hour, she was happy with the thirty bucks. Also, the brain-dead patients never complained. But Penny was outgoing by nature and liked to babble as she worked, and it was no fun talking to people who never answered, except to drool now and then. Even the regular nursing staff at Kabriel spoke only in whispers, as if they were caretakers of a graveyard. And in one sense Kabriel was like one huge tomb—none of the patients who checked in ever checked out. In fact, every one of them had been checked in by someone else. Sometimes Penny liked to imagine that late at night, when no one was watching, the comatose patients rose from their beds, donned Halloween masks, and did a long, slow dance to the rhythm of the wind blowing outside.

Yeah, Penny liked the money but the place had her spooked.

And nothing bothered her as much as Patient 111. First, the

woman didn't have a name tag above her bed as the others did. She was just lll — if she had been 666 Penny wouldn't even have touched her. Penny supposed she could have had one of the nurses check the files for her name, but she had never felt the inclination strongly enough. Also, lll was old and emaciated; a mummy with a dreary green hospital gown for bandages. There was so little flesh left on her that when Penny stretched her limbs, she feared one of them would break like a stick in her hands. It would just snap off with a dry brittle sound, and Penny would be left holding it and thinking, Oh shit. She wasn't sure how long lll had been at the clinic. When she'd asked the head nurse, Sylvia Thompson, Sylvia had only told her that lll had been there when she arrived at Kabriel eighteen years earlier. A long time to have a plastic tube rammed up your nose. Penny just wished someone would pull the plug on the woman. Every time she worked on lll she thought about it.

Then the big thunderstorm came late in the evening on the last day of April and nature itself pulled out the plugs. It was one of those storms people love to see roll in when there's nothing else to talk about. Clouds huge and black as evil mountains, lightning flashes bright as phaser fire. The rain came down as if it hadn't seen the ads for water-saver nozzles. Penny had a bitch of a time getting to the job. Then, after she had dried off sufficiently and rolled up her sleeves to work, Sylvia handed her a list of six patients to treat, and it included the infamous lll. Penny started to protest but thought better of it. She needed the job and the money. She didn't know anyone who wasn't hurting. Except maybe lll. She decided to do her first and get her out of the way.

The physical therapy treatment for a comatose patient was fairly routine. The primary goal was to stretch the major tendons and ligaments, which had a tendency to shorten during unending convalescence. Actually, in Penny's humble opinion, if any of the patients at Kabriel Clinic were to awaken miraculously, most of them would wish they hadn't bothered. Few would ever be able to walk or dress themselves, and certainly lll wouldn't have been able to get out of bed, even with a full-fledged brain transplant. Penny conscientiously stretched and massaged her patients, but she could have been working on Barbies and Kens for all the good she knew she was doing humanity.

She always started with the legs, but one end was as good as another. Working on lll's lower extremities, Penny tried not to glance at the old woman's face. Her legs were bad enough, knobby clubs with gray bristles. Penny quickly rubbed the bony sticks up and down to get the circulation going, then began to work the Achilles tendons. Few people realized the strength of that particular tendon and how much force it took to rupture it. But Penny barely leaned on Ill's toes to lengthen the tendons, worried that if the damn things did snap, the woman would suddenly sit up and vomit a bellyful of blood in her face. She feared that there was something very unsavory in the old woman, just waiting to wake up and make a mess of things.

Yet there was no logical reason for her fear.

Not one Penny could pinpoint, anyway.

She finished with the legs and moved to the arms, abdomen, and chest. To stretch a patient's spine, Penny would sit the person up and bend her forward as if she were a doll reaching for her toes. The move caused her to get a good whiff of whomever she was working on. Ill always smelled like spoiled milk, and that night was no exception. There was no explaining it because the woman never got milk through the nasogastric tubes that fed her miserable body. The smell reminded Penny of that of infants; in Ill's case, infants who had been left alone in their cribs for weeks.

Penny completed her therapy by manipulating the woman's neck. Turning Ill's head from side to side was like twisting the radiator fan on a rusty Mustang. Penny's worst concern about working Ill's neck was that one day she would be rotating the woman's head, slowly loosening the long tendons that ran into the skull from the shoulders, and suddenly be seized by an uncontrollable desire to break the woman's fucking neck. Just rip off her scrawny head, drop it to the floor, and kick it under the bed as if it were a punctured football. It was a thought she didn't share with anyone.

Yet, for all that, Penny believed that Ill had once been a beautiful woman. She could tell by her delicate bone structure, which was, in fact, all that was left on display, the bones, capped by a tangle of fine white hair that could have been stolen from a retired scarecrow. Penny didn't know the woman's eyes, their color, their size. They remained closed, and for that Penny was grateful. Never, never would she have reached over and raised the lids to peer under them. Not for ten dollars a treatment, anyway.

Penny was just finishing Ill's neck when the lights went out.

"Shit," she whispered, and immediately let go of Ill.

Kabriel Clinic was divided into four wings. Penny and Ill were in the south wing, which had ten beds—one long line of mechanical respirators and computerized EEG and EKG monitors. When the lights failed, Penny was alone in the wing with 111 and three other patients. Although fully half the patients at Kabriel could not breathe on their own, that night by chance 111 was the only patient in the south wing who had a plastic tube rammed up her nose. The steady hiss of the mechanical respirators was an unpleasant sound Penny associated with working at the clinic. But when that hiss shut off with the lights, she knew panic. Particularly as time went by and the backup generator didn't kick in, as it should have according to state regulations, and the nurses began to shout anxiously to one another in the halls. Penny couldn't hear every word that was being said, but the meaning was clear.

They, the staff nurses, and she, the part-time help, had to start breathing for the patients on mechanical respirators or many of the well-preserved vegetables were—in five minutes or less—going to turn into applesauce. For an instant Penny thought, That wouldn't be so bad.

She thought it for maybe one whole minute.

Finally, though, she realized exactly what she was being called to do. It was her worst nightmare. She was supposed to take a deep breath, lean over, and press her lips to the *thing* while exhaling slowly. The woman was only a thing as far as Penny was concerned, and Penny was not really heartless. From her perspective 111 was brain dead, and that meant she had no mind. Finished, end of discussion, no moral issue at stake. Why should she mess her lipstick and risk catching a disease to preserve a foul-breathed mannequin? No, she thought, she wasn't going to do it. She didn't want to do it. She had to go out with her boyfriend later that night, and if he smelled 111 on her he wouldn't hold her hand for a month, much less sleep with her that night. Bill was kind of a wuss when it came to cleanliness.

Yet all of Penny's thoughts were just thoughts. As she lowered her hands and felt under her trembling fingers 111's dry flesh and wavering pulse, she realized with a force stronger than simple reason that she could be directly responsible for a death. That she was, in a sense, ready to commit murder.

"Oh shit," Penny whispered.

Penny was trained in CPR. Every health professional in the state of Iowa had taken the class. The skill was simple, not something even someone as anxious as Penny was could forget. Yet it was a long way from remembering the basics of CPR to being an expert at it. The last person Penny had done CPR on had been George, in her initial class, and George had been the dummy.

Penny, however, did have one advantage with lll that she didn't have with George. lll's heart was still beating, she assumed. All she had to do was respirate lll until the power came back on. There was no need for rib-crushing maneuvers to massage her heart. Penny had broken George, trying to keep his plastic heart massaged.

Now that she was decided, Penny moved quickly. Leaning over, she opened the woman's mouth to check for obstructions. Finding none, she tilted the woman's head back, reached up with her right hand, and pinched lll's nose closed. In the dark Penny couldn't be sure if lll's lips were coated with gross substances, but she had to assume they were. With the back of her left forearm she wiped them off. Then, finally, taking a deep breath, she pressed her lips to lll's. The kiss of life for the brain-dead woman. She didn't taste like spoiled milk—more like a Kirby vacuum cleaner. Penny didn't so much exhale into the old woman's lungs as she felt the breath being sucked out of her own lungs. Penny filled lll's lungs once and then sat back up.

"Wow." She panted.

She took another deep breath and returned to her task. Once again she felt as if lll pulled the air out of her lungs rather than placidly accepting it like the living corpse she was. Penny's fear of the woman returned. As the seconds turned to minutes in the dark clinic, she felt a strange weariness overcome her, as if lll took not only her breath but something more subtle. Something inside her breath that reminded Penny of the soul she didn't believe anyone possessed. Yet she believed in lll's possession, in the something evil inside the woman. Penny struggled to keep lll alive even as she prayed for her to die.

Then the power returned, and with it the lights, the hiss of the respirator, reality.

Penny literally jumped back from lll. She spit out the taste in her mouth. The act should have shamed her, but it didn't. Once more the plastic tube started to fill lll's lungs. But the old woman still had Penny's last breath inside her. A last mouthful of life to exhale. As Penny's breath came out, lll's head rolled to the side and her eyes popped open to stare directly at Penny. They were blue, dark as the ocean during an eclipse, but to Penny they seemed black as a Halloween sky after all the children had gone home to bed.

A word flew out of the woman's mouth as she exhaled. One clear word followed by a second distorted sound. Perhaps a whispered sigh of pain. A sound of grief certainly.

"Child," the woman had said. Followed by the other sound, the word Penny preferred to believe, for a long time afterward, she hadn't heard.

The word that made her swear never to work on Ill again.

PROLOGUE II

THE VOICE HAD STOPPED.

The Cold One sat at the edge of the warm sea and watched as the bloated sun settled through a wide band of red clouds that resembled a fresh festering scar. The air was hot and dry, the rough sand beneath Its body moist. Yet for the first time in Its life the Cold One was not particularly aware of Its surroundings. The Voice had stopped, the words that made up Its worldly stream of being. Now there was nothing left for the Cold One except what It was. Yet that was the enigma, even to Itself. Still, it didn't bother the Cold One. Nothing ever had, and It doubted anything ever would.

Yet in the silent void there was cognition. It came in an instant, though it had probably always been there—Its purpose. The Cold One slowly stood. A crab crawled over Its bare foot, the right one. The Cold One stared down at the small creature, perhaps curious as to what it would do, perhaps not. The crab rose on its posterior legs and leaned toward the big toe with its claws. The Cold One felt a pinch, Its body did. Blood appeared on the toe. A wave came and the foam washed away the crab. The toe continued to bleed, a bit. The Cold One turned and walked toward the old road a mile inland. The sun beat down but the Cold One did not perspire.

It was far south. Here the roads were poorly tended, and travelers few. The Cold One had to stand by the side of the road a long time before a car appeared on the horizon. The Cold One had originally come in a car of Its own, but someone had stolen the vehicle while It sat on the shore of the sea. It had come to the sea, in this particular spot, because that was what the Voice had done. The Cold One had not felt commanded by the Voice—because It felt nothing—but had merely followed the Voice because that is what It had always done. But now that the Voice had stopped, the Cold One reasoned, It would follow the Voice no more.

The approaching car was expensive, sporty, the type middle-age men bought to feel younger. The Cold One registered the fact without judgment. It saw that the man behind the wheel was approximately forty-five, chubby, tan, with a wide mustache that made his mouth appear fat. His shirt was open in a sloppy way and the hair on his chest was much whiter than the growth over his lip. He was coming from the south, heading north—the direction It wished to go. The Cold One noted all this from a distance of half a mile. Since birth Its senses had been more acute than a human's.

The Cold One stuck out Its thumb to hitch a ride. Half a minute later the car came to a halt beside It. The car was a red convertible, coated gray with dust from the dry road. The driver perspired heavily, but smiled as he placed his arm on the top of the driver's door and checked It out. The Cold One smiled in return.

"You're a long way from nowhere," the man said.

"Yes," the Cold One answered. "I went for a stroll down to the water and some bastard stole my car while I was gone."

The man shook his head. "That's a bitch, but to be expected in these parts. I can give you a ride. Hop in."

The Cold One considered. The man had a reliable car that would probably take It as far north as It wished to go. But this man was no ordinary tourist. The Cold One smelled cocaine on his nose, his breath, a stash of it in his trunk. It was obvious the man intended to take the drug across the border and into California, which could cause problems for the Cold One if the man was apprehended. On the other hand, the Cold One thought, It could kill the man, bury his body and his drugs in the weeds, and take the car for Itself. It was very easy for the Cold One to kill. It was much stronger than humans, and It didn't mind killing, although It got no pleasure from the act either. The Cold One was not even sure what pleasure was.

"What's your final destination?" the Cold One asked.

"Los Angeles. Where are you heading?"

"Malibu."

"Do you want to alert the authorities here that your car's been stolen?"

The Cold One shrugged. "The authorities might have been the ones who stole it."

The man reached for a cigarette. "Ain't that the truth. Well, it's up to you. If you want a ride, I'll give you one. You'd be a fool to wait here for your car to reappear magically."

The Cold One considered further. It had another alternative. It could *change* the man. This act, this change—It had never done it to anyone before. But now that the Voice had stopped, it was time. The Cold One knew this fact without logic or reason or thought. The idea was just there like the crab on Its toe. The man would be Its first. It smiled again.

"That would be great," the Cold One said. It walked around to the other side of the car and climbed in. The man put the engine in gear. They rolled north, toward the States, driving with the roof down. The sun drifted closer to the horizon but the air continued to bake. The man smoked his cigarette and wiped the sweat off his fat mustache and glanced over at the Cold One.

"I'm burning up," the man said. "I wish the AC on this damn thing worked." He paused to study It closer. "How do you stay so cool?"

The Cold One leaned back and closed Its eyes. "It's the way I am."

Breathe
Softly

ONE

❖

P ETER JACOBS WAS dreaming when the phone rang and awakened him. He was one of those people who knew he must dream but rarely remembered any of them. But this dream would stay with him. Later he supposed it was because he came out of it so suddenly. Yet he also wondered if it was the nightmarish quality that caused the dream to linger. Certainly, at that point in his life, when he did return to the normal world, the madness started.

In the dream he was fishing with his best friend, a girl he didn't know in real life. They were on a wide lake surrounded by mountains. The evening sun was just setting behind one of the peaks, casting a red glow over the mirrorlike water. They were completely alone. In every direction, there was no sign of people or buildings. His friend sat in the bow of the large sailboat, her rod in her hand, her line in the lake, her blue jeans rolled up, and her legs lazily swinging back and forth over the gunwale. The girl was pretty, he realized that much, and he knew she was an old pal. But he wasn't sure of her name, and that bothered him.

So did the absence of wind. The main sail hung slack like a pretty dress without a woman's body to fill it out. They were going nowhere fast, and soon it would be dark. Yet the lake was serene and he was happy just to be with his friend.

"Any bites?" he asked. He didn't know how long he'd been standing, but from the stiffness in his legs it could have been hours. She glanced back and smiled. She wore a white sailor cap perched at the back of her head as if she were a child. Her sunglasses had black, wide frames, her hair was long and dark. She was about his age, thirty.

"One will bite in a minute," she said.

He chuckled. "You can feel it coming?"

Her grin was mischievous. "Of course. Always. Watch."

He watched for less than a minute when her line jerked a couple of times and ripples fanned out in the flat water. He hurried over and was by her side as she lifted the fish out of the water. It was a catfish, the barbels smoothed flat as if with styling mousse. It wasn't moving. She set it on the deck of the boat and removed the hook with a yank hard enough to make him jump. Assuming it was dead, he picked it up. Even though the fish was cold—as cold as if it had lain overnight in a chest of ice—it was alive. Its eyes were, at least, as they stared back at him and blinked. Blinked! He had never seen a fish blink; they couldn't, could they? The pupils were blank inside. He quickly dropped the blasted thing.

"What's the matter?" his friend asked.

"That thing's alive."

"I would hope so. Put it in the chest. We'll eat it later."

Suddenly he didn't feel serene. Besides the weird fish, the reflection of the evening sun on the water bothered his eyes. Not the glare, but the odd shade of red. He knew the boat was not sitting motionless in a huge pond of blood, but he had to remind himself of that fact. She threw her line back in the water.

"I'm not going to eat it," he muttered.

"Why not?"

He shook his head. "Because it keeps looking at me."

That amused her. "I'm looking at you."

"Yeah, but I don't plan on eating you."

She wrinkled her nose. "A pity." She reached out and placed a hand on his shirt over his belly. "Won't you?" she asked.

He smiled uneasily. "You keep fishing."

She let go of the rod, but it remained balanced on the railing. "I don't have to. They come to me automatically."

"Why?" He really wanted to get off the boat now. He didn't like this person who was supposed to be his best friend and whose name he couldn't remember. She moved her hand lower.

"Because I'm their mother." She paused. "Won't you?"

"Won't I what?" he asked, although he knew she had not changed the topic. She tugged on his zipper. He let her for a moment before pushing her hand away. But her fingers came right back to the task. "Stop that," he said.

"Won't you?" she asked.

"And stop asking me that."

She smiled again, then reached up and removed her sunglasses. Her eyes were not blue or green, but gray like the fish's, with blank, unfocused pupils. Slowly she blinked. He stood paralyzed by the horror of it all. She yanked his zipper down as she had torn the hook from the fish's mouth. Then she touched him, his bare flesh—so cold and slimy her fingers, like slippery scales that had just been taken from the ice. Yet he felt a fire begin to burn deep inside—in a place where he had stored up fuel for ages.

"Won't you?" she asked for the fourth time as she lowered her head.

Peter Jacobs did not wake screaming, even with the phone ringing in his ear, because he thought the phone was his alarm, and that was a reassuring sound. He was relieved to be conscious and far from the fishy woman. He coughed as he reached for the phone; he could almost smell her on him. He was mildly disgusted that he had an erection.

"Hello?" he said.

"Is this Mr. Peter Jacobs?"

"Should be, yeah."

"This is Chuck. I hope I didn't wake you. I know I should call you at your office, but I didn't want to talk to you there. I have a story for you, Mr. Jacobs, if you want to hear it, and I think you do."

Peter yawned. The voice was cool but hushed, an easygoing fellow who could be hiding in an attic. "Could I hear it after a shower and coffee?" Peter asked.

"I don't have much time and my story isn't long. Just relax. Imagine you're dreaming and that I'm the voice of your subconscious. I'm a normal guy. I don't lie unless I have to. I'm calling you of my own free will. I don't want any money for my story, I only want to be heard. Can you hear me, Mr. Jacobs?"

"I'm listening." He wondered how the guy got his home phone number. The paper wouldn't give it out anymore, he was sure, not after he'd yelled the last time. This was not his first call of this type. He wrote a column entitled "Wouldn't It Be Nice?" that chronicled high points in ordinary people's lives: someone winning the lottery; another person miraculously finding a lost love; etc. In the last year the column had gone into syndication. He was currently in fifty markets around the country. He was becoming something of a celebrity: Peter Jacobs, the happy-time reporter. Yet Chuck didn't sound all that happy.

"I stopped in a favorite bar of mine a couple weeks ago," Chuck said. "You know the Rosita on Hawthorne, not far from the water? It's a happening place. I go there to drink beer. I used to drink more than my fair share—that is, until I met her. Now I don't know if I'll drink again. My life's taken a whole new direction. She did that for me. She did a lot of things for me."

"What was her name?" Peter asked, bored. Getting-laid stories came to him daily. He was tired of hearing about them, particularly since he hadn't had sex in a long time, not since Lisa, Sad-Eyed Lisa. He noted that the erection from his dream had subsided.

"She didn't tell me her name," Chuck said. "I asked her but she said that was confidential. She smiled when she said that. She was a looker—better than anything I'd looked at in my life. I was surprised when she chose to sit by me. We had a few beers and talked—I did most of the talking. She was quiet, but her eyes were full of life. I couldn't stop staring at them. Even when I tried to look away, I couldn't. They were hungry eyes, and they made me hungry for her. But they made it hard for me to breathe, too—if you know what I mean."

"What *do* you mean?" Peter asked, wondering why he didn't hang up. Chuck's tone had changed slightly, becoming tense in the space of two sentences. But the next thing Chuck said made Peter tense.

"Lots of people are having trouble breathing these days. Look at that young girl, Cindy Trells. She must have had a hell of a time breathing after they finished doing what they did to her. I never seen anything like that before, have you, Mr. Jacobs?"

Peter sat up and pressed the Record button on his answering machine. Chuck had his undivided attention now. Two weeks ago twenty-year-old Cindy Trells had been found dead and mutilated in a big green trash can behind a supermarket. Peter remembered reading about the case. Cindy's throat had been ripped out, and Chuck didn't sound like your everyday normal guy.

"I never have," Peter said carefully. "Could you tell me what happened to her?"

"I'd love to, I really would. I could tell you a lot about that gal. She was a bleeder, not like some of the others. But that's not why I called—it's not important anyway. It's just one of those things that happens when things are changing too fast. Am I going too fast for you?"

"You're doing fine, Chuck," Peter said, trying to keep his voice calm. "Tell me more."

"Well, we had a few beers and then I asked her if she'd like to go back to my place. She said sure. She said the word like it would be her pleasure. I was thinking it would sure be my pleasure." Chuck fell silent.

"Then what happened?" Peter had to ask.

There was a long pause. "Then it happened. What can I say?"

"You had sex with her?"

"No."

Chuck's no sounded wounded. "If you didn't have sex with her, what did you do with her?" Peter asked.

Another long silence. Chuck was breathing loud now. "I'd never read about it before. But she told me I'd like it."

"Like what?"

Chuck coughed—no, it was more of a gag. But then he recovered. "I want to tell you, I really do. I want the whole world to know about it. I think they will, too, but not before you, Mr. Jacobs. You're going to be the first to know."

Chuck hung up. Peter stared at the receiver as if he had just been slapped by a fish. Then slowly he put it down. He wondered if Chuck liked fish. Cold and uncooked. The call had almost been an extension of his dream.

Peter forced himself out of bed, showered and shaved. He ran the water hot, even for him. In the kitchen he found his roommate, Matthew Bill, studying the Thomas Guide road atlas. He and Matt went way back, to their preteen years at Baker Home, an orphanage in Nebraska located on the edge of a cornfield so large they had both wondered why America couldn't feed every hungry person in the world. Peter noticed, as he put on his coffee, that Matt had the atlas upside down.

Matt was retarded—not terribly so, but on tests he scored two and a half standard deviations below the norm, which put his IQ at around sixty. He was capable of taking care of his basic needs: washing, dressing, shopping for essentials if he had to. He also had a paper route—

the same paper, the *L.A. Times*, that Peter worked for—and could drive a car. But his route had been causing him problems lately. Matt, with Peter's help, had carefully memorized every house the *Times* had given him when he started on the job. Matt had trouble with written addresses, but once he could associate a house with a specific visual cue—a colored fence, a cracked door, a particularly nasty dog—then he never forgot to throw a paper there. Lately, though, the paper had been running a special, three months for the price of one, to get new subscribers, and Matt had been receiving, on average, one new client a day, or one bewildering pink slip after another. It was a bit much for him, and Peter hadn't had time to do the route with him. Or else he'd been too lazy to do it. Matt got up at three in the morning to deliver his papers on time.

"You have the book upside down," Peter said to Matt, referring to the Thomas Guide. Peter reached for the bread. He usually had toast in the morning, with a hard-boiled egg, but he had been going easy on the eggs lately because he had done an article on a chicken farmer and the guy had showed him where those white jewels really come from. And here Peter had always thought the Easter Bunny brought them. He and Matt did have a few things in common. Matt turned the map book the other way.

"I know why I keep missing this street," Matt said. "It's spelled wrong."

"Who's spelling it wrong? The paper or the map makers?"

Matt looked up at him with his perpetual frown. "Both of them."

It was hard to find many people who thought foolish innocence attractive, but Peter liked to watch Matt as he would his own child. Never mind that Matt was six four, two hundred and twenty pounds of uncertain animation. His body had the strength and lack of coordination of a high school lineman on extra-strength steroids. He had a flat face; he'd run into a few things with it. But his teeth were straight and incredibly white—he brushed and flossed several times a day. His dark-brown hair was always combed, and his clothes were always clean and pressed. It was true, he looked slow and talked even slower, but he was never anything but friendly.

Before his success with his column, Peter had worked with mentally handicapped children, which he found satisfying—at least Monday through Wednesday. It had been the weight at the end of the week and that special fatigue that came from overtaxed patience that had driven him to look elsewhere for a paycheck. Peter believed one of the reasons he kept Matt close was his guilt about having left the other kids. But he had his own life to live, he thought as he sat beside Matt at the table.

"Give me the pink slip," he told Matt.

"They gave me two of them."

"Give me the one you're having trouble finding."

Puzzled, Matt withdrew both slips from his pocket. "I have both the papers here, Pete. I just can't find one of the houses."

Matt was the only person Peter let call him Pete. "I understand. Give me the paper that has the address on it of the house you can't find."

Matt studied both slips, then shoved one forward. "It's this one— Maple Street. There aren't no maples on my streets."

"Maple Street doesn't have to have maple trees on it to be called Maple Street. It's just a name." Peter studied the pink slip, then the road atlas. Matt was on the wrong page. Also, the new house was at the edge of Matt's route, an area Peter believed Matt didn't know. Holding the atlas out so that his friend could see, Peter traced the turns Matt would have to make to find the place. Matt tried to mimic him with his own thick index finger but ended up wrinkling and tearing the Thomas Guide. Peter closed the book. He had bought it for Matt the previous Christmas, but Matt had yet to find an address in it.

"Was this house supposed to get a paper this morning?" Peter asked.

Matt considered. "I was going to bring them a paper."

"Do you have any papers left over?"

"Yes. Six of them." Matt added shyly, "I sell them."

Peter was surprised. "You sell the extra papers? When? Where?"

"At the corner." He added proudly, "For half price. I have regular customers."

"Better not tell your boss."

"No."

"Give me one of the extras. I'll drop it off at the new house on the way to work. Maybe after work I can take you out and show you where it is."

Matt grinned. Patience had its rewards, Peter thought. The joy on Matt's face when he smiled always touched Peter. "We'll find it together, Peter, and I'll remember it always." He looked hopeful. "Maybe it will have a maple tree in front."

"It's possible," Peter said. "Anything is possible."

Matt went to take a nap. Peter finished his breakfast and removed the tape from his answering machine before going out the front door. He didn't plan to play it for anyone; he just thought he might want to hear it in the car. Again.

On the Santa Monica Freeway, though, Peter didn't think of Chuck, but of his morning nightmare and how it reminded him of Lisa Cantrell, his last love. Or was she his lost love? He had lost something special when Lisa had said good-bye, yet perhaps not something he hoped to find again in the future. He had cared for Lisa, but wasn't one to repeat a mistake. The pain she left him with made him feel he had done something wrong.

He had met Lisa at the Griffith Park Planetarium on a Sunday afternoon. He had started the day out in the park, but later decided to hike up to where the astronomy shows played. A program was about to start as he arrived, something about the origin of the planets. He bought a ticket and walked into the dark domed room and sat down. Lisa was sitting alone on his right; she caught his attention because she was loading film into her camera. With the low-level light, he couldn't see her well except to know that she was short with wavy dark hair. The show was to start in a minute.

"You can't take pictures," he said. "At least not with a flash."

She glanced over. "Will they kick me out?"

"Maybe. Using a flash in here is like using a flash on a movie screen. It'll wash out whatever they're showing."

She chuckled and put her camera aside. "Of course. I should have thought of that. You must think I'm an idiot."

Later he was to think it was nice he met her under the circumstances that he did because it was her voice, more than anything, that enchanted him. Although an American citizen from birth, she had grown up in Sweden and England. The combination of accents was intriguing, very sexy.

"Not at all," he said. "I once went scuba diving in Hawaii and bought one of those small disposable cameras to take pictures underwater."

"It wasn't waterproof?"

"It was, but I took it down to sixty feet, too much pressure. It exploded in my hands, scared all the fish away."

"Did it scare you?"

"Not as much as other things."

"Such as?" She had turned toward him. She sounded genuinely

curious so he decided to give her a genuine answer, although he was evasive by nature. His eyes were adjusting to the dim light and he could see her more clearly.

"Pretty women," he said.

It was a nice line to begin a relationship. The show started a moment later and they had a late lunch afterward, sitting on the grass overlooking smoggy L.A., eating hot dogs and feeding the birds. Lisa was finishing chiropractic school. She had entered the field because she had broken her back as a teenager and was nursed back to health by an eighty-year-old osteopath who lived next door to her in London. Lisa moved stiffly, but out in the sun she was cute: a vivacious brunette, with freckles and dimples, slight but nicely proportioned. He was interested, and she definitely seemed to like him.

In the beginning they did all the things couples do: dinners, movies, camping out. After three months she moved in with him and Matt, which made for an interesting combination. Lisa liked Matt but was bent on teaching him something new every time she saw him, a new word or phrase or task, which made Matt wary of her. She didn't have Peter's experience to know that slower people just liked to sit around and space out like everybody else sometimes. Peter tried to tell her but she wouldn't listen. Lisa was into excelling and thought everyone else should be, too. In a sense she was still recovering from her broken spine. Push, push, push—he could practically hear her old doctor's voice in her head when he lay beside her at night. But still he loved her.

He might have pushed her too hard, though, once when they were making love. They used condoms and one climactic afternoon the thing broke. The happy sperm punched through the rubber as if they were on their way to a party. Of course it was the wrong time of the month, or the right time depending on one's priorities. Lisa was happy when she found out she was pregnant, and Peter told himself he was OK with it. Funny, he had never known Lisa was Catholic until that day.

Then they left the scenario of normal couples behind. In the fourth month of Lisa's pregnancy they went to a movie, an action film where people got shot as often as they hawked products. They had popcorn and soft drinks and everything was rosy until Lisa started bleeding. Peter kept his cool and rushed her to the hospital. Although he didn't tell her so at the time, he knew she was having a miscarriage. She wasn't in the mood to talk, not even moan in pain. A strange silence had settled over her, a watchful wariness. She was watching him as if he were an alien force that had infected her. *What did you put in me?* Her blood was all over the seat, seeping through her clothes. He was never able to get the stains out.

She did have a miscarriage, then she left him. That simple, that vague. The day she checked out of the hospital, she called a cab instead of him. He wasn't home at the time—he was at his office—although Matt was. It was Matt who helped her pack her things and disappear. She left him a note, though, he had that much to be grateful for. *Sorry, Peter. It can't work. Please don't call me. Lisa.*

Great, he thought. Life's a bitch and so was she.

Yet he didn't hate her for what she had done. He was the tired cliché: not mad but hurt. He hurt so bad he felt as if he were the one who had lost all the blood. He bought another car right away.

Lisa Cantrell. Only a year ago. But maybe the damage was to last longer, he didn't know. Maybe not; these days he didn't know if he cared to know. He didn't think about her as much as he used to.

Peter delivered Matt's paper and then drove to his office downtown. The paper had given him a corner room on the tenth floor when his weekly fan mail had passed four hundred pieces. The view was fine if you liked insurance skyscrapers framed by mountains, which didn't offend Peter's simple tastes. He had a secretary, Mary Gonzales, whom he shared with two *real* reporters, which is what they called themselves. It was something of a joke, between them and him. He gathered happy stories from happy people. It would have been nice if his interviewees remained happy, but more often than not they appeared miserable just remembering when things had been better.

His column had begun by accident. Four years earlier he had been working two jobs: supervising retarded children downtown from seven to noon, Monday through Friday, and teaching writing at an Orange County high school afternoons, the last two periods of the day. His normal-IQ students were more demanding, but they weren't much better writers. Then again, he really didn't believe creative writing could be taught, only stumbled upon by a few.

He fancied himself a writer, but had never constructed anything as challenging as a novel. He had this fear—intellectually he knew that he couldn't be the only one suffering from it, yet still he felt that the phobia was unique to him—that he would write the bulk of a book and then reread it and be seized by the uncontrollable desire to burn it. Then, after his masterpiece was in ashes—or after all his discs were erased—he'd decide it could have won a Pulitzer. He didn't know why he had such strange thoughts. Maybe they were the stuff of brilliance, or maybe he needed Prozac.

Anyway, he got the idea for "Wouldn't It Be Nice?" one evening when he was watching CNN and every top story was depressing, including the sports scores. Right then he sat down and wrote a piece about how his next-door neighbor had been reunited with his childhood sweetheart after a twenty-year gap. It started with the guy getting mugged at the Santa Monica Pier and then begging passersby for change to take the bus home. The piece was particularly sweet because the heroine of the story had given him all her change without knowing who he was. Then recognition and nostalgia had set in and the two of them ended up getting married.

But Peter had not rushed out to his local paper to try to talk them into running the story. A fellow teacher, with whom he played basketball, came over the next day and spotted the article on the coffee table. He submitted it to the *Times* without Peter's permission. The paper wanted it and any similar follow-up stories. Seemed the editors appreciated his style—touching sentiment laced with barely concealed cynicism. The hero of his first story was still begging change from his wife.

The column took off. He was able to get Matt a job at the paper. Life was good. Then Lisa left. Life was good for short periods of time, Peter thought. He never read his own column when he opened the paper in the morning.

Mary winked at him as he made his way to his office. She had a basketful of letters for him but he waved her away. He seldom received usable stories through the mail. Most of his columns came to him word of mouth, from friends or friends of friends. Also, the majority of stuff that came in the mail didn't ring true. He had been meaning to write Ann Landers a letter about it.

Mary always hit on him, and he would have filed a major civil suit against her charging on-the-job sexual harassment if he hadn't enjoyed it. Many women courted his attention now that he was young, handsome, and successful—never mind that he'd possessed the first two qualities all his life. But he didn't enjoy the attention as much as he would have earlier in life. The personal philosophy of the Wouldn't-It-Be-Nice Man said it was because he was thirty years old and the high school homecoming queen was already married and getting fat and some dreams were only dreamed for a time and if by chance they did come true, then it was usually too late.

The money was good, though. He had a great stereo in a hot car. And he still had his handsome face, and could fool them all. He looked like a patient listener—a doctor with a good bedside manner, a priest who would never think of molesting children. With his golden curls and arresting green eyes, his great body and smooth voice, he was the dating game contestant to take home to Mom. But if he had a few days off he didn't shave and seldom showered. He would don his oil-stained leather jacket and cruise the Coast Highway on his 900 Harley. The sensation of speed was one of the few thrills that got him going. Twice he had outrun cops, and one other time had written a column on an officer's daughter to get out of a hundred-mile-an-hour speeding ticket.

But he had to work today. He was only two columns ahead of publication, and in the newspaper business that was nothing. Sitting at his desk, he wondered if he *should* open his mail. He turned on his computer and dug through his files and found the nothing he expected to find. Then he heard a knock behind him, where no knock was possible, and knew in an instant he had found the solution to his problem. There was a window washer blocking his stunning view of the First Interstate building. This was not just any window washer. This guy looked as old and grizzled as corporate America. Peter figured anybody who had survived that many years dancing high above greater Los Angeles must have a story to tell. He waved the man inside, and when that didn't inspire a coherent response, he wrote a sign and held it up to the window.

COME INSIDE AND I'LL BUY YOU LUNCH.

The old gent was agreeable.

Turned out, over a few beers at a corner café, that Mr. Roberts had once fallen from the fifth-floor window of the Pasadena Hilton— right into the deep end of the hotel swimming pool. "Hurt my pride some," Mr. Roberts said, remembering back. "But not a bone in my body." It was a print, Peter thought. He wouldn't let the guy go back to the job, though, not after forty-eight ounces of Bud. Mr. Roberts didn't feel like working anyway.

It was in the afternoon, after his early but extended lunch, that Peter put Chuck's tape into the player on his desk. He ran it through a couple of times and felt worse for the experience. Cold actually—

even with the June sun pouring through the recently washed windows. He picked up the phone and asked his boss, Ed Foley, if he could go see him in his office. Sure, Ed said, he wasn't busy.

Ed was Peter's boss only in the sense that the hierarchy at the paper felt he should have one. In reality Ed seldom asked what he was working on and even less frequently edited anything he wrote. All Ed cared about was that he got his column in on time and that people kept reading it. If either of those two criteria was not met, Peter knew, Ed would fire him. They were on friendly terms, but not close.

Ed had a smaller office than Peter's. It was cramped, cluttered with enough paper to make a tree sigh for all the wasted wood. Peter had been able to postulate that Ed stayed where he was because the tight dimensions worked some kind of psychic magic on his bulging perimeter. The guy was six two and three hundred pounds. He liked pizza, everybody's pizza. He smoked fat cigars that filled up only a corner of his wide mouth. He was a good newsman with a keen ear for the next story. He wrote fast and hard, breaking an average of one computer keyboard a month. Peter liked him well enough. He handed Ed the tape without preamble and told him to listen to it. Ed did so carefully, three times.

I'd love to, I really would. I could tell you a lot about that gal. She was a bleeder, not like some of the others. But that's not why I called—it's not important anyway. It's just one of those things that happens when things are changing too fast. Am I going too fast for you?

"I take it this Chuck called you?" Ed asked as he turned off the cassette player.

"This morning, at home."

"What did I miss before you started recording?"

"Not much. He said how he met this woman in a bar. That's the same woman he talks about at the end of the tape."

Ed shook his head. "Scary voice. You know the story on Cindy Trells?"

"Just what I read. Torn to pieces, her body dumped in a garbage can behind a supermarket."

"Let me tell you a few things you may not know. Shut the door, please, would you? Thanks. Have a seat." Ed got comfortable as Peter took the chair in front of the desk. Ed continued, "My friends in the

L.A.P.D. tell me Cindy Trells is part of a bigger picture. There's a new serial killer in the area. He's done at least three people, maybe six. Or else there are two killers and they've done three each. The M.O.'s are different but they have a fingerprint that ties them together. Otherwise the police have no leads. Scary shit, huh?"

"Scary like Chuck?"

"Yeah. You've got to take this tape to the police. For your own safety if nothing else. If Chuck's got your number, he could have your address as well."

"The thought occurred to me." Peter paused. "There's been no mention of a serial killer in the paper."

"My sources asked me not to. Not yet, at least. We have an agreement on stuff like this. But you could be the one to break this story wide open. If Chuck is the one, he's contacted you, and it sounds like he's going to contact you again."

"Why do you think he chose me?"

"I have no idea if you don't."

Peter shook his head. "I don't frequent his bar." He considered further. "The police will want to put a tap on my phone."

"Probably."

"I hate getting involved."

"Doesn't every patriotic American? You already are involved. I know you, if you think you could have helped but didn't and someone else dies you'll feel guilty. Call the cops now. Call your friend—Amos. He's been assigned to this case. They've got about twenty detectives working on it."

Peter knew Lieutenant Amos Rodrigues through Amos's daughter, Madeline. The previous year she'd been one of the only kids in California to get a perfect score on the SAT. He'd thought her story worth printing. Her father had been ecstatic to have his daughter in the paper and took Peter out to dinner. The two of them talked about motorcycles, and one thing had led to another and they ended up riding together a few times. Yet Peter hadn't seen Amos in a few months.

Peter stood. "Can I have my tape back?"

Ed popped it out and handed it over. "Are you going to call him?"

"Probably. But I won't write about it."

"Why not?"

"You mean why not be a *real* reporter for once? The question reminds me of the night I wrote my first column, the feeling of unreality I had watching the regular news."

"You're too idealistic, Peter."

Peter was at the door. "No. I just don't need people like Chuck in my life."

He closed the door when he got back to his office. He didn't ring Amos but Matt instead. Matt was happy to get the call. Peter had only recently given him his own phone. Peter was surprised by how relieved he was to hear that Matt was OK. Only then did he realize how much Chuck had disturbed him. He talked to Matt for a few minutes before dialing Amos. His detective friend wanted to know what was up. Peter played him the tape. There was a long silence.

"Can you come down to the station immediately?" Amos asked.

"Right now? Is that necessary?"

Amos sounded tired. "Yeah. Somebody was busy again last night. It might have been Chuck."

Peter knew he had no choice. "I'm on my way."

They were in Lieutenant Amos Rodrigues's car on the Santa Monica Freeway, heading toward Pacific Palisades. Amos had been waiting in his car outside the station when Peter drove up. He'd told him to jump in—they were going to the scene of the latest crime.

"I was on my way there when you called," Amos explained. He had on a gray sport coat, a blue tie; his handgun rode conspicuously on his right hip. He was not a handsome man, although his Hispanic profile was strong and proud. He was short, fit. At forty he could run a five-minute mile. His right eye was plastic, a reminder of a violent childhood; it was always staring but fortunately in the right direction. His black hair was thick, always neat. He moved with confidence.

"Your people are there already?" Peter asked.

"Sure. The body was found an hour ago. The guy was just sitting behind the wheel of his car dead."

"Was he shot? Knifed?"

Amos frowned. "Somebody did something to him." He nodded. "We'll see when we get there. Remember, this isn't reporter business, not this afternoon."

"No problem." Peter wanted to change the subject. "How's Madeline?"

A safe topic. Amos loved his daughter maybe more than a father should in such a crazy world. He talked during most of the trip and Peter had to make only an occasional grunt. Amos was animated; he used his hands frequently to make his points. He was originally from El Salvador and had seen pain in his days. His two brothers had been executed by death squads before his eyes. He had moved to Los Angeles fourteen years earlier, and his rise in the department had been nothing short of meteoric. There was talk—actually Amos had done the talking—that he would soon be a captain. He'd solved a number of cases that had been rotting in the L.A.P.D.'s basement files. That was a hobby of his, to read and research old files.

But he liked the fresh ones as well and listened to the tape twice on the drive.

Their ride ended at a cul-de-sac on a winding road studded with expensive houses. The cul-de-sac was at the top of a hill with the finest view of the coast money could buy. Two black and whites were parked behind a metallic green Mercedes. Down the street a number of onlookers stood on a porch and watched. Peter checked the time—two-fifteen. He had to assume the man had died during the night and wondered why it had taken so long for the body to be found. Of course, he thought, maybe his sitting upright in a Mercedes had delayed things. Peter climbed out of the car with Amos and walked toward the two uniforms. One of them—he looked like a high school senior—spoke to the lieutenant.

"The medical examiner is working the body now."

"Do we have prints?" Amos asked.

"McCoy was here and dusted. I don't think he lifted anything exciting."

"Do we know the victim's name?" Amos asked.

"He was found with his wallet on him." The officer pulled a notepad from his back pocket. "James Crosser; age thirty-nine; occupation architect; address seventeen Stanford Street, Santa Monica. He had a wife and two kids. Mrs. Crosser's been contacted. Seems they had an argument last night, close to eleven. He left to get a drink and never came home."

"Did Mr. Crosser favor a particular bar?" Amos asked.

"Mrs. Crosser didn't know." The young officer wiped the sweat from his upper lip. "She was very agitated. They hadn't been married long, and their kids are still young."

"What were they arguing about?"

"Money."

Amos considered. "Contact her again about his drinking habits. Get photo I.D. and circulate it in the bars around here and near his home. Also, show the liquor stores in the area his picture. Tell Mrs. Crosser that I'll be calling her later today."

"Yes, sir." The officer turned and climbed into his car.

"Tragic," Peter said.

"You should have seen Cindy Trells," Amos said, "and her father, when I brought him the news." He nodded toward the Mercedes. "Let's see what we've got."

The man, the body, was sprawled across the steering wheel, face-down. He was balding; even at a quick glance he appeared older than his thirty-nine years. Of course, Peter reminded himself, no one looked so hot dead. The man had obviously dressed quickly; a rumpled green sweater, baggy gray slacks. His skin was very white. There was a small amount of blood on his sweater at the rib cage. His left hand lay across the top of the steering wheel, and his wedding ring looked as if it were about to slip off. Death had shrunk his fingers.

As the officer had stated, the medical examiner was working the body. Peter knew the M.E. His name was Blank; Amos had told stories about him over dinner. Blank wore a blond punk crewcut. He was tall and gangly and remarkably pale. It was no exaggeration to say he resembled a cadaver. His hands were large, with fishlike fingers. He wore white latex gloves. It was eighty degrees and he had on a black turtleneck, a tiny gold crucifix around his neck. Amos said Blank was brilliant; his testimony in court was often devastating. Amos said he could scare a jury into believing him just by smiling at them.

Blank seemed unaware of their presence. Peter watched as Blank took samples from under each of the man's nails with a slim metal instrument and deposited what he found in separate plastic envelopes. Amos let him work without speaking. When he finished that task, he pulled up the man's sweater, but not without first checking the label. Amos had told Peter that Blank had a fetish for dead people's clothes. He liked to dress up in them. Blank frowned as he studied the bloody red hole in Mr. Crosser.

"What is it?" Amos asked.

"A feint," Blank replied. "This man was dead when he was poked."

"Are you sure?" Amos asked.

"Ninety percent. I'll be a hundred percent sure after the autopsy."

Peter was curious. "How?"

Blank looked up. His blue irises swam in a red sea. He must have partied late when he was all dressed up. "Sorry?" Blank said pleasantly.

Amos gestured. "Blank, this is Peter Jacobs, a friend who got a strange call this morning. I'll play it for you in a minute. Peter, this is our M.E."

They nodded, but didn't shake hands. Peter repeated his question. Blank answered with his right hand over the hole in the man's skin. "It's a question of gravity. A dead person's blood ends up at the lowest points. By the time this guy was poked, most of his blood was down in his legs and buttocks. That's why he didn't bleed."

"But he did bleed," Peter said. "There's blood right there."

"Not as much as you'd expect considering he was poked through the heart," Blank said. "Also, there are few burst capillaries around this wound." He touched the messy hole with the tip of his latex finger. "You see the mangled tissue is relatively white."

"Then how did he die?" Amos asked.

"I don't know," Blank said.

"He's like the others?" Peter asked.

Blank shrugged. "I can't answer that on the grounds it might incriminate me."

"The other three, or all six?" Peter persisted, taking the response as an affirmative.

Amos shook his head in disgust. "Ed's been talking. Tell him that I said he's not to. But I'll answer your question if you promise to keep quiet. This guy died like three others we found in the last month. There is another set of three that died in a more obvious way. They were torn to pieces—as if by a wild animal. At their crime scenes we were able to obtain a number of prints. One of the prints matches a print we found on a man who died last week—like this man here."

"What is the sex of the victims?" Peter asked.

"Four males—now five—two females," Amos said. "Cindy Trells was the youngest at twenty, but none of the victims has been over forty."

"I don't know how you guys keep this out of the papers," Peter said. "Or frankly, why you bother. Don't tell me you're trying to avoid a panic. A thousand people are murdered in the L.A. area each year."

"We're afraid of looking incompetent," Blank said. He lifted up the dead man's head and studied the face, feeling the tone of the cheek flesh. Mr. Crosser's mouth hung open; he'd had expensive dental work.

"The moment the phrase serial killer goes out, things get crazy," Amos said. "We're trying to keep a low profile until we can at least get a grip on what's happening. We have no substantial leads. Blank, when did this man die?"

"Between three and five in the morning. Probably close to four."

"What made the hole in his chest?" Amos asked.

"I don't know," Blank said. "Not a knife."

"What would you guess was the cause?" Peter asked.

Blank paused in his examination. "A finger."

"A person couldn't poke a finger into someone's heart," Peter said.

"A martial arts champion could," Blank said. "But I don't think such a person picked this man up last night."

"Then what are you saying?" Peter asked.

"That I'm confused," Blank replied.

Amos spoke to Peter. "Let Blank hear your tape of Chuck."

They retreated to the lieutenant's car, leaving Mr. Crosser alone behind the steering wheel of his Mercedes. Blank wore a faint but excited grin as he heard the tape. Maybe Chuck was his kind of guy, Peter thought. Blank listened to the recording twice before commenting.

"Sounds guilty as sin," Blank said.

Amos shook his head. "He didn't say he murdered Cindy Trells. And he didn't have any details of the crime not found in the paper, except the thing about her being a bleeder."

"Which is significant," Blank said.

"*Could* be significant," Amos said. "Could be coincidental bullshit. Peter, how could he have obtained your number?"

"It was listed when I first started at the paper four years ago. But not since then."

"I think he'll call back," Blank said.

"Why do you say that?" Peter asked.

"A serial killer often feels the need to have someone to tell his story to," Amos said. "To let the world know how clever he is. Even how horrible. You tell stories for a living. Blank is suggesting that Chuck wants you to tell his story."

"But my column is only about happy events," Peter said.

"The irony might appeal to Chuck," Amos said. "And Chuck

sounds like he needs some happiness in his life. Take the woman he describes. Their encounter didn't sound pleasant."

"She could have been one of his victims," Blank said.

"She could be his partner," Peter said.

"She could even not exist," Amos said. "She could be a mean imaginary mother in his twisted psyche. Whatever, it is unlikely *she* killed James Crosser." Amos paused. "Peter, do you want to help us?"

Peter knew what that meant. His phone tapped, his conversations recorded. An effort made to set up a meeting with Chuck. The waiting, the wondering. The worrying about Matt. Peter was surprised he wasn't concerned for his own safety.

He glanced back at James Crosser. A petty squabble, a late-night drive for a drink. Two young kids and a dead father. What a waste. Especially if it were to happen again.

"What do you want me to do?" Peter asked.

Amos briefed him. There were no surprises except that Amos offered him round-the-clock protection. Peter declined, thinking it early in the game for such drastic measures. He didn't want to freak out Matt, who scared easily.

Before leaving with Amos, Peter got Blank alone for a moment. He asked the question that had been bothering him from the start, in many ways the only question that mattered.

"If this guy didn't die from the puncture to his heart," Peter said, "how do you think he died?"

"My best guess?"

"Yeah."

Blank raised a thin, colorless eyebrow. "I think he was smothered and didn't resist." He paused. "None of these nonbleeder cases shows a single sign of struggle."

TWO

❖

THERE WAS A lot written about gangs and gang violence in the papers, Jerry Washington knew. It made him laugh, because no one in a gang was writing the news. If they had been they would have said more about what it was like to be given a choice between dying and dying. Jerry felt as if he had been flying since he was six years old, when his best friend's older brother had pulled a gun on him and asked how fast he could run. The papers called the gangs surrogate families. Jerry supposed there was truth in it in his case, since his father had beaten him regularly until he died, overdosing at thirty-eight on dirty smack. But Jerry never wanted to be a gang member any more than he wanted to be an enemy of a gang.

He had gone through the usual initiation rite on his twelfth birthday. Kill someone, preferably white, or at least fuck them up bad. His conscience had been somewhat soothed by the screams of his victim as he fled because he knew the guy was still alive. He was eighteen now and wanted out, but simply being in the barrio was like being on the eternal inside. He didn't want to hear his own screams, even though he did sometimes in the middle of the night when he woke from a bad dream. He'd been having a lot of those lately.

But maybe there was a way out.

The day he met Susan Darly had been one of the darkest of his life. Freddy "Fist" Forum, unelected but still much-respected leader of the Black Ties, South Central's bad-ass answer to the Brown Mother Fuckers and Company, had told him that he had decided the shit was to come down on Clear Gell, a pimp and drug dealer. Fist's complaint about Gell was simple. Gell sold drugs in Fist's territory and didn't pay his property or state tax. Fist wanted Gell's balls laid up against a door frame and the door shut tight. Fist ordered Jerry to do the job because he believed that Jerry no longer liked getting his hands dirty. Fist thought Jerry and a couple of stooges from the low ranks would be perfect to put a little red in Clear Gell's genital shampoo. Fist gave Jerry his own personal piece, a .44 Magnum, to help Jerry on his way. Fist also told Jerry that if Gell wasn't dead by sunset, somebody else would be.

Clear Gell lived in a small white box south of the projects that could have had the words CRACK HOUSE over it in neon for all the camouflage it attempted. There was no sense making up a subtle plan of attack, Jerry thought as he drove toward the place with Willie and Willie's half-baked little brother Harold. Clear Gell knew Fist wanted his ass, if not his balls. These days he was doing all his business with Mother Goose in hand, Gell's affectionate name for his double-barreled shotgun. Jerry figured they might just as well ram the front porch with Willie's Camaro and simply open fire. Willie was sick of the car anyway, and maybe they'd get lucky. They were going during the day because that was when Clear Gell slept. Imagine that, Fist had said with a smile. Jerry discussed his idea with Willie and Harold as they closed on ground zero.

"Which way are we running afterward?" was all Willie wanted to know.

"Toward Hawthorne," Jerry said. "We can catch Sammy for a ride back."

"I'm too tired to run," Harold said from the backseat. "I was up all night doing business. I don't want to wreck the car."

"You were up all night with your lighter up your nose," Jerry said. "We can't walk up to Gell's place and knock. He'll shoot first. He's got that place boarded up good. We've got to ram the porch and start shooting. Put your seat belt on."

"There ain't no seat belt back here," Harold said.

"Then maybe you won't be running too far," Jerry said.

They came to Gell's street a few minutes later. Willie was driving and knew his own balls were on the line with Fist so he wanted Gell's bad. He aimed straight at the front porch and hit the accelerator hard. Jerry saw his life flash before him, and it was pretty depressing.

"Not so fast!" Jerry yelled. What a fucked plan. Willie's reflexes had been slowed by too many years of reds. He didn't hit the brake until they were in Gell's front yard. By then they were doing forty.

The force of the impact almost knocked Jerry out, even with his seat belt on and his feet braced on the dash. One moment they were in the sun and the next the sky was raining boards and glass. Dust flooded the front seat. Something deep inside the mangled Camaro engine squealed a metallic death cry. Jerry was not only dazed but seeing red and black. But maybe that was because it was still dark in what was left of Gell's home sweet home. Jerry forced himself to stay alert by reaching over and slugging Willie, whose head was just wandering back from the cracked steering wheel.

"We've got to get out, man," Jerry said, pulling his piece from his belt.

"It's too dark," Willie mumbled.

Jerry hit him again. "Gell's just outside the car. Put your piece in your hand or you'll die."

The remark sobered Willie some. Jerry glanced over his shoulder and saw that Harold was already out his door, his gun in his hand. But, shit, Harold didn't know where he was going and immediately ran into a wall that probably hadn't been there five seconds before. Jerry turned the handle and smashed his passenger door with his shoulder, but it wouldn't budge. Not an unforeseen possibility. He dived out the window and landed in a pool of glass pellets, blood running down his scratched arms. He was in what used to be the living room. It was a good thing he was down when the first blast came out of the dust cloud. Mother Goose's shot exploded the plaster just six inches above Jerry's head and christened him with Christmas snow. Jerry instinctively rolled to the left, closer to the steaming Camaro. He smelled gasoline.

"Die, motherfucker!" Willie yelled. Or maybe it was Harold; the brothers sounded alike in the middle of combat. Jerry heard three weapons firing: two pistols and one pissed bird. Gasoline had dripped all over him now and there were sparks flying in the holocaust. Jerry leapt up in time to see a charging Harold lose the top half of his skull. The spray of brains did nothing to clear Jerry's vision or calm his racing heart. Jerry knew a fear right then that told his bladder he didn't have to die holding a full load. Jerry pissed his pants good as Harold crashed to the floor.

"Motherfucker!" Willie was yelling. Jerry's vision finally cleared enough to see Willie dash down a truncated hallway from where he supposed Gell had been firing, and down which Gell must now be fleeing. Jerry didn't know anything, really. He just chased after Willie. There was no sense stopping to check on Harold.

Jerry caught up with Willie at the end of the hall outside an open bedroom. Jerry bumped him forward a foot or two—he came up on him so fast—but Willie had already taken the shot to the groin an instant before the contact. Willie went down shooting, though; he had balls even if his were gone. Jerry heard a scream from the bedroom. Sounded as if Mother Goose had stopped laying her golden eggs. Jerry peeked around the corner and saw Gell holding up a hand to an eye that poured out a river of red. Clear Gell had been shot in the head and was still alive. Jerry raised his gun and fired directly at him from a distance of twenty feet. He hit a picture of the Madonna on the wall against which Gell labored. Gell removed the hand from his messy face and watched as the sacred picture hit the floor. An expression of profound sorrow swallowed his features. Then he followed his personal deity to the floor and lay still. Jerry knelt beside Willie.

"We've got to get out of here, man," Jerry said.

Willie was a fallen soldier. Roll him onto his shield because there was no sense rolling him onto a stretcher unless the white coats had transporters to beam them there. Jerry knew he was talking shit. Willie grabbed his arm, and the blood and sweat pouring off his face made for one sorry sight.

"I'm hurt bad, man," Willie said.

"Yeah, you one messed up motherfucker," Jerry agreed. His tone was light but his eyes burned. He had not grown up with Willie but had known him long enough not to want to see the guy's intestines wrapped around a JC Penney belt. Jerry wondered if he should put a bullet in his head.

"You've got to help me, man." Willie groaned and squeezed his eyes shut. His whole body trembled. His voice rose. "I's not feeling good."

Jerry patted his back. "Stay down. I'll get you a doctor."

Willie wept. "I don't need a doctor. I need a priest. Get me a priest, Jerry." He grabbed him with remarkable strength for a dying man. "I see the devil! I see him coming for me!"

"There ain't no devil, you stupid nigger." Jerry leaned over and whispered in Willie's ear. "Say to God that you're sorry for your sins and that you don't want to be going to any fucking hell hole."

Willie sucked in a burning breath. "I'm sorry, man." His voice fell to a whisper and his grip on Jerry faltered. "I'm sorry, Jesus."

"He forgives you," Jerry said. He watched as Willie let go of him altogether and lay back on the filthy floor, silent. Jerry added softly, "Somebody's got to."

Jerry tossed a match to the Camaro's gasoline as he said good-bye to Clear Gell's establishment. The fire engines rang and the smoke rose behind him as he ran toward Hawthorne Boulevard. He was covered with blood and guilt, but in that part of town hardly anyone looked at him.

Sammy gave him fresh clothes and didn't ask questions. Jerry told Sammy to call Fist and tell him that Clear Gell's balls were now fried eggs. He gave Sammy the .44 to return to Fist. Jerry hoped Fist had squeezed enough blood out of him and that they could call it quits. But he doubted it would be that easy.

Jerry walked out of Sammy's house and caught a bus that took him to Malibu.

Jerry liked the beach. The water and the sea gulls didn't have his kind of problems. Nor did the rich bodies lying on the sand. He went down to Malibu whenever he got the chance, which wasn't often, and pretended that he was a part of a sane world. When he immersed himself in the surf he imagined that he was receiving a baptism that no organized religion was ever going to bestow on him.

He was coming out of the water not two hours after giving last rites to Willie when he met Susan. He caught her Frisbee. He had to catch the damn thing, it was about to hit him in the head. He always had good reflexes, even if he couldn't shoot straight. He looked around for the Frisbee owner and saw blond hair and innocence so fresh and sweet he couldn't understand why white people hadn't learned to package it. The Frisbee girl smiled at him as if he'd never hurt a soul in his life.

"Sorry," she said.

"No problem," Jerry said, shrugging. He had confidence around girls when he wasn't with other gang members because he knew he had the body and the face. He was built the way his survival demanded: pumped upper chest, long tapered legs that should have been winning races on a track rather than running from burning buildings. His eyes were dark, slightly blue; his easy smile a great lie to flash at a hard world. He smiled at the girl as she nodded down the beach in the direction of enough glare to make whoever she was pointing to as visible as a babe on the far side of Mercury. "What's your name?" he asked.

"Susan."

He tossed her the Frisbee. "I'm Jerry. Are you prejudiced?"

"Why?" She looked eighteen, his age. Her bikini was yellow, tissue size.

"Because I want to ask you out," he said.

"And if I say I don't want to go out with you then I'm prejudiced?"

"That's right."

"I can't go out with you."

"Why not?"

She pointed to his soaked pants. He had taken off his shirt and rolled up his pant legs before going in the water, but it didn't change the fact that he didn't have a bathing suit on.

"Because you look ridiculous with those on," she said.

He reached for his zipper. "If I take them off will you go out with me?"

She giggled. "Don't!"

He undid the top button. "The word is yes or I keep going."

She stopped laughing and folded her arms across her chest. "Keep going then. At least then I'll know if the saying is true."

"What saying is that?"

"Once you go black you never go back."

He let go of his pants. "Proof of something like that don't come cheap. Sorry, Susie, I can't take my pants off for you, not on a first date. But let's go out. I'm not as dangerous as I look."

"You don't look a bit dangerous to me." She considered him. Her friend down the beach could have washed out on the tide. Susan had blue eyes too, but much lighter than his. There was a warmth in them he hadn't seen in maybe a hundred years. The unexpected tenderness had an unexpected effect on him—he began to shake. He was smart enough to know he was still in shock. Crashing into buildings and jumping out into clouds of plaster dust and shooting people—the stuff of bad movies, but a daily occurrence around the projects. Who the hell did he think he was flirting with a girl who could have grown up on another planet? He lowered his head and dragged in a couple of deep breaths to stop his trembling. Foam washed over his feet. He noticed that he still had Willie's blood under his fingernails. He felt a hand on his shoulder and was surprised when he raised his head to find that it belonged to Susan.

"What's the matter?" she asked.

He shrugged. "Nothing. Hey, sorry to bother you. I have to go."

She grabbed his arm. "Wait. Tell me what's wrong."

"Nothing's wrong. Everything's cool. I have to go."

She let go of him, her face solemn. "Yes."

"Yes, what?"

"Yes, I'll go out with you."

"Why?"

"Because I want to."

"Why?"

"Because you look like you need a change of pace." She glanced in the direction of her invisible friend. "And so do I."

That was a month ago, and life had changed big time for Jerry. Although four weeks to the day they had met they were back on the same beach in the same spot at the same time of day. Jerry knew that on the beach, they weren't far from Susan's house. Her father was a big lawyer, her mother a platinum credit card junkie. Jerry hadn't met either and didn't care. Her parents were going away for the weekend, and Susan said she and Jerry could sleep in their bed. She told him the saying was true, at least in his case. She wasn't going back. She was only seventeen and still in high school but he wasn't worried about being arrested for statutory rape. For once in his life he was having fun.

Susan had given him the incentive, but he had made a few hard decisions of his own. The Clear Gell hit had made no more impression on the police than an inner-city basketball game that got out of hand—no surprise. But Jerry had used the hit for leverage with Fist. He had told Fist that there were rumors going around about who had ordered the hit, failing to mention, of course, that he had started the rumors. Jerry told Fist that he wouldn't remember a thing about that day—even if he was arrested and charged with first degree—if Fist would forget about him. It was a good time to ask for a favor while making a threat, and with Fist it was always smart to package the two together. Even though he'd lost two soldiers, Fist was delighted with the results of the hit. He told Jerry he could walk where he wanted. It was important to get an official decree. If Jerry had simply tried to hide from Fist, he would have been hunted down and slaughtered no matter how long it took.

Jerry had not left Clear Gell's house empty-handed either. He had rummaged through the pusher's drawers after saying good-bye to Willie and found a wad of five thousand bucks. With the money he got himself an apartment on the low-income side of Santa Monica and bought a Honda Civic with an odometer that had been twice around the hundred-thousand-mile mark, but which was still running. Those two moves had used up over half his cash, so he quickly got a job working sixty hours a week at a 7-Eleven. He pulled the graveyard shift, and didn't mind as long as none of his old pals wandered in. But Fist had promised it would be hands off, and the guy usually kept his word, as long as it didn't cost him anything.

Jerry saw Susan practically every day.

The sane world was Jerry's world, at least for a while. It was good, as he lay on the beach beside Susan late that Friday afternoon in June—not three hours after Peter Jacobs had asked M.E. Blank how he thought James Crosser had been killed—and waited for Susan's parents to leave, that Jerry had no clue about all the strange things that could enter that sane world.

Unnatural things. From all directions.

It was Susan's idea to go for a last swim.

She was in a good mood, but restless, eager to do three fun things at once. Even though she had a fabulous tan, she didn't like to lie on the beach, which was Jerry's idea of fun after working all night and going for one long swim. Some days he'd sleep four or five hours straight on the sand.

There was a swell out of the south that afternoon, four-to-five-foot breakers that looked twice that height when you were in the water with them. They had already been bodysurfing once and had come out early because Susan kept losing her suit. She found some string, though, and tied it down, and wanted to get wet one last time, she said with a leer, before she got real wet. But he wasn't crazy about the idea. He sat up reluctantly as she tugged at his arm.

"It's getting pretty rough out there," he said, studying the surf. The waves had jumped a foot, maybe two, since he had lain down, and the tide was coming up onto the steeper incline of the beach, which made for a wicked undertow as the foam rolled back out. There was also a riptide, heading north. When they had come out of the water the first time, they had had to walk half a mile back to their towels. Jerry had once been pulled out far on a riptide and had almost drowned. He had a lot of respect for the ocean's moods.

"Come on," Susan said.

Jerry yawned. "You slept all night while I worked. I'm tired, and if you get in trouble out there I won't have the energy to save you."

She stood and kicked sand on his legs. "I grew up on this beach, brown sugar. I could outswim you any day. I'm going in even if you don't." She tossed her blond hair in the orange sun and surveyed the pounding surf. "I love being turned upside in the curl. It makes all the blood go to my head. Better than sex." She glanced at him. "Almost."

Jerry got up slowly. "All right, I'll come. But if the riptide's pulling out, we're coming right back in."

Susan bounced as they walked toward the water. "If it's pulling out, we get to go to Hawaii sooner than we expected," she said.

They reentered the water during a pause in the sets. Jerry decided he had been overcautious, even when the next waves came in, because they weren't that high. But half an hour later, the sun now touching the edge of the world, the sets abruptly pumped up the punch. Susan wasn't bragging—she was an excellent swimmer, and he was no slouch himself, but it was all the two of them could do to keep air in their lungs. They let one big wave after another pass without even trying to ride them. Jerry called over to Susan that they should go in.

"We have to take one of the big ones before we do," she yelled back.

"These suckers are eight feet tall."

"Wuss!"

"We could be thrown to the bottom and break our necks." A true statement, even though they were treading water way over their heads.

"Pussy!"

Susan did not know it but where he came from that kind of insult was worth a knife in the back. Still, he laughed as they bubbled to the top of a huge swell.

"We'll see who's wearing the pussy," he called. "You have to take the wave I take."

"Deal! Then I'll beat you to the shore!"

"I'm going to beat you on the shore, babe."

"Whew! Love it!"

A few minutes later a monster appeared. Technically a wave is measured from behind, and this one would have been a ten footer.

But from their perspective, running out of gas in the churning foam, the white-crowned motherfucker was as tall as the World Trade Center. Susan had challenged his manhood. He pointed to the wave. That was it. Smooth sailing, sister. Susan yelled back her affirmative. Break a leg, brother.

Jerry moved into position and gave a furious kick. The wave picked him up, then it put him down, hard and fast. He was flipped head over heels faster than he could shout, which he did anyway, and ended up with a mouthful of water. The force of the wave as it crashed was every bit as strong as the impact of Willie's Camaro on Clear Gell's front door. Every inch of his skin was pulverized with foam; the saltwater could have been forced into each of his pores. The air was crushed from his lungs and he ached to draw in a breath but didn't dare. His head went one direction, his spine another. There was nothing to do but ride out the storm.

A minute later, gasping for air, he surfaced fifty yards from shore. He didn't see Susan right away; he didn't see anyone foolish enough to be in the water. He was not worried, though. More waves were rolling in. It was hard to see over them. He figured Susan had missed the wave, or else chickened out. In either case he believed she was still out and didn't search the beach for her. He walked toward the shore, exhausted.

A couple of minutes later he got worried. Standing on the sand, he saw no sign of her in the water. True, another incoming set was obstructing his view and the light was fading, but her blond hair should have stood out against the deepening gray. Fidgeting, he scanned the beach. If she'd come in ahead of him, she would have hung around to gloat over beating him. Because of the riptide, their towels were a quarter-mile south of where he had come in. She wouldn't have run back there, he was sure of that.

Yet there was no Susan.

"Shit," he whispered.

Maybe she had caught the wave, and it had speared her into the ocean floor. Knocked her out, or at the very least dazed her. She could be drowning this moment, he thought, but could be saved if he could get to her in time. The nearest lifeguard was as far away as the towels. What was best? Run for help or dive back in? How long did it take to drown? Five minutes? He hadn't seen her in four.

In the end he raced back into the water. But all he found were more waves and a stronger riptide. He began to believe that the tide had taken her out to sea, yet he had his doubts; it wasn't taking him out. His worry was now a thing of terror.

"Susan!" he screamed.

In the end his exhaustion forced him back to the beach. He trudged toward their towels. His only hope was that she had somehow pulled a magic act and got to shore. His guilt was a bleeding wound. He had known it wasn't safe to go back in and still he'd let her go. He couldn't imagine what it would be like to tell her parents she was dead. He should never have got involved with her. He was a Black Tie and would always be; he poisoned everything he touched. Moving and getting a job had changed none of that.

She wasn't at the towels; he hadn't really expected to find her there. Before he could plop down and give into total despair, however, he noticed a group of people gathered farther up the beach, *opposite* from the direction he had come. They appeared to be standing around someone on the ground. It was two hundred yards to the group and he ran it in twenty seconds.

It was Susan, sprawled on her back, her hair plastered over her face, her skin the color of ash. A long-haired woman in a one-piece black bathing suit was giving her mouth-to-mouth resuscitation. Jerry fell to his knees beside them both. He grabbed Susan's hand. So cold, the flesh.

"Is she alive?" he asked desperately.

The woman paused and glanced up. "Did you call an ambulance?" she asked in a calm voice.

"Someone is calling," a man said behind Jerry.

"Good," the woman said. She returned to the resuscitation. Each time she exhaled, Susan's chest rose, but only with the forced air. Jerry let go of Susan's hand and touched the woman's arm.

"Tell me if she's alive," he pleaded.

The woman nodded between breaths. "Her heart's beating."

"Why isn't she breathing?" Jerry asked.

An important question, maybe the magic one. As if in response Susan suddenly let out a choked gasp. The woman quickly rolled her on her side and slapped her hard on the back several times. Susan dragged in another ragged wheeze, then another. The people murmured their approval. Tears of relief flooded Jerry's face. The woman with the black bathing suit looked at him once more.

"She'll be fine now, I think," she said.

THREE

❖

J ULIE MOORE ENTERED the elevator at the U.C.L.A. Medical Center and pushed the top-floor button. She wasn't late for her interview but felt rushed. She was paranoid about being even a few minutes tardy. She had grown up on a farm in Kansas, and her father had been as strict about what time the cows were milked as he was about what time her boyfriend brought her home at night. He had once locked a guy in the barn for keeping her out after midnight. The fact that the U.C.L.A. campus was fifteen hundred miles from her father was one of the main reasons Julie had chosen to go there. That was seven years ago, and she was still at the university, now working on a Ph.D. in psychology. Her doctoral dissertation was entitled "The Psychology of the Near-Death Experience." Julie was at the hospital to interview a woman who had died for fifteen minutes the day before.

Exiting the elevator on the fifth floor, Julie strode to the nurses' station. Claire Montgomery, her subject, had been transferred from intensive care to an ordinary hospital room that afternoon. Julie knew from experience that the nurses had to be handled carefully. A patient could be capable of completing an hour interview, but an RN would say only five minutes.

"Hello," Julie said to the lone nurse on duty. "My name is Julie Moore. I'm here to see Claire Montgomery."

The woman set aside her paperback novel and Camel cigarette. Illegally smoking in a hospital and reading Jackie Collins while on duty. Julie figured this woman couldn't give her hell. The nurse—

Tina Thompson, her name tag said—was fortyish, wearing yesterday's makeup, tomorrow's problems. She coughed wearily and checked her watch.

"It's after eight," Nurse Thompson said. "Visiting hours are over."

"I know, but with classes and my job I was unable to come earlier. And I won't be able to interview Claire over the weekend."

"You can't talk to her on Monday?"

"I'm here to discuss something that happened to her yesterday. She's elderly, so the longer I wait, the less clear the facts will be in her mind."

"I know who she is. The woman who supposedly died and came back." The nurse ground out her cigarette. "We get a few of those now and then. I don't know why they bother."

"You don't know why they bother what?"

"Breathing again, if it's so great on the other side." The nurse regarded her with mild disdain. "What are you, a reporter for the *Enquirer?*"

"I'm a graduate student doing a paper on NDEs—near-death experiences."

"You believe in that crap?"

"I have an open mind."

The woman shook her head. "If you'd seen as many people die as I have, you wouldn't."

Julie stiffened, thinking of Patricia, her sister. Twelve-year-old innocence—not immune to locked brakes, skidding tires, full impact. Julie had been there, seen no soul leave, heard no angels singing.

"I've seen my share," Julie said.

Something in her voice made the nurse raise an eyebrow. She picked up her book. "You can talk to Claire as long as you're gone when I take my break in half an hour."

"Thank you. Which room is it?"

"Five-oh-one. End of the hall on your right. If she saw Jesus, ask her what he thought of the Holocaust."

"I'll try to work the question in."

Julie found Claire propped up in bed, watching TV. The woman had the room to herself, which would simplify the interview process. Julie had known Claire was in her late seventies but was still surprised by how tiny she was; a shriveled black doll with cotton candy white hair and bright eyes sunk into a vein-traced skull that perched on her bony neck with birdlike timidity. Yet when she spoke her voice was clear, if not a bit dry.

"You must be Julie," Claire said. "Come in and have a seat." She flicked off the TV—she'd been watching a Simpsons rerun—and gestured to the chair beside her bed. "I'd offer you coffee but, this late, room service only offers morphine and sleeping pills."

Julie chuckled and took the offered chair, setting down her briefcase, which held her notes and cassette recorder. "The nurse at the station might be able to bring you a cigarette if you wanted one," Julie said. She shook the old woman's hand, feeling the brittle bones beneath the parched skin. "It's a pleasure to meet you, Claire. I'm sorry it's so late."

"Don't worry about me. I don't fall asleep till after two or three in the morning, if I sleep at all." Claire smiled. Her stained dentures fit poorly but the expression was nevertheless charming. "That Nurse Thompson walks around in a cloud of smoke and she knows it's against the rules. She told me she's just begging for the hospital to fire her so that she can sue them. She'd probably win, she's a tough gal."

"You must be one tough cookie yourself surviving what you've been through. Do you mind if I set up my recorder? I'm hopeless when it comes to taking notes."

"Go right ahead, Julie. It's my pleasure to have company on a Friday evening. The only one who visits me is my nephew, Tim, and he lives in San Diego. He only comes on Saturdays." Claire sighed. "I used to love Friday evenings when my Billy was alive. We'd dance down at the Hopkins' on Florence every weekend. Do you know that place, child?"

Julie removed her cassette player from her briefcase and checked to make sure she had fresh batteries. "I'm afraid not. I'm not originally from L.A."

"For all I know they tore down the place years ago. Where are you from?"

"Kansas. Gayley. It's small town twenty miles south of Wichita."

"Do you know many people in L.A?"

"Few."

Claire nodded. "No boyfriend, huh?"

Julie blushed as she connected her microphone to the player. "Does it show?"

"Gosh, I didn't mean it that way. You're a pretty thing—all that

blond hair and good skin. You look as if you could have a key ring full
of boys in your pocket and still have room for a real man hanging on
your rabbit's foot. It's just that I don't think I ever worked a Friday
night in my life."

"This is fun for me," Julie replied. But Claire had hit home with
her remarks. With each passing year, Julie had fewer friends, particularly of the male variety, and the twin excuses of too much work and
school gave her no comfort. She knew enough psychology to realize
that her loneliness was moving close to a clinical diagnosis. Yet she
was bright, she was attractive—enough people had told her she was
and she was inclined to believe them. Besides her blond hair and
good skin, Julie was spunky with a spark in her blue eyes. As a senior
in high school, her speech teacher had encouraged her to study
broadcasting, because he felt she had the bone structure and voice of
an anchorperson. But she hadn't the confidence, and had gone into
psychology to find it. She was high strung in tense situations and never
ate enough, which made her too thin to try to slay her internal demons all in one stroke by posing for *Playboy*. Not that they had called
lately.

Claire watched her. "This may be satisfying for you, but fun is
something that gets your blood pumping a lot harder than it is now.
You need more color in your cheeks, girl. Get out and have a good
meal. See a movie. Get laid."

Julie laughed. "I'll see what I can do about that last one on the
way home." She positioned the microphone closer to Claire, using
the woman's food tray—which swung out from the wall—for support.
"I'm going to turn this on now if you don't mind."

Claire waved her hand. "It makes me feel like a celebrity."

Julie pushed the On button and spoke in the direction of the microphone. "This is Julie Moore speaking with Claire Montgomery on
June seventh at eight-fifteen P.M. This is the twentieth interview in a
series dealing with near-death experiences. Claire, you may start
speaking now. Begin where you wish and tell your story in your own
words. I'll save my questions until you're done."

"Could I have a sip of water first?"

"By all means."

Claire drank from the glass beside her bed. She glanced once at
the recorder, once out the window at the view of Westwood Village,
then took a deep breath and began.

"It happened yesterday morning. I've been in the hospital for my heart. It don't beat like it should—it's always skipping and jumping in my chest. My doctor brought me into the hospital to run tests and try to stabilize it. He's been saying for a while I need a pacemaker, but I've been resisting 'cause I don't want anybody putting anything inside my body that needs batteries." She laughed softly. "That's not a joke, Julie. Call me superstitious but I figure that one day those batteries have got to run out."

Julie smiled. "I understand."

"Anyway, my doctor prescribed new medication to help with my heart rhythm. He admitted he was experimenting on me, but I didn't mind. At first the medication worked fine. I could breathe like I haven't been able to in years. Then there was a messup. I don't know if it was the nurses' fault or the pharmacy's. I don't suppose it matters. My medication got switched. My valve that was supposed to be opening was closing before the other end was opening. This morning my doctor explained what went wrong, but I don't know all the technical details. Anyway, a few minutes after I took my pills I felt as if I had a hundred-pound weight on my chest. My heart started hammering something frightening. Drawing a decent breath was like pushing a car uphill. The pain was awful. It spread out of my chest and into my arms. I could hardly work my hands. But I managed to push the button to call the nurse. If I hadn't done that, I would have died, no question about it." She paused. "But I died anyway, that's what this story is all about, isn't it?"

"It's your story," Julie said. "Please continue."

"I was conscious when the nurse rushed in. It wasn't Thompson but this other gal who likes women instead of men. She told me when I first got here, and I said that was fine as long as she didn't try kissing me. Anyway, she tried asking me what my symptoms were, but I was in no state to talk. She checked my pulse and went running for the doctor. It was then I felt a huge pop in my chest, as if the pressure had just got so great my ribs exploded. Then I blacked out.

"When I woke up I wasn't where I was supposed to be. I mean that in a way that I imagine would be hard for any sensible person to believe. But sure as there are jets flying in the sky, I was floating above my body. The nurse was back with a doctor and a respiratory therapist, and they were down below me working on my body. I figure I must have been up somewhere near the ceiling. They were shocking me with a pad and sticking needles in my arms and it didn't bother me one bit. I felt great, more free than I had ever felt in my life. Because they were only doing those things to my body and I wasn't in my body. In fact, I saw right then that Claire Montgomery wasn't that old bag of bones at all, but some kind of spirit. One that could fly. I felt like flying right then.

"Just the thought swept me out of the room. I passed through the walls as if they didn't exist and floated down the hallway. I saw Nurse Thompson sitting at the station and went over and tried to get her attention by calling her name. I even went so far as to tug on her uniform sleeve, but she didn't know I was there. She was reading her book and sneaking a cigarette, and I could have been the wall standing there. A funny thing happened, though, when I touched her. It was like I could read her mind for a moment. And I can state for the record that Thompson is no lesbian. The two naked men she had in her mind and the things they were doing to her body—she must have seen on a porno movie. She couldn't have done something like that in real life, I would think, and still be able to sit down the next morning.

"It was about this time I noticed there was something odd about the ceiling. It was there like always, but there was something else layered over it, some kind of dark opening, oval shaped, maybe ten feet across at the widest. I don't know why but I couldn't stop staring at it—once I got Thompson's nasty thoughts out of my mind. Then all of a sudden I slipped into it. I didn't intend to, it just happened. Then things really got interesting.

"I felt like I was flying in the Shuttle, I was moving that fast. But even though everything was black like space, there were no stars. I don't know how long I was in that tunnel. Ten minutes, an hour. Time didn't mean anything to me. I wasn't the least bit scared—the opposite. I rushed forward with great excitement. I knew the tunnel would end and I would enter a wonderful place. There was a faint light up ahead, getting steadily brighter.

"I exited into a wide open space, so big I imagine all the galaxies in all the sky could fit into it. It was filled with a wonderful white light. How can I explain that light? It was brighter than a thousand suns, but not hard to look at. It was softer than the smoothest velvet, but powerful too, like nothing could have stood against it. I mean that literally. The light was alive, conscious. There were so many living beings in it and yet I was unable to focus on a single one. There were patterns of some kind all around me: intersecting triangles, circles, and spirals. They weren't flat, though, but three dimensional, maybe four dimensional. These shapes were alive, too. They had a purpose—I don't know what, but I was so happy to see them. It was like they were blue-prints for the universe I had left behind.

"I was saturated with joy. I could have floated in that place for eternity, but a being of some kind came to me. I couldn't make out what he looked like. I couldn't describe him to you. I couldn't even tell you if it was a he or a she. I just became aware that there was someone before me who loved me and whom I could trust. The love coming from this being was stronger than anything I could have imag-ined on earth. He embraced me to the core of my being without touching me. I felt I belonged to this being, that we were one, but I wanted to worship him as well. I know that sounds confusing but I wasn't confused right then. I felt as if all my questions had been an-swered without my asking them.

"My whole life flashed before me. I say flashed because it was not as if I viewed it incident by incident. It was as if the whole of my stay on earth were simply there before me. The most interesting thing was that whenever I had helped anyone—the act could have been minor—the influence was the greatest. For example, when I helped a child at a store find his mother—that simple act had sent out a positive vibration into the whole universe. I could see the effect of every action I had taken, like visible waves that rippled out. Ironically, the things I had considered my most important accomplishments in life, like being the only one in my family to graduate from college, meant little or nothing as I viewed them. All the time I appraised my life, the being remained silent beside me, never judging me. I was my own judge. The experience answered a big question for me about how God is described in the Bible. Even before the experience I could never imagine a God of love judging his children. I never judged my children.

"Finally the being had a question for me. Without using words, he asked if I wanted to stay where I was or go back to earth, back to my body. I didn't have to think for a moment. I wanted to stay. Who would have been crazy enough to leave? The being seemed to under-stand my response. But then there was a flash of light in that ocean of light. The being vanished, my joy left me. I felt myself falling, falling, down the black tunnel, faster than I had climbed it.

"Then there was another flash of light; this one hurt. I felt myself jump forward. I was in my body and there was a sheet over my face. My chest was on fire and both my arms ached. I brushed aside the sheet and called for the nurse. The woman-lover came running in the room and turned white when she saw me. 'You're dead,' she said. I just smiled at her, though I wasn't feeling too happy to be back. 'If I'm dead, sister,' I said, 'then we both need life insurance.' "

Claire laughed softly. "I thought that was a funny first line for a born-again to make." She paused. "That's my story, Julie. I hope you don't think I'm crazy or that I made it up. It's what happened to me, even if I can't tell you what it means."

Julie did not speak right away. Claire's story had held her mesmerized, and she tried to analyze why. There was the obvious fantastical content of her tale, but Julie had heard many NDEs and Claire's was not unusual. In fact, Claire reported several of the classic experiences. Julie realized it was the way Claire's voice changed as she spoke—particularly when she reached the end of the tunnel—that had intrigued her. Claire's choice of words had become more eloquent. Her delivery had taken on a vitality. Her old eyes had shone. There was a glow in them still as she regarded Julie.

"A penny for your thoughts," Claire said.

Julie shook herself and consulted her notes. "You told your story well. There are a few questions I'd like to ask. The first one: when you were hovering over your body and observing the doctor and respiratory therapist working on you, were you in a position to see in detail the procedures they used to revive you?"

"Like I said, I saw them apply the shock pad and put the needles in my veins."

"Had you ever seen such procedures used before on dying patients?"

"Sure. On TV."

"Are there any other details of the procedures that you noticed that you hadn't seen on TV?"

"None that I can remember at this time."

"When you were floating on the ceiling and down the hall, did you notice unique features of the building that you hadn't noticed before? Such as a tiny stain on the ceiling? The inside of a closet?"

"No. I was having too much fun to worry about such details."

"When you went through the dark tunnel and emerged on the other side, did you meet anybody that you had known on earth?"

"No."

"You mentioned that your husband is deceased. Did you meet him?"

"No. I would have recognized him if I had, even without his body."

"The being that you did meet—would you say that he had been a human who was now on the other side?"

Claire was thoughtful. "I don't know. If he had been human, he must have been the most incredible man who ever walked the earth."

"Would you say that he was Jesus or any other religious figure?"

"I was raised a Baptist and he reminded me of the way I was taught Jesus was supposed to be. Filled with love and light. But I couldn't say he was Jesus. He never told me his name."

"Did he convey to you any knowledge that you didn't have prior to meeting him?"

The question brought a frown to Claire's face. "I don't remember anything—but now that you ask, there was something he wanted me to bring out."

"That he wanted you to bring out? To say?"

"Yes."

"To whom?"

Claire blinked, looked startled. "Maybe to you."

Julie forced a laugh. "But you didn't know me until today."

Claire spoke softly, her face grave. "But isn't that the very question you're asking me? And maybe the answer as well."

"I don't understand what you're saying."

Claire slowly nodded, more to herself, as if realizing something. "I was supposed to tell you something. I remember that now. Only I can't remember what it was—exactly."

Julie felt flustered and had to make an effort to keep her voice even. "Claire, did the being say to tell Julie Moore so and so? Did he specifically say my name?"

"No. I told you, he didn't speak with words. But you were there, somewhere in that space, in that light, in all those strange and wonderful shapes and colors."

"What was I doing there?"

"Nothing. You weren't really there. It was like you were part of the plan."

"What plan?"

"I don't know."

"Claire, when I first walked in here, did you feel I was part of the plan?"

"No." Claire wasn't defensive, quite the opposite. She seemed almost relieved. She added, "But your questions brought the feeling back to me."

"But you don't know what you're supposed to tell me?"

"No."

"You don't seem very upset with the fact that you can't remember."

Claire gazed out the window. "Maybe I wasn't supposed to tell you anything with words, just as the being didn't tell me anything with them. Maybe it's enough that I am here with you now, just as he was with me for a little while."

Julie tried another approach. "Whatever the being wanted me to know, do you feel it was a positive message?"

Claire hesitated. The question seemed to strike another chord, but not one of peace. She lowered her gaze and stared at her wrinkled hands. "After this experience, I'm not afraid to die, Julie. Can you understand how important that is to me?"

"Yes. Certainly."

"I no longer believe there is death for anyone, no matter what their religion. I no longer believe there is a devil or hell. When I was on the other side all I saw was light. I think that's all there is, in the end. Just the eternal light of God. I don't think anyone needs to be afraid."

Julie spoke with reluctance. "You're trying to tell me that the being conveyed to you there was no reason for me to be afraid? Specifically me?"

Claire studied her. "Yes."

"Is something going to happen to me?"

"Yes."

"You feel sure of that? A moment ago you couldn't remember any message from the being."

"It comes to me as we speak about it."

"What's going to happen to me?"

"I don't know."

"If we talk more about it will you know?"

"No."

Julie sharpened her tone. "How can you be sure? Your story keeps changing every few seconds."

Claire reached out and took her hand. "Don't be upset with me. I'm not trying to scare you. I never thought about who you were or what message I had for you before you walked in this room. I planned none of this. But now I *know* I have to tell you this. There is, ultimately, no reason to be afraid. No matter what walks in this world, beyond it is the light of God. We will all go back to that one day."

Julie flashed a thin smile. "Sounds like a pleasant sermon. I would like to believe it."

"It's not a belief. It's my experience." Claire let go of her hand and sat back, as if her heart were troubling her again. "Do you have a sister?"

"No. Why do you ask?"

"No reason." Claire reached for her glass and took a sip of her water. Her glow had left her. Now she was just old. "Do you have any other questions?"

"You mentioned that the being asked if you wanted to stay and you conveyed to him that you did. Did he explain that wouldn't be possible?"

"No."

"But you didn't stay. You came back," Julie said.

"Yes."

"Do you have any comment on that incongruity?"

Claire thought a moment. "No."

"Is there anything else you'd like to add to your story?"

"No. Except that I'm sorry if I scared you. It wasn't my intention."

"You didn't scare me. I've done many interviews such as these."

Claire's smile was kind. "I understand, Julie. I hope you meet a nice young man soon. Someone to take care of you."

Julie turned off the recorder. "I can take care of myself."

Claire turned away and seemed to shiver. "I'm sure you can."

Julie stopped at the nurses' station as she left. She had not asked Claire all her questions, but was anxious to get away. Thompson hadn't gone on her break yet. She was still reading her book. Julie nodded to the glitzy title.

"Any good?" she asked.

The woman looked up. "The story is silly. But the dirty parts are fun. They're the only reason I read books like this."

Julie froze. "Interesting," she whispered.

"What's interesting? Sex?"

"Yeah. I love it." Julie turned. "Thanks for letting me talk to Claire. Have a good night."

In the elevator Julie's hands were trembling. Twice she missed the ground-floor button. Her reaction appalled her. Claire was just an old woman, she told herself. No supernatural being on the other side had predicted doom and gloom for Julie Moore. There almost certainly wasn't another side.

"Why do I do these interviews?" she muttered.

To hear what became of Patricia? That was too simple an answer. To finally complete her degree and get a high-paying job? Too cynical a response. Because even an atheist was always thinking about God? Maybe that was closest to the truth. Whatever, Claire's story had hit her hard.

Before leaving the medical center Julie stopped to call her chairperson, Professor Stephen Adams. He was her advisor for her Ph.D. An Englishman in his late sixties, he possessed knowledge on many esoteric subjects, from kundalini yoga to past-life regression to tea-leaf reading. It had been Adams who had encouraged the subject matter of her dissertation. Yet Adams was not simply interested in her collecting accounts of NDEs. The literature was chock full of them. Personally he was fascinated with details that people observed while outside their bodies that could later be verified. That was why Julie had asked Claire some of the questions she had. Yet her paper remained "The Psychology of the Near-Death Experience" because she was, after all, a psych major. Adams had asked her to call after she interviewed Claire. He had briefly spoken to the old woman earlier that day.

Julie dialed his number. Adams answered promptly and, briefly, she reviewed Claire's story. She left out Claire's warning. Adams seemed pleased, if a bit distracted.

"Anything we can show to the physicists?" Adams asked when she was done. He wanted independent collaboration of Claire's tale, something rarely found in an NDE.

"Well, the doctors do say she was technically dead," Julie said.

"Anything else?"

Julie hesitated, thinking of Nurse Thompson's comment about the dirty parts, Claire's remark about the nurse's sexual fantasies. But she feared to rehash the coincidence, feeling it would give the other things Claire had said more weight than she was willing to grant at this point.

"No," Julie said.

"I'm glad you called now. A few minutes ago I spoke to a friend of mine, a doctor, at the center. He told me that Dr. Morray is there right now. He saw him in the basement, in the morgue. See if you can catch him."

Julie knew Dr. Lawrence Morray by reputation. He was a well-known cardiologist and one of the pioneers in the NDE field. For years he had collected accounts of people who had come back from the dead, well before any of the popular books appeared. He had published several papers—using his position as a department head at a prestigious medical teaching center—in respected journals when NDEs were seen as nothing more than hallucinations. Yet his major book on the subject never materialized. Word had it that he had suddenly lost interest in NDEs and burned all his research. But Professor Adams didn't believe the stories. He felt Morray had his research tucked away somewhere and that Julie could save herself a tremendous amount of leg work if she could study it. Adams had tried approaching Dr. Morray directly, but his efforts had been rebuffed.

"If he wouldn't talk to you, what makes you think he'll talk to me?" Julie asked.

"He likes pretty young women. His wife is half his age and a real dish. Offer to buy him coffee. Sweet-talk him. Act sincere and make him feel important."

"I try to do that with all the men I meet. It doesn't work." Julie sighed. She was tired and she had to be up in the morning to open the bookstore. She worked twenty-five hours a week at a Crown in Santa Monica. This on top of her dissertation research and a couple odd classes. Her student loans just didn't cut the big three: tuition, food, and rent. She was almost always tired. "Can I walk into the morgue?" she asked. "Won't they kick me out?"

"The dead people? They never complain."

"Huh."

"Give it a shot, Julie. Morray's a character, brilliant but brooding. You might be able to reach him. No one on the planet knows the subject better than he does. One of his partners once said he thought Morray let some of his patients die just to bring them back."

What a wonderful medical recommendation, Julie thought. She agreed to try to meet the big man. Hanging up, she wondered if she'd see any dead bodies in the morgue. She hadn't seen one in a long time.

The medical center was huge, spread out over many buildings.

Reaching the morgue was not simply a matter of pushing the basement button. Julie had to ask for directions and even so, she got lost twice. It was half an hour after she spoke to Adams that she found herself in the long silent hallway that dealt with the center's continuing difficulty with human mortality. Yet even here there was no sign that said Morgue. In the distance she spotted a lone man approaching. He was tall and seemed to dream as he walked. Without seeing a name tag she knew instinctively that she had found Morray. She let him come to her.

"Excuse me, are you Dr. Morray?" she said in her most professional voice. He paused to study her, and she did the same. He was a picture of many burdens, an old sixty. The wrinkles on the top half of his face seemed to form from an invisible sack of earth placed on his oversize balding head. His mouth was thick lipped; it seemed locked in a constant straight line. His dark eyes were intelligent but world-weary, as if they had stared too long at lost patients. His white coat was flecked with drops of dried blood.

"Yes," he replied cautiously. "Who are you?"

She offered her hand. "Julie Moore. I'm a Ph.D. candidate. What a coincidence I should run into you. I've been looking for you for some time."

He shook it reluctantly. "Why?" he asked simply.

She swallowed. She had not prepared a speech and his presence was intimidating. "I heard you burned your files but I didn't believe it," she blurted out.

His face hardly moved. "You're a student of Professor Adams?"

"Yes, sir. I am doing my doctorate on NDEs."

"I'm not interested."

"But you don't know what I'm going to ask." She jumped in front of him as he started to step past her. "Please, I know you must be as tired as I am and want to go home. And if you don't want to show your research to me, I understand. But I'd like to ask you a couple of questions about the field. I've been doing research on it for a year and some things still puzzle me." She paused. "There's no one I feel I can ask who knows as much as you do about it."

He appeared to resign himself to her questions with great reluctance. Yet a flicker of curiosity shone in his eyes. "What do you want to know, Ms. Moore?"

"So many of the accounts I hear of NDEs are so similar that I wonder if it's because so many stories have been in the media. But you investigated NDEs before they were popular. Were the accounts similar then?"

"Yes."

"Could you elaborate?"

He spoke as if he were lecturing a student. "The experiences of floating above the body, of passing through a long dark tunnel, of entering a realm of serene light, of watching a review of one's life, and of encountering a divine being were typical. Several accounts contained all of these variables. The majority contained one or more."

"How do you explain that?"

"I can't."

"But from your extensive research, you must feel there is an afterlife?"

"No."

His answer surprised her. She was stunned by how much it upset her. She strove to regain her balance. "But for many years you heard glowing accounts of life on the other side. You traveled all over the country to hear them."

"I heard stories from people whose hearts and respiration had stopped for extended periods of time, periods modern medical science would consider unusually long. The stories were often told with great wonder, and many people's lives were profoundly changed by their experiences. But my research never proved the existence of an afterlife for the simple reason that multiple subjective accounts containing numerous similarities do not constitute scientific proof. Above and beyond that, none of the people I questioned had ever died. They had close brushes with death. Find me a person who has been dead three days and let me question him, and then ask me if there is proof of an afterlife." He checked his watch. "Until then, my wife is waiting for me."

"Just one more thing. Why did you suddenly abandon your research?"

"I felt I was wasting my time."

"Do you feel I am wasting my time?"

"Yes. Certainly you are wasting mine."

"I do apologize. May I ask one more question, Doctor?"

"You have already asked that, Ms. Moore."

She forced a smile. He was not a cheery character. "May I see your research someday? At your convenience? I'd just like to read it. I wouldn't use it without permission."

He drew in a weary breath. "You appear young and healthy, Ms. Moore. Why are you so interested in death?"

"I could have asked you the same question twenty years ago. That was when you started your research, wasn't it?"

The question had touched deep. Dr. Morray was thoughtful, yet the mood was not soothing, for his thoughts seemed as dark as the air around him. "There was a personal tragedy in my life," he said finally.

"Someone close to you died?"

"Yes. But it was actually . . . thirty years ago."

"And it sparked your interest?"

"*Sparked* is a poor choice of a word, Ms. Moore."

"I'm sorry." She almost mentioned Patricia then, but something held her back.

Morray shrugged. "Since then I have seen a thousand people die. Their bodies stop functioning and it's the end for them. That's all I know, no more than any other man or woman." He added, in a more gentle voice, "Maybe someday you may look at my records. You're right, I didn't destroy them."

"I'd appreciate that very much. When would be a good time?"

He was already walking away. "Catch me sometime here or at my office. Have a good evening, Ms. Moore."

"You, too, Doctor."

Julie drove home. It was close to ten, not too late to catch a movie, she thought. But she was tired and hated to go alone, although she'd been doing a lot of that lately. She was a great fan of films; it was her main form of entertainment. She usually went in the afternoon, when the prices were cheaper and not having a date didn't brand her a social leper. Buttered popcorn and a medium Coke were sometimes lunch. A movie had to be terrible for her not to like it. Science fiction and horror films were her favorites, but she liked love stories as well — where a golden prince appeared at the door of the rent-controlled apartment in Santa Monica and offered to pay half. What a story.

Julie pulled into her designated parking spot and climbed out and frowned at the metal showing through on her Ford Escort's front tires. What did four new tires cost? Two hundred bucks? She had two choices: she could fast for two months and die of starvation or else perish from a blowout on the freeway. In either case, she'd see a cool white light.

"Yeah, right," she muttered.

Her place was a box. She had a TV and a VCR, but hadn't used the VCR since it had eaten her copy of *Alien*. She had a number of books, mostly textbooks and *New York Times* best-selling paperback novels. She read her share of trash and liked the dirty parts as well as Thompson. Her lack of sleep had not diminished her sex drive, nor had her latest six-month abstinence. It was really ridiculous when she thought about it. A blond, blue-eyed, twenty-nine-year-old from Kansas who couldn't get laid in big, dirty Los Angeles. She didn't know why she just didn't go out to a bar and pick up the best-looking guy in the place.

Of course, there were reasons, and AIDS wasn't the least of them. But even assuming the guy had walking papers, she'd never slept around, because unless she was really relaxed or really drunk she couldn't have sex. It would hurt too much. She had no major sexual psychological traumas. She had never been raped or abused, and there was nothing wrong with her physically. Her problem was simply a slow, wet fuse. It forced her to be in a committed relationship, or else become an alcoholic. But booze also had a tendency to make her throw up. God had dealt her a difficult hand, there were no two ways about it.

Yet it wasn't as if she never got asked out. At school, eating lunch on the grass, guys stopped to talk to her, not often, but at least on great hair days. But she had to have a reason to say yes, and she seldom gave them time to give it to her. She didn't think of herself as picky but rather discriminating. Usually they were male children: freshmen or sophomores. She would have been happy with an undergraduate senior.

In her apartment Julie had dinner: a bowl of corn flakes and a banana. She ate a lot of fruit; it was cheap and easy for her to digest. She had a nervous stomach and was plagued by heartburn. She always kept a roll of Rolaids or Maalox in her purse. Eating her exquisite meal, she watched TV, the news. There had been another murder in L.A., some poor man with two kids. It seemed there had been a lot of killings lately. The newscaster said the police had no suspects.

Once more she debated with herself about running out to see a movie, but a huge yawn settled the issue for her. Better to sleep and be fresh for work tomorrow, she thought. She undressed, trudged into the bathroom, and closed the door. She preferred to shower at night rather than in the morning. It allowed her to sleep in an extra half hour. If there was no God behind the white light people saw on the other side, at least there were warm beds and soft pillows on this side. Her idea of bliss was to still be in bed at ten in the morning.

Julie was in the shower and washing her hair when she heard the noise outside the door, inside her apartment. At least she assumed it came from inside the apartment. It sounded as if someone had bumped her coffee table. Immediately she turned off the water and quietly reached over and locked the bathroom door. For the life of her she couldn't remember if she'd locked her front door, but doubted it. She had an innocent farm girl's bad habit of trusting that people were basically good-hearted even when the media blasted the opposite into her skull day after day. Her blood roared in her head; she could hear it clear enough over the roaring. She believed she might be in danger.

"Hello?" she called, her voice thick. "Someone there?"

There was no answer, but she thought she heard the sound of steps on her wood floor; the boards creaking with the weight of a body considerably heavier than her own. A rock 'n' roll drummer took over the pounding in her head. Her fear leapfrogged through ten levels and landed in the region of pure terror. A wave of dizziness swept over her and she had to lean against the tile wall, still dripping wet. It was the news, she told herself, all the talk of murder that had her spooked. The chances were that she hadn't heard a thing. That there was no tall dark man with a long silver knife waiting outside the door.

"Jesus," she whispered.

Yet she did not believe that. She had heard something, even if it wasn't Ted Bundy. She dragged in a series of deep breaths, trying to calm herself. She had to think. She refused to end up another statistic. Her research was filled with them; many of the people she interviewed were old and sick and died shortly after she talked to them. Claire had been old.

"You're trying to tell me that the being conveyed to you there was no reason for me to be afraid? Specifically me?" "Yes." "Is something going to happen to me?" "Yes."

Her predicament was compounded by three factors. She had undressed outside the bathroom and had nothing to wrap around her except a medium-size towel. Her nakedness added to her feeling of helplessness. Also, her bathroom backed up against the studio on the other side of the hall. Her only window to the outside was a miserable opening Bart Simpson would have had trouble crawling through. Of course, she could shove off the screen, stick her head out, and shout bloody murder, but that raised a third problem. She wasn't absolutely sure there was anyone outside the door and she dreaded making a fool of herself. Even in the face of death, it made no sense but there it was.

Julie dried herself hastily and made a quick quiet search of her medicine cabinet and bathroom drawer for a potential weapon. Tampons, cotton balls, lipstick, Vaseline, Valium—she had it! She could open the door and ask the tall dark man with the long silver knife if he would please drink her glass of drugged water before he laid her out and opened her up. It had been a warm day; he might be thirsty.

"God," she whispered, weeping silently at the absurdity of her thoughts. She was going to die; the black tunnel was calling. She would fall into it and miss the white light and all the good memories. Tall and Dark would slit her jugular and she would fall into an abyss. Dr. Morray knew reality when it died in his arms, don't give me any of that happy-time New Age bullshit.

Julie found a razor blade—one of the single-edged disposable kind—in a blue plastic holder. Not a formidable weapon, but it was all she had and it would have to do. She broke the plastic that held the blade and lifted it out and held it up to the light, cutting herself in the process. Not a happy time to see the red stuff, she thought. No shit. She wrapped one end of the razor in blood-stained toilet paper, leaving a half inch of the metal exposed. Wrapping her towel around her, she put her ear to the door and steeled herself. She believed she heard someone breathing not fifteen feet away. Tall and Dark might have been sitting on the edge of her bed, his nose to her sheets, enjoying the scent of his next victim.

Her plan was simple. She would throw open the door, swing with her blade at whoever was there, and then make a beeline for the door. If he grabbed her, she would let out a scream that could be heard at the beach. Here goes, she thought. Be brave, be strong. Don't die, don't cry. One, two, save my ass, Jesus, and maybe then I will believe in you. Three, four, just open the fucking door.

Julie threw open the door.

A man sitting on her bed jumped up in the dark.

He lifted his arms. She took two strides forward and swung with her blade.

Made contact; the guy let out a cry.

She whirled and leapt for the front door. Her towel fell off and she didn't stop to retrieve it. Her hands found the knob and twisted it left, twisted it right, finally got the damn thing to open. She had one naked leg in the hallway when Tall and Dark spoke at her back and she realized he was more like Brown and Pumped.

"Shit, Julie, you cut my hand," he complained.

Julie stepped back inside and shut the door. Pissed and feeling like a fool.

"Stan," she said with disgust.

Stanley Fraiser's entry into her life was another symptom of her deep-seated trauma brought on by her father's humiliation of her high school boyfriend, or else a bad call. She had met him at the bookstore where she worked. He was buying a book; she had assumed that meant he read. She should have taken more careful note of the title: *Warbirds of WW II*. He had squeezed her number out of her by talking about all the movies he had seen lately, which she, of course, had seen as well. He had promised to take her to a movie on their first date, which was the last promise he kept to her.

All right, in her defense, he wasn't an intellectual, but his body was the stuff of orgasms. She had noticed that on day one in the bookstore. He worked out incessantly; he had pectorals bulging from his ass. He ran on the beach wearing nothing more than a colored jock strap. His face was tan and perfectly handsome, if lacking in distinction. He had good hands; and knew how to relax her without alcohol.

He was a dead end, though. He worked two part-time jobs: as a waiter in a sushi joint and as a clerk in a hardware store. God knows she was no stranger to low-paying employment, but the problem with Stan was that he had no desire to get ahead, and probably hadn't the intelligence to do it. She had gone out with him three months, twice a week, before she saw a sample of how poorly he wrote. He'd left a note on his door for a friend but she read it instead and had a hard time believing he could misspell *back*. She tried talking to him about it but he became defensive. So he couldn't spell, he said. That's why they had invented computer spell checks. The only problem was he didn't own a computer and hadn't the slightest idea how to operate one.

He borrowed money from her, which he seldom repaid. Julie considered herself generous by nature, but when he took the twenty that made the difference between her being able to buy gas and having to ride her bike the six miles to school, she blew up. He soothed her feathers by giving her a back rub, but he ruffled them again before the night was over by asking if he could move in—just for a couple of months. Seemed he was behind on his rent, but not his gym member-ship. She said no. She gave him a bigger no the next night when he asked if she wanted to go out.

That had been the last time she had spoken to him. Six months ago. Stan had been her last sex, steroid assisted. Pitiful.

Yet here he was, holding on to his bleeding wrist and looking at her as if she should apologize. She strode over and picked up her towel and covered herself.

"You bastard," she said. "What kind of stunt are you pulling?"

"What are you talking about? I just came over to see you and you cut me." He held it up for her to see. She had in fact nailed his left wrist; it was bleeding badly. She set her blade down on her desk. "Give me something to stop this," he complained.

"Try pressure."

"Julie!"

"Shut up. I'm getting dressed first, then I'll look at your cut." On top of everything else Stan had been a hypochondriac. She sure knew how to pick them. She grabbed the red skirt and white blouse she had worn all day and shut herself in the bathroom.

Five minutes later she reemerged with a Band-Aid on her own finger. Stan was over at her small kitchenette, constructing a tourni-quet out of paper towels. She had bandages and rubbing alcohol in her hands.

"Come here and let me see it," she said coldly.

He had on blue jeans and his work T-shirt: Gabe's Hardware. He sauntered over and sat down in the chair at her desk. He offered her his bloody wrist. She had sliced it all the way across and it looked deep. She began to roll the bandage around the wrist.

"I think you need stitches," she said.

"Great. Drive me to the hospital. Pay for it."

She stopped. "You didn't just drop by and get cut. You sneaked into my house and waited for me in the dark to come out of the shower, hopefully nude."

"I didn't sneak in. I knocked and you didn't answer."

"Maybe. But I called out while in the bathroom and you didn't answer."

"I didn't hear you."

"Bullshit."

"What do you want from me, Julie? I'm the one who's hurt."

"I don't want anything from you, except for you to leave."

"Why are you so mad at me? Did we part on such bad terms?"

"No, Stan. But you scared the shit out of me. How did I know you weren't a murderer? What if I had accidentally slit your throat? I was aiming for it."

Stan looked down at his wound. "My hand feels numb."

"More reason to see a doctor." She continued wrapping his wrist. "But I'm not going to drive you. I'm tired and I have to get up for work in the morning. What brought you here anyway?"

"I just came to say hi."

"And?"

"You have become such a bitch, you know that?"

"You caught me at a bad time, Stan."

He looked at her, trying for sincerity. "You look good, Julie. I've missed you." He paused. "Have you missed me?"

She sighed. "A little, yeah. How have you been?"

"Not so good. A lot of money problems. How are you doing in that department?"

"Stan. I can't give you a loan. The tires on my car are worn to the metal and I can't afford to replace them."

"I just need a hundred bucks. I can give it to you next month."

"No way."

He glanced at his hand. "You know, Julie, you've injured me. I don't know how bad. You might want to be a little nicer to me."

She stopped dressing his wound and stood stiffly. "Get out. Now. Or I call the police."

He stood slowly. Ordinarily Stan had a pleasant if somewhat vague expression on his face. Now his anger was visible. He must need the hundred badly, she thought. He held up his left arm. The partial bandage was already soaked.

"You're going to be hearing from me about this," he said in a cold voice.

She laughed. "Really? Is that a threat? I'm going to call the police right now and file a report. You can file your own version. I wonder who they'll believe, seeing as you're bleeding all over *my* floor." She poked him in the chest. "Go drop a barbell on your brain. It might shock it into normal functioning."

Stan left. How tragic that he slammed the door behind him. Julie cleaned up the mess he had left. She didn't call the police because she didn't take his threat seriously. But she hoped the feeling returned to his hand, if it was in fact numb. She wouldn't have intentionally hurt him, even though he'd scared the shit out of her.

Julie undressed, turned out the light, and went to bed. She intended no one any harm. Why would a supernatural being who lived in the light of God think she deserved to suffer? It made no sense, she thought as she fell asleep. None at all.

FOUR

❊

D
R. LAWRENCE MORRAY had lied to Julie Moore when he had told her he was on his way home. Even though it was ten o'clock on a Friday evening, Dr. Morray was seeing a patient in his office at the U.C.L.A. Medical Center. Ten was late even for him, though it wasn't unusual for Dr. Morray to schedule appointments from six in the morning to nine at night. He worked an average of eighty hours a week, sometimes a hundred. He was seldom home. There was nothing there for him except his wife.

His patient was a sixty-year-old printer named Pino Carbone. Carbone had emigrated to the United States from Sicily thirty years earlier but still had a heavy accent. He had become Morray's patient by accident. Two years earlier Morray had been leaving the hospital via the emergency back door when Carbone had been brought in suffering from what appeared to be serious heart failure. There had been a huge gang fight that same night and the ER was crowded with bleeding Hispanics and African-Americans. Morray had offered to treat Mr. Carbone when it became clear that no doctor could see him for at least an hour. Morray had listened to his heart and checked his blood pressure and had immediately given him a thousand-dollar shot of a potent blood thinner. The medication had dissolved the blood clot forming in Carbone's arteries and saved him a much more serious heart attack. Nevertheless, the man's heart was scarred. Even though he was out of intensive care in a week and back on the job in six, he continued to be plagued by angina, chest pain. He had called Dr.

Morray that day and said he was feeling worse. Morray had agreed to see him at ten that night because it was his first opening.

When Dr. Morray was through examining Carbone, he had him put his shirt back on and brought him into his office. He had put Carbone on the treadmill and been forced to take him off after a minute; the man was already turning blue. He had also monitored his heart closely. Dr. Morray believed himself a master of diagnosis with a stethoscope alone. He didn't need to perform cardiac catheterization—which produced moving X-ray pictures inside the heart and arteries—to know that Carbone's right pulmonary artery was more than ninety percent blocked, not to mention most of the other major arteries and veins in his heart.

"Give me the bottom line," Carbone said as he took a seat in the chair in front of Dr. Morray's desk. Morray's quarters at the medical center were spartan; the bulk of his personal books and tools were at his private office in Malibu. He did have a lovely view of Westwood Village, however, the many movie theaters and restaurants. He had been to neither in many years. Carbone was still panting from his short jog on the treadmill.

"You need a quadruple bypass. If not, you'll drop dead sometime in the next six months." Dr. Morray spread his hands by way of apology. "You wanted me to be blunt."

Carbone drew in a deep breath and paled. Dr. Morray was familiar with the reaction. No other organ in the body—when it started to fail—invoked the fear that the heart could. A doctor could tell a patient his kidneys or liver were shot, and the intense dread would seldom be there. Dr. Morray estimated that more than half his patients made themselves considerably sicker by constantly worrying about their hearts. Yet there was no easing their worries. The heartbeat, next to the inhalation and exhalation of breath, was what people connected with life. Dr. Morray had met few people who were not terrified of dying. Carbone looked scared.

"You're taking about them sawing open my chest," Carbone said. "I don't want that."

"Do you want to die? The main arteries and veins in and out of your heart are virtually closed."

Carbone shifted uneasily in his seat. "I read about this laser they're working on. They slide it into the heart through a big vein and melt the cholesterol away."

"That's still in the experimental stages."

"What about the balloon? And this Roto-Rooter thing?"

"Balloon angioplasty is the correct name for the first procedure. It involves threading a catheter through an artery in the arm or leg. When the catheter reaches the plaque deposit, a balloon at the end of the catheter is inflated to compress the plaque and widen the artery so that the blood can flow freely again. Rotational atherectomy is the name of the second procedure. In it a rotablator—a motorized cutter with a diamond-studded burr—works in the arteries to shred plaque into smaller pieces that can float away."

"Are you experienced in both procedures?"

"Yes. But I don't recommend them in your case. Your blockage is too severe."

"What's the downside of the procedures? Say things go bad?"

Dr. Morray listed them on his fingers. "Possible reaction to the dye. A blood clot at the artery entry site requiring surgical removal. A blood clot in the coronary artery treated. Spasm in the wall of the coronary artery. A perforation or tear in the artery wall. A stroke, heart attack, heart arrhythmia, or electrical disturbance of the heartbeat. Or death." Dr. Morray paused. "Is that enough for you?"

"But these things usually don't happen, right?"

"That's true, but I still think you should get the bypass."

Carbone was doubtful. "You know my printing business is my own. I've been having trouble obtaining medical insurance. It's a stretch for me to pay for this office visit. How much would this operation cost?"

"Between the operation and the postop care I'd say fifteen thousand." Dr. Morray raised his hand when Carbone started to protest. "You cannot wait to save the money. Have the operation and if worse comes to worst let Medicare worry about it."

Dr. Morray realized he might have said the wrong thing. Carbone was a proud man who liked to pay his way. The printer straightened in his chair.

"What are my chances of surviving the balloon, the rotablator?" he asked.

"I told you, I don't recommend it. I don't base my recommendations on whether a patient can afford the preferred treatment or not."

"But you do feel it is better for me to try them than to do nothing at all?"

"Of course. If you do nothing, you will die."

"What are my chances?"

Dr. Morray shrugged. "The procedures are done in an operating theater, in case you do have a heart attack, so that you can be opened up immediately. Your chances of surviving both procedures would be better than ninety percent. But a more important question is how successful will that treatment be in solving your problem. I believe it will not solve it. At best it will give you a couple of years of easier breathing. Then you will be right back where you started."

"But then I can worry about dropping dead in a couple of years." Carbone coughed. Dr. Morray knew he was accumulating fluid in his lungs, a classical result of failing cardiopulmonary functioning. "Doctor, I think I'll try these things first. Then I'll change my diet and start walking again and, who knows? I could be fine."

"You will not be fine. Do not delude yourself. But you can be well if you get the bypass. You could live another thirty years."

Carbone was stubborn. "Maybe I'll have it done. I'm just saying I want to try the others first. A friend of mine had them done and he's doing fine."

"Your friend was fortunate, but you are not your friend. You don't have his body." When Carbone didn't respond, Dr. Morray asked, "Is your decision based on finances or a fear of the pain from bypass surgery?"

Carbone hesitated. "Both. I don't know which bothers me more." He leaned forward, the cold light of fear clear in his eyes. He'd been having trouble breathing since he walked into the office. "Would you do the balloon and the rotablator on me? You saved my life once before, I trust you."

Dr. Morray sighed. "I will do them if you force me to do it."

Dr. Morray lived in a luxurious hilltop home in Malibu with an unobstructed view of the coast in both directions. He had bought the four-thousand-square-foot ranch-style house twenty years earlier and it had since gone up in value five times. But maybe it had lost a chunk of that equity with the recent fires. During the dry months there was considerable flammable brush on the slopes that stretched away from his backyard and swimming pool. Yet Dr. Morray had no intention of selling it, and didn't care what it was worth anyway. He'd made a million and a half the previous year and just let it sit in the bank—that is, except for the forty percent he sent to the IRS. Money, fame, prestige—these meant little to him. When he examined his life, he had to wonder what he did care about. It was an examination he didn't often undertake.

He found his thirty-year-old wife, Sara, floating naked in the Jacuzzi in the backyard. When he had met her five years earlier, he had thought she could give his life new meaning. He had fallen in love with her as he had no other woman, except his first wife, Sandra. He had met Sara at the Armand Hammer Museum in front of a Van Gogh. The painting was a sad work, like most of Van Gogh's, he thought, but shimmering with color, the reds and oranges on fire. Sara had come up behind him and spoken just the opposite of what he'd had in his mind.

"It's so cold," she said.

He had turned, and saw for the first time her creamy skin, her hair so black it had to be dyed but wasn't and her eyes, especially her eyes, dark but luminous. Her summer dress was white and short; the low neckline granted a glimpse of the top of her breasts, large and lovely, faintly freckled. Yet she was pale by Los Angeles standards. Her rich red lips seemed to be painted on, even though it was clear she wore no makeup. Immediately he felt as if he knew her, although she did not look familiar.

"Why do you say that?" he asked. "The colors are so bright."

"But the strokes are dark. I'm an artist, I see it."

He nodded. "Van Gogh didn't have the happiest life."

"Few artists do."

"Are you talking about yourself? Are you unhappy?"

She chuckled; the sound echoed softly through the empty wing. Her voice had character beyond her years. Or maybe it was pain—her laugh had an edge to it, a turbulent mystery. She stepped closer to the painting, away from him, yet it was as if she moved to get a better picture of the whole of him. She continued to smile but her expression was reflective.

"What's your name?" she asked, ignoring his question.

"Dr. Lawrence Morray. Yours?"

"Sara."

"Just Sara?"

"I don't know you, Dr. Morray." She paused. "But you look familiar. Have you been on TV?"

"Not in many years. Even then, only a couple of times."

"Why were you on TV?"

"Some research I was doing."

"Hmm. You're a researcher. What do you research?"

"I'm not involved with research at this time. Presently I'm a cardiologist. I see patients and teach at the medical center up the street. What do you do?"

"I paint."

"Do you paint for a living?"

"Yes. I'm very good. They should display my work here."

"Is there somewhere your work is on view?"

"Yes. In bookstores. I do covers for books."

"It's good that you're successful. You don't look old enough."

She flashed another smile, this one clearly full of fun. "I fool people that way all the time." She tossed her long hair. "My last name is Smith."

He didn't know why she let him take her for coffee. He was clearly twice her age, and it was obvious his status as an important physician didn't impress her. She didn't ask much about his work. She didn't talk much about hers. Even though they spoke openly about many things, she had an elusive quality that made him unsure how she felt about the world as a whole. Her wit was subtle but pervasive; even after several years of being with Sara, he still didn't know when she was joking or being serious.

She had depth, though, even if she permitted no one to explore the bottom of it. She reminded him of Sandra in many ways, but it was not a comparison he willingly made. His past was best left buried. He told Sara on their first date that he had been married before, but she had no apparent interest in the first Mrs. Morray. But after only one afternoon in her company, he wanted her to be the next Mrs. Morray. Her eyes had hypnotized him along with her mouth. She had a habit of teasing the tip of her tongue over her teeth, which he found very sexy.

He asked if he could see her again and after a long pause she said yes. They were married a year later. But the twelve months before the wedding turned out to be their best time together. Every day, just a bit, he found himself losing enthusiasm for Sara Morray, or perhaps it was for life in general. She was still the same. She still laughed at his occasional joke; still smiled when there was no reason to smile. But he believed he finally had the answer to the question he had asked her in front of the Van Gogh. Her grin was filled with rich color but the strokes were all wrong. She wasn't happy. She hadn't married him for love, but out of some deep inner compulsion that he didn't understand. They slept together in the same bed, but he believed neither of them ever dreamed of the other.

He came up from behind her as she floated unclothed in the bubbling water and stared down at her magnificent body. Despite the distance in their marriage, they continued to have sex frequently. They never discussed why they did. Pleasure was not always an end in itself, he thought, even for the cynical, and he was pretty cynical about most things. Sometimes he believed she was trying to get pregnant, despite the fact that she never stopped him from wearing a condom. She'd had a miscarriage at the end of the first year of their marriage. The memory was painful for him, for many reasons, but she had recovered from it well.

Sara liked the water hot. The steam swirled around her lush breasts. Her nipples—pink with the heat—peeked through the strands of long dark hair that floated down from her head. She had her eyes closed and could have been asleep, except that he knew she slept very lightly.

"Are you hungry?" she asked.

"I could eat something." He stared out at the dark expanse of the ocean. "Have you eaten?"

"I was waiting for you." Out the corner of his eye he saw her open her eyes and sit up. She studied him for a moment. He could always feel when Sara's eyes were on him. "You look tired," she said.

"I'm not tired," he lied. "What did you do today? Did you paint?"

"I sketched, went to the beach." She stood and reached for a towel. The steam, in the flickering blue-white light of the Jacuzzi, rose around her flesh in an aura. "There was a lot of excitement," she explained, her expression remaining reserved. "A young girl almost drowned; it was close." She paused and in a single fluid motion swept the towel around her shoulders. Sara was always graceful, especially naked. "If a woman had not given her mouth-to-mouth on the spot, the girl would have died. The girl's boyfriend was there. He wept when she started to cough."

"He must have been relieved."

Sara approached and touched a bloodstain on his white coat. "You shouldn't be out like this. Makes you look unprofessional."

"In my profession people are always bleeding." He looked down at her and she flashed him a faint smile. Going up on her toes, she kissed him briefly on the lips. He reciprocated a moment too late and kissed the air. "Do we have any steak?" he asked.

"I can make you steak." She turned for the house, the bottom of her rear showing under the edge of the towel; the smooth curve of eroticism, in another time. "Would you like wine with your meal?" she asked.

"Yes, please."

She went inside. Dr. Morray stared at the dark ocean for a few minutes more. Almost drowned. It was close, she had said, and he knew just how narrow the line between the living and dead could be. Like the pause between inhalation and exhalation. Stretch it out too long and maybe you saw God, or maybe just heard the dirt thrown on the top of your coffin. He felt a chill that brought sweat. The ocean water was warmer farther south, he remembered, but sometimes a cold current ran through it.

He turned and walked into the house. While Sara cooked, he sat in the laboratory he had constructed in the north corner behind the garage. Test tubes and beakers stood around him like the silhouettes of toy soldiers preparing for a battle to be decided by a child. He didn't turn on the light. The darkness was his shawl against the psychological frost that had followed him into the house. But he had come to the wrong room for reassurance. He sat in the dark in front of a two-foot-square wall safe. It was locked up tight, had been for several months.

Yet he thought he heard something move inside.

FIVE

❊

T HE COLD ONE sat in the sun on a bench by the beach. A
young mother sat beside It, holding a female infant while a
male child approximately two years old played at her feet.
The Cold One had met the mother a few times before at a nearby
grocery store. The woman had red hair, a bad complexion, and a sore
back from her recent pregnancy. Her husband worked in Hollywood
as a sound editor. He'd been working unusually late, the woman con-
fided, since she'd lost her figure. The woman was distressed.

"It's not that I think Tom's having an affair," she said. "But I
worry with all those pretty young things at the studio that he might
start having one." She shook her head and stared at her plump legs.
"I've just got to do something to get my body back in shape. I forget,
do you have any children?"

"Two. A boy and a girl."

"When did you have them?"

"Some time ago."

"You look in incredibly good shape. What did you do to get your
figure back?"

"It just happened for me."

The woman shook her head. "You're lucky. I would die to be you
right now."

The Cold One smiled. "Now you are being overly dramatic." It
felt a scratching on Its calf. The Cold One had on white shorts, a blue
halter top. The two-year-old was trying to get Its attention. The mother
reached out to stop the boy.

"Robbie, leave her alone."

"It's fine," the Cold One said. It reached down and picked up the boy and set him on Its lap. The Cold One could feel the blood pumping inside the child, the breath going in and out of the tiny nostrils. This creature was alive, It understood that. But the boy was not alive in the way that It was alive. For the child felt things. He had needs and desires. He cried when he was hurt, laughed when he was happy. But even though the Cold One did these things, It didn't do them for any reason.

"I think he likes you," the woman said.

"Children always do." The Cold One caressed the top of the child's head. It knew that if It were to squeeze slightly on the bone tissue with Its fingers, the child's skull would crack and the brains would be exposed. Then the child would stop breathing and the mother sitting beside It would be upset. In fact, the woman could suffer what humans called a nervous breakdown and be ruined for life, even though nothing physical had been done to her. Such was the power of human emotions, the Cold One thought, and the weakness of them. The Cold One wondered if one day It would ever experience emotion.

But perhaps It was already, It wasn't sure. Was curiosity an emotion? Since the Voice had halted inside six weeks ago, It had been pondering what It was, why It did not behave as humans did when It was clearly inside a human body. It had bought a book on physics and had been reading it before the red-haired woman had arrived. It had found the section on the laws of thermodynamics interesting, the three fundamental laws that were supposed to govern all of nature. Energy could be neither created nor destroyed. Entropy— randomness—always increased. The Cold One saw entropy as a basic problem for humans, all living things. Biological life was an expression of order in a universe that was constantly growing more random. Life could stand against entropy for only a short period of time. In the end it would lose.

The Cold One wondered if It might be the embodiment of entropy. It was an interesting idea. It had nothing against life on earth, but since the Voice had stopped It understood that by Its very nature It would destroy all life. It was only a matter of time. It leaned over and kissed the top of the child's head.

"I'm sorry, I must run," It said. "I have an appointment." The Cold One set the child down and smiled as the little boy immediately picked up some sand and tossed it into the air. It knew that before the child grew to adulthood he would be dead or like It. The Cold One stood, leaving Its physics book on the bench. The woman with the red hair squeezed Its hand.

"Please don't repeat anything I told you," the woman said. "I just felt the need to unburden myself. I say more than I should when I feel that way."

"Your secrets are safe with me," the Cold One assured her.

The Cold One walked south along the beach in the direction of Sunset Boulevard. From horizon to horizon the sky was blue; the water sparkled with the myriad reflections of the sun. Yet It knew the sky It saw was different from the one the humans around It saw. For the Cold One could see the stars even in the middle of the day, the black space that was always overhead. Humans often spoke, particularly in literature, about the light of the soul. But the Cold One never saw that light, only a darkness as deep as that which lay beyond the stars. It stared up at the sun as It walked, the glare not bothering Its eyes. A tiny black dot traced a line across the brilliant orb. It was the planet Mercury, the Cold One knew. It had followed the movement of all the planets since It had become conscious. It occasionally wondered if It had come from out there somewhere. The city was trapped in the middle of a heat wave but the Cold One was unaffected by the temperature.

Near the intersection of Sunset and Coast Highway, It came across a preacher that It also knew from previous meetings. He stood outside a restaurant called Gladstones, talking to a small group. But he excused himself when he saw It and hurried over. The Cold One paused to allow the preacher to catch up. The man, in human terms, was not the holy-roller type, but a sincere and personable young man who was interested only in spreading the good word of Jesus Christ. He had read the Cold One bits and pieces from the gospel and the Cold One had listened with interest. In particular the Cold One found Revelations intriguing. If It was not related to the second law of thermodynamics, It wondered if It might not be the Antichrist. It didn't really mind one way or the other, but had decided that It did want to know. It might affect Its long-range plans. But It had not asked the preacher if It was the Antichrist.

"Hi, how are you doing?" the preacher asked. His name was Craig Westmore. He was thirty-five years old and had thinning reddish hair that he kept rigid and in place with excessive hair spray. His frame was much too thin by normal standards, and his face was prematurely wrinkled—perhaps from the sun, perhaps from his quirky nature. He had an intense expression that could often look confused. He was not an intelligent man, the Cold One understood, but most humans would have called him kind. The Cold One wondered if It, too, would be called kind and decided that, normally, the answer would be yes. The preacher was happy to see It. He carried his leather-bound Bible in his right hand.

"I'm well," the Cold One said. "How are you?" Humans always asked questions like this, although they had no interest in the answers. It continued Its walk south. The preacher followed.

"Wonderful," the preacher replied. "I'm glad you came by. I haven't seen you in a few days. Have you been busy?"

"Yes. And you?"

"The work of the Lord never ceases. Have you thought more about what we discussed last time?"

"Yes."

"Do you have any questions for me? I would be honored to answer them for you. I consider you very close to entering the house of the Lord."

The Cold One nodded. "I was curious about the Antichrist. You said he is to come soon, that he may even be on earth already. Does your Bible say exactly where he is to appear first?"

"The Bible's not clear on that point. Most modern scholars believe it will be in the Mideast, but I'm unconvinced. We know for sure only that his arrival will signal the beginning of Armageddon and the close proximity of the return of Christ."

"Is Christ the one who is supposed to slay the Antichrist?"

"Yes. He will cast him down into the hell from which he arose." The preacher opened his Bible. "I can read you the Scriptures that deal with this topic."

The Cold One raised Its hand. "It's not necessary. I'm sure you know them well. Tell me, why is the Antichrist portrayed in the Bible as a man? Could he come in female form?"

The preacher laughed as if It had told what humans called a joke. "No. The Antichrist is clearly male. God, too, is always seen as masculine."

The Cold One teased. "It sounds to me as if the Bible were compiled by men."

The preacher became serious. "I think it's time that you made a firm commitment to accept the Lord Jesus Christ as your personal savior. There's no guarantee of salvation for you until you do."

"How do I do that?"

"You just have to pray to Jesus to enter your heart. If you are sincere, he will come. It's that simple."

The Cold One stopped walking. "Can we do it here? I don't have a lot of time."

The preacher's face broke into an expression of delight. He gestured to a nearby bench. "Have a seat. Close your eyes and repeat this prayer after me. Feel it with all your heart."

The Cold One sat on the bench beside the man. His expression was earnest—he truly expected something amazing to happen. The Cold One, of course, expected nothing. It shut Its eyes as the man spoke in an affected voice, as he tried to sound old and wise. The Cold One spoke also, but in a normal voice.

"Blessed Lord, I call upon you to accept my soul. I am a sinner, I am a fornicator. Only you can forgive my sins. I ask you to do so now that I may have you enter into a clean heart when you enter into my life. From this day forward, I will be your servant. The works of Satan and his servants I reject totally. I pray to you, Jesus, to save me. You are my savior, my only savior. Bless me now in the name of the Father, the Son, and the Holy Spirit. Amen." The preacher paused. "You may open your eyes now, child."

The Cold One opened Its eyes. "Are we done?"

A beatific grin broke across the preacher's face. "We are done for all of eternity. How do you feel?"

"Fine."

The preacher laughed. "But don't you feel free?"

The Cold One stood. "I suppose. I do not feel bound."

The preacher stood. "That's what I'm talking about. The joy of the freedom of the Lord is something you will begin to experience from this moment on. I envy you, this your first day of being born again. What's important now is that you go deep into a study of the Bible. I will be happy to help you in this." He looked It over and his breath faintly quickened with excitement. The Cold One understood this as a sign of sexual interest. It often received such signs. "Anything I can do for you will be my pleasure."

"We will talk later. Now I must be going. Thank you for your prayers."

"All thanks goes to Jesus. Amen to you, Leslie."

"Amen to you, Craig."

The Cold One was going to meet the man who had driven It from Baja. Only the man was not a man anymore. Neither was he like the Cold One, and that was part of the Cold One's difficulty. The Cold One had discovered It could not easily replicate Itself as It had initially believed. It had tried a number of times and failed. Either the humans died or they became murderous beasts, devoid of self-control. They were sterile, too, not able to pass on Its breath to others. They acted brain damaged, which the Cold One was beginning to believe they were. It wasn't as if human brain cells died only when they were deprived of oxygen for more than five minutes. The damage also occurred, the Cold One knew, when a human was deprived of a *living* breath. The Cold One had given Its human plenty of air, but no life. Perhaps it was the breath of entropy, the exhalation of the Antichrist. The Cold One did not care much for titles. Being born again had not changed Its disposition.

Still, the Cold One continued to make *bastards* — as It called the ones who survived Its embrace. They had their uses because they were usually subservient to Its wishes. The Cold One was not worried about Its inability to replicate Itself. It never worried. And It had a backup plan. Life on planet Earth would cease — it was inevitable.

The Cold One met the bastard known as Ralph near the Santa Monica Pier. Ralph was one of the more stable of Its bastards, which was not saying a lot. He had, since his transformation, developed a compulsion to drink warm blood. The Cold One knew of the folklore surrounding vampires and wondered if a being such as Itself had ever walked the earth before and created offspring. Yet It felt no compulsion about anything, and none of Its bastards was affected by the sun. It had instructed Ralph to drink only the blood of stray animals. From newspaper articles on recent violent murders, It did not believe all of Its bastards were obeying Its instructions to be careful.

Ralph was sitting under a tree on the grass as the Cold One walked up. He immediately jumped to his feet when he saw It. Besides being the most stable of Its bastards, Ralph was the most afraid of It. The Cold One had changed Ralph slowly, and the process had been very unpleasant for him. He had begged for It to stop, as if the Cold One might respond to screams. When the Cold One had matters all arranged, It would destroy all Its bastards or, perhaps, have them destroy themselves. The Cold One suspected that Ralph knew this as well.

Ralph was thinner than when he had picked It up six weeks earlier, and that was only a small part of the ruin he had suffered. Most humans would have said he looked like a homeless person on a ten-year binge. He was filthy; he stank. He hadn't changed his clothes since they'd met. It had told him to go home and act normal, but Ralph had immediately eaten and killed his ten-year-old daughter — in that order. The child had yet to be reported missing because the mother lived in another state. The Cold One had been surprised when It had first visited Ralph and found him sitting naked in the middle of his living room with his daughter's bloody clothes and bones strewn about. It had told him to wash while It had gone out and rented a machine to shampoo his carpet.

"Hi," he said, his voice cracking pitifully. He shifted uneasily from foot to foot. He had only one shoe. He feared to look directly at It. His eyes constantly darted toward every child that walked by, every dog that ran on the nearby grass path. The Cold One understood. Everything alive repulsed him and made him ravenous. It came close and reached out Its hand and put it on his shoulder. It squeezed hard enough to bring pain.

"Be still," It said. "Listen closely. I have a job for you."

The Cold One spoke while Ralph stood with his head lowered and his eyes closed. He couldn't stop trembling. But when It was done he nodded that he understood. Once more the Cold One cautioned him to control himself, then It walked away. It would have sighed when It glanced back at Ralph from a quarter mile away, if It ever sighed. Ralph had caught a sea gull and ripped the bird's head off. People watched as he poured the blood down his throat. The Cold One wondered if It might need someone else to complete the task It had given the man. Maybe someone a little more alive.

SIX

❧

A WEEK HAD GONE by since Chuck called Peter Jacobs. A week of waiting and dread. But then one morning, the same time as before, his phone rang. Peter knew it was Chuck before he picked up. His gut tightened. He was just glad the ringing had not awakened him from another nightmare of the young woman with the staring fish eyes.

"Hello," Peter said.

"Is this Mr. Peter Jacobs?" The voice had changed in the last seven days. It was thinner, at the same time coarser, as if Chuck had just downed a margarita with sand in it.

"Yes," Peter said. He pushed a button on the electrical box Amos and pals had set up. Chuck's call was now being traced, yet a trace took time, usually several minutes. It was Peter's job to keep him on the line as long as possible.

"This is Chuck," he said. "I hope I didn't wake you. I know I should call you at your office, but I didn't want to talk to you there. I have something to tell you, Mr. Jacobs, if you want to hear it, and I think you do."

Almost the exact words as before, as if Chuck had memorized a script. Peter sat up in bed and spoke warmly. "I would love to hear what you have to say, Chuck."

"We have to meet, you and I, we have to talk. There is so much you have to hear. The world is changing, it won't be the same any-more. You're an important person. You can understand how important my words are." He paused. "You do understand, don't you, Mr. Jacobs?"

"Yes. I would like to meet you. When and where would be a good time?"

"Tonight. At the Museum of Natural History beside USC. You are familiar with the place?"

"Yes. But could you please give me a more specific location and time? The museum is large."

"Specifics, Mr. Jacobs, blur when your breathing slows down and your heart leaks blood. You understand?"

"Yes," Peter whispered.

Chuck hung up. Peter set the phone down. It rang one minute later. Amos was on the line. He sounded excited. "Forget my skeptical words the other day. He pegged James Crosser's hole in the heart, as well as the others."

Peter was thoughtful. "Yeah, he did it in a subtle manner. But you know, the guy doesn't sound that smart to me."

"Are you suggesting that he isn't working alone?" Amos asked.

"You're the detective. Were you able to trace the call?"

"No. You weren't on the line long enough. Not that it will matter if he visits you at the museum tonight."

"Do you honestly think he will come?"

"It's impossible to predict with someone like him. If he doesn't come, he might send you a message."

"How?"

"It could be anything." Amos paused. "It could be a rifle bullet shot from a distance. I tell you that because now we're entering the stage where things can get scary. You don't have to go if you don't want to."

"Has anyone else died in the last week?" Peter asked.

"Not that we know of."

"But you think he isn't finished?"

"No. This guy will go until he's stopped. I know that much about him."

Peter swung his legs over and put his bare feet on the floor. He'd been sleeping with the window open lately, Chuck notwithstanding. It had been hot the last few days. But he'd asked Matt to keep his window locked. He had bought his friend a fan to stay cool. Matt had not asked him why, for which Peter loved him: the innocent trust and obedience.

"Sure, I'll go. I promised Chuck, didn't I? How are we going to work this?"

Amos outlined a plan in which Peter would be wired for sound, while a dozen detectives in plain clothes milled around. The museum management would be contacted beforehand. Amos knew the museum was open later than usual, till nine, because of a special exhibit. Amos had already taken his daughter, the perfect SAT girl, to see it. He thought Peter should be at the museum as early as six o'clock. Just in case.

"I want you armed as well," Amos said.

"I've never used a gun," Peter said.

"This afternoon I'm going to teach you how to shoot."

"But I have to go in to work."

"Peter," Amos said patiently. "This week *you* are the news."

Julie Moore sat in Professor Adams's office, upset. It was ten in the morning and she had just come from the U.C.L.A. Medical Center. She had gone there for another interview with Claire Montgomery. She had left the old woman the previous week without asking the effect her NDE had had on her outlook on life. Unfortunately, the nurse on duty had told Julie that Claire died in her sleep the very night Julie had seen her. Julie had tears in her eyes as she poured out her story to the chairperson of her department.

"Why does it bother you so?" Adams asked. "Many of the people you've interviewed have died shortly afterward. It's to be expected. Many of them are very ill or old."

Professor Adams's office was a composite of New Age books and pieces mixed with Old World spiritual artifacts. On his desk he had a stone gray Shiva *lingam* from India; a quartz crystal from the mines of Arkansas that had been carved into a pyramid; and a miniature skull from a Dogan shaman in central Africa. Although Adams collected the stuff, he was not obsessed with it. He had once told Julie he kept it only to impress his undergraduate students. Adams was impressive in his own right, to Julie at least. In films she always loved the proper English gentleman, and he fit the bill nicely. His suits, as well as his groomed hair and trim mustache, were gray. He had tons of shoes from all over the world and never wore the same pair twice in the same week. His eyes were also gray, warm and alert; he seldom met anyone without immediately complimenting him or her on some small thing. He was loved and respected by most of his students. Julie thought of him as a modern Van Helsing. His knowledge on the most arcane of subjects was vast.

"I just connected with her in some way," Julie explained. "I just assumed I'd see her again."

"You didn't sound that taken with her when I spoke to you after the interview."

"We didn't part at a smooth point in the interview. That was another reason I wanted to speak with her again, to tell her that I appreciated her talking to me about her experience."

"Did you have an argument?"

Julie shrugged. "She touched a personal nerve in me."

Adams smiled. "And you don't want to talk about it. That's fine. But tell me this—do you feel guilt over her death?"

Julie felt shocked by his insight, although this was not the first time he had called her on something she thought safely buried inside. "I do feel guilty," she admitted. "But I don't know if it's because I feel in any way responsible for her death."

"Then what could it be?"

"I don't know."

Adams was reflective. "Then try to remember that she is now in that wonderful place she described to you, beyond all suffering."

Julie made a face. "It's a pleasant thought."

Adams chuckled at her skepticism, not that he was bent on converting her to a specific philosophy. As far as she could tell, he accepted almost everyone's beliefs as valid. He did not like fanatics, however, those of strict dogma, anything that narrowed the mind. She had talked to him a couple of times about her sister's death, how the experience had alienated her from religion rather than brought her closer to her father's faith. His words were always comforting. Simply sitting with him she felt herself relaxing. He reached over and picked up the skull on his desk.

"Why do people who have NDEs experience such joy?" he asked suddenly. "Have you ever asked yourself that question?"

"The obvious answer is that for a short time they are dead and floating in some kind of heaven." She paused. "But you're not looking for that answer."

He stared into the skull's eyes. "It's not because they're dead. It's because their breathing has stopped."

"Isn't it the same difference?"

"Not at all." He set the skull back down and grunted as if the empty eye sockets had given him the insight he needed to explain his theories. "In the Himalayas yogis and their disciples practice different forms of *pranayama*, breath control, and *kriyas*, rhythms of breath, which naturally allow them to enter a state of breathlessness. When the inward and outward breaths cease, they experience mystical ecstasy, not unlike that of people who almost die. The difference is that yoga is a lot easier on the body than being hit with a car or choking on a chicken bone. Meditation is, too. You can enter a high state by calming the breath—working with the mind via the body. Or you can do the reverse—calm the mind and the breath will naturally calm. But both ways the breath is involved. It is the breath that links the inner and the outer world. I sometimes think the yogis in India are light-years ahead of us psychologists. They go straight to the source of bliss and get drunk and then all their problems vanish."

"But don't they practice for many years before achieving higher states?"

"Yes."

"And who is to say their higher states are anything but subjective illusions? What insights into reality have they brought into the world?"

Adams raised an eyebrow. "If they can show one how to be happy, that is insight enough for me. But I didn't bring you here to discuss these things. You said Dr. Morray offered to show you his records. I want you to get them before he changes his mind."

"He offered to let me look at them. He didn't say I could take them home with me."

"I don't mind if you study them in his home. But I would like to see them myself."

"You believe they're at his house?"

"Yes. I doubt he keeps them at one of his offices." Adams pulled open a drawer in his desk. "I have his home number here. Why don't you call him? You cannot imagine the work that he could save you on your dissertation."

"Only if he allows me to quote his research."

"Let's take things one step at a time." He scribbled a number on a scrap of paper and handed it across his desk to her. "I wouldn't mind if you called him now."

"I doubt if he'll be at home right now."

"His wife might be. She can tell you when he gets in."

Julie smiled. "Are we being a little aggressive?"

"I am. Dr. Morray has always fascinated me. I'm not sure why. It must be something other than the research he did. You're my way to get close to him. I'm using you, Julie, what can I say? But if you don't want to call him, that's fine, too. Just don't expect to be awarded a doctorate from this university."

Julie laughed and reached for the phone. "Since you put it that way, I feel divinely inspired to call." She punched in the number and played with Adams's pyramid while Morray's phone rang. A woman answered. She sounded young and pleasant.

"Hello?"

"Mrs. Morray?"

"Yes."

"This is Julie Moore. I met your husband at the hospital. I'm a graduate student at U.C.L.A. and your husband offered to let me see some records that might be of help with my dissertation. Is he at home now?"

"No. He won't be home until eight this evening."

"Would it be all right if I called back then?"

"What are these records?"

"They involve near-death experiences. I'm sure you're aware that your husband researched the field extensively years ago."

"No, I wasn't aware of it."

Julie was taken aback. What did those two talk about? She hoped her disclosure wouldn't annoy Dr. Morray. "Would it be OK to call back? I don't want to be a pest."

"Why don't you just come by this evening? We have so few guests these days. It would be good for my husband to have company. Let me give you our address. You have a pen?"

"Yes. But don't you want to ask him first?"

Mrs. Morray's voice was smooth. "No. Just come. It'll be fine. We live at One Twenty-one Malibu Lane, off Coast Highway, two miles north of Pepperdine."

"Got it. Thank you, Mrs. Morray."

"Sara, please. It'll be nice to meet you, Julie."

Julie found Adams watching her after she set down the phone. "Piece of cake," he said.

"He doesn't know I'm coming."

"His wife will smooth over any difficulties."

"It was nice of her to invite me. Do you know anything about her?"

"She's an artist and looks like a model. I once met her at a party. You'll have competition for the doctor's attention."

Julie nodded, remembering Dr. Morray, his flat voice, his haunted walk. "It's not as if I want to try to steal him away from her," she said.

SEVEN

❊

"I FEEL LIKE THE Bionic Man," Peter Jacobs told Lieutenant Amos Rodrigues and Blank. Peter still didn't know Blank's full name or if he even had one. He wasn't sure why the medical examiner was present. Amos was busy checking out the power supply to the wire under Peter's shirt. They were in a men's room inside the museum. The time was five minutes after six. "Can this thing electrocute me?" Peter asked.

"There isn't enough power," Amos said.

"It could give you a nasty shock, though," Blank said. "We once had a snitch wear a wire to a drug buy. The guy was scared. His perspiration caused the wire to short out. He screamed and the Colombians got suspicious. I did the autopsy on the guy. They had cut his throat from ear to ear."

"Thank you for sharing that with me," Peter said dryly.

"Just don't want you to sweat too much," Blank said.

"It's hot!" Peter protested. "Of course I'm going to sweat."

"You'd sweat more if you had a sport jacket on," Amos said, satisfied with the condition of the wire. He gestured for Peter to button up his shirt. The absence of the coat was a major issue; it made it hard to camouflage both the wire and Peter's weapon, a miniature snubnosed .38 that he had taped to his right leg, close to his sock, for lack of a better place. "You'd also look more suspicious," Amos added.

"What if Chuck runs up to me and stabs me?" Peter said. "Maybe I should wear a flak jacket."

"The snitch I told you about wanted to wear one," Blank said.

"Would you stop that," Amos said wearily. He studied Peter with his good eye. "If you want to change your mind it's not too late."

"Sure it is. All you cops would laugh at me." Peter shook his head. "It's at times like this I miss teaching." He nodded to the medical examiner. "What are you doing here, anyway?"

Blank was dressed entirely in black as usual. "You never know when my services might be needed," he said, not smiling.

Julie Moore sat in her car down the street from Dr. Morray's and worked on her makeup. Ordinarily, she was a casual dresser. But she thought the doctor would appreciate her dressing up for him. She had on a blue suit and bright yellow scarf. The suit was the best piece of clothing she owned. Her father had bought it for her the previous Christmas. She wasn't a master of makeup; the lipstick she had with her made her look somehow terminal, at least in the yellow overhead light. Off to her left, a quarter of a mile down a shrub-covered hill, was Coast Highway, and just beyond that the ocean. Sober red light struggled to cling to the horizon in the west. The sun had been down half an hour.

Julie was just about to start her car and drive the remaining hundred yards to the Morray's residence when Dr. Morray coasted by in a gold Lexus. She saw him but doubted he noticed her. She watched as his garage door opened and then closed after the car disappeared inside. He was late, she thought; it was half-past eight. She decided to give him a few minutes to relax before banging on his front door.

A few minutes later, however, the garage door opened again and the Lexus pulled into the street. It took off in the opposite direction, away from her. Julie understood in a moment what had happened. Morray had come home tired and hungry and his wife had sprung Julie Moore on him. He had probably fled the house to enjoy a quiet meal in a restaurant. It made no sense to follow him, but she started the car and chased after him anyway. She thought it remotely possible that he might return to the hospital and she could bump into him again and apologize for being such a pest. In reality, she was just upset that she had annoyed him and wanted to smooth things over as quickly as possible. Of course her chasing him might make him angrier.

Once on the Santa Monica Freeway, Dr. Morray bypassed the exits that would have taken him to the hospital or to a bunch of good restaurants for that matter. He continued onto the Harbor Freeway, took that south, and got off at the exit for Exhibition Park. His movements continued to puzzle her as she followed him into the parking lot for the park. Where was he going? The Coliseum? The Sports Arena? The museums?

Julie felt like a fool when she saw Dr. Morray's wife, Sara, climb out of the Lexus and stride toward the museums. So much for deductive reasoning, Julie thought. Sara Morray had on a red summer dress and carried an oversize black briefcase in her right hand. Even in the harsh white light of the parking lot, there was no mistaking her. She was very beautiful, as Adams had said. Julie did a sudden turnabout. This might work out for the best, she thought. Maybe Sara Morray was the one she should talk to, anyway. The woman had sounded so delightful on the phone. Julie could tell her the whole story of how she thought she was following her husband. Sara would probably get a good laugh out of it.

Julie climbed out of her car to chase after the woman, who was heading in the direction of the Museum of Natural History.

The plainclothes cops were clearly growing more disappointed the later it got. Peter could tell by their expressions as they passed him in the museum hall, though, of course, he made no effort to try to talk to them. He was disappointed that his main emotion was relief that Chuck hadn't shown because he liked to imagine that a part of him was always up for danger and adventure, but in reality he just wanted the night to be over so that he could go home.

It was possible, however, that Chuck was in the museum but they had missed each other. For that reason Peter kept moving. There was also the even greater possibility that Chuck had put in an appearance, noticed the dozen plainclothes detectives milling about, and immediately split. Peter thought that some of the officers looked as if they were personally related to ex–Police Chief Darryl Gates.

At nine o'clock sharp the lights began to flicker. Peter was entering the dinosaur section then. He had already been to the special Egyptian exhibit and been suitably impressed. He didn't believe in reincarnation but had experienced déjà vu studying the mummies and hieroglyphics etched on the stone blocks. He had wanted to reach out and touch the ancient letters, as if their meaning might become clear to him with such a simple act. But the signs warned to keep hands off. The display had inspired him to want to visit Egypt and the pyramids. He hadn't traveled much, and never out of the country.

Since the movie *Jurassic Park*, he imagined the dinosaur exhibit would be the most popular in the museum, but there was only one person present as he strolled around the bones of a huge *Apatosaurus*. The woman appeared to be an employee of the museum because she was sitting on a bench and sketching the dinosaur, oblivious to the fact that the place was closing. He hadn't struck up a conversation with anyone, partly to keep himself available for Chuck and partly because he knew his every word would be recorded. But he wanted to talk to this woman as soon as he laid eyes on her.

Her hair was long and dark, straight—she wore it loose over her shoulders. Her bangs were also long, brushing her eyebrows. She tossed her hair from her eyes, a gesture he found instantly attractive. She had a young face and her body, despite being lush, gave the impression of teenage vitality. Yet the impression was at odds with the mature grace with which she carried herself. Her red dress was lovely; the portion of leg it revealed, divine. She frowned as she worked, unaware of him, and pursed her red lips as a child would, or maybe a sensual woman. Peter had often thought it strange how eroticism for him was so closely akin to innocence. Not that children excited him sexually. Yet, if asked to describe her in the moment he saw her, he would have said she was as much a young girl as a mature artist. He stepped behind her and saw that her sketches were excellent.

"Hello," he said. He would have reached under his shirt and torn off his wire if he hadn't been afraid of shocking himself. Goddam that Blank and his stories. She turned and raised her head to him. She had the biggest eyes.

"Hi," she said after a moment's hesitation. "Do you work here?"

"No. Do you?"

"In a manner of speaking." She gestured to her sketch pad. "I've been hired by the museum to redesign the dinosaur environments." She nodded at the *Apatosaurus*. "He looks like he's in a room in downtown Los Angeles, doesn't he?"

"How do you know it's a he?"

She smiled—the expression made her so kissable he almost asked her out right then. Damn the wire, he thought. At least there'd be no chance of his forgetting her phone number. She didn't wear a ring.

"That's a good question," she said. "If it's a she dinosaur I'll have to completely change my design."

He pointed to her bench. "May I?"

"Of course."

He sat down. "How did you get this job?"

"I belong to a couple of civic committees. One of them is concerned with Los Angeles and the arts." She shrugged. "A woman on the committee is the wife of the curator of this museum. He asked me for my help."

"Do you make your living as an artist?"

She was amused. It was a tired and clichéd expression but it was as if her eyes danced. Circles around him, that was for sure. "I make my living being beautiful," she said. "But I enjoy painting and do get paid for it. If that's what you want to know, Mr. —?"

"Jacobs. Peter Jacobs."

She offered her hand. "Sara. Are you *the* Peter Jacobs?"

"Is there only one of me in the phone book?" He briefly squeezed her hand. Her fingers were long and delicate.

"There is only one of you in the paper," she said. "I read your column from time to time."

"Not always?"

"You're writing faster these days."

It was an accurate observation, even if it did wound him slightly. "I'm saving myself for my novel," he said.

"Are you working on a book?"

He took a chance. "I might start one tonight."

She laughed softly. The sound put Lisa's gaiety to shame—so soft, Sara's voice, yet so mischievous. He definitely had to get her number.

"And I suppose I'm the one who's inspired it?" she said.

"Did I say that?"

"Are you writing a book?"

"No. I mean I would, but I have nothing to say."

"Then you should write about me. My life's been unusual."

"In what way?"

She gestured around her. "I often find myself sitting alone late at night surrounded by dinosaur bones." She paused, measuring him with her eyes, which was both thrilling and nerve-racking for him. He realized that since he had seen her he had forgotten all about Chuck. "Then a handsome young man suddenly appears. And I feel like I've slipped into a time warp."

Her words were encouraging. "Where do you live?" he asked.

"By the beach."

"Which beach?"

She was coy. "It's all one ocean, Mr. Jacobs. Where do you live?"

"Sixty-two twenty-two Saunders Avenue, Venice. I'm almost always home in the evening."

"But not this evening." She glanced around. The lights had stopped flickering—now they were going out. She closed her sketch pad over the baby *Apatosaurus* cuddling its father or mother, as the case might be. "What are you doing here?" she asked.

"I came to meet someone."

"Where is she?"

"He didn't come."

"He? Are you disappointed?"

It was time for a bold step. "Not now. I'd like to talk to you some more, Sara. Could I buy you a cup of coffee?"

She stood and her whole demeanor changed. Suddenly she appeared uncomfortable. "I'd like that. But tonight's not a good time for me. I was supposed to get here earlier, when the lights were still on, and finish working on this. But I had car trouble and was delayed." As she spoke, lights went out behind her and they were almost plunged into darkness. Peter cursed the timing. The absence of light seemed to add to her disquiet. "I really should be going," she said.

He jumped to his feet. "May I walk you to your car?"

She was already moving away, sketch pad and briefcase in hand, in too much of a hurry to put the pad away. He took this as a bad sign.

"That's not necessary, I'll manage," she said. "I hope we meet again, Mr. Jacobs. I'll be reading your column more closely in the future."

"I hope to see you, Sara," he called after her. Then she was gone.

Amos and Blank caught up with him a few minutes later. They ushered him into the same bathroom they had used earlier. Amos was clearly disappointed, Blank amused. Peter knew without asking that they had been listening over the wire.

"You didn't even get her last name," Blank said.

"What would you have done?" Peter asked, annoyed.

"Take off your shirt," Amos said. Peter began to unbutton it.

"I wouldn't have taken no for an answer," Blank said. "I never do."

"That's because you work with dead people all day and they never argue with you," Peter said.

"There's a lot to be said for the dead," Blank agreed.

"Would you two stop," Amos said, and began to untape the wire. The adhesive took hair with it as it came off, making Peter wince. "Do you know how much tonight's operation cost the taxpayers?" he asked.

"Maybe Chuck did show and we scared him off," Peter said. "Half your men and women look like extras from *Dragnet*."

"That's what I told Amos," Blank said. "I think I should be given a gun and put on the streets. No one would mistake me for the heat. Not with my handsome face."

"Chuck didn't show," Amos said confidently. "We had video cameras focused on every entrance to the museum, and I studied every face that came through the doors. There was no one here tonight who could have talked the way he talked on the phone."

Peter noted that Blank treated Amos's observation with respect, which made Peter inclined to believe it, although he wouldn't have been able to connect Chuck's voice to his appearance had he been shown a mug shot of the murderer with the taped conversations running in the background.

"What do we do now?" Peter asked.

"Wait till he calls again," Amos said.

"Or until he kills again," Blank added.

Julie Moore observed the conversation the man had with Sara Morray, although she wasn't close enough to hear their words. When the lights went out, she didn't follow Sara to the exit. Her attention was drawn to the man when two other men caught up with him and escorted him to a rest room. It made her wonder what was going on. The one guy looked like a cop, she thought, the other an undertaker. Yet the man Sara had been talking to—he looked just fine. They stayed in the rest room a long time, longer than she was willing to wait even to solve the mystery. Nor was one guy's pretty face incentive enough for her to wait any longer. Stumbling around in the dark outside, wondering where the hell her car was, she ran into the man.

He was more handsome close up, even in the poor light. He must have been hot; his long-sleeved dark shirt was half unbuttoned. He walked by her and nodded slightly. She had to speak to get his attention.

"Excuse me," she said, joking. "Do you know where my car is by any chance?"

He turned. His hair was light, she could see that much, his body trim. "Did you park in the front lot or the back?" he asked.

"The front, I think. Which way is that?"

He pointed. "That way. But your car's probably been stolen by now. They steal all the cars in the front lot. You probably shouldn't waste your time looking any further. Just call a cab."

She took a step closer. "I hope you're joking."

"Who's the one who's joking? Do I look like a parking lot attendant?"

She giggled nervously. "No, as a matter of fact you look like the gardener." She paused. "That was a dumb joke. Sorry. I felt like I knew you because I saw you in the museum a few minutes ago when those two men dragged you into the rest room. I thought they were going to kill you."

"And you didn't scream for help?"

"I don't like to get involved." She offered her hand to show she'd been kidding. "Julie Moore."

He accepted her hand. "Are you hitting on me, Ms. Moore?"

It was good it was dark; her cheeks suddenly had enough blood in them to make a vampire forget the jugular. "I'm just trying to find my car," she said.

The man glanced around. She could practically read his thoughts. They were close to the museum, true, but they were still in south-central L.A.—at night. Dangerous territory, each road marked and claimed by blood spilled in gang fights. She didn't know why she trusted this man instinctively, but she did. Perhaps it was the way he held himself, the inner strength he conveyed.

"I'll help you find your car," he said. They walked around the building, opposite from the direction she'd been heading. "My name's Peter Jacobs, and, yes, I write for the L.A. *Times.*"

"I don't get the paper. What do you write?"

"Trash." He laughed and shook his head. "This isn't my night."

"Don't say that. It could improve—all of a sudden."

"How?"

Julie thought of her stark apartment and watching movies all alone and bald tires and settling for Stan even when she knew he was a flake and how something had to change if she was to keep from going nuts. She also thought that it was her life and she was the only one to change it. She said something then she never guessed she would have said.

"We might not be able to find my car and then you'll have to give me a ride home and on the way there we'll stop and I'll buy you coffee to show my appreciation and we'll have a wonderful talk." She had to take a breath. "It's possible."

He studied her, cool as a celebrity. "I've been wanting a cup of coffee."

They ended up at a Denny's in Santa Monica, not far from both their residences. Julie's car had been found and she followed him to the coffeeshop. His column must pay well, she thought—he drove a new black Jaguar. When they were seated, she explained that the only reason she didn't get the paper was because she was broke. Better he think she was poor than uninterested in world events. She told him she watched CNN.

They talked about many things. His success impressed her, his wit surprised her—until she learned he had taught high school. Peter Jacobs was cool and sophisticated, and also mischievous with a good sense of humor that made even more sense to her when he explained that he lived with a handicapped young man whom he had known since they were kids. Yet she had the impression his humor was on the surface, that he took life very seriously. There was something about him that seemed tragic—an odd word to apply to a man who had a fabulous job and the looks of a soap opera star. Yet the impression struck her from the start and wouldn't leave. It was clear that, like Dr. Morray, Peter Jacobs had a lot on his mind.

"What were you doing at the museum?" she asked. He had only ordered coffee, but she was having apple pie and ice cream with her caffeine. She hadn't eaten since lunch.

"Visiting the Egyptian exhibit. Did you see it?"

"No. Actually, I got there late. I saw you near the dinosaur exhibit."

"I stopped to talk to a woman."

The way he said "a woman" made her pause. She'd been wondering whether he knew Sara Morray. Obviously he didn't, and she asked herself if she wanted him to know such a beautiful lady, married or not. She liked Peter, quite a lot actually. She spoke carefully.

"Who was she?" she asked.

"Her name was Sara. I didn't get her last name." He paused. He had a way of studying her with his green eyes that made her feel exposed. He didn't do it often, though, turn up the scrutiny, but now was an exception. "Do you know her?" he asked.

She felt a stab of guilt. "No."

He held her eyes a moment before continuing. "She was making sketches for the museum. It seems they're going to redesign the dinosaur exhibits."

"Sounds interesting. Who were those men who dragged you into the men's room?"

He smiled. "They didn't drag me in. Just a couple of friends."

"They were there to see the Egyptian exhibit as well?"

"Yes."

"One of them looked like a cop."

Peter coughed. "Really? They're both in the newspaper business."

"Do they write?"

Peter studied his coffee. "Those two guys think they make the news." He looked up and shrugged. "They're just friends. Why were you at the museum?"

"Just somewhere to go. I must go back to see that Egyptian exhibit."

"Yes. What are you doing your dissertation on?"

She had told him she was in the Ph.D. program in the psych department at U.C.L.A., but hadn't gone into details. " 'The psychology of the near-death experience.' "

His eyes widened with interest. "Have you had one?"

"No."

"What led you to the subject?"

Her ice cream was melting. She tried unsuccessfully to mush it closer to her pie but her hand was trembling. Why had his question touched such a chord in her? She had been asked it many times before. Of course, she'd never responded with anything about Patricia, except to Professor Adams, who was practically her personal shrink. Yet she had already lied to Peter about Sara Morray and didn't want to lie again.

"My sister died when I was sixteen. She was twelve." She shrugged, but the gesture did nothing to steady her voice. "I often wondered what happened to her—you know, besides the fact that she was put in a box and put in the ground."

Peter was silent for a moment. "Put in a box and put in the ground. The words sound so sad. I suppose it is sad—but it's going to happen to all of us one day." He reached over and held her hand. "I'm sorry. I shouldn't have brought it up."

She slipped her hand away, not because of his touch, but to wipe her eyes. It amazed her how painful the memory of Patricia still was. She shook her head.

"I brought her up. It doesn't matter, it was a long time ago. But I suppose the loss influenced my dissertation." She paused, reflecting. "The trouble is, I've begun to doubt my research will prove anything."

"What are you trying to prove?"

"That there's life after death. I know that sounds presumptuous. Jesus had a hard enough time proving there was, and who am I? But I'd be lying if I said that wasn't the ultimate thrust of my research."

"Then you must have faith that you'll succeed."

She shook her head again. "No. I want it so that we don't need faith. That we just know, one way or the other." She stopped. "Have you ever lost anyone close to you?"

"I spent most of my earlier years being shuffled from one orphanage to another. I haven't had many people close to me."

"That must have been tough for you."

His answer surprised her. "I wouldn't say that. I never felt cheated by not having a mother or father. I always felt— I'm not sure."

"Say it."

He sat back. A note of weariness entered his voice. "How do you know I was going to say anything important?" he asked.

"Because I'm only six months shy of a doctorate in psychology." She lowered her head. "But you are not my patient. I'm sorry."

"I always felt like I didn't deserve parents," he answered finally.

She nodded. "Many orphans do."

"No. I didn't feel like the others."

"What do you mean?" she asked.

But that was one question Peter Jacobs would not answer.

EIGHT

❊

T WO WEEKS HAD elapsed since Susan Darly scared Jerry Washington to death by almost drowning in the Pacific Ocean. During that time he hadn't seen her. She'd stayed overnight in the hospital and then went home for the rest of the weekend, Jerry had to assume. He knew for a fact that she'd checked out of the hospital the day after her ordeal. But Susan hadn't called him, and when he phoned, her father said Susan wasn't to be disturbed and hung up. Jerry didn't understand what was happening. He couldn't imagine Susan blaming him for her near drowning. He hadn't even wanted to go back in the water.

Susan attended Malibu High. It was Friday, the last day of classes for the year, and Jerry figured if he didn't catch her now he might never talk to her again. He drove to the school at lunchtime. Malibu High was fenced in but there were open gates, so he just walked in. He quickly spotted her, and some guy. They were standing together under a tree by a row of vending machines. Jerry thought he knew who the guy was although he'd never seen him before. Susan had once described her previous boyfriend to him—a classic football jock: six four, two hundred and fifty pounds. "Blond and dumb, like me," Susan had said with a laugh. Ted was his name. Jerry felt his blood heat as he watched Ted put his arm around Susan. No one messed with his girl and got away with it. Jerry sauntered over.

Susan saw him coming and her reaction surprised Jerry, or rather, her lack of one. Her face was strangely blank, as if he were someone she only barely recalled. The same could not be said for

Ted. He immediately put some distance between himself and Susan. He had eighty pounds on Jerry, but Jerry knew how frightening he appeared when he was mad. Plus he assumed Ted had heard about him.

"How come you haven't called me?" Jerry demanded, stopping ten feet from Susan, fifteen from Ted, who had retreated to the far side of the girl. Susan's expression changed only slightly at his question. She didn't look well; the skin under her eyes was dark and she was thinner.

"Jerry," she said flatly.

Jerry glanced at Ted. "Don't you have business somewhere else?"

Ted took a step closer to Susan. "I'm talking to Susan. Do you have a problem with that?"

Jerry was on him in a flash, his right hand around his throat, his left index finger two inches from Ted's eyes. The streets had taught him to move fast. He let Ted breathe, but just barely.

"Listen to me, motherfucker," Jerry said. "Stay away from Susan or I cut your balls off. It's that simple and it's no bullshit." He released Ted and shoved him back. "Get out of here."

Ted nodded weakly and left. Jerry turned, momentarily alone with Susan, although students across the courtyard had been observing him. A teacher or security person would appear soon, Jerry knew. He didn't have a lot of time. He stepped closer to Susan; again she hardly reacted. The whites of her blue eyes were jaundiced. He caught a whiff of her breath—he assumed that was what he smelled—and wondered what she was eating. Not something healthy or fresh. She stared at him as if he were someone moving on a screen.

"Are you seeing that jerk again?" he demanded.

"No."

"What are you doing then? Why haven't you called?"

"Who?"

"Me! Susan, what's wrong with you? You look stoned."

The remark amused her, and she allowed herself a faint smile. "I am not myself," she said in a soft voice. Soft in the sense of low volume. Her tone was anything but gentle—more the quiet hiss of a snake before it strikes. He didn't like her eyes. They were not *hers*; they watched him as if he were a piece of shit, or worse. She licked her lips with a coated tongue. "You look good," she said.

"Come on, let's get out of here." He grabbed her arm. "We have to talk."

She shook loose; the sharp movement of her arm almost sent him tumbling. He backed up a step and stared at her in shock. In that moment the sun could have blinked, the foundation of his reality was so shaken. She was strong, stronger than he was. How was that possible? Her smile broadened and became even more distasteful. It was not an expression of pleasure but a cold and calculated gloat. She took a step toward him, and he consciously had to resist the urge to flee. He didn't understand why his girlfriend was more frightening than Clear Gell and Fist put together.

"I don't have to do anything," she said. "Except what pleases me."

Jerry swallowed. The sun was hot on his skin, but with her eyes on him he broke into a cold sweat. It was as if something sharp and metallic were projecting out from her hollow pupils to cut and dice his insides.

"There's something wrong with you," he muttered. "The near drowning—it did something to you. Let me take you to a doctor."

She reached out to touch him. Her hand came slowly, giving him time to observe that maybe it wasn't a hand at all, but more a claw. Her fingers touched his left temple and a chill settled over his brain. She caressed his hair; it would have felt better, perhaps, if she'd just yanked it out at the roots.

"I don't need a doctor," she whispered. "I need a transfusion."

He trembled—he who had cut open young men with a switchblade. All because of her touch and the thing he sensed in her, the terrible thing. In that moment Jerry did not believe that he was talking to a human being.

"They can give you a transfusion at the hospital," he mumbled.

She drew back her hand and let out a bloodcurdling cackle. "The streets will run with blood," she said. "There I will be *transfused*. I will walk the streets at night, Jerry. I will not forget you."

She laughed more and walked away. Jerry left the campus in a hurry. He took the Coast Highway to the freeway and drove aimlessly until he came to a deserted field, where he pulled over to the side of the road and vomited into a tumbleweed. Even the midday sun, blazing straight overhead, couldn't stop his shivering.

When he was recovered he had more questions than answers. Yet he had to believe, as he had told her, that her brush with death was responsible for the change in her. That she had been altered in some basic way he didn't even debate with himself. As far as he could tell, she was like a fucking vampire.

Yet she was also his girl and he cared about her, more than he had ever cared for anybody in his life. He had to help her, as best he could. He had to speak to the doctors who had treated her at the hospital. Maybe they had experience with what people went through when they almost drowned. He climbed in his car and drove back toward the coast.

Two weeks earlier the ambulance had taken Susan to Malibu Memorial. Jerry had, in fact, ridden with her and the paramedics to the clinic. She had been wheeled directly into intensive care and he was told to wait. Still not convinced that she would survive—she never spoke in the ambulance, although her breathing had stabilized—he'd called her parents and caught them just before they left for the weekend. But when the twin assholes had arrived at the hospital and seen his black skin, they had the clinic security guards kick his ass out. So it was with more than reluctance that he reentered the hospital and inquired at the front counter for the doctor who had treated Susan Darly two weeks before. The young white woman with the fat face remained seated at her desk and responded to him as if he were something that needed disinfecting.

"Are you related to Susan Darly?" she asked.

"Yes. I'm her brother. She was here two weeks ago, and she's still not feeling good. I want to talk to the doctor who saw her."

"If you're not Ms. Darly's legal guardian, then I'm afraid I cannot release any information from her medical records, including which doctor saw her." The young white woman with the fat face returned to stacking the papers on her desk. "Have a good day, sir."

Jerry wasn't in a pleasant mood. Although he hadn't displayed his temper since he'd moved from south-central L.A., his anger, like his memories, had not simply vanished with his change in address. He leaned across the counter. "Listen, you bitch. I'm going to see Susan Darly's doctor and you're going to tell me who he was. If you don't then you'll be checking into this fucking hospital yourself and not checking out until the summer is over. Do you understand me?"

Things might have gone badly for Jerry and the woman if a man in a white coat, who was reading a magazine in the reception area, hadn't spoken up. "Excuse me," he said. "Are you here about Susan Darly?"

Jerry stuffed his hands in his pockets. He was too close to hitting somebody, he realized. He couldn't help Susan if he was in jail. The woman stood and fled through a door behind her.

"That's right," he said. "Do you know her?"

The man stood. To Jerry, he looked rich, well educated, typical Malibu. Yet his expression was sympathetic. "Yes," he said. "I'm Dr. Stevens. I treated her when she was brought in." He paused. "You're not her brother."

Jerry drew in a breath. "I'm her boyfriend. I'm not here to cause trouble. I'm just worried about her. I saw her today for the first time since her accident and she's acting weird."

Dr. Stevens was interested. "How so?"

"She's behaving like a fucking zombie." Jerry gestured helplessly. "Her eyes are spooky, man. She looks like some kind of devil."

Dr. Stevens considered. "I thought she was showing signs of shock even the day after her trauma. I was reluctant to let her go but her parents insisted. Is it possible you could persuade her to come back in? I'd like to examine her."

"No way," Jerry said. "She won't listen to me. But I don't think her problem's physical. I think something's snapped in her mind. Don't you have somebody who knows what happens to people when they almost die?"

"You mean a psychiatrist?"

"I don't know. Somebody."

Dr. Stevens became quiet and thoughtful. "There is a woman who's been here a couple of times to interview people who've had near-death experiences. I understand she has almost completed her doctorate. I can't remember her name but she struck me as competent. She might be a good person for Susan to contact."

Jerry nodded, willing to try anyone who might help. "How do I get in touch with her?"

"She gave me her card. I have it in my office. Wait here and I'll be back in a minute." Dr. Stevens was gone five minutes, but when he returned he had the woman's card, which was all Jerry cared about. He handed it to Jerry. "Her name's Julie Moore. This card has her home and office numbers. Put the two of them together and get back to me with how Susan's doing." The doctor was a good man; he gave Jerry a reassuring pat on the back. "Don't worry, son. She's been through a trauma and is recovering. In all likelihood her problem will disappear with time. It's a secret doctors like to keep quiet, but time does take care of most problems."

Jerry thanked him, walked outside, and climbed in his car. He studied the woman's card, deciding to call Ms. Moore as soon as he got home. He was grateful for the doctor's words but didn't believe them. Once more he remembered the way Susan had stared at him as she licked her lips, as if he were something to feed on.

"There I will be transfused. I will walk the streets at night, Jerry. I will not forget you."

Jerry thought that time would only make the situation worse.

NINE

❀

A WEEK AFTER COFFEE at Denny's and only hours after Susan Darly touched Jerry Washington, Peter Jacobs and Julie Moore went on their first official date. Peter took her to a movie — he knew she was obsessed with them. They saw a French film subtitled, except for the main title, which wasn't translated, so they never did learn what they were watching. It was about a man who had three identical brothers. Peter liked it, except the ending; the director left it a secret which of the brothers survived. Julie enjoyed it even more than he did, but then she had a working knowledge of French — except even she couldn't translate the title. He kidded her about her fluency as they drove to a restaurant. He liked that about Julie — he could tease her and she teased back. Lisa had been sensitive in that department.

They had Indian food at Nizam's, in Peter's opinion the best Indian restaurant in Los Angeles. He ate Indian food regularly but Julie was a novice, so he had to order for her: *biryanni* chicken and rice; vegetable *samosas*; sweet *lassi*; *popadams*. Julie was in heaven. It was a whole new culinary experience for her, and she couldn't believe how much better rice tasted with a few spices added. They ate until they felt they'd have had to be rolled out of the restaurant.

It was only ten o'clock. Julie suggested seeing another movie. Peter wasn't surprised, and would have gone along except he was tired. The problems with Chuck had caused him to fall behind on his work, and he'd had to go in early the last couple days to catch up. He wanted to go home and sleep, but then Julie asked if she could at least see his place.

"Just to be sure you're not married with five kids," she said.

He laughed. "I just have one big kid."

Matt, however, wasn't at home. Peter wasn't concerned. Recently he'd told Matt to leave him a note whenever he went out, and there was a scrap of paper lying on the kitchen table that had the word *arcade* misspelled.

"He usually goes to the arcade Fridays and stays until closing," Peter explained as he handed her the note.

"Has he had his IQ tested recently?" she asked, studying Matt's note.

"Yes."

"It's around sixty?"

"Yes. How did you know?"

Julie smiled. "Sometimes I think you don't appreciate how much we psychologists know. After I got my master's I worked for the state for a year testing IQs. I still do testing, on occasion."

"If I wrote a couple of words on a piece of paper could you tell how smart I am?"

"I've been reading your column since we met. You're plenty smart."

"But I want an IQ number. A hundred and five? Two hundred and five?"

Julie pretended to scrutinize him. "I have to research how you excel in *all* areas of life before making such an evaluation."

"That sounds like a come-on if I ever heard one."

She laughed. "And not a very clever one. Do you know I don't know my own IQ? I'm too close to the tests, so it's useless for me to take them."

"I would put it at an even hundred."

"A hundred is average!" Julie protested. "You think I'm a dumb blond?"

"No. You said it yourself—a hundred is average. What's wrong with being average?"

His words caused her to pause and consider. "You think I'm trying too hard? Trying to prove something?"

"You're the psychologist." He let the remark hang for a moment. Of course, he had spotted right away that Julie was desperately trying to prove something by working herself to death at school and on her job. He had no problem with that and even admired ambitious people. He was just concerned that her motivation for excelling was confused. Throughout the evening she talked about how domineering her father had been, and yet her eyes shone when she spoke of how proud he was of her. Peter had never had a father, but he did have a problem with people who lived their lives to please *anyone* else. He did whatever he did because he wanted to. Reason enough. He added, "There's nothing wrong with getting ahead as long as you're happy when you get there."

She gestured to his nice place. "You're there already. Are you happy?"

"I'm not unhappy, which I think is the highest I can aspire to." He held up his hand when she started to interrupt. "But I do enjoy things. I do have fun times."

"When?"

"When I'm eating at that restaurant we visited tonight. When I'm caught up on my work and know that I can take a week off and do nothing. When I'm riding my motorcycle along the beach and the sun is out and the water is blue. Then I'm happy."

"What about love? Romance? Does that make you happy?"

He hadn't talked about Lisa, even when she spoke about a guy named Stan, who really sounded like a piece of work. It wasn't his habit to talk about feelings, but all her years of psychology had taught her how to draw him out. He realized with a start that he did like her, and was somewhat surprised because he hadn't been sure if he wanted to see her again after their talk at Denny's. The problem was not Julie Moore, however, but the mysterious Sara. Had he not met them within half an hour of each other, he probably would've been content with Julie. She was intelligent and attractive. He was pressing her to look at what motivated her, but on the whole whatever skeletons she had buried in her closet appeared manageable. Julie was a nice girl, really, and he liked nice girls.

Yet if nice girls were supposed to go to heaven, bad girls were supposed to go *anywhere*, and he supposed what was missing in his life was a fresh horizon. By no means had Sara impressed him as a tramp, but there had been something in her sidelong glances and in the toss of her hair that made him feel she was no ordinary woman. Yet that was just the superficial level of his attraction. He had no idea why she intrigued him so much. Maybe it was because when he sat beside her he felt as if he'd sat down in another reality.

He had tried to find out from the museum what her last name was, but they wouldn't release the information. He understood. He was considering asking Amos to identify her. The museum couldn't say no to a lieutenant with the L.A.P.D. But he wanted to understand his interest before he acted on it—although he knew he wouldn't have a new insight until he saw her again. Obviously he couldn't ask Julie for her opinion.

But Julie—what was he supposed to do with her? She was waiting for him to answer her question about love and romance, and he supposed if the night continued much longer she'd wait for him to kiss her. She had dropped enough hints, which he found endearing, her innocent enthusiasm. He did want to kiss her, to make love to her. He had no difficulty having sex with a woman he didn't love, as long as he liked her and she didn't press charges in the morning. He'd had a couple of those as well, when his column had first hit.

"I like love," he said.

She chuckled. The kitchen was suddenly cramped, for both of them, he knew. "You don't love it?" she asked.

"What are you asking? About sex or love?"

His question made her nervous. She wasn't good at hiding her emotions, not the master that he was. His remark also might have offended her. She lowered her gaze as if sad.

"Sometimes they go together," she said.

"You're a romantic, I knew it."

She glanced up and stared just a beat too long. "Yes. Yes, I am. Aren't you?"

He shrugged. "I'm cold as ice, can't you tell?"

She shook her head. "I don't believe you."

"Why not?"

"You have too much hot Indian food in you to be cold." She paused. "And I don't like cold people."

He kissed her then, partly because he couldn't think of a response, partly because it seemed like a good time, and mostly because he wanted to. Her mouth was very warm. Julie Moore was pleasant to sink into. She slipped her arms around him and her hands found their way to his hair. He loved having his head rubbed. Time went by—a few satisfying minutes. He touched her left breast and she sighed with pleasure. Her breasts were not big but firm; her whole body strong. He remembered that she often rode her bike to school to save money on gasoline. The thought of Sara slipped from his mind. Nice girls were good enough, he decided—for now.

They went into the living room, to the couch. They should have gone into his bedroom, but that move seemed more of a commitment than he was willing to make. The couch was cozy enough. She unbuttoned his shirt. He was still sore in a couple of places from the wire Amos had ripped off, but she soothed his wounds with the tips of her fingers. He undid her blouse, her erect nipples surrounded by goosebumps. He thought maybe she was cold, and considered it his duty to warm her. He leaned his head down.

"Zeus," Matt said.

Peter snapped his head up quickly. He let go of Julie in the process and she fell to the floor. The living room had thick carpet, and she landed safely on her back. She pulled her blouse closed as he sat up. Matt stood above them, a huge teddy bear in his hands and a dazed expression on his face. He offered Peter the toy.

"I won this for getting over a hundred thousand on Flying Saucers," he said. He glanced down at Julie. "Hi."

"Hello," she said from upside down. "Are you Matt?"

"Yes."

"I'm Julie Moore. Pleased to meet you, Matt."

"Julie," Matt pronounced carefully.

"Are you OK?" Peter asked Julie.

She began to button her blouse. She was a cool girl; she was smiling. "Fine, thank you. Give me a moment to get myself together."

"Sure," Peter said. He accepted Matt's toy and climbed to his feet. "Come with me a minute, Matt."

"Did I do something wrong?" Matt asked as they headed for the kitchen. "I left you a note."

Peter led him to the door that exited into the garage. Peter parked his Jaguar inside and made Matt keep his truck on the street, even though they had a two-car garage. Matt had scratched his last car. Peter set the teddy bear down on the floor. He spoke patiently to his anxious friend. It was important with Matt to make a point immediately or else he learned nothing from it. It was also important to reassure him before scolding him. Matt was extremely sensitive.

"I'm glad you left me the note," Peter said. "I saw it when I came in and wasn't worried because I knew where you were. That was very good. I'm also glad you did so well at Flying Saucers. But there's something you have to be careful about in the future. If I'm alone with a woman, if we're kissing or hugging or stuff like that, don't try to sneak up on us."

Matt was worried. "I didn't try to sneak. I tried to be quiet."

Peter held up his hand. "That's what I mean. Sneak was a poor choice of words. If I'm alone with a woman, particularly if we're close together, you know, make some noise before you enter the room. You don't have to be quiet."

Matt hung his head. "I'm sorry."

Peter squeezed his shoulder. "It's fine. It's all right. You did nothing wrong. I just want you to understand so that in the future you'll know what to do. That's all. Remember, we learn by making mistakes."

Matt nodded, feeling better. "I make noise if you are kissing a woman. I do not sneak." He paused. "Do I make noise if you're touching her titties?"

"You don't come in the room if I am touching her titties. You leave immediately if I am."

"If I can see them and if you're touching them?"

"Yes. Did you see Julie's?"

"Her titties?"

"Yes."

Matt grinned. "Yes. They were nice. I liked them."

Peter had to laugh. "That's nice. Just don't tell her you saw them. Women are shy that way."

Matt nodded firmly. "It'll be a secret between us?"

Peter let go of his friend's shoulder. "Yes. It'll be our secret."

The romantic mood was ruined for the time being. Peter asked Matt to talk to Julie for a few minutes before he took her home. It was after twelve and Peter was exhausted. Before leaving he ran into the bedroom to use his bathroom. He'd drunk three beers with dinner. After coming out of the bathroom, he noticed the light on his answering machine blinking. He was quick to check his messages these days, in case Chuck had called. It was Lieutenant Amos.

"Peter, give me a call as soon as you get in. We've had another incident."

Amos left a couple of numbers where he could be reached. Peter tried his home. Amos answered immediately and didn't sound as if he'd been in bed.

"Hello?"

"Amos, this is Peter. How bad is it?"

There was a certain lifelessness in the lieutenant's voice that Peter had not heard before. Amos was bringing his work home with him, or worse, he was afraid his work would visit him at home. There were no two ways about it; he sounded scared.

"It's real bad. There's been another murder. We found a teenage boy ripped to pieces in the Santa Monica Mountains. We have a tentative suspect, an eighteen-year-old kid, but I don't think it's him. Before coming home I questioned him for two hours and got nothing."

"What makes the kid a suspect?"

"He was at the victim's school this afternoon and had a run-in with him. A squabble over a girl. I'm sure it's just a coincidence."

"What were the kids' names?"

"Ted Rawley was the kid murdered. Jerry Washington's the suspect, and Susan Darly was the girl they fought over."

"Jerry Washington," Peter whispered. "I've heard that name before."

Amos was interested. "Where?"

"I don't remember. Just recently. Wait a second, Julie Moore told me."

"Who is Julie Moore?"

"A woman I met at the museum last week."

"I thought that woman's name was Sara something?"

"This is another one."

"How many women did you pick up that night?"

"I'm irresistible, what can I say? Julie told me that a Jerry Washington called her this afternoon. It seems his girlfriend had a near-death experience and is now acting weird. Jerry wanted Julie to talk to her."

"What does Julie Moore do for a living?" Amos asked.

"She's completing a doctorate in psychology. Her dissertation is on near-death experiences. She also works in a bookstore."

"Did she talk to Jerry?"

"I don't think so."

"What time did he call her?" Amos asked.

"She's in the next room. I can ask her if you want."

"It's not pressing. Ask her later and get back to me. Anyway, I don't know what it could have to do with the murder of the boy."

"Still, it's an extraordinary coincidence that I should be with someone tonight who was contacted by your only suspect. When you consider *I've* already been contacted by the murderer." Peter considered. "Maybe Jerry did kill Ted. Was he able to account for his whereabouts at the time of the murder?"

"No. He said he was at home resting. But I have experience interrogating people. Ninety-nine percent of the time I can tell if a suspect is lying. I could swear Jerry was telling the truth. Also, he's young and black. His voice doesn't sound anything like Chuck's . . ." Amos's voice trailed off. "There was one thing he said that made no sense."

"What was that?"

"Jerry said Susan, his girlfriend, probably killed Ted."

"How was Ted killed?"

"Blank has no idea, and Blank *always* knows how someone died. His best guess is that Ted was ripped to pieces by an extremely strong man. Like Cindy Trells and the others who were mutilated."

"Does Jerry know that Ted was ripped to pieces?"

"Yes. He still said he thinks it was his girlfriend."

"Interesting. Why did you call me?"

Now Amos sounded weary. "I needed to talk to someone who isn't a cop. Peter, what's going on here? We have two serial murderers with totally different M.O.'s, linked by a single print."

"You're the detective. You're not supposed to like coincidence. I want to explore this connection between Jerry and Julie and me."

"What is the connection? I don't see one."

"Neither do I. But this is a big city. People don't just happen to run into each other for no reason. You said you still have Jerry in custody?"

"Yes. But we won't be able to hold him unless we're ready to charge him. And we can't do that. We have no proof."

"Maybe I can have Julie call him tomorrow and talk to him myself." Peter glanced up the hall. Matt was showing Julie his baseball cards. "Why don't I call you tomorrow? Will you be home?"

"In the evening. There'll be no days off until this is solved. The chief received a visit from the mayor today. Things are heating up. The papers have got to connect all this crap—it's just a matter of time. I'll probably be reading about it tomorrow morning over coffee. Has your boss pumped you for information?"

"Yeah. But I told him there was nothing new."

"It doesn't matter. The shit is going to hit the fan. Ted's father is a big-shot real estate developer. Of course he blames us for his son's death."

Peter expressed his sympathy. He told Amos to get some rest. They exchanged good-byes and Peter returned to the living room. Matt was talking about José Canseco. Peter practically had to drag Julie out the door to get her free of Matt. The two hugged before parting. Peter was glad they hit it off.

"I think a lot can still be done for Matt," Julie said when they were alone in the car together. "To raise his IQ, I mean."

"What?"

"For one thing he should be going to school."

"He doesn't like school."

"Oh? Another thing—he could use some of the modern IQ-boosting programs that are on the market. I noticed you have a PC with a CD-ROM."

"He'll only use the computer to play games."

Julie paused. "Is something bothering you, Peter?"

"No. Yes." He shrugged. "It's a long story. You mentioned someone named Jerry Washington earlier in the evening. That he'd called you. Do you think you still have his message on your answering machine?"

"It should be there."

"Could I listen to it when we get to your place?"

"Sure. If you tell me what this is about."

"Can I tell you after I've heard the message?"

She was watching him. "Sure."

Julie's place was as claustrophobic as she had said. Santa Monica had rent-controlled apartments, but sometimes saving money on rent backfired on the tenants. Maintenance was neglected. The plaster on the hall walls looked as if it had been through one earthquake too many, and the carpet in her studio could have been purchased secondhand from a bankrupt airport terminal. Julie was obviously hesitant about his seeing her humble dwelling, but he made up a quick story about a slum he used to live in before he hit it big. Peter often did that without a twinge of conscience; he lied to save other people's feelings. At least she was neat, he thought. Without Matt his place would have been a mess. Matt loved to clean, especially to use the vacuum. Peter had bought him a vacuum the previous Christmas and it was his favorite gift.

The message was still on the machine.

"Hello, Ms. Moore, this is Jerry Washington. You don't know me and I don't know you. A doctor at Malibu Memorial gave me your number. He said you were an expert on what happened to people when they almost died, how they changed and shit like that. The reason I'm calling—my girlfriend almost drowned and now there's something wrong with her. She's acting like some kind of animal. I don't know what to do. If you could call me back when you get in, I'd appreciate it."

Jerry left his number, thanked Julie, and hung up. Peter sat thinking for a moment. Amos was right—the kid didn't sound like Chuck, or like any voice Chuck could reasonably imitate. Jerry also didn't sound like a murderer. Peter knew that was a huge leap to make based on a brief message, but he knew he was a good judge of character. Jerry had come across as genuine. His girlfriend was in trouble and he wanted her helped.

Yet that very evening Jerry had told the police his girlfriend was guilty of murder.

"You didn't call him back?" Peter asked.

"No."

"Do you know when he called?"

"No. I figure he called somewhere between two and four this afternoon. I was tired when I came in and wanted to take a nap before we went out. I was going to call him tomorrow."

"Is it common for people who have had near-death experiences to react like Jerry describes?" Peter asked.

"No. I've never heard a case like this." She hung her purse on the back of her desk chair and sat down on the twin bed. Her blue eyes looked tired; the easy pleasure of their evening vanished. "Why are you interested in Jerry Washington?"

"Because he was picked up this evening in connection with the murder of a kid named Ted Rawley."

"*What?* This boy who called me?"

Peter sighed. "If I tell you the whole story you'll be upset with me."

"Why?"

"Because I lied to you the other night."

"Why you were at the museum?"

"Yes."

Julie absorbed the information quickly, without obvious irritation. Peter's respect for her rose another notch. She was one of those people who could let little things go. She nodded and patted the bed beside her.

"I forgive you ahead of time, Peter. Please, sit down. Talk to me."

He told her the whole story, from the beginning: Chuck's first call; the two series of murders; the different M.O.'s; the connecting fingerprints; Chuck's second call; the failed rendezvous at the museum; Amos's story that night. Julie paled as he described James Crosser's wound and was clasping her hands together by the time he finished.

"But why is this Chuck calling you?" she asked.

"I don't know. Amos thinks it's because I write for the paper. He says Chuck wants me to tell his story."

"The police were all over the museum that night?"

"Yes. A dozen of them."

"They saw no one suspicious?"

Peter shrugged. "Billy Graham looks suspicious to me. Chuck could have been there without our knowing it."

Julie stood, then sat right back down again. She kept looking at her fingers, avoiding his eyes.

"What about the woman you were talking to?" she asked.

"Sara? She works for the museum. I told you that."

Julie gave him a quick glance. Her pale skin colored; she was embarrassed. "I also lied to you about something," she muttered.

"Why you were at the museum?"

"How did you know?"

"You got there so late. It didn't sound like you saw anything." He paused. "Are you Chuck?"

She laughed briefly; it sounded forced. "No. But I didn't go to the museum that night to enjoy the exhibits. I followed Sara Morray there."

"Who is Sara Morray? To you, I mean."

Julie took a deep breath. "It's silly to be caught in a lie."

"You weren't caught. You volunteered the information. Besides, remember, I lied to you. We're even. Who is Sara Morray?"

"She's the wife of Dr. Morray, a well-known cardiologist. Years ago he did extensive research on NDEs. He's one of the world's foremost experts in the field. Last Friday evening I went to his house to see if I could study his files. I saw him come home and then a few minutes later drive off again in the same car. I decided to follow him. But it wasn't until I was in the museum parking lot that I realized I'd been chasing his wife."

"But you went inside the museum. Did you want to talk to her?"

"I thought I did. I thought she could help me get closer to her husband. But when I got inside, and saw you talking to her, I changed my mind."

"Why?"

"I don't know."

"Why were you afraid to tell me her identity?"

Julie gave him a wan smile. "Because you looked happy talking to her. And she's so pretty."

"There was no reason for you to be jealous. I have a dozen beautiful women chasing me. What's one more?"

Julie snorted. "You sure know how to make a girl feel special."

Peter gave her a comforting hug. Yet inside his thoughts were in turmoil. The coincidence factor had risen another notch. He had gone to the museum to meet a murderer. Instead he had run into a woman, Julie, who was soon to be independently contacted by someone who was connected to one of the murderer's victims. What were the odds of that happening? One in a million?

More coincidences occurred to him. These were less direct, more tenuous; nevertheless, they formed a disturbing pattern. Ted was dead. Jerry had known Ted. Jerry and Ted had also known Susan, who almost died. Susan had in fact had a near-death experience not long before her friend Ted was ripped to pieces. A curious jumble of events to be sure, Peter thought, but added to the fact that he just happened to run into *the wife of one of the world's experts on near-death experiences* when Chuck was to meet him at the museum.

Was this all coincidence? Was he using circular logic rather than linear deduction? Peter was too tired to know. But there did seem to be a common denominator in all this—one to be slipped into the equation.

Dr. Morray.

Peter knew he couldn't go to Amos with his ideas. But it was the cardiologist alone who linked the two seemingly random series of events. Perhaps it was Dr. Morray's hand that had made the print that linked the two sets of murders. Peter was determined to find out.

Or was he just determined to see Sara again?

She had not acted like a married woman.

He wondered how married she was.

"Do you have Dr. Morray's home phone number?" Peter asked casually as he finished hugging Julie. His timing might have been poor, but it was a question he had to ask eventually. Julie was no dummy. She gave him a long hard stare.

"Whose number?" she asked.

"Don't be jealous. I think the police will want to talk to Dr. Morray. If nothing else, he might have insight into what's going on with Jerry's girlfriend."

"The police can ask me about that. I'm an expert on the subject as well."

"Why are you taking that tone?"

"What tone?"

"You sound mad, Julie."

"I'm not mad. I'll give you the number." She reached over, opened her desk drawer, and took out a scrap of paper. She handed it to Peter. "Are you happy now?"

"Jesus." He slipped the scrap of paper into his pocket and put a hand on her shoulder. "What would a psychologist say about all this?"

Julie chewed her lower lip and stared at the far wall. "A male psychologist or a female one?"

"A male, of course. Someone objective."

She smiled faintly. "I'm just another girl to you. You want me for sex and the phone numbers I can give you."

"Who said anything about sex?" Peter asked innocently.

She groaned and buried her face in her hands. "I go to all this trouble to impress you and you can't even be bothered seducing me," she muttered.

He patted her on the back as she bent over. "You don't need to impress me, Julie. I'm not that great a catch. Being able to write funny columns doesn't make me special."

Julie sat up and shook her head. She was not crying but her eyes were damp. "You are more special than you realize."

"What makes me special?"

She stopped and brushed a hair from his eyes. "You have magic."

"What magic?"

"Magic is magic. It can't be described."

Peter nodded. He did understand—magic was what he felt when he met Sara Morray.

Yet his attraction for Sara didn't diminish his affection for Julie.

He wanted to see her again, get to know her better. He wanted to go home now, though. He didn't like to leave Matt alone with Chuck possibly peeking through the windows. Peter still had the gun Amos had taught him to shoot. However, he didn't know how he could leave quickly without offending Julie more. She was staring at him again.

"You want to go home," she said.

"I thought I was supposed to get sex first."

She laughed softly, sadly. "You must think I'm pathetic."

"I like pathetic women. They're easier to control. You're perfect for me."

She sighed. "What a way to start a relationship." She paused and lowered her eyes once more. "If this is a start."

"Who knows? Let's neither of us have too many expectations. More times than not they lead to disappointment." He put his arms around her and kissed her cheek. He whispered in her ear. "Did you hear what Matt said when he saw your breasts?"

She nodded. " 'Zeus.' He was impressed."

"I was impressed."

She snuggled her head into the crook of his shoulder. She was nice to hold. Matt would probably be fine, he thought. It was just one night.

"Are you staying?" she asked.

"I'm staying," Peter said.

TEN

❁

T HE COLD ONE sat in the preacher's car and listened to the gospel program on the radio. The preacher was driving It to his house. The preacher had met It at the beach an hour earlier and had insisted It had to have several of his books to "stabilize her recent rebirth." The Cold One had no pressing business, so It had agreed to look at the material. It did want to read more about the Antichrist because It still had no idea what it was.

"I live in Orange County, in Anaheim," the preacher said, reaching out to turn down the radio. A woman with poor pitch was singing praise to the Lord. The Cold One didn't understand why most of the deities humans worshipped were in constant need of compliments. Their gods, the Cold One thought, were usually as troubled as the humans.

"You drive a long way to go to Malibu," the Cold One said.

"Orange County has plenty of ministers. And I feel the people on your side of town, the rich and famous, are in special need of the Lord's help." The preacher, Craig Westmore, glanced over at It. "I enjoy coming to see you as well."

The Cold One nodded without comment. By the change in the preacher's breathing rhythms, the alteration in the odor of his exhalations, It understood that powerful hormones had just been excreted into the preacher's bloodstream. The preacher wanted to have sexual intercourse with the Cold One, but was afraid to broach the topic for fear of committing a *sin*. The Cold One understood the human concept of sin well; almost any powerful desire invoked the feeling of sinning in most people. It supposed It was a sinner, since It had killed several people. But It was comfortable with the label, which probably made the term not applicable. It wondered what It was going to do with the preacher when It was done with him.

The preacher nodded to the radio. "Do you enjoy this kind of music?"

"It's all right."

"We can listen to rock 'n' roll if you'd rather. I'm not such a fundamentalist that I think anything with a strong beat is the work of the devil."

"That would be fine."

The preacher flipped the dial, searching through the bands. "I don't suppose you'll be impressed with my house. It's nothing like the places you see in Malibu. But it's mine. At least, I'm not renting anymore." He located a Beatles song and left the dial there. He sat back and rolled down the window. The air conditioning in his car didn't work. "I bought it three years ago. My mother left me fifty grand." He paused. "She died of cancer."

"That must have been hard for you."

The preacher nodded. His eyes were damp; he was a sensitive soul. "She was the light of my life, my mom. I used to see her every day. When she passed on I almost lost my mind. It was only the Gospel that got me through the ordeal. The knowledge that I will see her again in heaven."

"Do you honestly believe that?"

The preacher glanced at It as if stunned. "Yes. The existence of heaven is one of the cornerstones of my faith. Don't you believe in heaven? All who are born again must."

"I don't know." The preacher was lying. It could always tell when a human was. Secretly the preacher feared his mother was just rotting in a grave.

The preacher nodded. "This is why you must read religious books. I'm glad you're with me today. If you don't strengthen your faith at the start, Satan will pounce on you in an instant. There's nothing he likes more than to claim the soul of someone recently saved. It's that much greater a victory for him."

"Is it possible your mother went to hell instead of heaven?"

The preacher laughed nervously. "My mother was a strong

Christian woman! She spent an hour every day in prayer. No, she's in heaven at the right hand of Jesus enjoying her just reward." He nodded to himself as he focused on the road. "She's happy."

"You don't sound happy."

The preacher drew in a deep breath and sighed. "My life is hard sometimes."

The Cold One reached over and squeezed his leg. "When you join your mother it will be easier."

A half hour later they reached the preacher's house. It was as he had described, of modest structure and decoration. Yet it was private, at the end of a cul-de-sac, separated by wide stretches of yard on either side. There could be plenty of noise inside and the neighbors wouldn't hear. The preacher parked and led It inside.

"Can I get you something to drink?" the preacher asked as It sat down on the living room sofa. The Cold One studied the religious paintings on the wall, the scratches on the aged furniture. The house smelled of fast food and dried semen. The Cold One understood that the preacher frequently masturbated.

"Yes, please," It said.

"Is orange juice OK?"

"How about a cold beer?"

The preacher chuckled. "As a matter of fact, I do have an old bottle of wine I was saving for a special occasion." He looked doubtful. "But I don't want to give you the wrong impression. I want to set a proper example for you."

"Don't worry, Craig. Am I not already saved?"

He brought out the wine. Ice and glasses. They toasted the spread of Christianity and the return of the Lord. The preacher seemed to enjoy the wine; he had three glasses, the Cold One only two. He brought It several books as well, but spoke little of them. The alcohol seemed to have dampened his enthusiasm for religious literature. The Cold One didn't mind. It could study the books later. It set down Its glass of wine and moved closer to the preacher. It touched his leg near the top. It smelled another blast of excreted hormones on the human's exhalation. The alcohol had loosened his inhibitions. The preacher wanted to screw, It knew, in the worst way, and his Jesus would just have to forgive him tomorrow.

The Cold One considered an experiment. It knew lust, as much as the desire for sleep and food, was the basis of most human behavior. Yet even though It was in a human body, It never needed to sleep and ate only because the act was expected of It. Nevertheless, It had begun to wonder if It might not be capable of experiencing one of the big three desires. It wanted to seduce the preacher to see if It felt anything. Of course It doubted that It would.

It smiled. "Craig?"

He grinned. Because of the alcohol, his expression appeared comical. "Yes?" he said, taking another sip of wine.

"Fuck me."

The preacher sat up hurriedly and put his glass down on the floor. "Excuse me?"

It put Its arm around him and leaned over and lightly kissed his ear. It spoke in a soft urgent voice. "I want you to fuck me, Craig. I want you to do it to me ten times in a row."

The preacher began to protest but It kissed him then, and he showed how feeble his resistance was when he kissed It back. The Cold One knew how to kiss in a manner most humans would have considered sensual and passionate. It did have experience with sex; It had just never had what humans called *good sex*. On the other hand, maybe what It needed in order to feel something was *bad sex*. It knew that as far as human sexuality was concerned, bad was often good. Yet the concepts of good and bad meant nothing to It. The Cold One began to pull off the preacher's shirt. It took the preacher's right hand and placed It on Its left breast. The preacher caressed It and moaned softly with pleasure.

"Do you love me?" he whispered between passionate breaths.

"Sure."

"Tell me you love me."

"I love you."

"Did you know I loved you from the moment I first saw you?" the preacher asked.

"Shh," the Cold One said. It finished removing the preacher's shirt and reached down to unbutton his pants. His penis came out hard and throbbing. The Cold One teased the organ with Its finger-nails and the preacher leaned his head back and groaned. Already he was feeling so much and still the Cold One felt nothing. It pulled off his pants and stroked his testicles. The preacher slipped off the couch and onto the floor. He reached out to pull It down beside him. The Cold One smiled and raised Its hand.

"Let me catch up to you," It said, and reached around to pull off Its blouse and shorts. It stood above the preacher totally naked, straddling the man. The preacher looked at It as if caught in the midst of religious fever.

"Sweet Jesus," he whispered.

The Cold One knelt beside him and kissed the head of his penis. The simple act had a profound effect on the man. His spine arched off the floor. His breathing accelerated so rapidly it sounded as if he were about to have a heart attack. The Cold One could hear the man's heart pounding inside his chest as It continued to suck the man's penis. It had never done this before, but had read about the act in a book. The book had spoken of how stimulating it was for both the male and female. Still, It felt nothing. The man began to shout softly.

"God! God! God!"

The man had an orgasm. The Cold One had not intended for him to climax so swiftly; It had wanted to complete sexual intercourse from start to finish before deciding if It was capable of experiencing lust. But as the preacher's sticky seminal fluid squirted onto his thin abdomen, the Cold One knew It would be some time before the man would be ready to attempt sexual intercourse again. It was not disappointed. Yet It did not want to spend any more time in the preacher's house. It moved close to the preacher's head and stroked his thin red hair. The man was smiling.

"That was wonderful," he said. "Thank you."

It leaned over and kissed him lightly on the forehead. "I enjoyed it."

"Did you?"

"Sure."

He touched Its hip. "Did you mean it when you said you loved me?"

It grinned. "I don't know what love is."

The preacher took Its remark seriously. He wanted to give It a quick sermon, perhaps to feel better about the sin he had just committed. "You know when you love someone it causes you pain to be separated from them. For example, I love my mother and it hurts me that she is gone. I love Jesus as well and can hardly wait to get to heaven to be with him." He paused and touched Its thigh. "And I must love you because I couldn't wait to see you again. That's the main reason I drive over to Malibu, to see you."

This was a new concept for the Cold One, that love could be gauged by the pain it brought. It continued to stroke the man's hair. "Do you think I love you?" It asked gently.

The preacher closed his eyes, his expression one of contentment. "I think so. I don't think a born-again woman like yourself would have done what you just did unless you were in love."

The Cold One continued to be intrigued. "So if my love is genuine then I should feel pain when you're gone? Like your mother is gone? That would be a test that my love exists?"

The man continued to swoon under Its soft touch. "Yes."

"Before your mother died, did she suffer pain?"

"Tremendously. The cancer spread throughout her body before she died."

"Did her pain cause you pain? Because you loved her?"

"Yes. Terrible pain."

A second experiment occurred to the Cold One. Suffering was another concept It understood only intellectually, not from experience. It leaned over and kissed the man lightly on the lips.

"If my love for you is real," It whispered, "and you were to suffer horribly before you died, then I should definitely feel pain. Is that correct?"

The preacher opened his eyes and laughed. "What are you asking?"

"For clarification. What is the answer to my question?"

He was amused. "I would hope if I were to die horribly that you would shed a tear or two. You would have to be a monster not to, Leslie."

The Cold One sat back and nodded. "Maybe I am a monster, Craig."

There were many ways to kill a human. A person could die from a wound to almost any part of the body, the Cold One knew. It surveyed the preacher's naked body and considered which area, if torn and broken, would cause him the most pain. Certainly the genitals, if ripped off, would upset the man greatly. The Cold One debated feigning more oral sex before biting off the man's penis. But then he might simply go into shock, and in such a state the human brain did not function clearly. The subsequent horror for the man might not be enough to stimulate any possible feelings of remorse in It. The Cold One reached for the bottom of the man's left rib cage instead. It probed for the first rib.

"That feels nice," the preacher said.

In a sudden move the Cold One stabbed Its left index finger through the man's skin. Before he could react, It curled the finger around the bone and cartilage and pulled outward. Three ribs burst through the flesh, making a noise like a log crackling in a fire. Their jagged bloody tips glistened in the warm sunlight that poured through the windows above the couch. The man tried to sit up but the Cold One held him down with Its right hand. Still, the man saw and felt that his side had been ruptured and began to scream. The Cold One put Its hand over his mouth. The scream choked in silence.

"This is already painful for you," the Cold One said. "But I don't feel anything. Maybe I don't love you. Let's see."

The Cold One returned to pulling out the ribs, one by one, with Its left hand. Beneath It the man struggled violently, but since the Cold One had ten times the strength of a normal human, the efforts were in vain. Strained muffled cries vibrated through the hand clamped over the man's mouth, through the man's jaw bone and even up into his skull. The man was trying to plead for It to stop, the Cold One understood. But now that It had started, there was no reason to stop, even if the experiment did not seem to be producing any results. The man would have to die.

Soon the Cold One had opened up the entire left side of the man, from near his waist to his collarbone. There was much blood, on the man, the floor—on the Cold One Itself. The Cold One saw the advantage in having performed the operation on the man while naked. Had It not, the cleanup process would have been more difficult. The man's white ribs stood straight up in the air like a row of large teeth. The left lung was visible, the spleen. Still the man lived, although his muffled screams had ceased. His flesh had gone completely white and his breathing was ragged. The Cold One could see he was going into shock. It removed Its hand from his mouth and leaned close to his face.

"There must be no love for me," It said. "I feel nothing."

The man opened his red eyes. "What are you?" he gasped.

"I don't know."

Tears ran over his face. He could see the cracked ribs sticking out. "Help me."

"No," the Cold One said.

Tremors shook the man's body. Blood trickled out from his mouth. Two of the ribs It had broken had pierced his lung. Urine poured from his penis and mixed with the blood and semen. His tears began to cease. He was bleeding to death.

"Why?" he whispered.

The Cold One sat back. "The sun shines because it is bright. Water is wet because it is a liquid. There is no why." It paused to tug on one of the bloody ribs. The man did not wince. His pain was almost over. The experiment had produced no results yet the Cold One had nevertheless found it interesting. It wiped Its hand on the carpet. It added, "There doesn't seem to be reason behind anything. Not a God, not a devil."

"Leslie," he said quietly, his eyes falling shut. "Kill me. Stop the pain."

"It's not necessary." It stood. "You will die soon enough."

The Cold One went into the bathroom and washed. Its clothes had been far enough away from the man so they weren't stained. It dressed quickly and searched the man's pockets for his car keys. It would have to drive back to the other side of town in the preacher's car. It was not concerned about disposing of the vehicle. It picked up the religious books on the couch.

The man was still alive as the Cold One opened the front door to leave. His eyes were closed, however; he was losing consciousness. The Cold One paused to look down at him once more. It had seen movies where the villain paused to study his victim before leaving. Sometimes, at such moments, the villain would display a twinge of conscience. But the Cold One could have been staring at a park bench for all It felt.

It walked out the door without saying good-bye to the Reverend Craig Westmore.

2
Rak

ELEVEN

✿

GOVINDA SHARMA WAS writing a letter to his dead wife's mother when the boy, Indra Kapura, brought him the news that his Master, Guruji, wanted to see him. It was Sunday, a day of rest for devout Hindus. Since returning to India six months earlier to work on a hydroelectric project for the American company Bechtel, Govinda had been putting in sixty hours a week as a quality-control expert on the medium-size power plant his employer was building in northern India close to the Ganges River. He worked without complaint. His wife was dead and there was little to fill his idle hours other than the memories of happier times. He had been composing the letter to Vani's mother for an hour and had written only five lines. The arrival of Indra was a welcome interruption.

Govinda had met Indra, and his younger brother, Pandu, his first day on the project. The boys had been employees of Bechtel then— gofers, only. They worked for everyone at the camp in a dozen different capacities but reported to no one. At least Indra didn't. More intelligent than his younger brother, but also more stubborn—Indra had been the first let go as the project moved forward. Govinda still used Pandu to take care of odds and ends for him: mail reports back to America; pass a message on to the construction foreman; fetch tea. Govinda missed Indra, though. Indra had returned to his father's house in the small town of Jyotir Math, high in the Himalayas.

It was Indra who had introduced Govinda to the Master.

Indra arrived with a knock at the door.

"Come in," Govinda called. Most of the people at the work site spoke English; only occasionally did he speak Hindi. Indra poked his head inside. His strong handsome face always seemed ready for mischief.

"It's me, Govinda," Indra said. "I have a message from Guruji."

Govinda turned quickly. Since his wife's death, he had become an atheist. He didn't believe in Lord Rama or Lord Krishna. He no longer studied the Vedas, nor did he perform any of his daily rituals. Yet at the mention of the Master's name, a man who was supposed to embody the very divine Govinda had rejected, he felt his heart quicken. He no longer trusted God but he couldn't help but love the Master.

"Come in, have a seat," Govinda said. "What is the message?"

Indra entered but didn't take the offered chair. Sixteen years old, he had the energy of youth, as well as the impatience of teenagers everywhere. Indra always spoke English to him. One day, he said, he wanted to move to America and become an astronaut. His dark face shone with excitement as he shuffled from foot to foot. Govinda cared for him deeply.

"Guruji wants to see you immediately," Indra said.

"Why?"

"I don't know. But Guruji said it was very important."

"Did Guruji speak to you directly?"

Indra shook his head. "Keshava told me Guruji wanted you."

Keshava was one of the Master's principal disciples.

"By immediately did he mean sometime in the next week?" Govinda asked. Even though he had been born and raised in India, he had completed his higher education in America. When it came to matters of time, he had a Western sensibility. *Immediately* to an Indian could mean sometime in the next year.

"He wants to see you now, today," Indra said.

"But you must know the reason."

Indra stopped fidgeting. "I do not. But I do know that Keshava was scared when he spoke to me."

Govinda sat up. "Is the Master in poor health?"

"No. I asked Keshava that. He said no."

Jyotir Math was eight hours by car, along roads so narrow and bumpy that the city was visited by only the hardiest tourists. Govinda did not look forward to the journey, especially since he was to be on the job early the next morning. But then he thought of the Master, the light in the man's eyes—so soft yet so powerful—and felt he couldn't say no. He stood.

"Find your brother," Govinda told Indra. "We'll leave in fifteen minutes."

Once the Master had asked Govinda, "Can you remember the day of your birth?" Govinda had replied that he couldn't. Then the Master had asked, "Do you know why you cannot remember it?" Govinda had said it was because he had been too undeveloped at the time to retain anything of value. But the Master shook his head and said, "You do not remember because you were never born. You have always been. You will always be." Then he pointed at a nearby lake, a boat crossing the water. "Many boats go across this water. Each one leaves a line, some bubbles, some foam. But then that line fades and the lake is once more the same. It is the same with the body you now inhabit. It is nothing but a line drawn on an ocean of consciousness. Many bodies you have inhabited. Many lines you have drawn on the water. But in the end, they have all faded. One day the line you call Govinda will be gone. Yet *you* will remain. That consciousness is *Satchitananda*—absolute bliss. It never dies."

The Master's words were beautiful, Govinda thought. If only he could believe them, at least for Vani's sake.

Govinda's earliest memory was of his mother and father rising at dawn every day to perform *puja* to Lord Shiva. Their home was modest—three rooms for eight children, two adults—but they had a small lingam and altar on the front porch. As the sun colored the eastern sky Govinda would stand with his parents as they anointed the gray phallic-shaped stone with ghee and sandal paste and milk and flower petals. As a child he didn't know all the words to the puja, but he had learned how to chant *Om Namah Shivaya* while the lingam was worshipped. The sound of the mantras followed him into the day, long after the ceremony was complete. Sometimes he thought he could hear the voice of God speaking to him in the chant. Comforting him in silence.

Then he had grown up. He had learned how to deal with the real world, or else he weakened his link to what was reality. Seldom as a teenager did he join his parents for morning puja. He felt the ceremony too dogmatic. Yet he envied the peace his parents found in it, even the memory of the peace he had once had. Still, he believed that Lord Shiva protected him and did pray to him from time to time.

He excelled in the village school, particularly in math and science, and was allowed to take college classes in Delhi, where his work was just as clever. By chance a representative from the Bechtel Corporation was shopping the hot stuffy college for a man or woman to get a master's degree in engineering at an American university and return to India to work for the company. Govinda was interviewed along with two hundred others. The company was willing to pay both tuition and living expenses. He must have answered all their questions correctly. He gave a prayer of thanks to Shiva when he was chosen. He decided his karma must be good.

Govinda adapted to Western life easily. Returning to the poverty of India—as his contract demanded—would be difficult. Yet it was always in the future, and the two years he spent in clean air-conditioned classes made the memories of his youth seem the stuff of a past life. Like most Hindus he believed in reincarnation as he believed in the need to breathe.

He was twenty-six when he met Vani, almost finished with his degree. It was at the party thrown by an Indian couple he knew only slightly. She greeted him at the door, wearing an orange sari, a red *bindu* dot on her forehead. Her eyes danced; he thought they sang to him. He compared her to Lakshmi, the goddess of fortune and beauty as he asked her name. He was shy; what else could a child from a small Indian village be? Yet right then he asked if she would marry him. "Maybe," she said. She thought he was funny.

They married six months later, the day after he graduated. He lived in a dream world filled with color then. Bechtel didn't want him to return to India, at least not right away. He had done so well in school they wanted him in their offices in Los Angeles. He was granted a green card and given a job that paid more in a year than his father could have made in a century as a village carpenter. He rented a home not far from the ocean and bought a Japanese car. Vani went to school and studied music. How she loved to play the flute! How he loved to listen to her play! Sometimes, when Vani performed a puja to Lord Krishna, he stood by her side and bowed his head, feeling not an ounce of betrayal to his personal deity. Had not Krishna himself said in the scriptures that his very own self was identical to Shiva? Truly, Govinda felt blessed by God.

Especially in the fifth year of their marriage, when Vani became pregnant.

Each month, as she grew in size, he took a picture of her standing in her underwear. He used a Polaroid because no film developer would see his wife half clothed. He marked each picture with the date it had been taken. As he penciled in the month on the back of the ninth one, he knew the next picture that popped from his camera would also contain his son. Vani had had an ultrasound and knew the child would be male. They even knew his name—Kubera, the god of love.

One night when he was working late, Vani walked to the store to buy a carton of milk. A car cruised by, filled with loud youths. A gun was pointed out the window. A shot was fired. Vani died, only a week short of her due date in a dirty street in a pool of blood. Kubera died. Shiva died. No, Govinda thought as he buried his wife instead of having her cremated as the scriptures demanded. Shiva had never lived. The mantras were meaningless sounds. The peaceful silence they granted was nothing but the emptiness between moments of chaos. There could be no divine intelligence at operation in the universe. Not, Govinda thought, unless it was sick. He buried Vani in a hole in the ground as an American would. He marked the spot with a stone tablet; no lingam, no *yantra*, no cross. He marked the place in his heart with tears he never shed.

A line on water, the Master said. For Govinda it was like a wedge etched in stone. There was before Vani and there was after Vani. The universe may have been made of absolute bliss consciousness, but for him, *after*, there was no joy. And it seemed there never would be.

He asked his boss for a transfer home. In his grief, India would be a place of refuge. He needed to get away. He was told about a hydro-electric project being built in the foothills of the Himalayas. There was an opening; it sounded like work he could lose himself in. He wanted to get lost, more than he wanted to launch a journey of rediscovery. He took the job.

He was in India a month when Indra took him to the Master.

Dragged him. Govinda had not wanted to meet the man.

His first sight of the Master surprised him. He had come expecting to see an old man with a long white beard sitting locked in the lotus position, with eyes half closed in mystical communion. Instead, he found a thirty-year-old man, with a long black beard, playing catch with children. He was laughing uproariously as the youngest children tugged at his white *dhoti*. He was a slight man, short by Western standards. But he moved with grace even in the midst of the wild ball game. The ball seemed to fly into his hands without his reaching for it. He glanced at Govinda as he approached. Just that one glance from the Master was enough to tell Govinda he was in the presence of a great being. Later he tried to analyze what he felt in that instant. The answer was like the paradox of the Master's supposed true nature. Govinda felt nothing around him, and everything. The Master was just present, yet totally present, in the moment. He was like all people at once, because he had realized the inner being that was the same in all, and yet he was no one, because he had dissolved the individual ego. In the Master's own words, he was *Hollow* and *Empty*. Sounded scary, to the uninitiated, yet the Master said when you learned to live like grass the gods came to do your bidding.

Govinda understood no such concepts at that moment, only that he immediately loved the man. Indra led him forward and introduced him. The Master stopped playing and took his hand. "Come," he said, and Govinda went with him.

The first afternoon the Master said nothing profound to Govinda. They talked about Govinda's job, the weather, food. The Master appeared curious about everything. Govinda spent an hour alone telling him about the latest Hollywood movies. The Master's eyes sparkled when he heard about the evil villains. Here he was a holy man who seemed most interested in bad guys. The Master laughed when asked why that was so. "It's all Brahman," he said. "It's all the supreme." He saw no difference anywhere.

Govinda didn't tell him what had happened to Vani. Yet that night, before he went off to bed, the Master placed both his hands on top of Govinda's head and said gently, "All who are born die. All who die are reborn. Don't grieve over the inevitable." Govinda had not known how to respond, but something inside him broke then and he wept the tears he had been unable to shed over Vani's grave.

The next day the Master taught him two spiritual practices. One was a form of meditation, a secret mantra, which he was taught to repeat effortlessly inside. He was also taught *Sudarshan Kriya. Su* meant "right" or "proper," the Master explained. *Darshan* meant "vision." A *kriya* was an "action" that was carried out by nature. Sudarshan Kriya was a technique that gave the proper vision of the supreme self. In practice, it involved breathing in a sequence of specific rhythms. But the Master emphasized that it was more than a breathing technique. Each rhythm of the kriya corresponded to different levels of existence: one to the body, one to the mind, another to the supreme being. The kriya set all levels of a human being into harmony through the different rhythms.

Even though Govinda already loved the Master, he didn't necessarily agree with the explanation. The Master laughed when he told him that. "Doesn't matter," the Master said. It would work whether he believed in it or not. So would the meditation. Govinda thought he had nothing to lose by giving them a try. First he did the kriya, then slipped into meditation using the mantra. He did each practice for about twenty minutes, as he was taught. At the end of the period he was not enlightened. No radiant light shone above his head, nor did angels come to serve him. Yet he felt as if a weight had lifted, as he had when he wept beneath the Master's touch. He felt relaxed, able to draw a deep breath without experiencing the tightness in his chest that had been there since Vani was shot. He decided then and there to continue with both practices. If he never found God—and he was certain he never would because the old man was simply not there—then at least his blood pressure would return to normal.

He had visited the Master three times since the first encounter. Each trip had been pleasant. Govinda told himself he returned because he enjoyed the man's company, which was reason enough.

Yet now the Master called him. And Govinda was dropping everything to run to him. He wondered at his true feelings as he still wondered, occasionally, about Shiva.

Govinda and Indra and Pandu sat in a rickety bus as it wound its way up the side of the Himalayas. Govinda had been unable to get a car. The bus was a mechanical nightmare of grinding metal and black smoke. Two feet off the side of the pitted road the cliff plunged a thousand feet onto pointed stones. Pandu, a year younger than Indra and much slighter, was green from motion sickness. Yet his eyes were wide as he gazed out the window—they were all enthralled. What man or woman born in India could not gaze at the Himalayas without wonder? Govinda was not superstitious, but even he felt the mountains to be more than stone and earth and snow. They were magnetic, somehow. When he entered them he always felt a clarity of thought he couldn't experience anywhere else in the world. They reminded him of the Master.

Yet the trip seemed to take an eternity. They left at eight but it was after six when they reached Jyotir Math. The village was tiny, best known for being the permanent home of the northern Shankara-charya, one of the four main spiritual leaders of India. The Master and the Shankaracharya were personal friends. The Master didn't actually live in Jyotir Math but in a small ashram located two miles farther up the mountains. Because Pandu had not seen his family in some time, Govinda told Indra to take his brother home while he spoke to the Master. Indra was disappointed; he wanted to see what the Master wanted. But it was uncommon for an Indian boy to disobey an elder whom he respected. Indra went off with Pandu while Govinda set out on foot for the ashram.

The ashram was modest by Western religious retreat standards. Two stories of white plaster and unfinished wooden support beams, it had twenty rooms that slept four each, and a single large meeting hall that opened onto a wide terrace that overlooked the city of Jyotir Math and the valleys and mountain peaks beyond. The Master lived apart from the ashram proper, in a small *kutir* that was shaped like an igloo with a pointed hat.

The Master's lifestyle was simple. He awoke three hours before dawn and meditated until the sun came up. Then he worked in the garden with everyone else until noon. There was a break for lunch and an afternoon chant. After that the children took regular classes, and the rest did what they wished: went to jobs in town or worked on the ashram or meditated. The Master didn't have many rules. In fact, he had none—people could do what they wanted. In the evening there was *satsang*, which meant to sit in the company of the truth. There would be another period of meditation, then the singing of *ba-jans*, mantras. Finally the Master would speak on some spiritual topic. Or else he'd just play, or they'd all dance. The Master was unpredict-able. He never went to bed till late, needing only a couple hours sleep at most.

The ashram had running water, unlike many hermitages in India. The streams that flowed down from the mountains were always cold and pure. Govinda had found his brief stays at the ashram com-fortable. On top of everything else, the Master was an excellent cook. Sometimes he would be in the kitchen all day, and end up with his dark beard coated with white flour.

Govinda was met at the front door of the ashram by a young man he didn't know. He was directed to the kutir. The Master was waiting for him, the man said. At the last moment Govinda realized he had brought nothing to give to the Master, as was the custom in India. He supposed, since the meeting was urgent, that it didn't matter. He hurried to the tiny house and knocked softly. He heard a "yes?" and stepped inside.

The Master sat cross-legged on the floor, as he often did. He even slept on the floor, on a couple of worn blankets and a white silk sheet. He looked up and smiled as Govinda entered with his hands folded in a prayerful posture. Immediately, with that special smile, Govinda felt the fatigue of the journey evaporate.

"*Jai Guru Dev,*" the Master said.

"*Jai Guru Dev,*" Govinda replied. The words meant "victory to the guru." When the Master said the words, he did not refer to himself but to all enlightened Masters in all parts of the world in all times.

"*Jai Guru Dev,*" Keshava said. He sat across from the Master, but in a chair. Ordinarily, in India, to place oneself above the Master would have been considered disrespectful, but in Keshava's case it was all right because he was old and arthritic. Besides, the Master didn't care one way or the other how anyone sat.

Keshava was a curious disciple. Although close to the Master, in his late sixties, and completely bald, he was something of a rebel. First, he ate meat, which no respectful Hindu ever did. He bought chickens and turkeys from the merchants who made the occasional trek up to Jyotir Math. He killed and prepared the animals himself. He also smoked cigarettes, although never around the Master. Finally, and this behavior was considered the worst by the rest of the disciples, he had taken a twenty-year-old wife five years earlier, and had recently fathered a child. Personally Govinda thought it was wonderful—the two seemed happy together. The Master kept Keshava close, perhaps to show that none of these things mattered to God. Govinda always had an interesting time with Keshava, who was well versed in Vedic literature. Keshava offered Govinda his chair as he entered but Govinda chose to sit on the floor between them.

"How was your trip?" the Master asked in Hindi. Govinda didn't know how many languages the Master knew, but they were many. The Master was fluent in English but Govinda replied in Hindi because it was the only tongue Keshava understood.

"Comfortable," Govinda replied.

The Master chuckled as if he knew better. "You brought Pandu and Indra with you?"

"Yes."

"Good, good." The Master reached into a basket and offered him a chocolate. "A devotee from Switzerland brought me these. They're very good. Have one."

"Thank you." Govinda accepted the candy, although he did not normally like sweets. But everything obtained from the Master was supposed to be *prasad*, blessed. To his right Keshava was clearing his throat, which he always did since he smoked so much. He ate tons of sweets, with his dead animal flesh. He had a belly.

"I suppose you're wondering why we sent for you," Keshava said.

Govinda nodded. "I am curious, but happy to be here." He stared at the Master, trying to see what was there, behind that serene smile. The Brahman, the eternal reality, or just a wonderful man? "I'm glad to see you again," Govinda said with feeling.

The Master nodded and said, "My Govinda, my Gopala."

Gopala, like Govinda, and Keshava for that matter, was one of Lord Krishna's many names. The Master was reassuring him he was an equal, no different from himself. Govinda always felt comfortable around the Master.

"An interesting situation has arisen," Keshava said, and his voice took on a serious tone. "We need you to follow someone for us."

"Follow someone? Why?"

"Because he's dangerous," Keshava said. "We have to see where he goes."

"Who is this person?" Govinda asked.

"Rak," the Master said.

"Who is Rak?" Govinda asked.

"You might be better to ask *what* is Rak," Keshava said.

"I don't understand," Govinda said.

"For five thousand years Rak has lived in a cave in the Himalayas," Keshava said. "He has not walked openly in the world since the days of Krishna. But yesterday he left his cave. As we speak he is walking out of the mountains. We want you to follow him."

Things were moving too fast for Govinda. He didn't know if he believed a word he'd just been told. "How can I follow him? Why should he let me?"

"He's blind," Keshava said. "Maybe he won't know you're following him."

"How was he blinded?"

"Krishna blinded him," Keshava said.

Govinda allowed himself a faint chuckle. He loved the Master, but had spent a long time in the West. He had a master's degree in engineering. He was a scientist at heart. A note of sarcasm found its way into his voice.

"If he's so dangerous, why didn't Krishna kill him? He was supposed to be God—."

The Master interrupted. "That is why we say he is dangerous. For centuries the Himalayan yogis have wondered why Krishna did not destroy him. We have always known he was in his cave. The answer could be that Krishna wanted him alive. Or perhaps the answer is more simple." He paused. "Perhaps even Krishna could not kill Rak. He is very powerful."

"I'm sorry," Govinda said. "I don't mean to be disrespectful, but I have trouble believing any of this."

"It is all true, Govinda," the Master said. He picked up a rose and gazed out his kutir window, east, in the direction of a towering snow-capped peak. He smelled the flower, but the fragrance seemed not to touch him. For the first time Govinda saw a hint of concern on the Master's face. "Rak is out there, alone, walking toward civilization. Finally, he returns to the world."

TWELVE

❖

THEY CAUGHT UP with Rak the second morning after Govinda spoke to the Master and Keshava. Govinda had Pandu and Indra with him. The Master had not said to bring the boys, but when the time had come to begin his pursuit, Govinda realized that he would have a much harder time watching Rak every second alone, even if the man was blind. Besides, the boys had wanted to accompany him once they heard he was going on an adventure. He hadn't explained all the details of what he was doing except that he had to follow a blind man who was potentially dangerous. In reality, that was the extent of the instructions he had been given. "Follow but do not interfere," the Master said. "Under no circumstances confront Rak. Report back to us by fax what he does."

Of course, Govinda did not tell the boys Rak's history. He didn't want to scare them unduly, and in any case, he didn't think they'd believe him. Govinda hadn't swallowed half of what he'd been told. What sane man would? A being five thousand years old who had dueled with God Himself and lived to tell the tale? Rak may be an extraordinary individual, but Govinda was sure he'd been born in the twentieth century.

They had camping equipment with them. Disciples at the ashram had donated it. The matter of Govinda's work had also been taken care of, at least for the next few days. A fax had been sent from the Shankaracharya to Govinda's boss, who was Indian, asking that Govinda Sharma be excused from his duties for the next week. Since the Shankaracharya was the Hindu equivalent of the Pope, Govinda was not worried about being fired.

They first encountered Rak as they moved around a solid stone wall that shot up a thousand feet. Rak was a mile ahead, following a stream Indra said eventually converged with the Ganges. The famous river was approximately thirty miles due east, gaining in size and strength as it was fed by the melting snow plunging down from the mountains. Govinda spotted Rak first and pulled out the binoculars lent to him by a devotee of the Master. The binoculars were high quality—miniature Nikons. He focused in on the supposed supernatural being and was stunned by Rak's appearance, although he had been told what to expect.

Rak was at least six and a half feet tall. Govinda could judge his size in relation to the stream, which also flowed not far from where they stood. In the West such a height was not uncommon, but in India Rak would be considered a giant. He seemed no more than thirty years old, fairer than most Indians—the color of desert sand before the sun rose—and powerfully built. His long hair hung braided over his massive shoulders like two coiled black snakes. His only clothing was a dark loincloth. He appeared to be more a god than a devil.

Yet he must have been blind, as the Master said. He carried a long stick in his left hand, using it as a white cane, feeling the ground before him as he walked. Still, he moved easily and rapidly, without hesitation. They were lucky they had spotted him when they did; an hour later and they would have missed him altogether. Govinda wondered, though, if it was luck. The Master had given them accurate directions as to where they could intersect Rak's path.

How had the Master known?

"We have always known he was in his cave."

Govinda lowered the binoculars. "That's him," he said to the boys.

"Let me see," Indra said. Govinda handed him the Nikons. It took Indra a moment to learn how to focus them. Then he gasped. "He's big. Pandu, have a look."

The younger brother accepted the binoculars and peered through the wrong end. Even after Indra corrected him, Pandu seemed to have trouble seeing through the glasses. After a minute he gave them back to his brother and turned to Govinda.

"He looks like a warrior from the *Puranas*," Pandu said.

The Puranas were a section of Vedic texts that dealt with the different ages of mankind, largely before Western recorded history. Chiefly they recounted the exploits of various *avatars*, incarnations of God, that had come to earth. Whole volumes of the Puranas were devoted to Lord Rama and Lord Krishna. Govinda found Pandu's comment significant because the Master had said that Rak *was* a great warrior from Puranic times, specifically from the days of the *Mahabharata*. The *Mahabharata* was an epic tale that contained the Bhagavad Gita, the Indian equivalent of the Bible. In it Krishna disclosed to his friend Arjuna on the battlefield of Kurukshetra the secrets of supreme knowledge. The Master had said that Rak was not mentioned by name in the *Mahabharata*; he was present at many key events, but not at the famous battle. By then he was blind, stopped by Krishna.

"Remember," Govinda said. "We are only to follow him. We are not to speak to him. In fact, I don't want him to know he is being followed. I want to keep a distance between us. We can still speak to one another, but in soft voices. Understood?"

The boys nodded. "Why is he dangerous?" Indra asked. "Did the Master say?"

"The Master said many things but asked me to keep them secret," Govinda replied. He held out his hand and Indra returned the binoculars. Once more Govinda raised them to his eyes. Rak had paused beside the river; he was standing very still, as if listening. Govinda felt fear prick at his spine, but quickly scolded himself for his foolishness. Rak couldn't possibly hear them from this distance. Govinda felt Pandu tug on his shirt and noticed the fear in the boy's big eyes.

"Does he know black magic?" Pandu asked.

Govinda smiled. "Of course not. There is no such thing. He's a man just like you and me."

Pandu gazed down at the rocky slope in the direction of Rak. The tall man had continued on his way. Pandu squinted his eyes as if trying to see better. "He doesn't look like you or me," the boy said.

They set out after Rak. The terrain was rough, with much loose stone, few trees, and occasional ice slicks. They were seldom slowed by snow, though, because they had dropped down three thousand feet from Jyotir Math, and by June—at their present elevation, a mile above sea level—the heavy layers of snow were confined to the tops of the peaks. Govinda didn't know exactly where Rak had started his trek, how far back in the mountains he'd been, but even in the summer in the Himalayas the temperature plunged at night. Yet Rak could have been naked for all the protection his loincloth gave him. Nevertheless, Govinda did not attribute his resistance to cold to anything supernatural. There were many yogis and *sannyasis* who survived year round in the mountains with little clothing.

The loose footing was a danger, not only because of the avalanche they could accidentally start that wouldn't stop until they were a thousand feet lower—and dead—but also because every time they stirred the rocks, they made noise, more noise than talking did. Govinda was the most at fault. The boys had grown up in the mountains and were as sure-footed as goats. Yet the few times Govinda slipped and started a miniature slide, Rak never paused to listen. Govinda maintained the mile distance and felt comfortable with it, although he knew he would have to narrow the gap before Rak reached a road. It was possible, in Govinda's mind, that the man would simply hitch a ride down the mountains.

That was assuming Rak knew what cars and buses were.

Govinda was in reasonable physical condition, but the day of pursuit was hard on him. He had set out early with the boys the morning after the Master's talk, and the night before—his first night camping in the mountains—he had not slept well. Indeed, he had not really rested since he had left his home. Fortunately, as soon as the sun set, Rak stopped beside the stream and sat down in the lotus position on a slab of smooth stone. Govinda found it interesting that Rak would halt as soon as the light faded and wondered if he might be only partially blind.

They set up camp above and to the east of where Rak sat. Govinda longed for sleep but offered to take the first watch. Again he was grateful for the binoculars. Without them, in the black Himalayan night, none of them would have been able to see Rak. As the boys snuggled into their sleeping bags and a million stars appeared overhead, Govinda sat up and continued to peer through the lenses at the motionless figure. There was something about the man that made it impossible for Govinda to quit staring at him. Like the Master, he was hypnotic. Yet unlike Guruji, the sight of him brought no sense of love to Govinda. Only intense curiosity. Many times since leaving Jyotir Math, Govinda wondered why the Master had chosen him to follow Rak.

Govinda watched him for hours—Rak never moved once. Not even to lie down. What mantra, Govinda asked himself, did someone like that meditate on?

Govinda woke Indra at midnight to take the next watch. Settling into his own sleeping bag, Govinda reflected on the tale Keshava and the Master had told him. But when he reached the part at the end— the story of Cira and Rak's birth—he purposely blotted out the memory. Some things were best not pondered in the dark.

"To understand Rak," Keshava had said, "it is best to examine what he brought to the world. What I tell you now, the Master has explained to me before. Also, as you know, I am versed in Vedic literature, and am particularly familiar with the scriptures that deal with Tantra, with which we will see Rak had much to do. But having said that, I must add that in no Tantric hymn will you find a *direct* reference to what I am to tell you. That is because the Tantra, like most scripture, is couched in highly esoteric language. For example, a particular verse might suggest a devotee obtain the fresh corpse of a young maiden for the purpose of sexual intercourse, and to serve as a table for the consumption of burnt goat's meat. At first glance that would not be something any sane man would do. Yet there is a hidden meaning in the verse that is more palatable. The fresh corpse of the maiden is representative of the dormant *kundalini*, the spiritual power residing at the base of the spine. The reference to having sex with the dead girl is another way of saying the kundalini has to be awakened. Burnt goat's meat is symbolic of the destruction of the seeds of anger in the mind. Unless a person conquers anger, he can never be free. That is what the Tantra is saying. Do you understand?"

"Yes," Govinda said. "But why is the instruction set down in such a symbolic manner?"

"To prevent a novice from embarking on such a path without a Master's supervision," the Master said.

"Is that what Rak brought?" Govinda asked. "A path to God?"

The Master thought a moment. "He brought a path. I will leave it to your judgment to decide where you think it led." He nodded to Keshava. "Please continue."

"The interesting thing about what I just told you," Keshava said, "is that if the Tantric scriptures are taken literally—if someone obtains a corpse of a girl and the ritual is followed to the letter—then strange and terrible things do happen. A fundamentalist view of Tantric is called the left-handed path, an idea I know many Western Christians would find ironic, or even blasphemous. But the point is this—there are two levels of meaning in these scriptures: the hidden understanding, or the path of light, and the surface meaning, that which we would call the path of darkness."

"Excuse me," Govinda interrupted. "I have read several Tantric scriptures. Almost invariably they are given in the form of Lord Shiva talking to his spouse, Parvati. Where does Rak come in?"

"You will see," Keshava said. "But let me say at the start that when Rak set down these verses, he equated himself with Lord Shiva."

"Rak never referred to himself as Rak," the Master said. "It was the name given to him prior to his birth by his mother, Cira. It was also the name Krishna called him."

"*Prior* to his birth?" Govinda asked.

"Yes," the Master said.

"I see," Govinda said, although he did not. How did she know she was to have a boy?

"I am not saying Rak wrote the entire Tantra," Keshava continued. "He was the original author. He started the tradition, so to speak. But let me leave the Tantra for a second and broaden the discussion. Because the essence of what Rak brought to earth is something not even spoken about in the world today. Yet it is very much in the world, even in the West, but hidden. Rak taught his followers a specific psychic ability called *Seedling*. I know the name is unfamiliar to you. Nowhere in the Tantra is it mentioned. Yet the left hand of Tantra leads almost invariably to it. I say almost because if the heart of the aspirant is pure enough, then the danger is avoided. But few who set out on the path ever recover from it, not in this life or the next.

"Seedling is the mental ability that allows one to dominate the will of another person. It is connected to two *chakras*, or centers in the body. You know about the chakras? I will explain them in brief. There are seven. Understand there is only one energy in the body, one kundalini, but when it flows through these different centers it manifests in different ways. When the energy flows *up* through a center, positive qualities dominate a person's life. When it flows downward, the opposite happens. The first center is at the base of the spine. It relates to enthusiasm for life or inertia. Someone who has no interest in life, no desire even to live, the energy is stuck in this chakra. But when the energy moves up from here, a person is interested in everything: art, music, writing. Life is worth living.

"The second center is at the genitals. It is connected to creation and procreation. When the energy is stuck here, the person can think of nothing but sex. Nude bodies all the time in the mind. But when it moves upward through the center, the person becomes creative. That is why artists and writers throughout time have instinctively understood the connection between sex and creativity. We will return to this center; it is one of the keys to understanding Seedling.

"The third center is at the navel. There are four qualities here: jealousy and attachment and generosity and joy. When you lose something or someone, or you feel jealous, you feel it in the pit of the stomach. But when the energy goes up here, you are happy. You've seen the statues of Buddha? He is usually portrayed as having a fat belly, even though he was not fat. That is because he was so full of joy. The same with Santa Claus in the West. He is always fat, but so generous, giving toys to all the children in the world.

"The fourth center is in the heart. Here there are three qualities: love, fear, and hate. Only one dominates at a time. You see these terrorists, they have so much hate, they are fearless. They can drive in with a bomb and blow themselves up as easily as an enemy—there is no love in them. When there is fear, though, there is no hate or love. Finally, when love rules the heart, hate and fear run and hide. For that reason love is the only thing that can conquer hate or fear.

"The fifth center is in the throat. Here there are two qualities: sorrow and gratitude. When you are sad, what happens? Your throat chokes. But when you are overwhelmed with gratefulness, what happens? The same thing. Tears flow in both cases, salty tears when you are sad, sweet tears when you are grateful.

"The sixth center is between the eyebrows. Here there are also two qualities: anger and alertness. Anger is not the same as hate. They don't have as much in common as most people think. Only an alert person becomes angry. Take a dull man. He doesn't care what happens. He doesn't worry about details. Everything is fine with him. But a perfectionist—his anger erupts in a flash. But when a person is angry, his alertness vanishes. Angry people make terrible decisions, when they're angry. They also get headaches because that is where the center of anger is—in the head.

"The seventh center is at the top of the head. It has only one quality, no opposite. Bliss or, if you like, wisdom. When the energy in a man or woman rises to the top of the head and stays there, that person is free from the pairs of opposites. He is enlightened. Do you understand everything I am telling you? It is important that you do before I continue."

"Yes," Govinda said. He found the description of the chakras fascinating because he could see the truth in them from his own experience. His skeptical guard relaxed a notch, yet it did not go away.

"This energy is called different things in different traditions," Keshava said. "We name it kundalini or *shakti* or *prana*. The Chinese speak of it as *chi*. The names do not matter—it is all the same. Various mystical traditions prescribe various ways to activate the energy and send it upward. Problems arise, of course, when it goes down. Someone may do a little yoga and then feel intensely lustful, unable to think of anything but sex. In that case the energy has become blocked at the second chakra. That is why a Master is absolutely essential on the spiritual path. A Master prevents you from getting mired along the way."

"Does Sudarshan Kriya raise the kundalini?" Govinda asked. It always had an energizing effect on him.

"Yes," the Master said. "Naturally, without effort, without danger."

"An understanding of the chakras is essential to understand Seedling," Keshava continued. "I will not go into detail describing the left hand of Tantra rituals. Suffice it to say they usually involve the invocation of a being into a form of some kind. It could be a corpse, a statue, or a yantra—anything that can serve as a focal point for the aspirant. The beings invoked are various: *yakshinis, nagas, dakshinis.* Each of these beings can confer a power to the person who invokes it or can give the person something directly. A dakshini can take the form of a beautiful man or woman and give intense sexual pleasure. The succubi and incubi in the Catholic tradition come from dakshinis. Nagas are like serpents and can be directed to kill another person. A yakshini can grant the power to see the future or make objects vanish. It is important to note that none of these beings is intrinsically evil. They are all simply forces of nature. They can be used both positively or negatively, in the same way atomic energy can be used to generate electricity to heat homes or to make bombs that kill people.

"Yet the temptation for a human to have one of these beings under his command is too great. Almost invariably the person misuses the powers granted. Also, the beings, once employed, always want something in return. Often it is something small: the perfume of incense, a little ash or ghee. Occasionally the being wants the life of the person who invoked it. You never know with these creatures. That's why it's best to stay away from them. That's why this path is called the dark path—few who set out upon it ever succeed.

"Rak brought rituals to earth that invoked a being that has no name in Vedic literature. For simplicity's sake, and because I know you have spent some time in the West, I will call it a dark angel. Understand I do not use the term *angel* as a Christian would. When I say a 'dark angel' I mean a creature that stands near the pinnacle of negative evolution. Everything is created by God and in the end evolves back to God. Western minds have trouble believing that something negative could be connected with God. They see Satan as separate from the divine, but the idea is nonsense because it implies a God who is not omnipotent. In the scheme of things, there is no good or evil. Everything plays a part in the drama. But for most people, especially for those on the spiritual path, there are things that are better avoided.

"Let's look closely at the idea of positive evolution and negative evolution and how a dark angel relates to them. A survey of the present world can give you a means of differentiating between positive and negative people. Positive people have love. They are most concerned with their fellow man. They enjoy nice things like everyone else, sure, but not at the expense of another. Negative people have little or no love. They are primarily concerned with satisfying their small egos. Their most noteworthy trademark is their self-absorption. Another is that they crave power, control over others. You see many movements in the world that on the surface profess to serve mankind, but they are really negative. There is hierarchy in them, one person is placed above the other. Negativity emphasizes difference, positivity emphasizes unity. There really is no difference between one religion and another, between one race and another, or between sexes. People are people. Beliefs are beliefs. A woman can do anything a man can. One is as good as another. But the influence of the negative, of beings like dark angels, tries to convince people to think otherwise.

"Seedling is the ultimate example of negativity manifest on the earth. Rak taught his people how to contact a dark angel—using the second and sixth chakras respectively—to dominate other's wills. A dark angel is a high being. It is what a human eventually becomes, after millions of years of evolution, if he or she chooses the path of self-service. To contact a dark angel one must raise the energy to the sixth center, *while at the same time maintaining the energy downward in the sexual center.* Seedling is intrinsically sexual. The person who employs it dominates through sex or rather, I should say, through the sexual aspect of the one energy in the body. It is not necessary for someone adept at Seedling to have sex with a person to take over his or her will. This may happen, but many times it doesn't. Yet the *influence* of sex is always there whenever the ability is used. Do you understand?"

"Partly," Govinda said.

"The dark angel is invoked into the sexual center, but first contacted at the sixth center, which is the plane of existence on which it lives. Therefore a person must raise his consciousness to a high state to use Seedling. Each center in the human body corresponds to a different level of evolution. That is what is unique about a human. I said a dark angel is the product of millions of years of negative evolution, but any man, if he is fortunate enough to meet an enlightened Master, can ascend through all the levels of evolution in one lifetime. The positive path is the easy way. It is filled with love and light. Personally I don't know why anyone would choose the negative path, but maybe it is their nature."

"You said Seedling exists in the world today," Govinda said. "How can that be? I don't know anyone in contact with dark angels."

"People who used Seedling in their past lives are born with the ability," Keshava said. "It is in their minds—they do not have to be consciously aware of it to use it. Most are not aware of it. You must have met people in your life who were able to completely dominate others. There was simply something about them that was hard to resist. They are always manipulative, eager to get ahead. Some might see them as powerful people, but inside they are cold. Love and Seedling are totally incompatible. Have you met such people?"

Govinda nodded. "I was just thinking about people who start these cults: Jim Jones of Jonestown, Guyana, and David Koresh of Waco, Texas."

Keshava nodded. "Perfect examples. The media offers theories as to how these men can totally dominate the minds of others. They say the followers are lost or stupid or had hideous childhoods. But in reality these men use Seedling. It is difficult for anyone to say no to them. You also may have observed that they are usually promiscuous. They use their followers in a sexual way. Many of America's charismatic preachers use Seedling, although just as many are good people. You can easily recognize the negative ones. They say it is God who works through them, but they are obsessed with their self-importance. They are convinced they play a major role in God's plan. People believe this. They say the preacher is a great man of God. What they do not understand is that God only has small roles for everyone. Many politicians use Seedling to get elected, then they use their authority to pass laws to create an elitist society.

"But let us not take this explanation so far that we create paranoia. Seedling is present in society, but not rampant. In fact, it is mostly dormant. What is left is usually a watered-down version of what existed in the past, especially in the days of Rak and, to a lesser extent, in the Middle Ages. Rak's closest followers could dominate almost anyone. It took a strong man or woman to resist. It is well the ability has faded. Can you imagine a society where people could consciously control others?"

"Is that what you fear?" Govinda asked. "That Rak will bring Seedling back to the world?"

"Yes," the Master said. "And other things."

"What other things?" Govinda asked.

The Master shook his head.

"We know the story of Rak's birth," Keshava continued. "We will tell it to you before we finish. But we do not know what his childhood was like. He first gained notoriety in the days of the *Mahabharata*, as an adult. His following was small for many years. We believe that was because he had to raise his core number of disciples to the level where they could use Seedling. Once he had accomplished that, there was nothing or no one who could stop his rise to power. He was both a sorcerer and a warrior. He stormed down out of the Himalayas, not far from here, and captured one village after another. He used swords and arrows, but it must be obvious by now that his real weapon was the manner in which he subjugated the wills of his enemies. In fact, Rak had few enemies once he swept through an area. It was because everyone joined him. If they didn't they were killed.

"Krishna and his brother, Balarama, confronted Rak in the area that is now known as Rajastan. Krishna had a great army by then—this was not long before the battle of Kurukhestra—but he had only his brother by his side when he met Rak. Maybe he feared he would lose too many of his people in a battle. Perhaps he was concerned Rak would be able to turn his own people against him. In either case Krishna must have known that ordinary weapons would not stop Rak and his followers. There were too many of them, and Rak was as deadly with his mind as he was with the sword." Keshava paused. "Have you heard of *pasupata*?"

"Yes," Govinda said. "From the *Mahabharata*. My father used to read the purana to me when I was young. Pasupata was one of the mystical weapons unleashed in the battle of Kurukhestra."

"You understand Krishna did not fight in that battle?" Keshava asked. "He was only Arjuna's charioteer?"

"Yes."

Keshava settled himself more comfortably in his seat. His arthritis was mostly in his spine. "You call yourself a scientist, Govinda. If you've heard about pasupata, it must have intrigued you. Or reminded you of something?"

Govinda nodded. "I remember the description of the weapon's power well. It created a gigantic fireball that instantly vaporized thousands of soldiers. Those who survived the initial blast later lost their hair and nails. Their mouths bled and they developed bloody diarrhea, constant vomiting, and skin sores. In short, all the symptoms of severe radiation poisoning." Govinda paused. "Once, while in school in America, I showed the description to a physicist friend of mine. It stunned him. When he was through reading it, he said to me, 'So we weren't the first ones to use atomic bombs on this planet, after all.' "

"Did you agree with his opinion?" Keshava asked.

Govinda shrugged. "Had the *Mahabharata* described the fireball as a towering mushroom, I would have been more inclined to agree."

"Mushrooms are not popular in India," Keshava said. "They never have been."

"I find the similarities in description interesting," Govinda said more carefully. "But that is not the same as believing that someone used nuclear weapons five thousand years ago."

"You know Rajastan is mostly desert these days," Keshava said. "Nothing much grows there."

"Much of it is desert, yes. But not all," Govinda said. "Rajastan covers a large area." He stopped again, finally understanding the direction in which Keshava was headed. "Are you saying that Krishna used pasupata against Rak in that area?"

"Yes."

"He blinded him with a nuclear bomb?"

"I would say rather that Krishna was able to start a nuclear reaction purely by the power of his divine will," Keshava said. "But, yes, he blinded him and at the same time destroyed the majority of his followers."

Govinda shook his head. "If Krishna was able to start a fission or fusion reaction above Rak's army, Rak would have been more than blinded. He would have perished with his followers."

"Yes," the Master agreed. "Yet Rak survived."

"But how?" Govinda asked. "Even assuming everything you have said already is true. No man could withstand such a blast."

"That's it," the Master said. "Rak is not a man. He is something else."

"What?" Govinda asked.

The Master nodded to Keshava. "Tell him how Rak accidentally entered the world." The Master's gaze strayed to the window once more. A cool breeze stirred the parted curtains. It was getting dark outside, cold. The Master added softly, "If it was an accident."

THIRTEEN

❋

T HREE DAYS ON the trail of Rak found Govinda and the boys in the jungles of Rishikesh. They were lucky to still be with him. Rak had hitched a ride on a bus ten minutes after encountering his first road, which had appeared on the third day of pursuit, still back in the Himalayas. Because Govinda had been keeping his distance, he and the boys had been unable to get on the same bus. They watched helplessly as it wound down the side of the mountain, Rak standing tall near the back window. What driver would have refused a blind man a ride? Fortunately, another bus came along twenty minutes later. This one was in better shape, or else the driver was very brave and reckless. They careened down the mountain at such speed that they soon passed the first bus.

Both buses had the same destination—Rishikesh, a small city famous for its high spiritual vibrations and many yogis and sannyasis. It was known as the Gateway to the Himalayas. For a short time they stood within a hundred yards of Rak in the bus terminal. They were not alone as they stared at him; he drew the eyes of every passerby. He had to be one of the most beautiful human specimens ever born, Govinda thought. This supposedly evil being. He appeared even younger up close, under thirty certainly. There wasn't a mark on his light-brown skin; indeed, it seemed to shine from within. Wooden staff in hand, Rak left the bus terminal and walked into the jungle. Night was near. As was his usual practice, he sat in the lotus position on a flat stone, this time beside the Ganges River, and closed his eyes as if meditating. Govinda had noticed at the bus station that during the day, Rak kept his eyes open. Once more Govinda wondered about the extent of his blindness. He had yet to see Rak lie down to rest. Govinda, Indra, and Pandu camped a quarter of a mile away from Rak, farther up the river. Govinda wanted to be close so that when Rak set off in the morning, they would not lose him in the jungle. The sand where they placed their bags was soft, the gurgle of the nearby water soothing. As usual Govinda offered to take the first watch. A crescent moon hung in the western sky. As Govinda watched through the binoculars, the silver moonrays glistened off Rak's body like the glow of radiation from an iron statue that had withstood an atomic holocaust. Pasupata, Govinda thought, nothing but a myth from the ancient past. Yet the *Mahabharata*'s description was interesting; he knew it had puzzled both Eastern and Western scholars alike since Hiroshima.

Close to midnight, the time Govinda would have had Indra or Pandu take over, a phenomenon occurred that made his blood run cold. Rishikesh was more jungle than town; naturally, there was much wildlife about, many birds and monkeys. Govinda could hear them in the trees. He knew there must be snakes as well, poisonous ones at that, and he had been relieved that Rak chose the riverbank to rest, away from the trees.

Yet now the snakes were coming, not toward them but toward Rak. As Govinda studied the blind man through the binoculars, a small black serpent slithered out of a tree and across the sand. Govinda believed he recognized it—a baby cobra, every bit as deadly as an adult. He jumped to his feet, the binoculars still in hand, ready to shout out a warning. But something stopped him—maybe it was the fact that the warning would have already been too late, he was never to know for sure. The snake slid into Rak's lap and curled around his spine. Heart pounding, Govinda quickly raised the binoculars just in time to see the snake caress Rak's ear with its forked tongue.

Yet Rak did not move. He sat like something dead.

And the snake did not bite him.

Another snake came out of the trees, and yet another, until soon there were a dozen serpents coiled around Rak, on his arms, his legs; one squeezing his neck, another two on his wrists. Watching, Govinda was unable to relax. His awe was as great as his fear. It made for a fantastic image, and a familiar one. In many holy paintings Lord

Shiva was portrayed as sitting in the lotus in deep *samadhi*, mystical union with Brahman, while snakes crawled over his body.

"But let me say at the start that when Rak set down these verses, he equated himself with Lord Shiva."

Not one of the snakes bit Rak.

Govinda woke the boys. He cautioned them to be silent and handed over the binoculars. Each took a look. Indra's eyes grew huge. Pandu went as pale as the moon.

"He has black magic," Pandu whispered.

"No," Govinda said. "They don't bite him because he doesn't move."

"Why are they all over him then?" Indra asked.

Govinda shrugged. "Better him than us."

"I want to get out of here," Pandu said, afraid.

"We have a job to do," Indra snapped at his brother. "We cannot disobey the Master."

"The Master gave the job to me," Govinda said. "I wouldn't mind if both of you moved farther upstream and camped closer to the bridge. I would feel better if you did."

"That is a good idea," Pandu said.

"We can't leave Govinda," Indra said to his brother. "He has to rest."

"Who can sleep with all those snakes so close?" Pandu asked.

"If you can't sleep, then you can take the next watch," Indra said.

"Don't be so hard on him," Govinda said. "I am as frightened as he is."

"I am not scared," Pandu said quickly. Then he lowered his head and swallowed thickly. "I am sorry, Govinda. I won't desert you. I can take the next watch."

"Are you sure?" Govinda asked. He was exhausted; the bus ride out of the mountains had been harder than the hiking.

"Yes," Pandu said. He reached over and kissed Govinda's hand. "I know the Master will protect us."

"He is with us," Govinda agreed. He didn't add that he doubted the Master knew the boys were with him. He cautioned Pandu to stay alert for any snakes that came their way and crawled into his sleeping bag, as Indra did. He was asleep in a minute.

* * *

He awoke to a muffled cry. His eyes popped open. There was orange light in the eastern sky. He sat up and understood in an instant what had happened. Pandu had fallen asleep sitting up and failed to wake Indra to take the last watch. Pandu had also not heeded his last advice. There was a baby cobra slithering around on his lap. The poor boy must have awakened just a moment before. He was trying so hard not to move—shaking all the while—that it broke Govinda's heart to watch. Indra sat up beside Govinda and started to scream. Govinda clamped a hand over the boy's mouth.

"Don't make any noise," Govinda whispered in Indra's ear. Then a bit louder, in Pandu's direction: "You will be fine if you don't move."

Tears ran down Pandu's cheeks. "Save me, Govinda."

Govinda let go of Indra, who was panting with fear, and slowly stood. The best help he could give Pandu, he thought, was to do nothing. Just keep him as calm as possible and hope the snake crawled away. If he tried to catch the snake with the tip of a stick and toss it aside, he would only aggravate the cursed thing. Yet he reached for a stick anyway to help Pandu believe that something was being done to save him. But Govinda only planned to use the stick to kill the snake once it was off the boy. Cautiously Govinda moved closer.

"Close your eyes," Govinda said softly. "Think of the Master. The Master and Shiva are one. Think of a statue of Shiva. Become like his statue. Snakes like Shiva, they never harm him. This one won't harm you if you don't move."

Pandu was having trouble breathing. His mouth hung open, dripping saliva; his diaphragm shook with tension. The snake nuzzled Pandu's belly with its snout, hissed softly; Pandu's movement troubled it. Pandu could not close his eyes, could not relax.

"Please." The boy moaned. "Get it off me."

"We have to let it crawl off," Govinda said, approaching to within fifteen feet.

"No!" Pandu cried softly. "It will kill me."

"I will not let it kill you," Govinda said. Ten feet away. Now he oscillated back and forth. Maybe he should try to hook it with the stick. Pandu was not going to last long trembling the way he was. Govinda noticed Indra out of the corner of his eye. "Stay back," he called quietly.

Indra's face was a mask of anxiety. "Do something."

"The best we can do is stay calm," Govinda said.

"I can't," Pandu cried. His words caught the snake's attention; it slithered toward his face. Seeing it coming, Pandu clamped his teeth over his lower lip; bit into the tissue. A drop of blood flowed from his mouth and hung as a suspended red tear on the tip of his chin. The snake paused and raised its head and teased the blood with its darting tongue. The taste interested the monster; it hissed loudly. Pandu's eyes swelled so large they looked as if they would burst from his head. The snake's mouth was perhaps six inches from the tip of his nose, watching him. Govinda watched him as well. He could see the boy was ready to crack. The stick it would have to be.

His decision came an instant too late. The moment he stepped forward to hook the snake, Pandu reached up with his right hand and grabbed it in the middle to throw it away. But there was never a man or a boy born with the reflexes of a cobra. Pandu had the snake away from his body and was on the verge of releasing it when the serpent snapped around in midair and bit his right hand, on the middle finger. Pandu and Indra screamed. Govinda dropped his stick and leapt forward. He caught the black thing by the tail and whipped it in a half circle over his head. Flesh tore as he did so; the snake's fangs had already sunk in deep. Govinda released the snake before it could bite again and watched as it disappeared into the water of the Ganges.

"Pandu!" Indra cried. He ran to his brother's side and clasped his injured hand. Govinda knelt by the stricken boy and studied the wound as well. The skin on the top half of the finger had been completely ripped away. The appendage was drenched with blood, and with something else: a dark blue venom that soaked into the mangled tissue before their very eyes. Immediately Pandu began to thrash. As a child Govinda had watched a man bitten by a cobra die. Cobra venom is particularly toxic; it paralyzes the central nervous system within twenty seconds. Govinda and Indra tried to hold Pandu down. The mysterious energy that gave life to the human body was in turmoil; feeling its power ebbing, it fought valiantly. Pandu's eyes rolled back in his head as his body convulsed in a single massive cramp. Green saliva leaked from his twisted mouth. A pitiful cry erupted from deep in his burning throat. The cobra venom was supposed to burn like the fires of the deepest hell.

"Pandu!" Indra cried again. His frantic eyes searched Govinda's face. Govinda felt the weight of the promise he had uttered moments earlier: I will not let it kill you. But all he could do was shake his head and hold on to Pandu. Finally, thankfully, the boy began to relax. For a moment his breath returned to normal as he settled into the sand. His eyes closed, he sighed—the sound peaceful. Govinda leaned over and kissed his cheek. He whispered in his ear.

"Think your mantra, Pandu. Be with God."

Pandu did not open his eyes, but nodded slightly. Then he stopped breathing and was still. Indra buried his face in his brother's chest and wept. Govinda's eyes did not burn with tears, though, not then. His gaze was cold as it swept the riverbank for Rak. He watched as the blind man stood from his trance and turned his head in their direction. He was a quarter mile away and Govinda did not have his binoculars, but he saw enough to know that the snakes had left Rak. And he understood enough to know that when one of them had departed, it had done so on a mission. In that moment Govinda did believe in black magic and the terrible story of Cira and her child. Rak seemed to nod in his direction. Then he stepped into the jungle and vanished. Govinda let go of Pandu and stood. This atrocious act could not go unavenged, he swore to himself.

"Indra, listen to me," Govinda said. Indra sat up and stared at him with vacant eyes. Govinda looked down at the devastated boy and at the body. That's all it was now, without the prana, and soon it would be even less—white ash floating on a warm river toward an ocean it might never reach. Govinda continued, "I have to go now. Rak must not get away. I will give you money. Hike upstream and get help for Pandu. Take him back to your parents. The Master will do a ceremony for him." He added softly, "The Master will take care of him."

Indra nodded weakly. He pointed to the place where the snake had struck. Even in death the blackened flesh looked painful. "It says in the Vedas that to be bit on the middle finger by a snake means that liberation is certain. Maybe Pandu sits with Shiva and Krishna right now." Indra paused; there was so much pain in his face, too much hope. One brought the other, Govinda knew. "Do you think that's possible, Govinda?" Indra asked.

Govinda reached down and squeezed the boy's shoulder. His next words came out spontaneously, but not without shame. He may have learned to believe in the devil, but he was farther than ever from trusting in God.

"All who are born, die," he said "All who die, are reborn. We need not grieve for Pandu." He gazed in the direction Rak had disappeared and added, "He is happy wherever he is."

* * *

The next twenty-four hours passed in a dream. Govinda followed Rak out of the jungle. Rak hitched another ride on another bus, but this time Govinda was only a few steps behind. He got on the same vehicle. Rak stood at the front, Govinda in the back. Together they rode to Delhi, to the airport—the bus was for tourists. As the sun began to set, Govinda followed Rak into the terminal. Rak still had on only his loincloth—Govinda figured Rak couldn't have money or a passport. Govinda, however, had both. It was his custom in India never to travel without a passport, and when the Master had called for him he had automatically placed it in his bag. Bechtel, his employer, had got him an extended visa; it was stapled to the inside of his passport. He could return to America whenever he wished. Of course the States were the farthest place from his mind when he entered the airport terminal.

Until Rak, staff in hand, spoke to the young woman at the Delta counter.

Govinda observed the exchange from a distance of a hundred feet. For several seconds the woman stared at Rak as if hypnotized. Govinda could not hear what Rak said because he spoke so softly. Then the woman set to work on her computer terminal. At no time did she ask to see Rak's passport, nor did she ask for money or a credit card. Fifteen minutes after Rak had entered the airport, he was handed an airplane ticket. The woman called to an assistant, a boy of about sixteen. He reminded Govinda of Pandu, although the two looked only slightly alike. For a long time Govinda knew many youngsters would. The boy led Rak in the direction of the gates. Govinda approached the woman.

"Excuse me," he said in English. "My friend seems to have got away from me. Maybe you have seen him. He's tall and blind?"

"Yes," the woman said. She was heavyset and had a faint mustache. Her dowry would have to be high to land a husband. "He was just here. I gave him his ticket."

Govinda smiled, although his guts were ice. "I hope you gave him the right ticket. We're traveling together."

"He said he was going to Los Angeles." She paused and frowned. "At least that's what I think he said."

"That's where I'm going as well." Govinda pulled out his wallet and passport. He handed the woman a gold credit card. "I do hope there's room left for me on the flight."

"You don't have a reservation?"

"No." He added, "Did my friend?"

Again the woman seemed uncertain. "He said he did." She turned to her terminal. "Do you two wish to sit together?"

"No." Again Govinda smiled. "You might have noticed how big he is. He takes up practically two seats. Traveling beside him is murder."

The woman nodded. "First class, business, or coach?"

"Coach. When does the flight leave?"

"In fifty minutes. Do you have bags to check?"

"No."

She was surprised. "All the way to America with no bags?"

"You may have noticed my friend had no bags either." Govinda paused. He had left his backpacking equipment with Indra. "Actually, I'm carrying his wallet. How did he pay for his ticket?"

This time the woman's confusion bordered on the painful. She winced; the lines on her forehead could have been caused by a throbbing tumor deep inside. There was now no question in Govinda's mind that what the Master and Keshava had said about Seedling was true. Rak had dominated the woman's will, without having sex with her.

"I don't remember," she said finally.

"It doesn't matter," Govinda said.

He charged his ticket on his American Express card. The woman pointed him in the direction of the gate. Along the way Govinda stopped and placed a call to his boss. He got his answering machine. Govinda said that he had to leave for America on an emergency and that he would call again at the first opportunity. He also told his boss to send a fax to his Master care of the Shankaracharya of Jyotir Math, and gave him the number. His message was brief:

Going to L.A. with Rak. Will let you know what happens.

Rak was aboard the plane by the time Govinda reached the gate. Govinda did not stop to wonder how Rak had gotten through passport control. One long stare would have been enough, and never mind that the guy was supposed to be blind. There was a question, however, that he wished he'd asked the woman at the Delta counter. Had Rak purchased a *round-trip* ticket? He had a feeling the answer would have been no.

Govinda passed Rak as he made his way to his seat in the rear of the plane.

Wearing only his loincloth, Rak looked comfortable in first class.

3

First
Love

FOURTEEN

❀

J ULIE MOORE MET Jerry Washington at the same Denny's where she and Peter Jacobs had had coffee ten days earlier. Jerry was working on a Coke, sitting in a corner booth. He waved her over; she had told him she would be dressed in green pants and a yellow top. She had guessed from his voice that he was African-American but was surprised at how frightening he looked, and handsome; for her the two often went together. Peter hadn't spoken to her since Saturday morning. It was Monday now; it had been a long weekend at the bookstore. She had only managed to get in touch with Jerry late Sunday night. Seemed the police managed to keep him locked up longer than Peter's detective friend had thought possible.

She hadn't called Peter, no way.

The bastard—she still thought he was the greatest guy, in bed and out. She hadn't needed to be drunk with him.

Julie and Jerry exchanged hellos and Julie sat down. Jerry had on a white T-shirt and blue jeans. He was very muscular; the veins on his biceps swelled through his shirt. His eyes shifted left and right as she studied him; a common trait, she knew, among people who had done time. Yet he had been in the slammer only one weekend, she reminded herself. The time must have dragged for him.

"Have you been waiting long?" she asked.

He shrugged. "Yeah. But I had nowhere else to go right now so it doesn't matter." He paused. "Are you a doctor?"

"Almost. In six months I'll have my doctorate in psychology."

She nodded at his Coke and signaled to the waiter. "I could use one of those. It's been so hot lately. It seems like it's never going to end."

"Where I used to live it never did end," Jerry said.

"Where was that?"

"South Central. Near the projects. Gangland."

"Were you in a gang?"

"Who wasn't? But I got out." He was reflective. "Susan got me out."

"She's your girlfriend who had the near-death experience?"

"I don't know what she experienced. I just know she almost drowned." He fidgeted—the topic obviously made him nervous. "Since then she's been acting strange—and I mean real strange. Have you seen that sort of thing before, miss?"

"Julie, please. I don't know. Tell me more details."

"First thing is her eyes—they're spooky. They remind me of an insect's—cold and hungry. She doesn't look at you like a human would. You see what I'm saying?"

Julie frowned. "I'm not sure."

Jerry leaned forward. He had clearly been bursting to speak to someone. "When I was in jail this weekend I gave this a lot of thought. How could Susan change so quickly? I kept asking myself. Then I got an idea. What if when she almost drowned her soul went on the other side and before she could get back in her body something else crept in?"

"I don't think that happens," Julie said carefully.

Jerry clenched his fists. "But listen! If you saw her you'd know she wasn't Susan. It wouldn't matter that you'd never met her before. The thing inside her isn't human. Look what she did to Ted."

"What did she do to him?"

"She ripped him to pieces up in the mountains. I know it was her that did it, I don't care what those fucking cops say. I tried to tell them. I said go to her house. Get her fingerprints. Compare them to the prints on what was left of that guy. But would they listen to me, a kid from the projects? Shit, they laughed in my face, then threatened to rearrange my face." He rolled his left shoulder; it seemed stiff. "Those motherfuckers."

"They didn't beat you, did they?"

Jerry chuckled and stared out the window. "They wouldn't call it beating, not in court. But let's just say that what they did hurt." He shook his head. "But I don't give a shit about that. All I care about is my girl."

"Excuse me for saying this, Jerry, but you're trying to get your girl arrested for first-degree murder."

He pounded the table. "I'm not! I'm trying to get her help. I know Susan couldn't hurt anyone. What I'm saying is she's not Susan anymore. Ain't you hearing me?"

"If she isn't Susan, what is she?"

Jerry sat back. His brief explosion had taken something out of him. Yet he rapped his knuckles nervously on the table. The ice in his Coke chinked like miniature bells. "A devil," he said in a quiet voice. "I think she's possessed."

Julie sighed. "Jerry, can I be straight with you?"

Jerry wore the expression of a weary soul. "You don't have to say it. I know I sound like I've lost my mind. Maybe I have lost it. All I know for sure is Susan's not Susan and Ted is dead."

"Were you there when Susan was pulled out of the water?"

"Not right away. I was searching for her farther down the beach." He paused. "I still don't know how she ended up where she did. It must have been a quarter of a mile from where we went in the water, and the rip was pulling the other way."

"Who found her?"

"I don't know, some woman. She was giving her mouth-to-mouth when I ran up. She probably saved Susan's life."

"Where were you when Ted died?" Julie asked.

"Resting in my place. I was waiting for you to call back."

"I'm sorry. I had a date that evening. In fact, my boy—my friend is anxious to talk to you."

Jerry took a sip of his Coke and shook his head. The waiter had yet to bring Julie her drink. "Why should I talk to him? You're supposed to be the expert on shit like this. But all you do is tell me what can't be wrong with my girl. Why don't you tell me what *is* wrong with her?"

"All right. It could be many things. You say she almost drowned. That's pretty traumatic. The effects of trauma don't always show up right away. She could have been fine while she was in the hospital and then when she got out she could have suffered a breakdown. It's even possible she suffered partial brain damage while in the water. That, too, could account for her odd behavior."

Jerry waved his hand as if he had already heard the rap. "Would trauma or brain damage give her super strength? You know, she's stronger than me now." He put a hand to his head as if it hurt. "I bet she was a lot stronger than Ted."

"I never heard of that before." When Jerry didn't respond, she asked, "How do you know how strong she is?"

"Because when I went to see her at her school, she shook off my hand and I felt like it had been slapped away by a speeding train, that's how." For the first time, Jerry looked her straight in the eye. "Listen, Julie, I ain't bullshitting you. I'm confused. I'm scared, too, and I don't scare easy. I think you can tell that by looking at me. I need your help. *Susan* needs your help."

"I'll be happy to speak to her if you want."

Jerry shook his head. "I don't want you to speak to her. Not after what happened last Friday."

"But I thought that was why you asked me to come this afternoon. If I don't see her, how can I help her?"

"I can't have you see her. I can't have that on my head."

"Have what on your head?"

"If she kills you."

Julie laughed. "I don't think that'll happen."

"I'm sure Ted didn't either."

Julie's Coke finally came. The timing was good; they needed to take a break. Jerry stared out the window while Julie rehydrated her system. She couldn't remember a heat wave like this since she'd moved to Los Angeles. Maybe it had something to do with the recent rash of murders. Jerry acted as if he were ready to hit somebody. He was frustrated, though, not hateful. She wished she could help him; she just didn't know where to start.

"Are the police still on your case?" she asked finally.

"Yes and no. They told me not to leave town or they'd come looking for me. But they don't think I did it."

"If it's any help, I don't think you did either."

He smiled thinly. "Maybe you can write me a letter of recommendation."

She spread her hands. "What do you want me to do? I'm a psychologist, not a psychic healer. There's no magic formula I can give you. If you won't let me talk to Susan, at least let me contact her parents."

"They're not answering."

"What do you mean?"

"I've called a dozen times since I got out. No one's answering at that house."

"Maybe they went away for the weekend."

Jerry shook his head. "That ain't it."

"What then?"

Jerry shrugged. "You think I'm crazy enough as it is. Maybe I was crazy to want to have this meeting." He started to stand. "I'm sorry I took up your time, Julie."

"Wait." Julie reached across the table and touched his arm. He jumped at the contact; he'd had a rough past, she knew. "Let's at least stay in touch. You can call me anytime. If I'm not there leave a message and I'll call you right back."

Jerry stared at her a moment as if surprised. "You're nice. I haven't met many people like you in my life."

She took back her hand and forced a smile. His words made her feel so sad. "They're out there if you look for them." She added, "I meant what I just said."

He nodded. "I'll call. I'll call after I see her again."

"Do you think you should?"

A tremor went through his body, but he mastered it quickly. His voice came out tired and beaten. "Somebody's going to have to go up to that house. It may as well be me." He touched his head again near the temples; he must have had a headache. "Good-bye, Julie."

"Take care, Jerry."

Julie sat for a few minutes and finished her drink. She noticed Jerry had left three dollars on the table to pay for the Cokes. That was nice of him, she thought. She hoped to see him again. She wondered if she could get Susan Darly's number from Peter through his detective friend. The girl might even be in the phone book.

Julie called Professor Adams before she left the Denny's. He'd been interested to hear the details of her meeting with Jerry. She had few facts to give him and consequently his comments were not very enlightening. Then, on the verge of hanging up, she poured out the story Peter had told her Friday night, and the possible connection to Dr. Morray. She knew she was breaking Peter's confidence by sharing the information, but she honestly felt she needed Adams's insight as to whether she should get further involved. Besides, she was pissed at

Peter. They'd made love three times Friday night, and she had come every time, a record for her. He could have at least called to tell her she'd worn him out.

Adams listened closely to her—he always did. He was capable of absorbing more information in silence than most psychologists could with a hundred questions. His first comment when she was done proved the point; she had said nothing about her feelings for Peter.

"I think you're crazy about this guy," he said.

"I'm not. It was just great sex."

"How great?"

"The best."

"You're crazy about this guy."

She slumped against the wall. "I suppose. But does it matter? What should I do with Dr. Morray?"

"Did you speak to his wife at the museum?"

"No. Peter did."

"What's that I hear in your voice?"

"Jealousy. Pure and simple. Tell me what I should do."

"You're asking me two questions. As far as Morray's concerned, you should call him again. He was the one who said you could study his records. As for Peter—I think you should call him, too. This is a new age, Julie. The sexes are supposed to be equal."

"I can't call him. It would be too humiliating."

Professor Adams laughed. "Nothing makes us find out quicker what we're really made of than a good dose of humiliation. I have to go, Julie, I have a student waiting."

"Thanks. Good-bye." She set down the phone and stared at it for a minute. Then she picked it up again. She had Dr. Morray's home number with her, but because it was the middle of the day, she didn't expect to reach him, just Sara. At least, she thought, that would be a start in the right direction.

But it was Dr. Morray who answered. He sounded out of breath. "Yes?"

"Hello, Dr. Morray? This is Julie Moore. I met you the other day at the hospital. I was wondering when would be a good time to drop by and maybe have a peek at those records we discussed."

His voice was curt. "Today would not be a good day."

"That's fine. Should I call back later? I don't want to keep pestering you."

"I am happy to hear you say that. I'm afraid the same could not be said for the reporter who's in my house right now."

Julie froze. "What reporter?"

"I don't know his name, and I don't care to know it. Call me another time, Ms. Moore, I have to go now."

He hung up. Julie slowly set down the phone. She felt sick to her stomach. She knew the reporter's name.

FIFTEEN

❋

"I LOVE THE OCEAN," Sara Morray said. "It reminds me of space. Both so vast, so unconquerable."

"You don't think space will be conquered?" Peter Jacobs asked.

Sara stared at him with her dark eyes and he felt as if he were staring into deep space. "It's not possible," she said.

They walked together along the beach, not far from her house. He had called her that morning and she had suggested he drop by for lunch; it didn't sound as if her husband was around. Curiously, she had not asked how he had obtained her number, or why he wanted to see her.

The day was blistering, even this close to the water. The paper said they were setting new record highs all week long. Peter had on gray silk slacks, a short-sleeved white shirt, no tie. He had yet to go in to work. Sara wore baggy green shorts, a white T-shirt with Mickey Mouse on the front. Her long black hair was pulled up in two ponytails, like a schoolgirl's. Her wooden sandals flopped against the sand. He had taken off his shoes and now carried them in one hand. She had been watering the front lawn when he arrived and had immediately suggested they go for walk. Only twenty minutes ago. Yet he felt as if he knew her, as he had when he met her in the museum. For a long time. He had forgotten how beautiful she was.

"You don't believe in the unrelenting nature of the human spirit?" he asked.

She laughed as if his question were a joke. "No."

"What do you believe in?"

She gave a sly smile. "That sounds like a personal question."

"It is."

She shoved him playfully away. "I hardly know you, Mr. Jacobs. Why should I tell you all my secrets? When you haven't shared any of yours with me."

"What do you want to know? You know what I do for a living. You know where I live."

She nodded. "Sixty-two twenty-two Saunders Avenue, Venice, California."

He was impressed, flattered that she'd memorized it. He thought she liked him. Why else would she have had him come over? Yet she was difficult to figure. Friendly, certainly, warm—an open door in many ways and yet, at the same time, a shadowed entrance. Her dark eyes sparkled but seemed to look through rather than at him. He believed Sara Morray would have scored high on Julie Moore's IQ tests.

"You have a memory," he said.

An inexplicable note entered her voice. It would have been easy to say it was sorrow, and perhaps accurate, yet it was like a sorrow she had long ago decided to welcome. "Sometimes I wish I didn't," she said.

"One of your secrets?" he asked gently.

"Yes, no. You must know that I'm married."

"That's what they tell me."

She did not ask who *they* were. She reached down and picked up a small stone, feeling it with the tip of her thumb as if to make sure it was smooth enough. Had she wished to skip it on the surface of the water, it would have been possible. The waves were glorified ripples; the huge swells of two weeks earlier had vanished. The sea seemed like a huge placid lake then, a mirror reflecting yellow glare. He had forgotten his sunglasses in his car.

He had not, however, forgotten his dream from the morning Chuck had first called. It came back to him then, the boat on the flat lake, the empty shore, the lifeless sails. The eyes of the woman, blank as those of a fish. What had stirred the unpleasant memory? He didn't know. Sara looked over at him.

"Do you know my husband is an important cardiologist?" she asked.

"Yes."

"What do you think of that?"

Peter shrugged. "That he must make a lot of money."

She smiled, a sad smile. "Have you heard the saying that money may not buy happiness, but it allows you to shop in better places for it?"

"No. But it's amusing."

"I think it's true, too, at least as far as my life is concerned. I have a good life. I want for nothing. I paint when I wish. I walk on the beach, I go for swims. My husband never tells me what to do. He seldom even asks me what I do." She paused. "I don't know why I'm telling you these things, Mr. Jacobs."

"Have you and your husband grown apart?"

She chuckled, without mirth, but also without bitterness. Clearly she was not happy, he thought, but it was as if she didn't mind. "We were never close," she said.

"Why did you marry him?"

"Because he asked me. I was young at the time. I had never been married before. It seemed the thing to do. That's how it's been with me, for a long time. I just do things. I don't think much about them."

"You seem so intelligent. I have trouble believing that."

Sara paused. She touched his arm. Her fingers were moist, with suntan oil perhaps, his skin with sweat. He realized then that one of the reasons her gaze was so penetrating was that she seldom blinked.

"Trouble yourself, Mr. Jacobs," she said, "if you want to know me better. I'm telling you the truth."

"Peter, please."

She laughed, letting her head fall back, the ends of her twin ponytails brushing the top of her bottom. It was difficult to be close to her and not touch her.

"Your last name is Please?" she asked.

"When I called you this morning it was." He paused. "You must wonder why I called?"

She continued to laugh. "Not at all. I'm sure the instant you laid eyes on me you were madly in love. And I'm sure you're hoping to have a passionate affair with me, and that you'll dump me the moment something better comes along."

Her manner was unnerving, even for him, and he wasn't easily intimidated. "In my defense—you only scored two out of three with that last remark."

She shook her head and continued to walk. "I saw you talking to that young woman outside the museum. I saw you walk her to her car. Looked like you two made a date."

"Looks can be deceiving." He caught himself. His usual flippant manner didn't impress Sara. He didn't know what would. Maybe the truth; she'd already been open with him. He added, "That was Julie. She's a friend, and we've since gone out once."

Sara walked into the water, let it play over her feet, the sand sticking to her sandals. Peter let her go; he didn't want to stain his pants. Then he joined her, what the hell. The bottoms of his feet welcomed the cool bath. Sara had her eyes lowered; she could have been searching for another stone, or perhaps a crab.

"Was she fun?" she asked.

"Julie?"

"Yes. You haven't gone out with me yet."

Yet. "We had a good time."

"When did you go out with her?"

"Friday." He added, "But had you been available, I would have called you."

She grinned, her eyes still on the sand. She continued to polish the stone in her right hand with her thumb. "What's Julie's last name?"

"Moore."

Sara raised her head. "Oh, I know her. What a coincidence. She called last week. She's a psych major at U.C.L.A. She wants to see some of my husband's records." She paused. "Should I let her see them?"

"Maybe you should ask your husband."

Sara shoved him again. "You give quick answers, Peter Please. But you never really say anything. My husband never says anything either. Did you know I never knew he had records on near-death experiences until Julie Moore called? What does that tell you about the state of our marriage?"

"Sounds typically American to me." He added, more seriously, "If you're not happy, why don't you get out? There are no children, are there?"

His question caused her to stop midstride. It was as if she had to strain her memory to answer. "I often dream about having a boy and girl," she said, her voice dreamy, her eyes set on the horizon. Then she shook herself, as if returning to her body. "I had a miscarriage three years ago. I still feel as if the baby is here."

He had spoken to no one about what he had gone through with Lisa. He didn't know why he suddenly wanted to tell Sara. "My girl-friend had a miscarriage a year ago." He paused. "Just before she left me."

"It upset her?"

"Yes. Very much."

Sara nodded. "My husband was more upset than I was. It still bothers him, in fact." She raised her arm, waiting for a pause in the small waves, and then let fly her stone. It skipped the surface of the water three hops before coming to an abrupt halt on the side of a sea gull's head. "Oops," she said.

The bird rolled over in the water. "I think you stunned him," Peter said.

"I think I killed him," she said matter-of-factly.

They returned to the house, an abode of the wealthy. The ranch-style home was modern inside: a wide-screen TV in the living room wall; marble tile on the kitchen floor; an intercom system throughout the house. The pool in the backyard was bigger than the one at his condominium complex. Steam rose from the bubbling Jacuzzi. He could imagine her in the water, naked, her wet hair draped down her back. She stared at him again.

"Would you like to see my paintings?" she asked.

He had to take a breath. He had never just grabbed a woman in his life and kissed her, but he was getting close. He wondered how she'd react. He wondered if he cared.

"Yes," he said. "Show me your paintings."

She had a rare talent. He recognized that the moment he entered her bright airy studio. It was a working artist's room; the canvases were stacked all over the place. She had twin easels, paints and brushes sit-ting on shelves, although the rest of the house was neat. Two subjects obviously enthralled her: the sea and space, she had said it already. She must have traveled extensively. There were watery coves in Tahiti, sensual in the evening light, and the Greek islands under a burning sun, the water such a hard blue it looked as if it could be walked on. Then she had haunting paintings of the planets, exploding nebula, the unending expanse of the galaxies. The outer space works were disturbing in a subtle fashion. It not only looked as if people would never go to such places, but that they were not welcome to even think about them. Her sea was so warm, he thought, her universe so cold. He wondered if she had those two sides. He picked up a painting in the corner, the only one that attempted to combine the two themes. The point of view was through a crack in the coral on a Pacific atoll, staring up through the blue water at the Milky Way.

"Do you like that?" she asked.

"I like all your work. Actually, I put that poorly. I'm amazed at your talent."

"I didn't paint that one."

"What? You're kidding. It looks like your work."

"It's the only one in this room I didn't paint."

"Who did?"

She hesitated. "An artist my husband admires."

"The style is very similar."

"Yes."

"Do you ever show your work?"

"I haven't in years."

"Why not?"

"I don't know." She shrugged. "I don't need the money."

"I'd like to buy one of your paintings," he said seriously.

She gestured to the rest of the room. "Take what you like. You don't have to pay me. Let it be a gift."

"That's very generous of you. May I decide what to take another time?"

"Yes."

Someone came in the front door right then. Peter knew who it was, yet his heart didn't skip in his chest. Dr. Morray was, after all, the official reason he was in the house. Sara did not appear worried either. Indeed, given the circumstances, her evenness was remarkable.

"Hello?" she called out in a calm voice.

"It's me," a gruff male voice responded. Dr. Morray appeared a moment later. He was as Julie had described: tall and balding, old for his sixty years, stooped with hidden burdens. Yet also intelligent, powerful; he was not a man who brooked nonsense lightly. He did not glare when he saw Peter, but his expression was light-years from welcoming. Peter did not flinch. It wasn't as if he'd been caught fucking the guy's wife. Not today, anyway.

"Hello," Peter said.

Sara spoke quickly. "Honey, this is Peter Jacobs. He writes for the *Los Angeles Times*. Peter, this is my husband, Dr. Lawrence Morray."

"Doctor," Peter said, and offered his hand. Dr. Morray shook it after a moment. The big man was taking time to adjust to the presence of a stranger. He had obviously just come from the office. He had his white coat on; it smelled of a chemical Peter could almost pinpoint. Formaldehyde, perhaps. Peter did not know if Dr. Morray was still involved in research.

"What do you write?" Dr. Morray asked.

"That column we sometimes read," Sara said. " 'Wouldn't It Be Nice?' You know the one—I read it to you last week."

Dr. Morray nodded. "About that window washer who fell into the swimming pool."

"A lucky man," Peter said.

"What are you doing here?" Dr. Morray asked bluntly.

Sara didn't rush to his rescue this time, probably wisely. "I met your wife at the museum last week," he said. "I thought it might be interesting to do an article on an artist who uses her talents to improve L.A.'s cultural centers."

Dr. Morray grunted. Peter didn't know if the man believed a word of it, and frankly didn't care. Already Peter didn't like Dr. Morray. There was an arrogance in his stance, a calculated coldness. Privately he thought the man capable of committing murder, which was not the same thing as believing he had. Peter set down the painting of the stars viewed through the colored coral. He was on the verge of excusing himself when the phone rang. Without a word Dr. Morray went to pick it up in the living room. Peter glanced at Sara, who had an ear cocked toward the phone. Her face was inscrutable.

"Is it a problem that I'm here?" Peter asked quietly.

"It's not a problem for me," Sara said.

"Should I be going?"

"That might be a good idea. I'll walk you out."

"That's not necessary."

She smiled. "But I want to, Mr. Peter Please."

Dr. Morray was setting down the phone as they made their way to the front door. He seemed annoyed and tired, but not just from the call and finding a stranger alone with his wife. It appeared as if the last twenty years had been unkind to Dr. Morray. This insight into the man was important to Peter. It made him feel less guilt about pursuing Sara to the next level. Obviously Dr. Morray didn't appreciate what he had in her.

"Who was it?" Sara asked.

"That woman who wants to study my records," Dr. Morray said.

This time Peter's heart blinked. Sara cast him an amused glance. "Julie Moore?" she asked.

"Yes. I wish she'd quit calling. I wish I'd never told her I had anything left to show her."

"Those are wishes that are easily fixed," Sara said. "Let me walk Mr. Jacobs out. I'll be back in a moment."

"It was nice to meet you, sir," Peter said.

Dr. Morray had already turned his back. "Have a nice day," he muttered.

Sara didn't speak until they reached his car, which Peter had accidentally parked a hundred yards down the street from the Morray residence. He hadn't been sure about the address. The wealthy were notoriously private. Numbers were not clearly posted in elite Malibu. Sara had left her sandals back on the front porch. She stood on the grass on the side of the road beside the muffler on his Jaguar.

"What did you think of my husband?" she asked.

"He doesn't look like your type."

"Do I have one of those? Besides you, I mean?"

Another suggestive remark. He had to capitalize on this one, and he had to do it now. Because if he didn't, he realized, this goodbye could be alpha and omega combined. What if her husband said, I don't want to see that guy around my house again? Peter would have said that if he'd been Dr. Morray.

Peter wished he'd heard what Dr. Morray said to Julie.

"Am I your type?" he asked.

Her answer surprised him. She leaned over and kissed him on the lips. Her breath was warm, her lips lush; it was a thrill, no two ways about it, three seconds of bliss. He was just reaching out to hold her when she pulled away. She reached up with her right foot and poked the inside of his left thigh. But her head was down, her face grave.

"I do like you," she said.

"And that troubles you? Because you're married?"

She glanced back toward her house. "I told you I didn't know about my husband's research into near-death experiences, and that's true. I know little that he does. He's a brilliant man, but secretive. He has a laboratory in our house, behind the garage. He's always in there, doing God knows what." She paused, concern touched her face. For a woman who often swam at the beach, her tan was negligible. She added, "Sometimes I think he dreams of creating a modern Frankenstein monster."

"That's an odd comment to make." Peter knew it could have nothing to do with the people who had been ripped to pieces, but nevertheless, it made him wonder.

Sara touched his arm. "There are things I want to tell you, Peter."

"Tell me."

"I can't. Not here, not now." Her dark eyes regarded him closely. Or else they focused on the space behind him—he couldn't be sure with her. What attracted her to him? Certainly not the things that interested other women. "I shouldn't have kissed you," she said.

"The neighbors might have seen?"

"I never think of them." She tossed her head as she had at the museum, only now her long hair was not free to dance. Her eyes narrowed on her house as if it were a cage. "You're right, I have to get away from him," she said.

"I didn't say that but I think it's a good idea."

She shook her head. "But I can't. The time's not right."

"When will it be better?"

"Maybe the next time I see you." She put her right palm on his chest and let him grasp it to his heart. Her touch made his vision clear; it was a piece put in a puzzle, her dark eyes windows into another realm. "Don't be gone long, Peter," she said.

SIXTEEN

❖

J ERRY WASHINGTON LEFT his meeting with Julie Moore more agitated than before. He wasn't upset with Julie; she had been as nice as any white person he had ever spoken to. Nor was he worried that he'd come off sounding nuts because he had worse things to occupy his mind. Like his last remark to Julie Moore. There was no sense waiting. He was going to Susan's house now, and he was scared.

Before he drove to Malibu, he stopped at his place and collected his piece—a Smith & Wesson .38 revolver, one of the most reliable weapons on the market. He had no intention of using it on Susan, but he also had no intention of ending up like Ted. He had to see why no one was answering that fucking phone before he went insane thinking about it.

Yet before Jerry left his apartment, he thought of Lieutenant Amos Rodrigues. The man had not been like most cops. He had drilled Jerry, but his questions had been straight. He had not been around when his partners had applied the muscle, and Jerry doubted that the detective would have approved. The blue suits had told him to keep his mouth shut on that point if he wanted to be able to piss the next morning; they hadn't wanted Rodrigues to know about their bone-stretching exercises. Jerry wondered if he shouldn't give the guy a call, have him meet him at the house. He had the man's card.

Then Jerry thought of Julie's confusion when he tried to explain what he believed had happened to Susan. He probably would get the same reaction from the lieutenant. The detective might even forbid him to go to Susan's house, and if he did, Jerry could be arrested again. Once they knew you'd been in a gang, they'd arrest you for squeezing a head of lettuce in a grocery store. He decided not to call Amos Rodrigues.

Jerry loaded his revolver and tucked it in his belt under his T-shirt. He couldn't wear a coat to hide it, not that day. For the last ten days the sun felt as if it had been stuck at high noon. Ever since they'd gone for that one last swim.

Jerry drove toward Malibu. He almost rammed a couple of cars along the way. The world was gray, the color of his options, a new experience for him. Because no matter how bad things had been in South Central, there had always been a thing or two he could do to make things better, or else get himself killed. Sounded like lousy options—he'd thought so at the time—but he'd gladly take them now. Christ, what was he going to do if Susan came at him with those weird eyes? Pull his piece and fire? He would as soon go back to jail. Why was he going to her house anyway?

He knew the answer as well as he knew the constant ache in his chest. His life had been a living hell since he had been old enough to notice that some people were white and others were black. A four-year-old's insight into truth, justice, and the American way, and how fucked it was. Then, on the verge of checking out, he'd had a month of normal life, and had found life was worth living, after all. He wanted that month back. He wanted years of it. He just couldn't avoid Susan, even if she was possessed.

And maybe, just maybe, she'd be better this time.

Susan's car was parked in the driveway as he pulled up. Her house was big and white; he imagined it filled with lots of rich goodies inside. He sat staring at it for several minutes. The bright white was at odds with the black cloud that seemed to hover low over it. How silent the street was, Jerry thought. It was as if the neighbors had holed themselves up inside, afraid of what had come onto their block. Jerry didn't have to ring the bell to know she was inside, and that she wasn't any better.

He climbed out of his car and shut the door. A front window curtain stirred, enough for someone to peek out. So be it, he thought. He touched his shirt over the spot where he had stashed his gun. It could have been unloaded for all the comfort it gave him. He walked toward the front door and rang the bell. Steps—it sounded as if Susan had gained two thousand pounds. He held his breath, his heart throbbing inside like an alien waiting to be born. He loved her, he told himself. He couldn't kill her, she wouldn't kill him.

She opened the door. She smiled.

But the smile didn't reach her eyes. They waited, they watched. They knew things he didn't want to know.

"Hello," she said. "Would you like to come in?"

He nodded and stepped into the house. She shut the door. A sound of finality. He glanced around; everything seemed to be in order: the couch and chairs stood upright, no B horror film on the wide-screen TV. Yet there was a faint foul odor in the air—it was hard to be sure, but he may have been smelling dried blood. He studied her. The whites of her eyes were the color of coral. Her smile remained fixed on her face, something scraped between dried lips.

"Would you like something to drink?" she asked.

"No. Are your parents here?"

"No."

"Where are they?"

"Out. Would you like something to eat?"

"No. I just want to talk."

"We can talk. What would you like to talk about?"

"Can we sit down?" he asked.

"We can sit. Where would you like to sit?"

Oh, God, he thought. She was still a fucking zombie.

He sat on the edge of a couch. She sat on a chair across from him. She had pink pajamas on, with bears and ponies playing with fat-faced white children. Her face was thinner than it had been at school on Friday. Maybe she hadn't been eating. He preferred to think she hadn't been.

"I guess you heard about Ted," he said.

"Yes."

"Do you know what happened to him?"

"He died."

"Do you know how?"

"From blood loss."

"You don't seem upset about that?"

"No."

"Where were you when he died?"

"I was with him."

"You didn't tell the police that?"

"No."

"Susan, how did he die?"

Her smile faltered. It was as if she were having trouble remembering. "We went to the mountains," she said softly. "I told him to take me. He didn't want to go. He wanted to go to an all-night party. But I didn't want to be there, I told him. I needed him alone." She paused. "I watched him die. He cried."

"What tore him apart?"

"Hands."

"Whose hands?"

She shrugged. "I don't know. It doesn't matter."

"It does matter. Susan, what's happened to you? Don't you know who I am?"

She nodded. "Jerry, my boyfriend."

"That's right, I'm your boyfriend. I'm here 'cause I'm worried about you. But you have to help me help you. My mind's messed up." He stopped. "What happened that day at the beach?" he asked. "How come you went under?"

"I was pulled under."

"What? By who?"

"That woman."

"Which woman?"

Susan's expression was stoned. "I was in the water. I was kicking my legs, ready to ride the big wave. Then there was a yank. I didn't know what it was. Felt like a shark. I couldn't move my legs. I couldn't stay on the surface. I felt myself going down and down. Arms went around me. It was her. She held me there a long time, until my lungs burst and the water flowed inside. Then she kissed me, and I kissed her. She gave me her breath. It was cold." Susan paused. "Then everything was different."

"How is it different?" he asked.

"You wouldn't understand."

"Try me."

"I cannot try you."

"Was this woman the same woman who gave you mouth-to-mouth on the beach?"

"Yes."

Jerry fidgeted. "This is too fucking weird. Who was she?"

"I don't know."

Something cold touched Jerry then. The exhalation of a polar bear. One that had just fed. Another whiff of something unpleasant in the air. He tried not to think what it meant, but maybe not all the blood was dried. It was hard to sit still, to be so close to her.

"Have you seen this woman since then?" Jerry asked.

"Yes."

"Where?"

"At the beach."

"Why did you see her?"

"She had to tell me things."

"What things?"

Susan shrugged. "You wouldn't understand."

"Did she tell you to kill Ted?"

"No."

"Did you kill Ted?"

"I suppose."

Jerry trembled. Tears burst from his eyes. He couldn't breathe, he simply couldn't draw in the air. It was as if he were being held down under cold water. Susan, his girl, was a fucking cannibal. "Oh, God," he whispered.

She stood and stared down at him. "It's the way it is," she said flatly.

"Where are your parents?" he whispered.

"Dead."

"How did they die?"

She took a step toward him. "Screaming."

He stood and backed away from her. "Why did you kill them?"

Her eyes were blank, her approach steady. "There is no why."

"You couldn't have killed your own parents, for God sakes!"

"I was hungry."

"No." He moaned. He backed into the wall. She was twelve feet away, ten. He drew his revolver and pointed it at her. She didn't blink. "Stop," he said quietly.

She didn't stop. "You cannot kill me," she said.

"I will kill you."

"No. I am already dead."

He cocked the hammer; his hand shook. But it was true what she said; he could see it then with the clarity sunlight brings to an unearthed grave. She was as dead as something that had been buried for days. He willed his arm steady. He aimed between her eyebrows. It would be a mercy, he told himself. He put four pounds on the five-pound motion of the trigger. Susan took another step closer.

"Don't make me," he pleaded.

She smiled, her lips pulled back over her teeth. He had not noticed before but she had something dark and meaty caught between her front incisors. "I want to make it with you," she said.

Jerry fired. An instant too late. Because as he pulled the trigger, she lashed out with her right foot. Her reflexes were supernatural. The blow caught his right hand and sent it crashing into the wall above and behind him. He felt plaster sprinkle down onto his head as he had at Clear Gell's. That special Christmas look. Only this time blood trickled down as well. Red holiday drops—one splashed his face. She had impaled his hand into the wall. His shot had gone into the ceiling.

He tried to pull the gun down to get off another round, but she was already on him. Besides, his right hand was useless. The gun slipped from his shattered grasp and fell to the floor at his feet. She lashed out again with her foot; he hardly saw the blow coming. He felt it, though, as the side of his left knee caved in. Cartilage, ligaments, bone—it sounded as if the whole mess exploded. In the space of two seconds she had disarmed and crippled him. He sagged against the wall. She put her right hand on his shoulder. Her touch was soft, even her eyes seemed to have lost their edge.

"I'm sorry," she said.

His pain was great then, his sorrow. He knew she was going to kill him and that there was absolutely nothing he could do. He wished then Clear Gell had gotten off another round before going down. He wished many things that would never be. She stroked his hair.

"Susan," he croaked.

"There's something of her left." She went up on her tiptoes and kissed his forehead. "But not much." Her right hand slid slowly around his neck. She pinned him against the wall. Yet her hold was loose; he was not choking. Her eyes strayed to his pants, his belt buckle. "Do you want me to go down on you?" she asked.

"No." He certainly didn't want that.

She popped the button on his pants with her left hand. "I can do it gently."

"No."

She pulled down his zipper. "But I can, Jerry, for you." She leaned over and licked the side of his face with a tongue studded with steel tacks. "I will make you happy before I make you sad," she promised.

She lowered her head.

It was a promise she didn't keep.

He was screaming even before her "gentle" turned to rough.

SEVENTEEN

❧

WHEN PETER JACOBS got home, he found Julie Moore in the kitchen talking to Matt. He knew something was amiss the moment he entered. He figured Dr. Morray had told her who was at his house when she called. Julie was not crying but her features were pinched. She stood up quickly from the table, as did Matt. There were notebooks and forms spread out over the table. Julie had been testing Matt.

"This is a pleasant surprise," he said cheerfully. He felt guilt, of course; it was a conditioned response. Yet intellectually he knew he had no need to apologize. He had just met Julie. They had made no commitments to each other. For all he knew she was seeing half a dozen different guys. Not that he really thought she was, but one never knew. The only aspect about the situation that gnawed at his conscience was that he had used Julie to get Sara's number. He had, in fact, lied to Julie to get it. That wasn't cool. Maybe he should apologize. He didn't want to lie to her again.

"Zeus," Matt said. "You're early."

"Better early than late," Peter said.

"If you want to catch the worm," Matt agreed.

"Did you get any pink slips for new customers today?" Peter asked.

"Two," Matt said. "I found one house. I think. I left the paper there. I could not find the other house. Julie said she might show me where it is."

"That was nice of Julie to offer to help." Peter looked at her. She wasn't exactly bursting with conversation. "How long have you been here?"

"Not long," she said.

"She's testing me," Matt said. "Do you know what the word *gigantic* means, Pete?"

"Very big," Peter said.

Matt grinned. "I said very, very big. Bigger than a house. I got that one right."

"Matt is doing well on the test," Julie said stiffly. "I think he's smarter than both of us. At least smarter than I am."

"Matt," Peter said. "Julie and I are going into my bedroom to have a talk. Would that be OK?"

Matt was interested. "Are you going to talk about me?"

"We're going to talk about us," Peter said, taking Julie by the arm.

"Are you two getting married?" Matt asked.

"Not today," Julie said quietly.

In the bedroom Julie sat on the edge of the bed. He sat on the floor at her feet. He liked the floor; he often did some of his best work there. He had shut the door.

"What's up?" he asked.

"Nothing. What's up with you?"

"You seem upset."

"I'm not upset," she said.

"Yes, you are. What did you do today?"

She shrugged. "Talked to Jerry Washington. What did you do today?"

"Talked to Mr. and Mrs. Morray."

"Sara? How was she?"

"She's fine. How's Jerry?"

"He's fine," Julie said, adding, "other than the fact that he thinks his girlfriend is in dire need of an exorcist."

"Tell me about him."

"Tell me about Sara."

He nodded. "You called while I was there. That's why you're upset."

"You're not my shrink." She shook her head. "I can't believe I gave you her number. I can't believe you asked me for it."

"Julie, it's no big deal. I went for a walk on the beach with her."

"With her and her husband?"

"He didn't come home until later."

She closed her eyes. "Fuck."

"We didn't do that," he said gamely. The remark didn't fly far. Julie continued to keep her eyes closed and now lowered her head. "Look, what are we talking about here?" he asked. "It can't be Sara Morray. I hardly know her. She's a married woman."

"You like her."

He hesitated. "I do like her. I like you, too."

She opened her red eyes. "Why didn't you call me?"

"I did, twice," he said honestly. "I got your machine."

"Why didn't you leave a message?"

"I hate leaving messages. I always feel like they can be used against me later in a court of law."

"Why didn't you call me at the store? You knew I was working. You knew I would have loved to hear from you."

Ah, loved, love—he had never said the words to her, of course, not even in the heat of passion. Nor she to him. But he could see Julie loved him already. She fell fast. But he did, too. He already loved Sara, even though he didn't think the infatuation healthy. She had some kind of hold on him. Even sitting here, trying to cheer Julie up, he couldn't stop thinking about Sara. What had she meant about her husband creating a modern Frankenstein monster? She had said so many odd things.

"I should have called you back," he said. "I'm sorry. I had a wonderful time Friday night." He reached out and touched her leg. "Hey, don't be so glum. It's not as if one of us is about to die."

She sniffed. "Do you want to go out together again?"

"Sure."

She nodded, thought about it. "Are you going to be going out with others?"

Sara was now a legion to be reckoned with. "I don't know. Maybe, maybe not. Why do we have to worry about that now?"

Julie forced a chuckle. "I seem unable to quit worrying about it. Why do you think that is, Peter? Am I so starved for love?"

"I don't know. I'm not your shrink." He paused. "It's natural. Don't be so hard on yourself. It was my fault I didn't get hold of you. After spending a night together, that was wrong of me."

"I accept your apology." She reached down and clasped his offered hand. Her eyes had brightened; her heart was forgiving. She really was a lovely woman. Under ordinary circumstances he would have considered himself fortunate to have met her. But these were strange days.

"Tell me about your meeting with Jerry Washington," he said.

She gave him a concise overview of the conversation. When she was done he was more confused than ever. Julie repeated that she had never heard of an NDE like Susan Darly's. Peter made a mental note to insist Amos go out to the girl's house, preferably in the next day or so. He asked for Jerry's home number and Julie gave it to him.

Peter pleaded that he had to work to do, and Julie said that was fine, she had schoolwork to do. He walked her out to her car and kissed her briefly. She was smiling as she promised to call him later. He couldn't remember exactly what he promised her.

Inside, Matt had fallen asleep on the couch. He was like a small child in many ways; he slept twelve hours a day. Peter removed his shoes and stuck a pillow under his head. Matt never stirred.

In his bedroom, with the door shut, Peter placed a call to his boss, Edward Foley. Peter didn't have work to do, not on his column. The previous week he had forced himself to get ahead. He could take off the next week and not be missed. But he wanted to talk to Ed because, like most good reporters, particularly the ones who had risen to their ivory towers from the hard streets, Ed had a network of sources: access to TRW computer files; friends inside the L.A.P.D.; unscrupulous private detectives; big-eared bartenders. Peter knew he had to handle Ed carefully, dangle the possibility of the story of the year before him—a solution to the string of killings—without giving him specifics. Unfortunately, the two specifics he could not avoid were Dr. and Mrs. Morray.

Dialing Ed's number, Peter had a moment of indecision. Who was he researching: the doctor or Sara? As Amos had said, Dr. Morray's link to the murders may not exist at all. Maybe Peter Jacobs was just horny.

Ed listened closely to his pitch. He was intrigued; he wanted to help. He said something again about the joy of real reporting and promised to get back to Peter with whatever he could find on Dr. and Mrs. Morray.

While Peter waited, Chuck called. Peter did not push the button on the little black box that alerted the police. He wondered at the lapse for it was definitely deliberate. Whom was he protecting? Chuck sounded cheerful enough, although his voice had deteriorated even further since their last conversation. He sounded as if he had throat cancer, but was enjoying the discomfort. He hadn't altered his format.

"This is Chuck," he said. "I hope I didn't wake you. I know I should call you at your office, but I didn't want to talk to you there. I have something to tell you, Mr. Jacobs, if you want to hear it, and I think you do."

"I don't know," Peter said. "I listened to you last time and you didn't show. Why should I listen to you again?"

"I was there in spirit, Mr. Jacobs. Do you believe in the spirit? It is important that you do if you want to understand why I kill. My spirit bleeds, my heart breathes. You might think it would be the other way around, but it is not. That is why things are the way they are."

"Are things so bad that you will have to kill again?"

"Bad is a relative term. I kill because it is my nature to kill."

"Well, why don't we get together and talk about it? I'll meet you anywhere that's convenient. If you want, we can try the museum again. How about tonight?"

"It's not necessary to meet again. Already we are very close. I see you when you sleep. I watch when you are awake. Soon you will understand, Mr. Jacobs, and the knowledge will fill you like a deep breath on a winter night."

Chuck was not one for long good-byes. Again he hung up. Peter went to call Amos but hesitated. What was the point? Chuck had refused to see him. Then again, Chuck's comment about watching him was far from comforting. Peter thought of Matt asleep in the next room. It might not be a bad idea to have an officer guard the condo. He just hated thinking about Matt's reaction. Matt wouldn't be able to sleep if he knew what was going on. If only there was another place to put him until all this blew over. Peter decided he'd have to look into that. Soon.

Curiously, Peter realized that Chuck no longer scared him.

It was as if he had already seen worse things than the crimes Chuck may have committed. Only he couldn't remember where.

Ed called back. He had little information, but he promised more later. So far he had nothing on Sara Morray. He said it was as if the woman had come out of nowhere. He didn't even know her maiden name. But he was able to tell him much of what Julie had already said about Dr. Morray. He was a rich and famous cardiologist. Over twenty-five years earlier he had embarked on an extensive investigation into near-death experiences. On the verge of publishing his research, he had dropped out of the field. He had an older sister living in San Francisco, an Esther Morray. Did Peter want her phone number? He most certainly did. Oh, yes, Ed said, there was one other thing. Sara was Dr. Morray's second wife. His first wife, Sandra, was deceased. She had died thirty years ago.

Peter found that interesting.

Sara had explicitly told him she was the original Mrs. Morray.

EIGHTEEN

❖

R AK WAS IN Delta's baggage area before Govinda Sharma
caught up with him. Govinda had to assume Rak had sailed
through customs; Govinda certainly had not. His lack of luggage had raised eyebrows. How come he had not brought even a
change of clothes with him? the customs officer had asked. Govinda
had made up something about his brother being in an accident and
his own confused state before leaving. He had been afraid Rak would
be out of the terminal before he could get free. The customs man had
finally let him go after placing a call to Bechtel to confirm that
Govinda Sharma had a valid green card.

Rak stood in the baggage area against a wall. Only his loincloth
saved him from the crime of indecent exposure. He had his wooden
staff in his left hand. Seeing him again—for the first time since they
had left India—Govinda thought him not so frightening. Rak may
have been tired because he stood with his shoulders slouched slightly
forward. His blindness was more apparent now than before. He reacted to the noises about him—the voice on the P.A. system, the banging of the luggage as it slid from the chute, even the cries of
children—but not in the smooth, effortless way Govinda had come to
associate with Rak's movements. Indeed, Rak appeared to be very
much what he was: a blind man newly arrived in a foreign country.
With no friends, no money to buy him a place to stay. Govinda had to
remind himself of what had transpired in India. The days in the
Himalayas, the night on the bank of the Ganges, the morning of the
cobra attack—all seemed like one far-off dream to him now. Yet noth-

ing cloaked the unexplainable better, Govinda knew, than a modern Western city.

Govinda found it curious how much more at home he felt in America than in India. The long flight had been a necessary break for him. He had slept most of the way from Delhi to Tokyo—their only stop on the journey—and then he had eaten and read magazines on the long leg across the Pacific, dozing periodically. Not once had he felt the urge to stroll up to first class and check on Rak, not even during their brief layover in Japan. A tiny and unimportant question had repeatedly surfaced in his mind—had Rak ordered the vegetarian meal or not, had he even eaten? Throughout the pursuit, Govinda had not seen Rak put anything in his mouth. Maybe he lived on prana, Govinda thought, the subtle life energy in the air. In the Himalayas there were supposed to be yogis who survived on nothing but kriyas and pranayamas.

Govinda had ordered the chicken and mashed potatoes on the flight. He had started eating flesh only after Vani's death, no doubt in defiance of his scriptural upbringing. He had thought of Keshava as he chewed on his drumstick. The food had been tasty.

Rak stood silently as people collected their luggage. Govinda moved to within thirty feet of him, studying him; the man had the power to draw him forward. But was it possible, Govinda asked himself, that he and Indra had been foolish to blow the incident with the snake out of proportion and into an act of supernatural retaliation? At the time the miracle had seemed self-evident. The cobras had flocked to Rak as if summoned, yet had not touched him. Then the baby one had come for Pandu. Only for Pandu, who was sitting watch. Yet the cobras might have gathered around Rak because he was a warm human body, and then failed to bite him because he had the ability to remain so still. Indeed, the cobra that had killed Pandu might not have been one of those that had climbed onto Rak. Watching Rak now, Govinda was tempted to approach and offer him a hand. Rak appeared to be waiting for someone or something that was not going to arrive.

Then something did happen, not something miraculous, but curious enough. One of the last people to receive his luggage from their flight was a tall young African-American. He looked like a basketball player, probably was; his T-shirt was stenciled with the University of Santa Barbara initials. He collected his bag and, as he was ready to leave, glanced over at Rak. Now that Govinda thought about it, the young man had cast Rak several curious glances. The young man tentatively approached Rak from the blind man's right. If Rak heard him coming, he gave no sign, simply continued to stare unblinking at the now-empty luggage carousel. The young man cleared his throat.

"Excuse me, sir," he said. "Do you speak English?"

Rak looked at him and nodded.

"Are you from India?" the young man asked.

Rak nodded.

"Is this your first time in our country?"

Rak nodded.

"Forgive me for asking, sir, but are you blind?"

Rak nodded.

"Is someone coming to meet you here?"

Rak shook his head.

"Do you have anywhere to go?"

Rak nodded. Ah, Govinda thought. Ask where. Where had Rak learned English? Certainly not from Krishna. The young man was concerned.

"Will you be able to get there?"

Rak nodded.

The guy was embarrassed, although it was obvious he had a good heart. "You'll have to excuse me once more, sir, but I feel compelled to tell you this in case you don't know. In America you can't walk around dressed as you are. People will stare and the police won't like it. I was just thinking in my bag here I have an extra shirt and pair of pants I can give you. They're old and worn but they're clean and I think we're about the same size. They should fit you." He paused, uncertain. He had Rak's eyes on him, something Govinda had yet to experience, and they were obviously affecting him. He was smiling but he had broken into a sweat as well. He added, "Would you like them, sir? Free of charge?"

Rak nodded.

"That's good. You'll fit in easier with clothes on, I'm sure." The man knelt and opened his bag. He took out a pair of old blue jeans and a light gray sweatshirt. Rak put on the clothes as he was handed them, the pants right over his loincloth. The service seemed to please the young man. At the same time he was anxious to get away. He began to back away the moment Rak was dressed, not even bothering to zip up his bag completely. He added, "You take care now, you hear? Watch out crossing the streets and all."

Rak did not respond. He simply listened until the young man was gone. He was still barefoot but Govinda doubted that would hamper him. He had walked through the snow of the Himalayas as easily as the blistering dust of Rishikesh. Los Angeles asphalt, even under a summer sun, would be nothing to him. Rak once more took hold of his staff and stepped out the door. It occurred to Govinda that perhaps he had only been waiting for someone to offer him clothes before he departed. Perhaps, Govinda thought, the young man had been *forced* to give him the clothes.

Rak exited LAX through what Govinda had called "the back way," out Lincoln Boulevard. Having lived in Santa Monica not far from the beach, Govinda had usually taken the boulevard when he went to the airport. He thought it an incredible coincidence that of all the spots Rak could have chosen in the world to visit, he had come to one of the few places outside India with which Govinda was familiar. It made Govinda wonder if the Master had known more of Rak's plans than he had let on.

Rak, however, did not stay on Lincoln, but quickly turned left onto Manchester, west, and headed in the direction of the ocean. Even the average blind American, Govinda thought, probably could have guessed the direction of the ocean from this distance, less than two miles from the water. Particularly with the faint salty breeze coming out of the west; which, however, did nothing to soothe Govinda's sweaty brow. He could not remember L.A. ever being so hot—it was as bad as India.

The young man's last remark to Rak quickly came back to Govinda. He watched as Rak struggled at his first few stop lights. Rak was obviously listening intently at each intersection, but even he could not always tell what each car from all four directions was going to do next. Twice he stepped into the street, against a red light, only to jump back as a car whizzed by. The tip of his staff was always in front of him, probing for permutations in the concrete. The obstacles slowed him down. He was not the master of this terrain as he had been in the mountains and jungle. Yet, Govinda thought, nothing stopped him. He still went where he wished.

They reached the beach. Rak crossed the Coast Highway and walked onto the sand near the water. He headed north, moving faster now. Waves came and splashed his feet and pants. Govinda allowed the distance between them to lengthen to a couple of hundred yards. He stopped at a refreshment stand and bought himself a Pepsi and a bag of peanuts, paying for the food with the few dollars he had hastily exchanged at the airport. He wished he had a hat and sunglasses—the sun was heating his brains. People were out en masse, and it wasn't even a weekend. It was a shock to see so many beautiful women with virtually nothing on. So many people for whom the body was the center of existence. He scooped handfuls of ocean water and poured it over his hair. Rak was walking very rapidly now. Was he closing on his goal? Govinda wondered.

Rak walked for six hours straight. By then it was almost sunset and they were on the beaches of Malibu. Govinda was ready to collapse when Rak suddenly stopped. At first Govinda assumed it was the time of day that made him halt; the sun burned the horizon like a Pasupata fed by the eternal. Yet Rak was not through walking, only done with the sand. He stood for a long moment staring up at the houses on the Malibu hills, sensing what, Govinda could not imagine. Then he set off toward the homes, leaving the beach, crossing the Coast Highway, taking a residential street that wound up into the rich real estate like a pathway to another land.

Rak, however, did not stay on the road. When it dead-ended at a wire fence, he vaulted the barrier as if it had been erected to keep out only animals and small children. He continued up the hill, climbing through the dried shrubs and grass with as much spring in his step as when he had first set out. On his tail, only a hundred yards back now, Govinda panted like a heart patient who had missed the elevator. Surely, he thought, Rak must know he was being followed. Certainly he didn't give a damn. What snakes were there in southern California? Rattlers? If one showed up soon Govinda thought he would offer his hand. He had never realized the pain fatigue could bring. Probably because he had never chased a five-thousand-year-old man before.

Finally Rak did stop. Near the top of the hill, overlooking the expensive homes and the darkening coast, Rak sat down in the lotus position on a flat stretch of dirt and closed his eyes. Less than a football field away Govinda fell to his knees. He did not need a sleeping bag to sleep. The ground was not shaking, at the moment; it was enough bed for him. He could not keep watch. If Rak was gone when he awoke, then so be it. The Master would have to forgive him. He had tried his best. He had to rest or he would die.

Yet Govinda did not think Rak would be gone when the sun rose.

Rak, he felt certain, was very near what he had come out of the Himalayas for.

Govinda tried not to imagine what it could be.

NINETEEN

❖

P ETER JACOBS TOOK the early shuttle to San Francisco to meet
Esther Morray, Dr. Lawrence Morray's older sister, two days
after receiving what was to be Chuck's last call. Peter had
wanted to visit the sister immediately after learning of her, but when
he had phoned her she had said she was busy and put him off. Peter
had presented himself for what he was, a reporter for the *Los Angeles
Times,* but had been vague about why he wanted to interview her. Esther Morray had sounded a bit senile. She had not asked specifically
why he was coming.

When Peter arrived and showed Esther's address to a taxi driver,
the man said it looked like a Berkeley address to him and that he
should have flown into Oakland instead. All Peter had was the street
address and the zip, and Ed Foley's words that she lived in San Francisco. No matter, the driver said, Berkeley was just across the bay.
Peter climbed in and they got on the Bay Bridge. The water all around
was beautiful; nevertheless, Peter wondered what the hell he was
doing.

Esther Morray lived in a second-floor apartment of a rundown
house on a street the driver said was a good place to buy drugs. Peter
had cash in his pocket; he asked the taxi to wait, which the guy was
happy to do. Peter took a backyard flight of splintered stairs to Esther's
front door and knocked. She took a long time answering.

She was at least fifteen years older than her brother, stooped
more from age than internal demons, with heavy bags under her eyes.
As she let him in, Peter realized he'd have to shout to be heard. Her

cheap furniture was old and smelled of dust and mold. This was the sister, Peter thought, of a man who made between one and two million a year. Dr. Morray did not deserve Sara. That's why he was here, Peter told himself. He sat down on a couch that could have been stuffed by friends of Matt and declined her offer of tea. She sat in a wooden rocking chair across from him. He had a feeling she spent most of her days there. She stared at him with vague brown eyes.

"You are a reporter?" she said.

"Yes, Ms. Morray. I work for the *Los Angeles Times*. I'm doing an article on your brother and his wife." It was possible, likely in fact, that Dr. Morray would learn of his visit with Esther and be angry, not that Peter cared.

Esther nodded. "Larry and Sandy."

"Larry and Sara." Peter paused. He knew the name Sandra Morray from Ed Foley's information. "Your brother's wife's name is Sara."

Esther was confused. "But Sandy . . ." Her voice trailed off, and she raised a hand to her head. "I'm sorry. I've never met Sara. But I know Sara, yes, he told me about her."

"Did you know Sandy?"

"Of course. Sandy was a wonderful woman. Pretty and sweet. We used to do many things together. I was with her when she bought her wedding dress."

"She was your brother's first wife?"

"Yes." Her face darkened. "She was so young."

"She died when she was young?"

"Yes. Only thirty." Esther sighed. "They were married three years. Then she was gone. Would you like some tea, Mr. — I'm sorry, I'm afraid I've forgotten your name."

"Jacobs. Peter Jacobs. No, thank you, Esther, I don't need any tea. Could you tell me more about Sandy? How she died?"

"She drowned."

"How?"

"In the water." Esther struggled. "Don't most people drown in water?"

"Yes. People usually drown in water, when they do drown. Was Larry with her when she drowned?"

"Yes. They were always together in those days."

"Do you know how it happened?"

"They were on a boat and Sandy fell in the water and drowned."

"How did she fall?"

"I don't know."

"Were they fighting?"

Esther shook her head vigorously. "They never fought. Larry loved Sandy more than life itself." Esther stared off into space. "He was never the same after he lost her."

"What do you mean?"

"He was lost. Have you ever lost someone close to you, Mr. Peters?"

"Yes."

"Then you know. If you don't want tea, would you like coffee? I can make a pot, if I have some. I'm not sure if I do."

"No thank you. Esther, did the police investigate Sandy's death?"

"The police? Why would they investigate? It was an accident."

"I understand. Where did this accident take place?"

"In the water. I told you."

"Where in the water? In Los Angeles?"

"No. In Mexico. They went there on vacation." Esther was suddenly sad. A tear crept down her ruined cheek. "I wish they had never gone. I still miss Sandy to this day. She was so kind. So talented."

"What was she talented at?"

"Painting."

Peter did not get anything else of interest out of Esther Morray, although what he had learned from her was enough to make him glad he had come. Or perhaps the word *glad* didn't really describe his state of mind as he left her in her rocking chair and went downstairs to ask his taxi driver to take him back to the airport. The more he heard and the more he learned of the people who had died, the more he believed that he had entered an illusionary phase of life. He felt as if he stood on a precipice above a valley cloaked in darkness, waiting for the sun to rise, for the cold wind to quit blowing. Yet he feared that when the light finally did come, the valley would not be a place of enchantment, but one of lakes filled with dark roiling liquids and narrow roads that led only into caves from which there were no exits. And even when the sunlight did arrive, he feared the cold would still be there, and that would be the worst thing of all. He shivered as they drove back over the bridge. So much water all around, he thought, to drown in. He thought of Jerry Washington's girlfriend then, the one whom the boy said was a monster. He had to call Jerry soon.

What he ended up doing at the airport before boarding the flight home, however, was call Ed Foley to see if he had more information.

Ed sounded excited, although he had only one particular bit to give Peter: the name and address of Dr. Morray's friend, a Dr. David Samuel. Seems the two had gone to medical school together. Dr. Samuel currently lived in Iowa. Peter took his number and pressed Ed to tell him what else was up, but his boss was noncommittal.

"Let me check it out first and make sure it's accurate," Ed said. "But if you want to fly out and interview Dr. Samuel, you can put it on the company card."

Peter found the remark curious. So far he had given Ed such scant information connecting Dr. Morray to the murders that he couldn't imagine the paper was willing to pay for travel expenses. Nothing Peter had uncovered so far pointed a finger at Dr. Morray, although it was interesting that he had been present when his first wife died. Ed also found the information noteworthy, when Peter reviewed his conversation with Esther. Again he pressed Peter to see Dr. Samuel.

"Shouldn't I call him first to make sure he wants to see me?" Peter asked.

"I can give you his number. But sometimes it's better to show up. It's easier to put down a phone than to slam a door in someone's face."

"What exactly am I asking Dr. Samuel? 'Did your old buddy ever kill anyone with his bare hands?' "

"You might want to ask that."

"Ed, if you know anything, tell me now before I fly halfway across the country."

"I told you, we have to check it out. But if it is true, then you'll want to be in Iowa anyway. Trust me on this. Just go."

"I'm going to buy a first-class ticket."

"Coach."

"Business class."

"Fine. Call me when you get there. I might have something for you by then."

They exchanged good-byes. Peter tried to get Dr. Samuel at the number Ed had given him, but a machine picked up. Peter didn't leave a message. He checked for flights for Cedar Rapids, found one on United that departed in ninety minutes, with a connection through Denver. He'd arrive in Iowa in the early evening.

Peter bought himself a first-class ticket.

He'd never been one to listen to people.

TWENTY

❧

J ULIE MOORE RANG the doorbell to Susan Darly's house and waited. For the last two days she had tried unsuccessfully to call the girl. She had been unable to contact Jerry Washington either, and that worried her. She suspected that he'd been picked up by the police again. She hoped they didn't rough him up any more, those fools. She'd been meaning to speak to Peter's detective friend, Lieutenant Amos Rodrigues, about the matter. At least Amos sounded like a decent human being.

A short blond girl with bloodshot eyes answered the door. Her movements were not slow; nevertheless, she gave the impression of being drugged. Her expression was a curious mixture: anger and glee, suspicion and cockiness. It seemed to shift through the spectrum of these emotions in the space of a moment, over a background of indifference. Julie could see why Jerry had said there was something wrong with her. Even without testing, Julie would have recommended close observation of Susan Darly. A fly buzzed around the girl's head.

"Yes?" she said flatly.

"Are you Susan Darly?"

"Yes."

"Hello. My name is Julie Moore." She offered her hand. Susan didn't even look at it. Julie took it back. "I'm a friend of Jerry Washington's as well as a specialist in what happens to people who have near-death experiences. I met with Jerry a couple of days ago. He told me how you almost drowned."

"Yes."

"Have you spoken to Jerry since then?"

"Yes."

"When?"

"I don't know."

"Did he come here to see you?"

"Yes."

"Was it today?"

"No."

"How was he?"

Susan blinked. Just once. "What do you want?"

Julie drew in a breath. The girl made her incredibly uncomfortable, and she had experience interviewing and testing the worst cases in juvenile hall. "I understand you have not been feeling well since your near drowning. I'm here to talk to you about that, if you want to talk. Also, I was hoping you'd be able to tell me where Jerry is."

"He's not here."

"I see." Julie paused. She believed Susan had suffered brain damage. "Are your parents at home?"

"No."

"Where are they?"

"I don't know."

"Do you know when they'll be back?"

"No."

Julie sniffed the air. There was a foul odor coming from the interior of the house. She couldn't place the smell, but hated to think of Susan wandering around aimlessly in it. Clearly the girl was not capable of taking care of herself. Julie didn't understand how the parents could have left her on her own. Susan's eyes had lost their glassiness in the last few seconds. Now they were focused and studying Julie.

"Would you like to come in?" Susan asked.

"Yes, if I may. I'd like to use your phone."

"I can show you where it is."

Susan moved aside and held the door open wide. Julie took a step inside and froze. The moment she put her foot across the threshold, the odor increased tenfold, and the elusive nature of its origin vanished. She smelled blood, lots of it, mixed with other morbid matter.

"You know, she's stronger than me now."

Julie turned her head and stared at Susan.

"I can't have you see her. I can't have that on my head."

The girl licked her lips. Grinning.

"Have what on your head?"

Eyes so cold. Like razors, Jerry had said.

"If she kills you."

Julie felt cold then. Worse than afraid.

"I don't think that'll happen."

"Susan?" Julie said softly, trying to keep her voice steady.

"I'm sure Ted didn't either."

"Yes?"

"How long have your parents been gone?"

"A long time."

"Where are they?"

"It doesn't matter."

"Where's Jerry? Tell me. It matters."

Susan put a hand on Julie's bare arm, fingered the skin as if testing the texture. "I took him to heaven," Susan whispered. Then she let out a single sharp cackle. Like the bark of a dog guarding the gate of hell.

Jesus Christ, Julie thought. She backed out of the house.

"I have to go," Julie said. Once more on the porch, the sun felt good on the arm Susan had touched. Yet Susan was reaching to grab for her again; her fingers stretched out like the claws of the junior prom queen who had taken to heart the last horror film she had seen at the drive-in with her werewolf boyfriend. Julie retreated another step.

"I don't want you to go," the girl said.

"I have a friend to meet," Julie said.

"Where?" Susan dropped her arm and moved onto the porch beside her. No, actually, she shifted a step past her, as if intending to block Julie from leaving. Julie was now certain Susan had no intention of letting her go. The girl seemed to enjoy the charade, but there was cruelty in her. Julie didn't know how she had failed to spot it at the start. They were standing on a porch in a rich area of Malibu, two young white females. The sun was out; there wasn't a cloud in the sky. Except for the bad smell, the setting couldn't have been more idyllic. Yet that smell spoke volumes, as did Susan's Jeffrey-Dahmer-I-look-like-I-eat-at-McDonald's-but-I-don't-really eye contact. Julie shot up her arm instinctively and pointed down the street.

"There he is!" she exclaimed. "Peter!"

Susan turned to look. Julie leapt off the porch and ran toward her car. Across the wide stretch of lawn she kept expecting to feel Susan's steel ligamented cyborg claw clamp down on her shoulder and rip out a chunk of tender flesh. Yet when she reached her car and finally glanced over her shoulder, she saw that Susan had not stirred from the porch. Indeed, the girl waved a nonchalant good-bye before stepping back inside the house and closing the door. Julie stood there for a moment trying to decide if she was one of the luckiest people on earth or one of the most foolish. Everything had happened so fast, she was having trouble assimilating what was real and what was imaginary. How much time had elapsed since she arrived? Two minutes? Surely not enough time to start believing in monsters. One thing was sure, though, she wasn't going to volunteer to treat Susan Darly again. That girl had too many flies buzzing around her head.

Julie got in her car and drove home. There was one message on her answering machine. She hoped it was from Peter, but it was from her dearest and most deadly rival—Sara Morray. The doctor's wife's voice was kind but to the point.

"Julie, this is Sara Morray. Please call me as soon as you get in. We should talk."

"About what?" Julie asked the machine. "Your husband or Peter?"

Julie couldn't stand the suspense. She dialed the Morray residence. Sara answered promptly. Julie said hello, identified herself, and apologized for missing her appointment with Dr. Morray the other day. Sara didn't seem to mind. She was cheerful enough, but a bit distracted. She did not, however, sound as if she were about to drop the bomb that she coveted Julie's boyfriend. Not that Peter was really her boyfriend, Julie thought. Where was that bastard today? She had called him twice that morning.

"Did I catch you at a bad time?" Julie asked.

"No. I was just painting."

Peter had said Sara was an artist. "I wish I could paint. I wish I could play a musical instrument, for that matter."

"I'm sure there are many people who wish they could psychoanalyze people the way you can," Sara said smoothly. "I do not mean that sarcastically. It's one of the reasons I called. I'm anxious to discuss your research on near-death experiences with you."

"You should speak to your husband. He's ten times the authority I am."

"I've tried. But he won't speak to me about it."

Sara sounded sincere, Julie thought. Really, the facts of the woman's great beauty and Peter's obvious interest in her were not reasons why she should automatically despise the bitch.

"Why do you want to discuss it?" Julie asked. "Have you had a near-death experience?"

Sara hesitated. "I'm not sure."

"Well, I'd be happy to meet with you sometime."

"How about now?"

"Now?"

"Yes. Are you busy? You could come for lunch. Just the two of us. I'm a wonderful cook." Sara chuckled. "At least my meals are always color coordinated."

Julie was tempted to say: But I just escaped from Malibu. The place has bad vibes. Ms. Suntan Homecoming has done it one too many times with the pale foreign exchange student from the German Black Forest. Julie still hadn't made up her mind what to do about Susan Darly. She was tempted to call Peter's detective friend and tell him the girl should be brought in for questioning, but worried he would snicker when she insisted that a SWAT team be sent. Yet she couldn't let that smell slide. It was one huge fact about the house, no matter if she had overreacted to Susan's manner. She prayed to God that Jerry was all right.

"Hmm." Julie grunted.

"Are you busy at the moment?" Sara asked.

"My usual answer to that question is yes. Between school and work, I'm always on the go. But this afternoon happens to be slow." Slow, my ass, Julie thought. Still, she considered the invitation. There was no sense arguing with her feelings. She had it bad for Peter, and the crush was not going to go away with additional therapy. If Peter did care for Sara—and Julie thought the odds of that were approaching one hundred percent—then it couldn't hurt to get a better idea what she was up against. Of course, that didn't mean she intended to compete for Peter's affections with any woman, perish the thought.

"I can come," Julie said.

"Wonderful. I'll be expecting you."

Sara hung up. Julie tried to reach Lieutenant Rodrigues. It took her some work just to find his department. He was out, his partner said. She left a message for him to call her when he got in. Heading out the door, she wondered if she should have added that she knew Peter Jacobs.

*   *   *

Sara was outside in the front trimming her rosebushes when Julie arrived. Julie almost didn't get out of the car when she saw her. Sara was not merely attractive, with all the right features carefully aligned by nature, she was a radiant soul, even wearing something as simple as a short blue sundress. Before Julie could find reverse, Sara approached the car with a dozen thorny roses in one hand, shears in the other. Sara's smile was magic; it could have sold magazines to both sexes. Julie found herself curious about the woman despite her best intentions to hate her.

"Hi," Sara said. "Did you have trouble finding the place?"

She didn't want to say that she had been there before, even though it had been Sara who had invited her. "No problem," Julie said. "I'm good with the Thomas Guide."

"I have one of those books. It's never helped me find a single place. Probably because I can never find the book."

"You should have two of them, and always keep one in your car."

"I have two cars," Sara said.

"Must be nice."

Sara took a step closer and scraped at the thorns on the stems of her flowers. "Have you ever received a bouquet of red roses and found yourself more interested in the missing thorns than the soft petals?" she asked.

Julie laughed, although in its own way it was a disturbing question. "I never have that problem. No guy ever sends me flowers."

Sara gestured to the rows of rosebushes that lined the driveway to the street. "I get flowers all the time. The earth gives them to me. But I think that when I pick them to bring them in the house, I ruin them." She stared down at the bunch in her gloveless right hand. A thorn had pricked her thumb; there was a spot of blood. Her expression was difficult to read, as was the meaning of her next words. "I think the thorns are as important as the petals," she said.

They went inside. Julie asked to see her paintings. Bad move for Julie's morale—Sara's talent staggered her. Compete with this woman? Julie asked herself. She figured she might as well compete for Leonardo's attention with Mona Lisa. Beauty and genius in one package; a rare combination anywhere in the world but virtually unknown in southern California. If Sara Morray wanted Peter Jacobs, then she'd have him. The deal could be locked and sealed at their next secret meeting. Julie was finding the whole afternoon depressing.

First Cannibal Sue wanted to have her for lunch and then Aphrodite asked her for lunch. Julie would have liked to have owned one of Sara's paintings, however; they were inspiring, particularly the ocean scenes. But she knew she could never afford one. There was no point in asking what they cost.

Sara appeared to sense her mood and inquired about her activities, listening intently as Julie described her research. Julie also described Professor Adams, and Sara seemed fascinated with his vast knowledge of esoteric subjects. She told Julie she definitely wanted his phone number as well. Sara was on the verge of talking about her own experiences when Julie mentioned how she still occasionally tested children for the state to pick up extra money and how she wished she could do more but didn't have the time. The comment piqued Sara's interest.

"What kind of tests do you give?" Sara asked.

"There are two broad categories that each involve a battery of tests. I test IQ and educational achievement level. Often I do both. I also test emotional stability."

"How do you do that?"

Julie shrugged. "With a battery of tests and my own personal observations on how the person behaves during the testing period. But specifically, as far as emotions are concerned, psychologists still rely heavily on the Rorschach Test, even though it's been around since 1921. You've heard of the Rorschach, I assume?"

Sara was uncertain. "That's the ink blot test?"

"Exactly."

"Do you consider it very accurate?"

"No one test is accurate. I draw my conclusions from an entire battery. Yet the Rorschach always gives insight. It's a totally subjective test. It is virtually impossible to fake responses."

Sara thought a moment. They were sitting in her living room. The west wall of the house was mainly windows, framing a gorgeous view of the coast. Julie could not imagine what a house like this cost. Maybe five centuries' worth of rent for her.

"Do you have this test with you?" Sara asked.

"As a matter of fact I do. I always keep my testing tools in the trunk of my car. Not that I use them that often these days. Why do you ask?"

"I'd like to take the Rorschach Test."

Julie shook her head, amazed. "You are rare, Mrs. Morray. Few people volunteer to take it. They fear the test will reveal too much about who they really are."

Sara smiled. "Not many things scare me."

TWENTY-ONE

❋

WHEN PETER JACOBS arrived in Cedar Rapids, Iowa, he called Dr. David Samuel. This time the man picked up. He sounded approximately Morray's age, guarded, more gruff than paranoid. Peter had barely introduced himself as a reporter for the *L.A. Times* when the man interrupted. What did he want?

"To talk to you about Dr. Lawrence Morray," Peter said. "I understand you two go way back."

"Who told you that?"

"A computer in the basement of our offices. I'm sorry, Dr. Samuel, that's the plain truth. But I'm not here to spy on you."

"You're here? Where are you?"

"At the airport in Cedar Rapids. I flew in to speak to you."

"Then you should have called first. I have nothing to say about Larry. I haven't seen him in thirty years nor talked to him."

"Did you two have a falling out?"

"In a manner of speaking. Why is the *Times* interested in Larry?"

"I would be happy to tell you the whole story when we get together."

Dr. Samuel chuckled. "You're smooth, young man, I grant you that. But I still don't want to get together. What happened between Larry and me—it's ancient history. It's nothing you'd want to write about anyway. I'm sorry you came all this way for nothing. Good-bye."

"Just a moment," Peter said, but the good doctor had already hung up. Peter felt more justified than ever in purchasing a first-class ticket. Maybe on the way home he would ask if he could fly the plane.

Just charge the lesson to my boss at the paper. He dialed Ed Foley next. Ed would tell him to drive out to Samuel's house, never mind that he didn't have an invitation. Peter might do it if he knew what to ask the doctor. An investigation needed a clear objective and he had none. Was he digging for dirt from Dr. Morray's past? Had the wicked doctor, for example, drowned his first wife? A tempting morsel. Peter knew if Sara heard that, she'd be out of Malibu the same day. But that didn't mean she'd be in Venice the next one. What was wrong with him anyway, chasing a married woman? He had never done that before. He was supposed to be trying to catch a murderer. He still felt guilty about not having informed Amos of Chuck's last call, not that the loon had said anything. Peter had asked a neighbor to stop in to check on Matt a few times during the day, make sure he was all right. He knew he had to get Matt another place to stay until the murderer was caught.

"He hung up on me," Peter said when he had Ed on the line.

"Why did you call him?" Ed asked.

"Because I call all my people before going out to interview them. It's a habit with me. They're usually happy to hear from me. Now what's the other reason I'm in Iowa? Tell me now or I get on the next plane heading west."

"Sandra Morray isn't dead," Ed said.

"*What?*"

"You heard me. She's alive near there in an intensive care facility, the Kabriel Clinic. She's been there a long time. Kabriel specializes in the care of brain-damaged patients. Get this, Peter: Sandra Morray has been in a coma for the last thirty years."

"Can someone survive that long in a coma?"

"Yes. No one has ever awakened from a coma after more than ten years, but there are a few people around like Mrs. Morray. I want you to get out to that clinic. Even if Dr. Morray is unconnected with the murders, we can do a fascinating piece on his near-death research and the fact that his wife is as good as dead but still alive."

"Won't we need his permission?"

"Are you being purposely naive or what?" Ed asked. "Of course not."

"I may be naive, but exactly how am I going to interview Sandra Morray when she doesn't have a functional brain?"

"I didn't say you are to interview her. Just go find out what you can about her. Buy a camera, take her picture. Ask to see her medical records. People love to read about people in comas. Tells you how boring the average man and woman's life is."

"I seriously doubt the people at the clinic will allow me to study her medical records."

"Tell them you're a doctor doing research on coma patients. Tell them you're family. Tell them anything, you're resourceful. Shit, you owe me. The airline called to confirm the charges for your plane ticket. What did you do, pay for sex with your own personal flight attendant?"

"I always wanted to be a member of the five-mile-high club." Peter chewed on what he'd been told. Thirty years lying in a bed. It was hard to imagine. Did people in comas dream? Did they suffer? Did they even exist? He was agnostic, which he honestly believed was the only true religion. Who knew anything really? Maybe just seeing Sandra Morray could tell him more about the afterlife than a room chock full of preachers. Maybe Julie should see the woman. He realized he was curious. He hoped it wasn't morbid curiosity.

"Are you still there?" Ed asked.

"I'll see her. But I won't take her picture."

"A picture would be nice."

"A picture might also buy the paper a lawsuit. You see, Ed, I'm not so naive. Besides, I will not invade anyone's privacy like that."

"The flash won't bother her."

"That's not the point. You forget I used to teach slow kids. Just because you're unaware of something doesn't mean it doesn't hurt you. Look at you. At the office you're oblivious to the fact that all the women snicker behind your back. But it rips me apart inside to see it happen. And I'm sure deep inside you know that you're fat."

Ed laughed. "You should be writing editorials. See what you can find out. I have several people still digging into Dr. Morray. If nothing else, he has interesting skeletons in his closet."

"How did you find out about Sandra Morray?"

"We searched for a death certificate and couldn't find one. You're not dead in this country until you have that little piece of paper."

"I don't know why they keep printing those things," Peter muttered, thinking. Did Morray know she was still alive? One would assume he did, surely, but the tale grew stranger and stranger. Maybe Dr. Morray had stashed her in the clinic and purposely forgot to pay her respirator bill. It was possible the wicked doctor assumed she was dead.

"Sometimes I think he dreams of creating a modern Frankenstein monster."

Did Sara know about Sandra? And while he was on the topic, whose painting had that been in her studio? A skeleton from a dark closet?

Peter said so long to Ed and rented himself the most luxurious car Cedar Rapids airport had to offer, a Cadillac Seville. It had a twelve-slot CD player with complimentary discs, a minibar stocked with tiny bottles of airline booze, and an Iowa road map, which he needed badly. Fortunately, after several minutes of serious study, he saw that the clinic was only an hour away. He could drive out to see Sandra, pay his respects, and be back in time to catch the last flight home. He was looking forward to calling Sara the next day and maybe—let's not fall into the bottomless pit of self-denial, Peter thought—having two hours of afternoon sex with her.

One thing about Iowa that he liked, he thought, as he got on the highway, was that it was surprisingly a whole lot cooler than Los Angeles. Indeed, from the clouds in the sky it looked as if it would rain any moment. He vaguely remembered reading something about a heavy thunderstorm the Midwest had had a few weeks back.

From the outside, the Kabriel Clinic looked purely utilitarian. A squat rectangle of red bricks, a place network executives might stuff game-show hosts in the off season. Peter was surprised to see iron bars outside the heavily curtained windows. They couldn't be there to keep patients in, he thought. The lawn was neatly trimmed; there were summer flowers, bushes with berries. He didn't even know if the place was set up to receive visitors. He'd already decided to use the family angle, even knowing I.D. would be a problem. He should have swiped Dr. Morray's wallet when he'd been at the house the other day. But he'd been too eager to get his hands on the wife. Peter didn't imagine he'd get far with the nurses.

On that point—at least at first—he was wrong. It was obvious the patients in this clinic didn't get visitors often, but when he strolled in and said in a hushed voice to the first nurse he encountered that he was there to visit his mother, she simply asked her name and went to check the records. She was back a moment later to lead him to a narrow wing with ten beds set along one wall. There was enough computer and medical equipment present to launch a hibernating voyage to Mars: EEG and EKG monitors, mechanical respirators, wired IVs leading into stainless steel implanted arm shunts. The preferred clinic incense was rubbing alcohol, a wise choice, since it largely covered the faint odor of decay. The nurse pointed to one of the beds. Peter saw the number above the patient before he saw the woman herself. An easy number to remember for hard-to-forget Sandra Morray.

111.

"Thank you, Nurse," Peter said. "Could I be alone with her for a minute?"

Certainly. The nurse excused herself and Peter moved to the bed. He had to force himself to get close to her. He had just seen the Egyptian exhibit, of course, the artifacts were fresh in his mind. It was no coincidence that the thought of a mummy should come to mind. Yet, in her own sad way, Sandra Morray appeared much farther along the path of decomposition than King Tut's cousin. Her face wasn't merely sunken and wrinkled, it had slipped through a crack in reality. Her skull seemed tense, as if it were trying to wrestle its way through the tissue layer of what remained of her facial flesh. Peter would have preferred to find a skeleton in one of the clinic closets than this monstrosity of modern medical science. A wave of revulsion swept through him. Why the fuck, he asked himself, didn't they let someone like this die? What did they keep her alive for? Possible cloning tissue? He should never have allowed Ed to talk him into this visit. Sandra didn't deserve it, no one did. He turned to leave.

A voice behind him stopped him.

"Excuse me, sir," a woman said. "Do you know this woman?"

Peter turned to find a twenty-five-year-old blond woman in a white uniform with a plain but wholesome face. She was panting slightly, perspiring; her short clipped hair, he saw, was a mess, partly because she was working hard, but mostly because it looked as if it had been cut by one of the clinic's patients. Her demeanor had an element of fear in it, of him perhaps, by his association with Sandra Morray.

"Yes," he said. "Who are you?"

"Penny Hampton. I'm a physical therapist. I work part-time here, taking care of the patients." She offered her hand. "And you?"

"My name's Peter Morray." He gestured to the bed. "This is my mother."

Penny Hampton quickly let go of his hand. She glanced toward the living corpse with undisguised anxiety. The hiss of the mechanical respirator cut the air, in and out, back and forth, plastic swords slicing to pieces the memories of the living dead. What a sound to have to hear for thirty years, Peter thought. Even if her brain were gone, her ears were still intact.

Penny wanted to tell him something but was afraid how he'd take it. Or perhaps she was simply afraid. She seemed unable to catch her breath. "What happened to her?" Penny blurted out finally.

"She drowned. Thirty years ago."

She swallowed. "You must have been young then."

The lies came easily. "Yes. I was an infant." He paused. "What's bothering you?"

"Nothing."

"You stopped me. You wanted to tell me something. Go ahead, I won't be offended. Has it something to do with my mother?"

She hesitated. "Yes. But I shouldn't talk about these things. The nurses will be upset. I could lose my job, and I need it. I need the money."

Peter's tone was reassuring. "I promise I won't tell them what you say. What is it about my mother that frightens you?"

Penny jerked back as if struck. "Why do you say that? That she frightens me?"

"It's obvious."

Penny accepted the remark reluctantly, then admitted the truth of it with a faint nod of her head. She glanced at Sandra then back at him. Her voice came out unsteady.

"It happened a few weeks ago. I was doing your mother's therapy. It was the last time I did it. I went through the usual routine: stretched her arms and legs, rocked her, massaged her all over. I was manipulating the bones and ligaments in her neck—I was almost finished—when the power suddenly failed. The lights, every one of them, went out. The dark was scary. But it shouldn't have been a problem. The clinic has backup generators to deal with emergencies. But for some reason they didn't kick in. In the space of seconds half the patients in the clinic needed mouth-to-mouth resuscitation to stay alive. Since I was closest to your mother I felt I should work on her." Penny paused and briefly closed her eyes. Clearly the memory was disturbing. "But I waited a minute before I began to breathe for her, more than a minute. I just let her lie there, dying."

"Why?"

Penny opened her eyes. "I don't know why. Something about your mother—I have never felt comfortable working on her. That's why I don't work on her now. I'm sorry, Mr. Morray, I know that must sound cold and unprofessional of me. I've felt guilty about it since." Her voice faltered. "I wonder if it's my guilt that has made it so hard for me to relax since then."

Peter's eyes narrowed. "You're having trouble relaxing?"

Penny nodded weakly. "Yes."

Peter felt as if he were in the role of a priest. She was confessing to him, hoping that her traumatic day would lose its hold over her. "And it started that day?"

"Yes."

"Do you have any other symptoms?"

She coughed. "Yes. I've become asthmatic. I never was before. I know stress can bring on asthma, though, I know that from school."

"It must have been a tremendously stressful event for you."

She shook her head. "Yeah, you can say that."

"What happened when you started to give her mouth-to-mouth?"

Penny jerked upright again. "Did I say something happened after that?"

"Did it?"

Penny spoke reluctantly. "Yes, I suppose. But I really shouldn't be talking about this. It's just that I thought you might be able to explain what she said."

"What who said?"

"Your mother."

"My mother spoke?"

"Yes."

"That's impossible. My mother has been in a coma too long. Are you sure?"

"Yes. I heard her. Right after the power came back on. Just as she exhaled the final breath I gave her." Penny was thoughtful. "It occurred to me later that when I gave her mouth-to-mouth, those were the first living breaths she'd had in her body in all this time. It made me wonder if that had something to do with what she said, that she was able to speak at all."

"What did she say?"

"Just two words. The first was clear. Her eyes popped open and her head rolled to one side. It was as if she saw me for a moment—that scared the shit out of me. Please forgive my language, I know she's your mother. Then the word came out of her mouth. She said *child*."

"Interesting. What was the second word?"

"I wasn't sure if I heard it correctly. I hate to say it without being sure."

"Just tell me what it was, please."

"*Cold*."

"Cold?"

Penny nodded. "Child, and then, cold. Cold child. Does that mean anything to you?"

"No."

"It was spooky when she said the words. You would have had to have been there."

"I suppose. Penny, may I ask you a personal question?"

"Yes. You're not going to report me, are you?"

"No. Don't think about that. I don't report people. But it's obvious to me that you're unhappy working in this place. Even given the fact that you need the money, isn't there somewhere else you can go? I mean, I'm sure many hospitals need physical therapists. Why do you stay here?"

Penny's eyes went back to Sandra Morray. Not a glance this time, more as if the vision of the living corpse pulled her. As if during their brief contact Sandra had cast a spell over Penny. Penny's own words confirmed what her body said already.

"I want to leave but I can't. I feel I have to stay close to her, to keep an eye on her." Tears suddenly sprang from Penny's eyes. She put a hand to her face and trembled. "Oh, God," she whispered.

Peter was by her side in a moment. "What is it? What's wrong?"

Penny couldn't stop crying. Couldn't take her eyes off Sandra Morray. "I even come in on my days off to see her. I never touch her. I haven't touched her since that day. But I can't do anything unless I first check to make sure she's alive." Penny's tone was desperate. "Why am I so afraid that she'll die? I want her to die. I'm sorry, but it's true. I've wanted her to die since the day I first saw her." With an effort Penny tore her gaze away from the old woman and buried her face in his chest. "But I'm afraid if she dies then I'll die, too."

He had been on the verge of leaving.

"That's OK," Peter said, trying to soothe the sobbing woman.

Now he knew he'd have to try to look at Sandra Morray's file.

TWENTY-TWO

❧

T HE TIME HAD come for Pino Carbone's angioplasty and rotational atherectomy. Dr. Lawrence Morray entered the O.R. and watched while the nurse prepared the leg area for the initial part of the procedure, the cardiac catheterization which would give them a moving picture of how the blood was flowing through Carbone's heart, or not flowing, as the case may be. Dr. Morray knew the picture would be bad and that he'd be working on the man for half the afternoon. He felt uneasy about having agreed to the procedure and had done so only because he knew Carbone was dead set against a bypass. Dead set, he thought, an ironic choice of words. Dr. Morray had an experienced heart surgeon and team available in the adjoining theater. At the first sign of trouble, he was going to have Carbone opened up. No one was going to die on him, not with Carbone's wife knitting in the waiting room.

"How are you this afternoon?" Dr. Morray asked Carbone as he moved into the O.R. The old printer gazed anxiously up at him from under his green hospital cap. Carbone would be awake throughout the procedure. Only the thigh area, where the instruments were fed into the inferior vena cava, would be anesthetized. Carbone had, however, received two grams of Valium that morning, to help relax him. It didn't look as if the medication had worked.

"I'm a little cold," Mr. Carbone said. "Is it possible to turn the heat up in here?"

Dr. Morray gestured to the scrub nurse. "No problem. We can make it like an oven if you wish. How did you sleep last night?"

"Lousy. How long will this take?"

"It depends on what the film shows. Three hours maybe."

Carbone acted depressed. "What am I supposed to do all that time?"

"Lie still with your arms by your side. Don't even move your hands unless you ask me first. Remember, you chose these procedures. If you'd done what I said, we could put you to sleep right now and you'd wake up a new man."

"Yeah. With a dozen staples holding my chest together. No thanks, Doc, I'd rather try this first."

Dr. Morray squeezed his hand. "We'll start in a minute."

Most patients were surprised that the incision through which cardiologists fed the cardiac balloon catheter was in the leg, so far from the heart. Dr. Morray had once seen a show on TV where the doctor had cut in the center of the chest, which was a curious way to go about it, besides being an impossible one, although the arm was sometimes used. But the inferior vena cava passed close to the surface of the skin in the leg. The required incision was usually an inch or less. Dr. Morray requested a scalpel, took a moment to set his mental landmarks on Carbone's body, and made the cut. Blood oozed from the wound; the sight of it never disturbed him.

Dr. Morray knew that had he gone into surgery, he would have been one of the best. His hands were dexterous, and he had the natural aggression of most great surgeons. To attack the body, to take out what was diseased, to re-form what was not right. Yet he had never seriously considered surgery because the heart, for him, was what made a human different from a rock. Even the sound of it, still, in his stethoscope, filled him with awe. Dread too, that the beat should stop, that there should be nothing but silence. In religion silence was often seen as a blessing, he knew, but for him it was the equivalent of nonexistence. He couldn't stand for it to be too quiet. Trips to the countryside, when he used to take them, would drive him insane. Sometimes, late at night, while Sara slept beside him, he would listen to his own heart through his instruments. Perhaps to reassure himself that he was in fact still a human being.

He knew his wife wondered about him sometimes.

She was not alone.

Dr. Morray deftly opened the artery with a minute incision and carefully fed the cardiac catheter into and up the large artery. Fluoroscopy provided guidance, a combination of released dye and X rays—

the result of which was projected on a black-and-white monitor above the operating table. Carbone could see what was happening as well, if he wanted to watch, which didn't seem to be the case. When Dr. Morray had the tip of his catheter at the heart, he spoke to his patient.

"I'm going to release a larger amount of dye now. It won't hurt but it may burn a bit. You will definitely feel flushed. Don't let it disturb you. It's natural."

"Since when did nature stick one of these things inside you?" Carbone grumbled.

Dr. Morray released the dye. The substance had a tendency to adhere to the plaque inside the arteries and veins. The effect was instantaneous; details of the interior of the heart leapt onto the monitor. The most dangerous place for a huge blockage was in one of the major arteries or veins, for the obvious reason that they carried the largest blood supply. Carbone's crucial right coronary artery—Dr. Morray noted with no surprise—was fully nine-tenths obstructed. If not for the recent development of the rotablator, which cut the plaque up into microscopic pieces and allowed it to float away in the bloodstream, Dr. Morray would have quit then and there. That was the main problem with balloon angioplasty; it merely squeezed the plaque against the artery walls. It did not actually remove the plaque as many heart patients erroneously believed. Also, in at least a third of the cases it scarred the artery walls and then the return of the plaque was virtually certain, but to an even greater degree. Still, on several of Carbone's smaller arteries and veins, Dr. Morray knew he would have to use the balloon technique. Although the rotablator was only the size of a wooden match, it simply could not fit in every nook and crevice. A pity, since—Dr. Morray saw—Carbone had significant blockage in every one of his major arteries and veins.

"What do you mean this won't hurt?" Carbone complained. "I feel like I have a blowtorch in my chest."

"The sensation will pass in a moment," Dr. Morray said, still studying the monitor. He was trying to decide which artery to clear first.

"How does it look, Doc?"

"Like you've been eating butter and eggs and doughnuts for breakfast every morning for the last sixty years."

"I like eggs," Carbone said.

"Most of my patients do," Dr. Morray said. He came to a decision; he would first clear the right coronary. Once he had the main supply to the heart opened, they could both breathe easier, especially Carbone.

Dr. Morray noticed that Carbone had closed his eyes.

"Are you feeling all right?" Dr. Morray asked.

"Yes." Carbone wore a faraway expression; it had come upon him suddenly. "I hear music."

"Oh?" The remark filled Dr. Morray with a curious disquiet, although he didn't know why. "What kind of music?"

Carbone sighed. "Beautiful music," he whispered.

"That's nice," Dr. Morray muttered.

Dr. Morray advanced the rotablator into the right coronary. The device removed the material narrowing the artery by rotating a diamond-crystal metallic tip at a very high speed. Dr. Morray had listed many possible side effects of the procedure to Carbone, but naturally the main one would occur if he accidentally cut the artery wall. Then Carbone would not have to worry about having a bypass; he would die instantly. Fortunately the right coronary was relatively large and Dr. Morray was one of only two dozen cardiologists in the world who could call themselves a master of the technique. While Carbone floated peacefully on the unstruck sounds of his sweet music, Dr. Morray shredded six decades of rotten nutrition into harmless mush. It was what he got paid to do.

Two hours later, using a combination of the rotablator and the balloon catheter, Dr. Morray had succeeded in opening all the main arteries and veins on the anterior side of the heart. He debated stopping there, while he was ahead, and waiting a day or two to see how Carbone felt. But he knew the small veins at the back of the heart, specifically the left innominate vein and the inferior thyroid vein, were still heavily compromised. He suspected that Carbone would still have pain. Like many people, Dr. Morray preferred to finish a job once he started it. He thought of what *he* would want—certainly not to be dragged back into the O.R. a second time—and decided to continue. If he could clear the two remaining veins, Dr. Morray thought, Carbone would be able to breathe as he hadn't been able to since he was thirty.

It was on the second of the two veins that disaster struck. Dr. Morray may have made a mistake in choosing the balloon size. Moving from the front to the back of the heart, he didn't change the catheter, thinking he'd simply not inflate the original balloon as much in the narrow posterior veins. The choice appeared smart when he freed the innominate vein without difficulty. But in the inferior thyroid there was a large chunk of plaque; here the blood labored through a space as narrow as a needle. The occlusion proved stubborn; he squeezed the plaque and still it refused to press down.

By now Dr. Morray was tired; his vision had begin to blur, as it often did at the end of a long concentrated procedure. He also had a headache. He hadn't slept well the previous night, plagued by nightmares of drowning, thoughts of Sandy. He realized his mind was not clear as he strained to make what would be his final important decision of the day. A single fact steered his thoughts. Despite the poor nature of Carbone's overall cardiovascular capacity, the man showed little calcification of his blood vessels, which would have made them less flexible. Dr. Morray decided the vein could survive a bit more pressure.

He gave the balloon another squeeze.

A judgment call.

The inferior thyroid vein burst.

The rupture showed on the monitor as the sudden spread of a dark cloud into Carbone's chest cavity. Dr. Morray did not need the anesthesiologist's anxious blood pressure readings to know that he was close to losing a patient.

"Get Dr. Stein!" Dr. Morray barked, calling for the heart surgeon.

Dr. Stein and his team swept in. Dr. Morray was relieved from duty. All he could do was stand in the corner while Carbone's chest was cut open and his breastbone sawed in two. Before Dr. Stein could get his hands on Carbone's heart, the printer suffered a coronary spasm. Dr. Stein called for the pads. Electricity jolted Carbone's body off the table. His heart started, it stopped, it started again, stayed that way for the moment. But Carbone's blood pressure continued to sink as blood poured out the back of his heart. Dr. Morray thought of Mrs. Carbone knitting in the waiting room. He would not tell her about the music her husband had heard at the start of the procedures. Nor would he mention how the remark had disturbed him. Dr. Morray, however, knew why the reference had made him uneasy. From his earlier NDE research, the investigation he had abandoned for fear he would find his dead wife and a pointed finger at the end of a black tunnel, he knew Carbone had already taken the first step onto the other side then.

Even before the inferior thyroid vein had ruptured.

"We're losing him," Dr. Stein said.

Even before the wicked doctor had killed another with his bare hands, Dr. Morray thought.

TWENTY-THREE

❋

J UST TELL ME what you see," Julie Moore said as she handed Sara Morray the first of the Rorschach Test ink blots. They were seated in the living room on the couch. Julie had her left leg folded under her, a yellow notepad and pen in her hands. Four feet away Sara stared at the picture with her beautiful dark eyes.

"A wolf's face," Sara said.

Julie made a notation and handed Sara the second card.

"A spaceship," Sara said.

Julie paused and made another note. There was red in the second card. Sara had not responded to the color. She gave Sara the third picture.

"A bow tie," Sara said.

Julie continued to scribble on her pad. Most people said a bug for the third card. Yet the initial spaceship response showed originality, which indicated a high IQ. Julie had no doubt Sara was intelligent. She handed her number four.

"An ink blot," Sara said after a moment.

A rather flat response, Julie thought. She gave her number five.

"A bat," Sara said.

Number six.

"A totem pole," Sara said.

Julie felt uneasy. The popular responses for number six were either an animal's fur or a rug. The former reply conveyed emotion — most people gave it because most people had plenty of emotion. The latter reply also related to people; only humans had rugs. Yet, even though a totem pole was not an unheard-of response, it was troubling in the context of Sara's other answers. Except for the wolf's face, Sara had not given one popular response. People who deviated too far from the norm generally didn't see the world the way others did. They usually had a problem with perceiving reality. More troubling, Sara had yet to give a response with a human in it. A classic interpretation of such a failure indicated an absence of empathy. Handing over picture number seven, Julie hoped Sara lightened up or else she was going to have to recommend that the woman check herself into a mental hospital. Sara stared at the latest ink blot without blinking.

"Rocks," she said.

"Rocks?" Julie asked, exasperated. "Anything else?"

Sara glanced up. "Should I give more than one response?"

"You can if you wish. Do you see anything else?"

Sara looked. "Just rocks."

Julie handed her number eight.

"A shield," Sara replied.

Again, Sara had not responded to the color in the picture. Number nine.

"A cow's face," Sara said.

Number ten. Julie prayed for at least one response that contained a person.

"A tower," Sara said.

Julie studied her notes and didn't like what she saw. Only one popular response out of ten indicated a pathological personality. The complete failure to see any humans in the pictures meant Sara suffered from an extraordinary feeling of social isolation. Then there was Sara's lack of response to color. The textbooks said that meant she was usually controlling, guarded. Julie glanced over at Sara's sweet smiling face and had to wonder. Honestly, Julie suspected even Cannibal Sue would have seen a person or two in the ink blots, maybe roasting on a stake, but at least not forgotten.

Yet Sara was a brilliant artist. How was it possible?

"How did I do?" Sara asked.

"Well," Julie said. "Let me ask you a question. How do you feel?"

"Fine."

"You're not upset about anything?"

"No. Why do you ask?"

"Well," Julie said. "Your responses are unusual."

"Could you be more specific?"

Yeah, you're certifiable. And the scary thing is, you don't show it, not even slightly.

"Well," Julie said for the third time. "Let's just say I've never tested anyone like you before."

Sara nodded as if that was to be expected. Her smile vanished, although she continued to stare at Julie. "I would prefer you didn't discuss my test results with anyone," she said quietly.

Julie forced a laugh. Somehow, since doing the test, Sara's gaze didn't feel quite the same. "Who would I tell?" she asked.

"Peter Jacobs," Sara said flatly.

Julie stiffened. "What does Peter have to do with you?"

Sara opened her mouth to speak. Unfortunately, she was interrupted. Her attention was drawn to the sound of car parking outside the front. A moment later Dr. Morray opened the door and walked in. Julie jumped to her feet with her notepad still in hand. The good doctor looked tired, annoyed. It was a wonder to Julie that she was glad to see him.

Govinda Sharma, sitting on a bluff overlooking Malibu Beach and a number of expensive homes, watched as Rak finally stood from his trance and began to walk down the hill toward one of the roads. It was the first activity Rak had pursued all day. As always, Govinda followed.

"Who are you?" Dr. Morray demanded.

"Darling," Sara said smoothly. "This is Julie Moore. You know her. She stopped by to have a look at your NDE research. While she was waiting for you she gave me the Rorschach Ink Blot Test. We just finished it. Julie won't tell me how I did, but since she suddenly seems a little scared of me I don't think I did very well."

Dr. Morray took a moment to digest what his wife had said. The ink blot pictures lay scattered over the couch. "Why are you testing my wife?" he asked.

"She asked me to test her," Julie said.

Dr. Morray glared at Sara. "Psychological tests are absurd. They only reveal what the tester searches for in the first place. You should not be wasting your time on them."

Sara smiled, unmoved. "Bad day at the hospital, dear?"

"No," Dr. Morray growled. "It was fine." He removed his white coat and added, "Today's not a good day, Ms. Moore."

"Excuse me, Doctor," Julie said quickly. "But would any day be good? Or do you just want to forget the whole thing? I seem to be annoying you, rather than furthering science."

Dr. Morray couldn't find a hanger in the closet and ended up tossing his coat on a chair. "Investigating NDEs does nothing to further science," he said flatly. "All it does is reinforce a state of denial about one of the main two truths in life. Those two are—we have to pay taxes, and we have to die."

Julie studied him. He was not merely angry, he was hurt. "Who died on you today, Dr. Morray?" she asked gently.

He wanted to snap at her, but only shrugged. "Perhaps psychology does have its uses, Ms. Moore. You are perceptive. One of my patients did die this afternoon. He was a fine man, and it's a pity that he won't live to see his grandchildren grow up. But in my business pity is something I cannot indulge in. Death doesn't care about it. That was one thing I was able to conclude from my years of research into near-death experiences. Now if you will excuse both of us, I would like to have a few words with my wife."

"Certainly," Julie said, leaning over to pick up her pictures. "I'll leave now."

"I wouldn't mind taking the test another time," Sara said. "We can have lunch then."

Julie caught Sara's eye and stared hard at her, trying to understand how the woman who stood before her could have responded the way she had. Psychological tests were *not* a waste of time. Sara could not have faked her responses, not unless she had inside knowledge of the Rorschach, which she obviously didn't. Julie tried to sense what was behind the woman's dark eyes, but feared her own sight was clouded because she hadn't forgotten Sara's last comment about Peter. She felt there was no logical justification—the results of the test and her jealousy over Peter notwithstanding—that she should suddenly feel that Sara Morray was her most deadly enemy. Yet there was something in Sara's eyes . . .

No, there's something missing in her eyes.

It was as if Sara stared at her from a place of nothingness.

"It doesn't work as well the second time," Julie said.

Sara smiled. Her mouth did. But her beautiful unblinking eyes—those mysterious windows of the soul—who had opened the curtains behind them? What would close them? Julie felt a chill then, deep inside.

"Perhaps you can give me another test," Sara said.

Julie tore her gaze away and stared out at the beach where Susan Darly had almost drowned. So close to Sara Morray's house. Gone to the other side, Dear Sue had, before returning to sunny California as a monster of the night. Was Jerry all right? She must hunt him down, as soon as she could, and be sure.

Hunt. Julie felt hunted right then. Standing in the center of telescopic sights.

"I have to go," Julie said. She finished collecting her things and said good-bye. Sorry I have to diagnose and run. Dr. Morray grunted and stood aside to let her pass. Sara offered to walk her out to her car. Julie assured her that it wasn't necessary. Yet Sara insisted. When they were outside and Julie was about to drive off, she asked Sara how she managed to stay so cool when her husband was upset. Sara smiled knowingly at the question, as if she had been asked it before.

"It's the way I am," she said.

Julie swallowed. "I can see that."

Julie started her car and drove away. She made it only as far as the corner before she had to pull over to collect herself. She trembled uncontrollably, and didn't know why. Her eyes burned with tears, but as the drops slid over her cheeks, she felt the coldness in them. First Cannibal Sue and then Evil-Eyed Sara. What the fuck was going on? Julie thought. What the fuck was next?

Not a good question to ask when the stars were obviously pissed.

A man who looked like Hercules tapped lightly on her car window.

"Yes?" Julie said, rolling down the window and staring up into his face and the glare of the sun. Even in solar silhouette, he was an incredible physical specimen: powerful profile, mountains of muscles, long braided hair, black eyes as piercing as iron swords. He smiled faintly—gentleness mixed with savagery, irresistible alchemy for her. It didn't matter that his ill-fitting clothes were ridiculous, or that his feet were bare. It didn't matter that she had just escaped from the jaws of someone pathological. Staring up at her new visitor, Julie found her thoughts of Sara Morray as blurred as a watercolor washed in the rain. "Can I help you?" she heard herself ask.

"Ma," he said in a soft voice.

"My name is Julie." She hesitated. "Do you speak English?"

He nodded.

"Can I help you? Are you lost?" He was obviously not from around there.

"Julie," he repeated to himself. He seemed to absorb the word, make it a part of himself. He raised his head and pointed back down the street. "You," he said. "Them."

"Are you referring to the Morrays? I have nothing to do with them." She added, "You don't want to either." When he didn't respond, she raised her hand to shade her eyes and moved her head to the side to get a better look at his face. He seemed calm and in control of himself, yet his movements were suggestive of blindness. He carried a crude wooden staff in his left hand. "Are you blind?" she asked.

He looked down at her. "Yes, Julie."

No one had ever said her name the way he did right then. It was as if he breathed life into her chest just by repeating it. She had not realized how smothered she felt while sitting with Sara. Her trembling began to subside. She felt a deep desire to assist this man, in whatever way she could. A natural desire to help the blind, she told herself.

"Do you know the Morrays?" she asked. "Sara? Dr. Morray?" If he was blind, how had he known which direction to point? she wondered. He stared at their house with her question.

"What you do?" he asked.

"What do I do?" She had to laugh. "Most of the time I run around aimlessly. I'm supposed to be a psychologist. I was just at the Morrays' house because I've been trying to see the doctor's records on near-death experiences. That's my particular field of study, and Dr. Morray is supposed to be an expert on it. At least that's what my chairperson, Professor Adams, tells me. He's the one who turned me on to Dr. Morray. But I have personal reasons for being interested in the Morrays as well. Dr. Morray's wife, Sara, is interested in my new boyfriend, Peter Jacobs. Well, Peter's not really my boyfriend but I wish he was. I wish Sara would butt out. Anyway, while I was sitting with Sara this afternoon I gave her the Rorschach Test, and I can tell you that she is one weird chick. You'd think she'd grown up on Pluto. She looks at color and sees shadows. I showed her people and she saw stones." Julie stopped herself. "Excuse me, I'm rambling."

The man nodded. Julie thought he must imagine her a fool. She hadn't just been rambling, she'd been trying to tell him in the space of twenty seconds her entire life story. She had almost succeeded. What had come over her? Yet her chaotic barrage of information seemed of interest to him. He absorbed it as he had the sound of her name—deeply and with consideration. He continued to stare in the direction of the Morrays' residence.

"Julie Ma," he whispered.

"When you say Ma, do you mean mother?"

"Yes."

She smiled. "I'm not a mother. I don't have any kids. I don't even have a husband, or boyfriend for that matter." She shook her head. "There I go again, babbling. Look, I'd like to help you if you want my help. You shouldn't be walking around here. You could get run over. Is there somewhere I can take you?" She paused. "Oh, shit!"

Dr. Morray had just left his house and climbed back in his car. He pulled out of his driveway and cruised in her direction. She ducked down; she didn't want him seeing her, didn't want him thinking she was spying on him. She'd had enough of both Morrays for this lifetime, and Professor Adams would just have to understand. Her strange new friend seemed to sense the importance of Dr. Morray's car. He turned as it passed, moving with the vehicle. Julie sat back up when Dr. Morray was out of sight. She did not believe the cardiologist had seen her.

"That was Dr. Morray who just drove by," she said.

"Yes."

"Do you know him?"

"Yes."

"Do you know his wife?"

"Yes."

Julie felt she had to ask. Even as she asked herself who the hell she was asking. A day of noteworthy personages. Cannibal Sue, Evil Eyes, and now Holy Hunk. She really had to try again to reach Lieutenant Rodrigues and tell him about these strange people. But the blind man carried with him a spiritual aura, a gravity of silence that begged for unanswerable riddles. He was like a wounded priest from a folk tale, a vanquished but not beaten victim from a forgotten legend. He was difficult not to stare at, even though he hardly looked in her direction.

"What do you think of her?" Julie asked.

Now he did stare down at her, and it was as if a cloud passed over his calm face—for a moment. A dark cloud that promised hard rain.

"She cold," he said.

Then he walked away. No good-byes. Julie watched him go, in

the direction Dr. Morray had disappeared. Not long after she noticed another fellow—he looked Indian—follow after the blind man. This second man glanced at her as he passed. He seemed on the verge of speaking to her. Julie certainly wanted to say something to him. Like, what the fuck is Hercules doing in Malibu, and why does everyone want to move here when there are earthquakes and fires and two too many weird women? But neither of them spoke, and the man's feet carried him away. To where, Julie didn't know.

"*Julie Ma.*"

Julie hoped she wasn't going to be a mother soon. When she'd slept with Peter she'd thought it had been the day before the start of her period. She'd told him he didn't need to wear a condom, as long as he was cool, which naturally he said he was. Only later had she realized her period was still a week away. Physically, she had been feeling a bit off since that night. It was probably nothing. Too much was going on in her life, she thought, to worry about tomorrow. What a strange character that blind man had been. It was almost as if with the loss of his vision, he had developed another sense. She didn't know why she felt the need to tell him everything she knew about the Morrays.

"*She cold.*"

"You got that one right, buddy," she muttered. "Whoever you are."

Julie restarted her car and drove away.

TWENTY-FOUR

❄

T HE FACADE OF Peter Jacobs playing Peter Morray came to a halt when he asked for the records of Sandra Morray and was in turn asked by head nurse Sylvia Thompson for identification. His failure to produce it, along with his expression of guilt, made her reach for the phone to dial the local police. His hand pressed over her hand did nothing to ease her mind, and in his own mind Peter could see things going from bad to worse. First Penny Hampton crying about her asthma, and next Sylvia and Penny running screaming into the night away from the illegitimate son of the coma witch. He had to think fast.

"My name really isn't Peter Morray," he told Nurse Thompson. "It's Peter Jacobs. I'm here on behalf of the Los Angeles Police Department."

The middle-aged woman with the bad case of too many brain-dead patients gave him an expression that said he'd better do better than that. Her hand remained resting on the phone near the numbers 911.

"I can prove it," Peter added.

"Please do so now," Nurse Thompson said.

Peter nodded to the phone. "May I?" he asked.

He called Lieutenant Amos Rodrigues, although he did not want to. Nurse Thompson allowed him to speak in private, excusing herself, probably to use the phone in the other room to call a more local set of law enforcement officers. Peter did not have a speech prepared.

"Amos," he said. "I'm here in Iowa checking out that lead I told you about on Dr. Morray. But I need your help. I'm in an intensive care clinic and I need to see the medical records of the original Mrs. Morray. I want you to tell the nurse here I'm working for the L.A.P.D."

Amos spoke with controlled patience. "Peter, I thought we decided that Dr. Morray was not a legitimate lead. But even if he is, you are not a cop. You can't just fly off to Middle America to investigate a man because you happen to find his wife attractive."

His remark set Peter back. But Amos was shrewd. Peter realized he should have known Amos would put his original interest in Sara together with his more criminal interest in the husband. Peter decided to play dumb; it worked so well for Matt.

"I don't believe I've ever met Mrs. Morray," Peter said.

Amos was losing patience. "You met Mrs. Sara Morray last week at the museum. We have checked into her story about being an employee of the museum and found it to be accurate. Somehow I think you checked, too. Am I right or am I right?"

"You're not giving me a lot of room to respond."

"What do you want with Sandra Morray's medical records?" Amos asked bluntly.

Sandra. Amos had been doing his homework. "I can't explain now," Peter said honestly. "There's just something funny about this whole family. If they're not murderers, then they've got really bad karma."

"Are you trying to humor me into helping you?"

"I'm trying to keep this nurse here from calling the cops. Tell her I'm your man. Whatever I find out, I'll let you know. I promise."

"Has Chuck contacted you again?"

Amos might know that he had, Peter thought. "Yes."

Amos was annoyed. "Why didn't you tell us? Why didn't you activate the trace? What did he say?"

"A crock of shit. He didn't want to set up another rendezvous. But he did say he was watching me. Which reminds me—can you have a man keep an eye on the condo while I'm gone? I'm worried about Matt, but I don't want Matt to know the guy's there."

"I'll take care of it. But you're not answering my questions."

"I'll answer them later. Amos, you know me. Trust me on this. Talk to this nurse. I'll have her call you in a minute. That way she'll know where she's calling. OK?"

Amos hesitated. "OK. Just remember in the midst of your romantic pursuit, don't push Dr. Morray into filing a lawsuit against the L.A.P.D. Understand?"

"If Sara Morray is interested in me, that's nobody's business but hers and mine."

"You could never be one of my men. There's no controlling you." Amos sighed. "Have the nurse call me in five minutes. I'll ask her politely for her cooperation."

"Thanks. How's Blank?"

"Wonderful. Last night he took me aside and told me confidentially that he thinks we have a werewolf loose in southern California. He had just done an autopsy on a preacher who had been brutally murdered in Orange County. Imagine that comment coming from the best medical examiner on the West Coast."

"Hey, maybe he's onto something. Give him my love."

Amos hardened. "You watch where you give *your* love. Dr. Morray's a big-time cardiologist. He treats many of L.A.'s power players. I'm warning you, don't fuck with him."

"Amos," Peter said pleasantly. "It's his wife I want to fuck. Catch you later."

Fifteen minutes later Peter sat in a corner of Kabriel Clinic and studied Sandra Morray's medical record. Penny Hampton had left for the day, the poor woman. She'd checked on Patient 111—as she continued to call her—before saying good-bye. That and taken a whiff of her inhaler. Peter could still hear her wheezing in his head.

The file he had in his hand on Sandra Morray started thirty years earlier. Curiously, the first entries were in Spanish, but then Peter remembered that Esther Morray had said Sandra's supposed drowning had taken place in Baja. It puzzled him that even the woman's sister-in-law should believe she had died.

He couldn't read Spanish and he didn't know what the original examining doctor had to say. Within one week of her accident, however, she had been moved to Kabriel Clinic. Two thousand comatose miles away. Odd, Peter thought. Why not place her in a clinic in nearby California? Particularly since she was Dr. Morray's wife and his practice was in California. Perhaps the first notes from an American doctor contained part of the answer. For they were written by Dr. David Samuel, Dr. Morray's schoolmate, the guy who said their falling out was ancient history. Apparently Dr. Samuel had lived in Iowa even back then. His diagnostic notes were brief. Sandra Morray had suffered severe cerebral trauma from a near-drowning episode. Her prognosis was poor. It was not expected that she'd ever regain consciousness. Her respiratory reflex was paralyzed and she had almost total renal failure. There followed more detailed instructions for her care, half of which were highly technical and Greek to Peter, although there was a mention of her need for regular physical therapy.

There was one note, however, at the bottom of page three. A scribbled afterthought, it appeared, although it struck Peter with the force of a freight train.

Sandra Morray had been pregnant when she was admitted to Kabriel Clinic.

Hastily Peter flipped through the file. On page six there was another scribbled note that hit him as hard. *Sandra Morray had carried the child to term.* Nine months after going into her coma, a cesarean had been performed. From what Peter could tell—another doctor had taken over Sandra's care by then and his handwriting was worse than Dr. Samuel's—the child had survived. A local adoption agency, Able Adoption, was mentioned.

What had become of that child?

Peter checked the time—it was almost seven. At present he had two channels to help him investigate—Ed's people and Amos. Efficient as Ed had been, Peter knew there was no way his boss would be able to demand an adoption agency release sensitive information from their files. Even Amos might have trouble getting hold of such details. Peter knew adoption agencies were notoriously skittish when it came to confidentiality. He was also hesitant to call Amos back because everything he learned from the adoption agency, Amos would also know, if not today then tomorrow. Yet he had no choice. He couldn't simply walk into the agency—even if it was still open at this time, which Peter doubted—and bluff his way into their records. Amos it would have to be.

Before Peter dialed the detective, he walked back and had another look at Sandra Morray. The woman had not changed position since their last meeting, nor was she talking in her sleep. The same was true for her brain-dead partners on each side. Still, Peter gave them a nervous glance before he reached over and pulled up Sandra's hospital gown. There was no perversity in the act, only simple curiosity. And it was true, her belly was scarred, proof of a cesarean.

Peter wondered if she had been raped *after* she had gone into her coma.

Thirty years ago. Down in Mexico.

Amos gave him hell, which Peter expected and accepted with the cool calmness of Sara Morray. Perhaps, Peter thought, during their first phone chat, he should not have mentioned his deep desire to fuck Sara. At heart, Amos was old-fashioned. Naturally the detective wanted to know why he should use the authority of his position to force Able Adoption to reveal who had adopted Sandra Morray's child. Peter didn't have a lot of reasons.

"If Dr. Morray does have a child he has chosen to ignore," he said, "the child may be able to explain why his mysterious father has taken to killing people."

"I cannot believe you just said that," Amos replied.

Peter scratched his head. "How about this. What if the *child* is the murderer?"

Amos was bored. "One more try."

"I can't think of anything else. Look, Amos, what harm can it do? You have to admit, if nothing else, it will be interesting to see where the trail leads. I told you the family's strange. Call the adoption agency. Tell them I'm stopping by. They're less than thirty miles from here."

"Are you going to write about this for your paper?"

"Of course not."

Amos lowered his voice. He did sound intrigued. "I didn't know it was medically possible for a woman in a coma to carry a child to term."

"It is. There have been two such cases recently in the papers. What shocks me is that Sandra Morray did it thirty years ago, when medicine was more primitive. Get me the name of the adoptive parents, Amos. They might still live out here. For that matter, the child might be here as well."

"If he is, he's not a child anymore."

"Or *she* isn't," Peter said.

Amos considered. "I'll see what I can find."

TWENTY-FIVE

❖

D R. LAWRENCE MORRAY was thinking about what his wife had said to him that afternoon when his secretary rang him in his private office and told him about the tall barefooted man who wanted to see him. Morray found the interruption annoying.

"Does he have an appointment?" Morray asked.

"No, Doctor. But he acts as if you expect him."

"What's his name?"

"I don't know."

"You don't know? Didn't you ask him?"

His secretary hesitated. "No. But if you could see him for a few minutes, I think it would be a good idea."

"Why? Is he old? Is he ill?"

"No. He looks perfectly healthy." She lowered her voice. "But he's blind, and I don't think he's from around here."

"Where do you think he is from?"

"Mars."

"Pardon?"

His secretary took a breath. "May I send him back, Doctor? He's not the sort of person to say no to, if you get my meaning."

He didn't have the slightest idea what she meant, but was curious. "Very well. Give me a few minutes, then have him come back."

Dr. Morray did not stir from behind his desk while he waited for his new patient. His mind continued to linger on Sara, a woman, he realized, he didn't even know.

"Why do you say that? The colors are bright."

"*But the strokes are dark. I'm an artist, I see it.*"

"*Van Gogh didn't have the happiest life.*"

"*Few artists do.*"

"*Are you talking about yourself? Are you unhappy?*"

She had never answered his question. Not after all these years. Yet this afternoon she had talked to him about herself.

After Julie Moore had left, Sara walked into the backyard and stripped off her clothes on the pool deck. It didn't surprise him; she was fond of swimming naked. He followed her into the backyard and watched as she dived into the water and swam the length of the pool, back and forth underwater, without surfacing. Sometimes he swore the woman didn't have to breathe. Finally she surfaced and walked toward him, still naked, the shower of sunlit drops on her exquisite skin a multifaceted prism of sensuality. They hadn't exchanged a single word since Ms. Moore left. She put her damp palm on his chest.

"How did your patient die?" she asked.

"In the middle of an angioplasty, I ruptured one of his major veins."

"He bled to death?"

He shrugged. "He had a heart attack. It was my fault."

"Do you feel bad?"

"Yes. But it happens. Why did you want that woman to test you?"

"To see."

"What?"

"What I would see." She turned her head toward the sea. "But there was nothing there. I could tell by the way she reacted to me afterward. I must have no imagination."

"That's not possible. You're an artist."

"Is that what I am? What else am I? Do you know?"

"Sara. What's this all about? Are you upset?"

"Have you ever seen me upset?"

"Yes."

She looked at him then. "No, you haven't. You think you have because I played the part. But I have never been upset. I never will be either." Her eyes strayed to the water. "I remember that you can't swim. Is that why you never join me?"

"You know I can't swim. What kind of questions are these?"

She tightened her hold on his shirt, smiled up at him. She had such a lovely smile, and her eyes, so large and dark, like bottomless wells in a child's fairy tale. Filled with strange magic. There was something so innocent about Sara, so pure and untouched. So still.

"Do you love me?" she asked.

"Sure."

"Have you ever loved a woman as much as you love me?"

He lied. "Never."

She nodded as if she knew it was a lie and lightly tugged on his shirt. "If I were to throw you in the pool now, Larry, would you drown?"

He had to smile. "I hope not. Why do you ask?"

"Because I remember."

"What?"

She let go of him. Her eyes strayed back to the ocean, then they closed, slowly, softly, almost reluctantly, as if perhaps they would never open again. Her voice came to him from far away and filled him with quiet dread that he did not wish to understand.

"I remember color. And the day it vanished. The day the sun set."

"Sara."

Her eyes remained shut. Her voice faltered. "Sometimes I hear a baby crying."

He had gone in the house after that. Into his place behind the garage. Then left for his office. Quickly. He had things to think about but not now.

Maybe later.

The tall, blind man with the bare feet opened the door to his office. He had not knocked.

"Come in, please," Dr. Morray said, glancing up. He stood from his chair as the man took two steps into the office. The man carried a wooden staff in his left hand and moved cautiously, although without fear. Dr. Morray was struck by his wide dark face; it could have been carved from stone, yet it shone with great power. His black eyes stared straight ahead without blinking. Dr. Morray hurried around his desk and offered the man a chair, which the man took, his long legs stretched out. "Would you like something to drink?" Dr. Morray asked.

"No."

Dr. Morray sat down once more behind his desk. "Have we met before?"

"No."

"What's your name?"

The man hesitated. He lowered his head and seemed to stare at his hands as if recalling the many deeds they had performed. Or else failed to perform, Dr. Morray thought. Yet there was no regret in his calm face. Dr. Morray didn't know why but already he liked this man, and wanted to help him in any way he could. Yet the man did not look like he needed a heart doctor.

"Rak," he said. His voice was very gentle.

"What can I do for you, Mr. Rak? Why are you here?"

Rak looked up. "Have story for you."

"A story?"

"Yes. Tell you."

Dr. Morray folded his hands on his desk. Under normal circumstances he would have laughed, or else asked the man to leave. But this man was far from normal, and this day was no better. Why had Carbone died so abruptly? How could Sara have spoken of things she knew nothing about? Dr. Morray studied Rak and wondered which of them saw the other more clearly. Despite his handicap, Rak carried with him a sense of authority and sureness Dr. Morray had never experienced before. It overpowered as did the ringing silence after the blast of a fatal bomb. Rak's presence intimidated and soothed at the same time. And Dr. Morray had seen many die and was not easily moved, by anything.

"I would like to hear your story," Dr. Morray said.

Rak told him. In broken English. In a soft voice that flowed like wine into the mouth of a man already intoxicated, already lost. As he listened, Dr. Morray thought that he was that man. That long ago he had drunk from a well and tasted a draught so cold that the chill was to remain with him for a lifetime. Rak was hypnotic without resorting to suggestion, beguiling without lying. Listening to him, Dr. Morray felt as if he were dreaming while awake, and understood that much that he believed real was only an illusion.

Yet the story was so simple.

The words clumsy to the ears. Perfect taken inside.

Dr. Morray felt as if Rak spoke in his mind.

"When I was young I swam in a lake near my home with other boys and girls. The days were hot and the water cold, and we would play for hours until the sun vanished. We never wanted to leave, even when the adults came to say it was time to come inside. But they could only tell

us, they could not force us to listen, for they would not swim in the lake. It was too cold, they thought, too deep. That lake exists to this day, it has not changed. But the boys and girls have changed. They are all dead, all but one. I remember him well. Tall rushes grew near the water, and this boy would hollow out the shafts and use them to breathe through as he dived deep into the lake. He would keep one end above the water and the other end in his mouth and inhale deeply while he peered into places no one had ever seen. That was his special skill, his secret knowledge. Others tried to imitate him but were never successful. They either almost drowned or else grew too fearful. As boys and girls do, they grew jealous of this young man. One day, while he held on to his longest pole and probed the lake's deepest floor, they yanked his pole away. They stole his air. They believed, of course, that he would hurry to the surface gasping for breath. But he never did and they never saw him again. They assumed he died. But it was they who died, in their time. He never did, even though he never took another breath. But what they did to him, it destroyed him in a sense. Never again was he to be part of the world. Always, for the rest of time, was he to wander in places far from humanity."

Rak paused. "Understand?"

Dr. Morray blinked and sat up. "Pardon? Yes, that was a nice story. Thank you for sharing it with me. Did I ask if you wanted something to drink?"

Rak stood. "You asked. I came. I go now."

"Really? Well, take care of yourself." Dr. Morray showed him the door. Then he returned to his desk and stared out the window at the cars and the buildings and the sun. He decided not to return home until it was dark. Until Sara was back. She had said something about being out late. Some business to take care of. He had business as well that needed finishing. A simple matter.

Ten minutes after Rak left, Dr. Morray had almost forgotten the story.

TWENTY-SIX

❁

T HE COLD ONE met with Its bastards at the end of a filthy alley
in Santa Monica. There were half a dozen of them, the rare
six that had survived the long, slow exhalation that never
ended and become the savage creatures that they were. One sat on a
smelly green Dumpster, two on the ground atop broken glass. Another
pulled bricks from the graffiti-covered wall of a nearby building. The
fifth paced back and forth like a mindless zombie. Only Ralph—who
sometimes was called Chuck—Its first, stood close to It, listening intently. Only Ralph appeared worried as the Cold One explained that
it was now time to run free. To kill and kill as long as possible.

"But we'll be stopped," he said. "We'll be killed."

The Cold One shrugged. "It happens, to them as well as to you."
It reached out to touch him. "Better death than me. Better to listen
than question."

Ralph cowered. "Where do we go? When?"

"A mall," the Cold One said. "A place filled with people. A place
you will find today."

The Cold One completed Its instructions and then bade the bastards to disperse quickly. It would not see them again and it didn't
matter. It needed them no longer. Very soon Its alternative plan
would ripen. All was well.

The Cold One had a car nearby but It continued to Its next destination on foot. The sun remained high in the sky, the hard stars behind the soft blue shone down upon It like a million red needles
pointed at a wax statue that refused to melt. Now there were other

shapes in the air as well. Phantoms of shadow that moved and changed with the wind. Flashes of light that shone from the corners. The Cold One did not know what these things were, only that humans didn't see them. But since these images, when they had appeared in the past, had not affected the Cold One, It paid them no heed now. It had no interest in ghosts any more than It had any interest left in the Antichrist. It had studied the preacher's books and found them poorly written and filled with illogic. It had read about the discovery of the preacher's body in the newspaper, the horror his physical desecration had brought to the people in his neighborhood. But because the article made no mention of It, the Cold One had not kept the paper.

The Cold One made Its way toward Julie Moore's apartment.

Julie, It realized, was a problem for several reasons. She was a sexual partner of Peter Jacobs—this fact was obvious—and it was possible she could draw his attention away from It in the next few crucial days, which was not permissible. Also, Julie suspected the Cold One of possessing unnatural personal qualities. It was possible Julie would share this information with Peter, or even with the authorities. Such acts might compromise the Cold One's designs. Better that Julie Moore die, It thought, and the sooner the better. Before Peter returned to town. The Cold One would take care of the death Itself. Not that It looked forward to or feared the act of Julie's murder any more than it anticipated or was anxious about the sun setting.

Yet once long ago, so it seemed, the sunset had brought It grief.

But that time was the property of the Voice. And the Voice had stopped.

After thirty years. The Cold One understood that the thoughts would not return.

They had set with the sun. In the deep waters south of the border.

At the door to Julie Moore's apartment the Cold One found two men. One was well muscled and tan with a bandage around his left wrist. The other was tall and thin with poorly fitting thick glasses. Apparently they had just tried the door and received no response. Yet the muscled one had a key in his hand. They studied the Cold One with uneasy interest. It smiled for their benefit.

"Are you here to see Julie?" It asked.

"Are you a friend of hers?" the one with the bandage asked.

There was something in the man's voice that indicated he was angry with Julie. The Cold One decided to adopt a similar attitude.

"I know her," It said. "I don't know if I would call us friends. What are your names?"

"I'm Stan Frasier," the one with the bandaged wrist said. "This is my friend and personal attorney, Dell Williams."

Dell offered his hand. Most humans would have described him as a nerd. "It's nice to meet you—?" he said. He wanted It to fill in the blank.

"Leslie," It said. "The pleasure is mine." It shook Stan's hand as well, then added, "I guess we're all here to see Julie, but where is she?"

"She better show up soon," Stan said grimly. "We've got some business to settle with her." He held up his wrist. "Can you believe the last time I was here she did this to me with a razor blade? She severed my median nerve. Half the inside of my left palm has lost *significant* feeling."

"You poor dear," the Cold One said, putting Its fingers to Its mouth. "And I thought *I* had a score to settle with her."

"Have you also been taken advantage of by this woman?" Dell asked seriously.

The Cold One looked disgusted. "Yes. But I'd rather not go into the details. I get so angry. Let's just say that Julie owes me big time."

Dell and Stan exchanged knowing looks. Dell spoke sympathetically. "That's what we're here for this evening. To try to work something out with her for what she's done to Stan. But from what I hear, it won't be easy."

"That key you have," the Cold One said to Stan. "Is it to her door?"

Stan hesitated. "Yes. She gave it to me months ago. She said I could stop by when I wished."

The men had been planning to "stop by" without invitation, the Cold One realized, and maybe go through her things before It had appeared. It held out Its hand for the key.

"I don't know about you guys," It said, "but I'm not going to wait out here for her. I'm going inside and relax in her favorite chair. Let me see the key."

Stan gave the key to the Cold One. Soon the three of them were in Julie's tiny studio apartment, drinking Julie's beer, laughing, and, of course, exchanging reminiscences of Ms. Julie Moore. The Cold One had a change of heart about sharing the details and made up a story about how Julie had borrowed her car and then banged it up and left it in front of her house without so much as an apologetic note attached. Now Julie, It said, was acting as if someone else had damaged the car after she returned it. It wasn't her fault and she wasn't going to pay a cent to have it repaired.

"Can you believe that bitch?" the Cold One asked.

Dell shook his head. "I think if all these matters were brought before a judge at the same time, we could have her wages garnisheed for the next ten years to cover damages."

"Yeah, that's what we have to do," Stan said. "I know she doesn't have much money now. But, shit, in a few months she'll have her Ph.D. Then she'll be making bucks big time." Stan became emotional. He held up his left hand and stared at it and suddenly there were tears in his eyes. "She ain't going to walk away and live on easy street and leave me with a crippled hand. No way."

Dell patted Stan on the back. "Take it easy, bud. You have the law on your side. She'll pay, don't worry."

Stan sighed and shook his head. "I just don't understand how someone can be so bitter about a relationship that she needs to lash out violently."

"It makes me sick what she did to you," the Cold One said in a strong voice. Then It sat up suddenly and set down Its beer as if It had just gotten a great idea. "Hey, do you two boys like to dance? I do, I love it. While we're waiting why don't we put on some music and we can dance. Just because Julie's a bitch doesn't mean we can't enjoy her home, does it?"

They were interested, naturally; the Cold One had sensed their sexual attraction to It from the moment they'd met. The day was getting on. The Cold One had decided It didn't have time to wait for Julie. It would *change* the men and leave them to deal with her. The music was important; it would drown out any painful noise.

Stan found a boom box in the closet; he knew where to look. Julie had tapes, stuffed without their covers into an old shoe box. The Cold One requested something loud—rock 'n' roll, It said. Stan slipped in a Stones cassette, "Love Is a Bitch," and turned up the volume. Dell offered his hand first, such a gracious young man. The Cold One swept him onto the middle of the floor and showed him a few nasty moves that had them both laughing.

The Cold One danced with Dell for several minutes before It suddenly began to kiss him. The intimate gesture performed in front of a wide-eyed friend with music blaring did much to stimulate the budding attorney. Stan hooted from the corner as It slipped Its tongue into the man's mouth. For his part, Dell acted as if he had died and gone to heaven; his penis grew erect and poked into the Cold One's belt.

"Hmm," Dell mumbled. As he started to pull back to catch his breath so that he could kiss It even harder, the Cold One reached up and grabbed the sides of his head and pressed Its mouth to his so firmly that not even a hiss of air could escape between them. Then the Cold One allowed the black magic to flow into Its breath, something It did only at times such as these. It allowed the breath that came from *below* Its lungs to enter into the man. The breath that was not composed of air, of oxygen and nitrogen and other gases that modern scientists could analyze and debate. This was the breath that was from the beginning, the moment of conception, the spark of life that had appeared out of nothing in the lifeless void. A spark that shed no light. The Cold One exhaled deeply into the man and he began to moan in pain, a pain so alien and horrible, the Cold One knew, that many human minds shattered at the first brush with it.

"Oh, baby," Stan said, happy for his friend.

The Cold One let the breath go in, then sucked it back out. Dell reached up with his hands to push It away, but It was too strong for him, and besides, the life was draining out of him, like the air out of a punctured ball. The Cold One swallowed what It had taken from him then pumped in another wave of air, a cloud of dry ice. The man shook in Its hands, his erection failed, and his bladder let loose. Urine poured onto the wooden floor through the hems of his pant legs. A sign, the Cold One knew, that he would not survive the change. It released Its grip on his skull and his head sagged onto Its shoulder, his bloodshot eyes open, still seeing, still feeling wave upon wave of incomprehensible agony. A gutted wail crawled from his gaping mouth, the prelude of a death rattle. It would not bother poking him in the heart, as It had the other failed bastards, to make him look as if he had died from some kind of normal cause. It released him and he collapsed in the puddle of his own piss. It turned to Stan, who had stopped smiling, who, in fact, looked very worried. It took a step over the contorted body toward him and held out Its hand.

"Your turn," the Cold One said.

TWENTY-SEVEN

❀

A N HOUR PASSED before Lieutenant Amos Rodrigues got back to Peter Jacobs with information on Sandra Morray's child. By then it was night in Iowa and Peter had abandoned any hope of flying home that evening. Amos had not been able to open the doors of the adoption agency for Peter—no one *touched* their files, Amos said—but he had done the next best thing, which was to obtain most of the information Peter needed. Peter took notes as he talked to the detective, numbering the salient points.

1. Sandra Morray's child had been adopted by a Mr. and Mrs. Randolph thirty years ago. The couple had lived in Iowa until thirteen years ago, when they died.
2. Their son—Clyde Randolph, who was also adopted—was currently a patient in a Denver mental hospital.
3. Mr. Randolph had a sister, Catherine Garoot. She was alive and living in Iowa City.
4. The adopted child's whereabouts were unknown. But her name was Ruth Randolph.

"We should be able to find her," Amos said. "But you may want to ask Randolph's sister about her. I assume you'll be paying Catherine Garoot a visit before you fly back?"

"Yes," Peter said. "Tonight, if I can. Do you have a phone number and address?"

"An address, no phone number. But the party's got to stop. If you do see her, you cannot pass yourself off as working for the L.A.P.D."

"I can't play cop or reporter? I'm losing all sense of identity. Seriously, Amos, I appreciate the information. Do you know how Mr. and Mrs. Randolph died?"

"No. Only that they died within days of each other. The husband four days after the wife."

"Odd," Peter remarked.

Peter took down Catherine Garoot's address and rang off. Before leaving Kabriel Clinic, he checked once more on Sandra Morray. Staring down at her, what was left of her, he was touched with sorrow. Yet now, like Penny Hampton, he did not pray for Sandra's death; quite the opposite, he hoped that one day soon she would awaken and see the world again and say a few words that would explain what happened to her the night she'd sunk into her long sleep. He wished he had a flower to leave her, a card that explained how sorry he felt that her life had been snatched from her. He felt guilt as he said good-bye, an inexplicable feeling of responsibility. Perhaps it was the reason he leaned over and kissed her forehead before leaving.

Perhaps not.

Knocking on Catherine Garoot's front door did not intimidate Peter. In the course of one day he had entered the mind set of an investigative reporter. He was hot on the trail of a story. Nothing was going to keep him from the truth. Nothing was going to stop him from winning the girl. He thought Mrs. Garoot would be elderly, as easy to handle as Esther Morray. The woman who came to the door appeared to be in her midseventies, but there the comparison to Esther ended. Catherine Garoot stood firm and erect. Her hair was dyed, no doubt, an attractive shade of red. Most significant, her dark-blue eyes were alert, taking him in as rapidly as he did her. Mrs. Garoot was old but not feeble.

"What can I do for you, young man?" she asked.

He had a whole line prepared—a big reporter from the *Times* tracking a murderous doctor. The words that came out of his mouth caught even him by surprise.

"I just came from Sandra Morray's bedside," he said. "What the hell happened?"

"Who is Sandra Morray?"

"Ruth Randolph's mother."

His remark made her face fall, but she let him in. A few minutes later they were seated in her small but tidy living room, drinking coffee and eating chocolate-chip cookies. He told her his story, beginning with Chuck's first call but leaving out the part about his wanting to make love to Sara Morray. He felt compelled to tell her the truth, had instinctively felt that unless he leveled with her he would get nothing from her. She sensed his sincerity, perhaps even the fact that he was leaving out a big part of the tale. When he was done, she leaned forward. His story had held her enthralled.

"I'm confused by Dr. Morray's connection to these murders," she said. "It seems you feel he is guilty by way of association."

"I'm far from having decided he's guilty. I regret if I gave you that impression. Your choice of words sums up my feeling. There is an *association* between him and what is happening. What his exact role is, I don't know. That's why I'm here. I'm trying to find out as much about him as possible."

"But I've never met the man."

"Yes. But you knew his daughter. By law, in fact, you are related to both him and his daughter." Peter set aside his cup of coffee. "I have been honest with you, Mrs. Garoot. Please tell me what you can about your brother and his family."

She fidgeted, something she had not done since he'd entered and something he suspected she seldom did. Mrs. Garoot had a calm inner strength. Yet the topic of her brother and his family disturbed her deeply. She glanced at a grandfather clock in the corner; time had been compressed with his question, made hard. She busied her hands pleating her long gray skirt.

"Where to begin?" she said. "Philip, my brother, was a fine man. He was a building contractor and specialized in custom homes for the well-to-do. He wasn't rich but he and his wife, Nancy, did well. Their marriage was sound. I'd call it stable, the two of them were more compatible than wildly in love. Personally I think those are the best marriages. They had no children, however. Nancy couldn't have any. They decided to adopt, with my encouragement I might add. That was thirty-two years ago. I know when it was because Clyde was thirty-one last month—he was their first child. They went through Able Adoption, and were given Clyde after a year of waiting. He was such a joy to them. I sat for him many times. He did cry half the night, as many infants do, but he laughed so much during the day that Philip and Nancy never regretted for a moment having him. After a year they put in a request for another child. This time, after another year of waiting, they got Ruth. She couldn't have been five days old when they brought her home." Mrs. Garoot paused and bit her lower lip. "I remember that day well. How I felt when I first saw her."

When Mrs. Garoot didn't continue, Peter asked gently. "How was that?"

Mrs. Garoot looked up. "You don't know me, Mr. Jacobs. I'm not a superstitious woman. Astrology, second sight, healings—all those things, I never believed in them. I suppose I still don't. But the instant I saw Ruth, I felt something I never forgot. I feel it even now as I think of her."

"What was it?"

"Dread."

"You felt dread when you saw a five-day-old child?"

"Yes."

"Why? Was she deformed? Did the comatose condition of her mother affect her development?"

"Not at all. Ruth was the most beautiful little infant I ever saw. Five days old and she had a head of wonderful black hair. Her eyes in particular were amazing—so wide and dark. You could see yourself smile in them." Mrs. Garoot paused and shook her head. "But there was something about her I didn't like. I didn't know what it was. She behaved like any other infant, although she was somewhat quiet. I didn't say anything about it, of course, and at first I seemed to be alone in my feelings. Philip and Nancy worshipped her. Even Clyde loved to stare at his little sister asleep in her crib. It was as if the boy worshipped her. And in time my own feelings of dislike for her went away. But not totally. It was seldom that I volunteered to baby-sit Ruth. Clyde, yes, but never the little girl alone."

"Please," Peter interrupted. "You have to be more specific. What was it about her that disturbed you?"

"She stared a lot."

"Lots of children do that."

"Not like Ruth. She stared at me as if I were an alien creature she was studying. But when you stared back at her, you saw—I don't know."

"You can say it."

"I can't, Mr. Jacobs. After all these years, I've been unable to explain to myself why Ruth worried me so. But besides her penchant for staring, I can add one thing you might find of interest, even if you don't believe it. It was hard to breathe around Ruth."

Penny, Peter thought. Mother and daughter. He hadn't told Mrs. Garoot about Penny either. "Could you elaborate?" he said.

"I felt as if I were smothering when I held that child to my chest. I got so I never did. I would give her a quick peck and take a step back. I wondered if I was allergic to her or something."

"Did your brother feel that way? Your sister-in-law?"

"No, but Clyde did, after a time. Let me continue my story. As Ruth grew, so did her beauty. Thirteen years old and she could walk in a room and turn the head of every adult male, and I don't mean that in a crude way. She would turn the women's heads as well, she was that darling. She was also a great talent."

It was Peter's turn to sit up. "At what?"

"She was an artist."

Peter coughed and reached for his cup of coffee. "Did she paint?" he asked.

"Yes. Wonderful paintings." She paused. "Are you all right, Mr. Jacobs?"

"Yes. Please continue."

Mrs. Garoot studied him, frowning, then went on. "Ruth had beauty and talent. But by the time she entered high school, it was apparent that something was wrong. She had no friends, not a single one. And it was not as if Ruth had an unpleasant manner. She was as sweet as any parent could wish. It was her kind disposition as much as anything else that filled me with guilt that even after all these years I could not love her as I did Clyde." Mrs. Garoot stopped again. "I think it was when Ruth reached high school that Clyde first began to have problems."

"What kind of problems?" Peter asked.

"As I mentioned, he, too, had trouble breathing around her. But it went much deeper for him, the older he got. By the time he was a senior in high school and Ruth was a sophomore, he had developed into a serious asthmatic. But his physical problems were only part of it. Understand, Mr. Jacobs, it's difficult for me to talk about my nephew this way. I loved that boy as much as I loved either of my own boys. But to put it bluntly, Clyde began to lose it. His thoughts turned dark. He became incredibly paranoid, fearful. He had a recurring nightmare where a black witch slipped into his bedroom while he slept and stuck long silver needles into his chest. His doctor passed it off as stress, related to his asthma, which seemed to get worse every week. Clyde took Quibron, Tedral—I used to know all the drugs. He swallowed pills by the handful and still couldn't draw in a deep breath, or let one out. Asthmatics have more trouble exhaling than inhaling. Did you know that?"

"No. Did Clyde blame his sister for his problems?"

"Not directly. How could he? Ruth was always nice to him. But by the time he was a senior, Clyde avoided her as well as he could while living in the same house. Often he'd ask if he could stay with me for the night, and I'd let him. His breathing and nightmares would be better. I remember one night we were sitting alone in this very room and the subject of Ruth came up. Right out of the blue he asked me, 'Who do you think her parents were?' He knew they were adopted. Ruth did as well. I told him I didn't know. Then he said, 'Do you think they were like mom and dad?' It was an odd question to ask and I brushed it off. But later I was to wonder if he was trying to tell me how much she disturbed him.

"Things went from bad to worse for that boy. Come his graduation day and he was in a hospital in Des Moines getting tests. Mental as well as physical tests. He didn't do well on them and the doctors recommended he go to another clinic in Chicago and stay for a couple of weeks. His paranoia was changing into schizophrenia. A psychiatrist would tell you that's not typical—the two conditions are fundamentally different. But by this time Clyde was seeing things and hearing voices. One day I'd talk to him and he'd seem fine. The next day he'd tell me about the demons hidden behind the sky. How the demons sometimes found a way to enter the world. How they looked just like everyone else, but weren't—not at all. He would whisper in my ear in a frightened voice, 'They're cold, Aunty. Cold as space. They're all around us.' "

"Did he ever say Ruth was one of these demons?"

"No. But when the chance came to go to the clinic, he wanted to go. An eighteen-year-old boy and he wanted to be put in a hospital so he could be away from her."

"Did he say that? That he wanted to get away from her?"

"No. But I knew it. I knew him. Please believe me, Mr. Jacobs, she scared him."

"What happened to Clyde?"

Mrs. Garoot looked distraught. "He never got better. He got only worse. He's hospitalized to this day. He can't breathe without a respirator. He still dreams of the black witch and her silver needles." Her eyes went far away. "He still talks about the demons."

"Do you talk to him?"

She shrugged helplessly. "I try, but he can't carry on a conversation. His grip on reality is all but gone."

"Does he ever mention Ruth?"

"No. But . . ." Her voice trailed off.

"What?"

"If he sees a woman with dark hair, he screams. That's what his doctors tell me."

"I see." Peter stirred his coffee—the sugar had melted ages ago. "So Clyde left at the end of his senior year. How did your brother and his wife take it?"

"As any parents would—badly. They blamed themselves. They couldn't understand why Clyde was so disturbed when Ruth was so normal. At least that's what they told me, but they said it as if they were trying to convince themselves. Because come Ruth's senior year, she still had no friends: no boys asking her out, no girls calling to gossip. Philip and Nancy would tell me it was because Ruth was so shy, so serious about her art. But I didn't believe it. The kids stayed away from Ruth for the same reason I stayed away from her. She was weird."

"Because she stared a lot?"

"Mr. Jacobs, I understand your wanting to defend this child. God knows I would do the same in your position. But you didn't know her. You didn't sit in the same room with her and feel as if you were sitting beside someone who didn't exist. That's maybe the best way to define Ruth. She was like an empty shell that something else lived through. That girl would smile at me and give me a big kiss and there wasn't a shred of warmth behind either gesture."

"I only ask because I'm trying to understand. Not because I disbelieve you."

"You may disbelieve what I have to say next. Come the middle of her senior year, Ruth started to talk about how she had to go to the West Coast—that it was time, she said. She kept this up day after day even though her mother and father told her she wasn't going anywhere until she finished high school. Even then I don't think they were going to let her run off to another state, not after losing Clyde the way they did. But for the first time in her life, Ruth was insistent. She said she was going. Her mother told me she caught her twice, packed and heading for the bus station." Mrs. Garoot hesitated. "The second time Nancy told me was the day before she died."

"How did she die?"

Mrs. Garoot gave another weary shrug. "The doctor said it was a heart attack."

"But you think differently?"

"If I have doubts about the diagnosis it was because of what my brother said. It wasn't because I disliked Ruth. But before I tell you what I have to say next, you have to understand that Philip loved his daughter. He didn't see anything wrong with her even when the entire school treated her as if she were a leper."

"What happened, Mrs. Garoot?"

She stared him straight in the eye. "My brother told me that the day he came home and found his wife dead on the floor, he also found Ruth kneeling beside her, kissing her. But not kissing her good-bye as a daughter would. Philip said Ruth had her mouth pressed against his wife's mouth the way a girl would over a lover's mouth."

"Maybe he misunderstood the act. Her mother had just died. Maybe Ruth was so distraught she didn't know what she was doing."

"My brother said Ruth wasn't the least bit upset that her mother was dead."

"Ruth could have been upset to the point of being in shock."

Mrs. Garoot shook her head. "My brother didn't think so. In fact, the day before Nancy's funeral he told me that he thought it was Ruth that had brought on his wife's heart attack."

"How? By kissing her?"

"He didn't say how. But he was bitter toward Ruth. He wouldn't allow her to attend the funeral. And then the next day, the day after that—it happened." Mrs. Garoot stopped. There were tears in her eyes. Peter gave her a chance to collect herself. He remembered what Amos had told him about the brief gap between the deaths of Mr. and Mrs. Randolph. Finally Mrs. Garoot added, "Philip died."

Gently. "How?"

She wiped at her face. "He killed himself."

Peter was stunned. "Why?"

Her voice rose. "I don't know why. All I know is he was alone with that damn girl when he took a shotgun and put it in his mouth and pulled the trigger. The police, those fools, say it was because he was upset over the loss of Nancy. That's what they wrote in their report. They hardly questioned Ruth, and of course she told them nothing."

"Did you question her?"

"No."

"Why not? You said she was there when it happened."

Mrs. Garoot wiped at her face again; this time a bitter swipe. "Because, Mr. Jacobs, I wouldn't have believed whatever Ruth had to tell me. The girl didn't wait for my brother's funeral. She boarded a bus for Los Angeles the day after Philip died. That was the last I saw of her."

"Do you have any idea where she is today?"

"No. All I know is the name of the family she stayed with while she was in Los Angeles and going to school. I know because she wrote me from their house. I never wrote back. I wouldn't go so far as to say this family adopted Ruth, but they took her in and helped her out. Remember Ruth was barely seventeen when her mother and father died. I don't know any of the details of how she met these people, whether she did it on her own or if the authorities put her in contact with them." Mrs. Garoot's voice turned grim. "But she adopted their name—Smith. She even signed her letter with the nickname Mrs. Smith gave her—Leslie. Yes, that's how it was on the outside of her letter. I didn't even know who it was from until I opened it." Mrs. Garoot added in a whisper, "Leslie Smith. Our little Ruth."

"You said Ruth knew she was adopted. Did any of you know who her real mother was?"

"No. Adoption agencies seldom tell you that. In those days I don't think they ever did. It's usually better not to know." Mrs. Garoot was reflective. "But it makes sense, doesn't it?"

"What makes sense?"

"Who Ruth came out of."

Peter shifted uncomfortably in his seat. "I'm not sure I follow you."

"To all extents and purposes, Mrs. Morray was dead when she gave birth to Ruth. From what you said, she couldn't breathe on her own." Mrs. Garoot nodded. "No wonder Clyde and I couldn't breathe around that girl. I wonder if it would have helped him to know that. I wish I could tell him now."

"Excuse me, Mrs. Garoot, but what would you tell him?"

She lowered her head and shivered. "Nothing."

"What did Ruth say in her letter to you? Why did she write?"

"She said she was where she belonged. Little else."

"Did she sound happy? Excited?"

"Ruth never sounded one way or the other. She wasn't what you would call emotional. I sometimes wondered if she had any emotions."

Peter felt as if he had exhausted the subject, as well as Mrs. Garoot. He wondered at the motive of his questions, the direction he was moving. He kept coming back to the fact that the more he learned about the family, the more he was drawn in. *They* fascinated him now, even though when he had left home it had been Sara alone who'd gripped his attention. He wondered what Sara was doing right now, if she was thinking about him.

It was curious how all three of these women had been—were—great artists.

"Ruth was the most beautiful little infant I ever saw. Five days old and she had a head of wonderful black hair. Her eyes in particular were amazing—so wide and dark. You could see yourself smile in them."

Peter was at the door and saying good-bye when he asked the question. He felt compelled to, even though he didn't want to. Didn't even know why the possibility of a yes filled him with dread. Of course, he never had trouble breathing around Sara, even when she'd stolen his breath with her kiss.

"Do you happen to have a picture of Ruth? One from high school perhaps?"

Mrs. Garoot's eyes widened. "Yes. I have her yearbook from her senior year. It came to me after she left. They took the pictures for it in February. She left in April." She hesitated. "Do you want to see her?"

No. I want to leave. I want to get out of this house and fly back to Los Angeles and screw Sara's brains out and pretend that people all over the city are not dying by being ripped to pieces by something inhuman. That is really what I want, besides Sandra Morray to return to life. I want that almost as much as I want Sara. But I don't care about Sandra's daughter, I don't want to see her daughter.

"Yes," Peter said. "Please."

Mrs. Garoot went for the yearbook. He remained by the door, his hand on the knob. He could get away quick, he thought, if the old lady really turned out to be the black witch with the silver needles. He had a sick feeling she was about to bring him something sharp and painful. A tiny detail that once inserted into his brain would make everything he had learned so far explode in his face. Mrs. Garoot was gone a long five minutes. That long without oxygen, he knew, and the brain died. He believed he held his breath the whole time she searched for Ruth Randolph's picture. He had always been able to hold it longer than most people.

Finally she returned and handed him the annual.

She suggested he turn to the R's. He knew that.

He knew a lot more than he was willing to admit.

Even when he saw the girl's picture. Seventeen years old. Thirteen shy of thirty. Beautiful, though, for any age. In any reasonable dimension. There was no reason to think then that Dr. David Samuel would talk to him now, even though in Peter's mind that conversation had just become an imperative. There was no reason for him to cry. So Sandra Morray had been in a coma for thirty years. So Clyde Randolph had been in a mental hospital for fifteen years. So Mr. and Mrs. Randolph had both been in the ground for thirteen years. Time was different in different states of consciousness, he thought, and time was fucked when you were fucked. Peter felt so screwed over when he saw Ruth Randolph's picture that he almost laughed through his tears. Such wide dark eyes staring up at him from the page. He probably could have seen his smile in them had he looked closer. But he didn't need to look to know Ruth Randolph resembled someone he knew.

"Sara," he whispered.

"That was Ruth's middle name," Mrs. Garoot said.

Peter closed his eyes and nodded. The implications were nightmarish.

Sara Morray was Dr. Lawrence Morray's daughter.

She had married her father.

TWENTY-EIGHT

❖

L IEUTENANT AMOS RODRIGUES and Medical Examiner Blank were enjoying a quiet dinner at an Indian restaurant close to Westwood Village when the call came in about the shootout at the Santa Monica Mall. Peter had insisted Amos visit the restaurant, saying Indian food was better than sushi. Amos had never tasted the food before and had difficulty ordering. He was afraid to leave the task to Blank, who had once taken him to a Turkish restaurant and tricked him into eating snails. The owner of the Indian restaurant, a gentleman named Mahesh, had suggested Amos try the tandoori chicken, which was turning out to be a good choice indeed. Amos had just offered some to Blank when his cellular phone beeped inside his coat pocket. Amos never went anywhere without the phone.

"It's probably Chuck," Blank said. "Since your friend refuses to return his calls."

"Peter never said Chuck left his number." Amos took out his phone and pressed the Respond switch. "Rodrigues," he said.

"Sammy here. There's a major shootout going on at the Santa Monica Mall. Sounds like our mystery maniacs might have come out of the closet."

Amos was already on his feet. "How so?"

"My details are sketchy, but whoever they are, they've already ripped at least three people to pieces."

"They?"

"It sounds like there are a few of them. The SWAT team's on its way. I'll be there in fifteen minutes."

"We'll be there in ten. Rodrigues out." Amos clicked off the phone. Blank was still eating. "Chuck and Company might be at the Santa Monica Mall."

Blank reached for his napkin. "Are there bodies?"

"Yes."

"I'm coming."

The mall parking lot was a riot of confusion. The red and blue lights of black and white units spun wildly. People were running and crying. Police strained to secure the site. Amos jumped out with Blank and tried to find out who was in charge. He spoke to the young officer who had met him at the Crosser murder and learned that he, Amos, was probably in charge. By chance the young officer had been eating at the mall when the panic started. Amos figured he'd know more than anybody.

"Give me the condensed version," Amos said.

The officer was pale. "I was eating at the Subway when I heard screaming. I ran up to the second level and saw six crazies attacking whoever happened to be around. Not hitting them or anything, but actually ripping their limbs off. I never saw anything like it. There was blood everywhere . . . and these people, no, these *things*—no one should be strong enough to do that to another person. No one should be." The officer wiped the sweat from his forehead—he was shaking badly. "I tell you, Lieutenant, they're like some kind of monsters."

"I knew it," Blank said with satisfaction.

"What happened next?" Amos asked, remembering that that kid, Jerry Washington, had said his girlfriend was stronger than she had any right to be.

"A man came running from a sporting goods store. With a shotgun and a pistol. He started blasting away and killed a few civilians in the process. Two of these animals went after him. He shot one of them four times before he went down. The other one got him . . ." The officer sobbed. "Tore his throat out."

"What were you doing all this time?" Amos asked.

"Watching," the officer croaked.

Amos put his hand on the man's shoulder. "I understand, son. Don't be ashamed. How many of these crazies are alive and where are they now?"

The officer straightened. "I don't know how many, but they're in the sporting goods store. They've got hostages."

"Is the SWAT team here?"

"No."

Amos and Blank went inside. The mall had been cleared, except for police. The sporting goods store was at the end of the south wing. Amos and Blank joined a group of six officers huddled beside a shoe store, a hundred feet from the murderers. The officers were jumpy, Amos saw, and he couldn't blame them. The end of the wing was littered with blood and bodies. It reminded Amos of El Salvador, the death squads, the insane nights. Not all of the bodies were still. The moans echoed through the deserted halls. Amos again asked about the SWAT team. No one knew when they would arrive. But they thought there were only two of the villains left alive: a male and a female.

"Have they made any demands?" Amos asked.

"They've shouted for us to stay back," one officer said.

"How many hostages are we looking at?" Amos asked.

"Maybe six," someone else said. He jumped. "Look!"

A teenage boy, his hands held high, walked slowly out the front of the sporting goods store. He wore cut-offs, a Beavis and Butthead T-shirt, and a nervous twitch that was close to a grimace. It was obvious he was trying not to look behind him, at his captors, or in front of him, at the pile of human carnage. The tension built in him with each step he took. It was clear he'd been told not to bolt and that it was all he could think of doing. Amos tried in vain to get a peek deeper into the sporting goods store. He had his gun out, Blank crouching low behind him.

"What's happening?" Amos muttered, more to himself.

"They're using the boy to make a point," Blank said.

Amos nodded. "I'm afraid you're right."

A few seconds later the tension grew too great for the boy, stepping over severed arms, sliding around torn entrails, and he bolted. He got maybe fifteen feet when two rounds of shotgun blasts spewed from inside the store. One shot caught the boy midback. The other took the top of his head off. The boy joined the pile. An officer behind Amos turned and vomited. Amos came to a quick decision. He was not waiting for the SWAT team.

Amos told the others they were starting, but they needed a plan. Some of the officers had a couple of ideas; they hadn't been completely idle before Amos's arrival. They'd questioned the mall manager and learned there was a ceiling ventilation system that ran the length of every wing in the mall. A four-foot-wide duct at the rear of the shoe store ran above the sporting goods store, too. There was also a back hallway with a door leading into the sporting goods store, but everyone quickly agreed the bastards would have secured that, if they had any brains, which had yet to be decided. The officers had the duct open in the shoe store with a ladder pulled under it. Someone could crawl through the duct and drop in on the bad guys. Is that what he wanted them to do? they asked Amos.

"Show me the duct," Amos replied.

"Do you want me to come with you?" Blank asked.

"Do you want to?" Amos asked.

Blank glanced in the direction of the bodies. A fifty-year-old woman, her lower right leg ripped off, her black wig slipping, crawled toward a Waldenbook store. Amos would have closed his eyes, for a moment, if the smell wasn't somehow worse in the dark. Blood, urine, feces, agony—in his worst dreams he had never imagined anything like this. Blank looked back at him.

"Sure," Blank said matter-of-factly.

Amos shook his head. "No way."

Amos didn't want to go alone just to play hero. But he figured if his plan didn't work he'd rather pay the price than sacrifice another man. His bravery was not a major decision; it was just a part of who he was, as his memory was a part of him. The part that never forgot he had been living on borrowed time since the death squads had come for his brothers and missed him asleep in the bathtub. That was not to say he had a death wish. He wouldn't go down without taking at least one of them, preferably two.

The vent was wide and clean. It could have been made for just such a sneak attack, if not for a Hollywood movie. It was dark inside, of course, but the penlight he carried between his teeth took care of that. There was one problem, however. As he crawled along the aluminum tunnel, he quickly lost all sense of distance. After two minutes of slow cautious movement, he had no idea if he'd traveled fifty feet or a hundred. He had no reference point, and for some reason his men had closed up the panel back to the shoe store. Perhaps they feared the zombies would take the duct—after they'd eaten the brave lieutenant—and drop down on them. Amos could not believe their stupidity.

The cries of one hostage came to his rescue, and he hoped, he thought, her noise would translate into her own release. He was on the verge of turning around and going back when he heard a woman weeping immediately below him. By chance he was only two feet from a possible panel opening. Using the small Swiss army knife he always carried, he deftly freed a corner of the panel and peered down. Yeah, looked like the back of a sporting goods store, unless Walden's was now offering a free basketball with every purchase of a *New York Times* best-selling hardcover. The weeping woman, twenty-year-old and brown haired, was alone and didn't look as if she'd be crying long. The side of her head had been split open, as if it had been hammered with a baseball bat. Cursing silently, Amos freed the entire panel and slid it aside. Ten seconds after swearing at God, he mouthed a quick Hail Mary and dropped into the storage area. The woman fell silent as he landed beside her. He leaned over and checked the pulse at her neck. She was dead. He pulled his .38 revolver from his belt. Their turn now, he thought. He wasn't in the mood to arrest and read rights.

Amos slipped off his shoes and socks and tried the door that led from the storage area into the store proper. It was unlocked, unguarded. Head low, he scampered into the ski equipment section. Did people buy skis during the summer? he wondered. Perhaps the season explained the signs proclaiming the amazing discounts. He heard voices over by the shoe section. The bad guys had the civilians cornered beside the Nikes and Reeboks. Amos maneuvered around several aisles, seeing a bit more with each glance, coming into better range with each step. The villains were a midforties man with a bad-hair day ex-concentration-camp look and a teenage girl who looked as if she'd resented her Barbie from the age of two. The guy had bloodstains around his mouth, the blond girl weird eyes the color of coral. Both the man and girl carried double-barreled shotguns and paced in front of the weeping hostages, a band of three twenty-something women and one old guy.

Seemed the old guy was mouthing off to his captors. The girl struck him on the side of the head with the back of her hand as Amos crouched lower beside a row of jock straps. She was strong, Amos thought. The old guy toppled as if struck with a bat and lay still in a pile. Amos had seen enough. He stood and, using both hands like the overpaid cops on TV, took aim with his .38. He would ask them if they wanted to see a lawyer when they were already bleeding. He was an excellent shot, with steady nerves. He fired and put a bullet in the top of the girl's back. Red blossomed over her pink blouse.

But she didn't go down.

"Shit," Amos whispered, and dived to the floor. The red-mouthed guy reacted like lightning. Amos was glad the jock straps were empty as he felt and heard them explode from the rush of steel pellets one foot above his head. He knew he couldn't stay where he was. These people didn't have normal reflexes. He'd have to put a bullet in the guy from behind if he was to get a shot into him at all.

Why hadn't that girl gone down?

Maybe they weren't people?

Amos got to his feet and, staying low, scampered down a few aisles to the camping gear section. There he hid behind a blue down sleeping bag and peered around the edge. At least the blond chick was having trouble staying on her feet. Playing backup for her partner, her shotgun still in hand, she wobbled unsteadily from foot to foot. Her breathing sounded labored and there was blood at her mouth, her own. The guy ran up and down the aisles, blasting at anything that didn't move. A nervous fellow. As Amos watched, he tossed aside his shotgun and pulled out a .44 Magnum. He made no effort to hide, yet still he was a difficult target because of his jerky movements and speed. Few people who'd grown up watching TV cop shows realized how difficult it was to hit any moving target with a handgun, even from a distance as short as twenty feet. Yet even knowing that, Amos made an important decision—he'd try to shoot the guy from halfway across the store, and in the head. He didn't believe he'd be the one left standing if the two of them met in the women's wear aisle. Raising his revolver, again using both hands, he took aim and fired.

It was the climactic shot of a splendid career. His bullet caught the guy in the face and he went down hard and fast. Quickly Amos shifted his aim to the girl. Incredibly, the girl had already spun and raised her shotgun in his direction. Before Amos could get off another round, he saw an explosion of orange light and felt something akin to an MX missile hit his left shoulder. The blow literally knocked him onto his back, which may have saved his life, because as he fell the heated air of another blast rushed past the tip of his nose. Didn't these people know it took a second to cock the shotgun before they were supposed to be able to fire again? Didn't they know they couldn't fly? Amos blinked in pain, and when his eyes cleared the girl was standing over him with her shotgun pointed at his face. An evil grin spread slowly over her face and there was something in the expression that reminded him of a line Jerry Washington had said about his girlfriend while he was being interrogated at the station.

"She smiled at me like she wanted to stuff me in a hotdog bun and smear on the mustard."

Amos realized he was staring up at Susan Darly of Malibu Beach and Malibu High. He realized that probably the reason he had been unable to find Jerry was because the boy had gone to visit the bitch after being released. He hadn't escaped. Staring down at him as if he were an insect walking across her freshly scrubbed floor, Susan methodically cocked the shotgun and depressed the trigger. The hammer slapped down, but hey, this time, no cigar. She carried in her hands a Remington *double* barrel. She lost her grin and frowned at the weapon. She was out of bullets. Amos wasn't.

"I'm a friend of Jerry's," he said as he took aim from flat on his back. His shoulder was a forest fire but the flames he could douse later. Susan didn't move an inch. "Have you seen him lately?"

"Yes."

"Where is he?"

"Dead."

"I thought so." Amos cocked his hammer. "So are you."

At the last instant she bolted to the right, but Amos had anticipated the move and his shot caught her in the side of the neck. Blood gushed over her, but in one final example of superhuman fortitude, she didn't drop but continued to stagger toward the others. Amos pushed himself into a sitting position and took aim again. He shot her low in the spine. He shot her in the left thigh. He shot her in the right shoulder. Finally, thankfully, she crumpled to the floor.

"Should have listened to you, Jerry," Amos whispered. "Sorry, man."

Time then lost its meaning for Amos. The hostages ran out. The police dashed in. The next thing Amos knew Blank was kneeling by his side and bandaging his shoulder and saying something about getting him to a hospital. Amos nodded wearily. Besides his shoulder killing him, he felt more exhausted than he could remember having felt. He prayed that it was over, although part of him tossed the prayer back laughing. No, it said. You haven't seen anything yet. Wait till the mother of these motherfuckers comes a-walkin'. Then you'll see how good a shot you are. Blank studied Susan's fallen form from afar as he patched Amos's wound.

"How many bullets did you put in her?" Blank asked.

"Five."

Blank shook his head. "Remember the Rodney King videotape? Another case of police brutality. The evidence is right there."

"It took all five to stop her."

"Really?"

"Yes."

Blank saw he was serious. He glanced at Susan again. The girl's right leg still twitched. For probably the first time in his life Blank was worried.

"I don't know if I want to do the autopsy on that girl," he said.

TWENTY-NINE

❁

T HE INSTANT JULIE Moore saw Stanley Fraiser sitting on the
bed in her apartment, she knew there was something wrong.
For one thing, Stan hated loud music, and he had her boom
box up to his ear with the volume dial twisted past midnight. Another
clue was that he seemed to have pissed all over her wooden floor. He
didn't stand when he saw her, just smiled like something that had
crawled out of the ground for the first time in the twentieth century,
and set the boom box aside.

"Hello, Julie," he said.

She sniffed the foul air. "Stan. What are you doing here?"

He stood awkwardly, not moving like the Stan of three-hour-a-
day workouts. More like a I've-been-sleeping-in-my-box-too-long Stan.
He seemed both burdened with stiffness and charged with unnatural
speed. Besides that, he looked like shit.

"I'm here to welcome you," he said.

Julie took a firm stride into her apartment. He must be stoned,
she thought. Didn't matter. She wouldn't allow him to intimidate her.
She pointed toward the door.

"You get the fuck out of here right now or I call the police," she
said.

"OK," he said. "No problem." He stepped toward the door.
"Have a nice day." He moved past her and put his hand on the door.
"Sorry to bother you." He slammed the door shut and turned on her.
"Sorry, I have to kill you now."

Julie didn't pause to do even a fraction of a second analysis of him. Susan had almost eaten her. Sara had seen rocks where everyone else saw cute cuddly animals. The events of this day had prepared Julie well for an attack from her zombie ex. She lunged for the bathroom. Stan didn't even try to catch her. She slammed the door shut and locked it tight. Her heart shrieked in her chest. She was so scared she couldn't find her voice to scream. Outside, she heard Stan slowly approach the door. The music, a Stones cassette, continued to blare.

"Julie," Stan called. "Open up or I will huff and I will puff and I will kick your ass in."

"Go away," Julie whimpered.

Stan seemed to have his face right up to the door. "I can't do that. Dell told me you owe me. That I have to take what's rightfully mine."

She coughed. "Who's Dell?"

"He's the ornament sitting in your bathtub."

Julie looked over. The curtain was closed, but it was a thin blue vinyl affair and it didn't disguise the fact that there was indeed a body sitting in her bathtub. Julie's voice came back to her in a rush. She let out a bloodcurdling scream just as the bathroom door exploded in a rain of splinters and ruptured hinges and Stan walked in and stared down at her. She didn't even know how she had come to be on the floor.

"Dell told me you'd try to keep me from what is rightfully mine but that in the end I would be victorious," Stan said. He glanced at the mirror and flexed his swollen biceps. "If I get any better than this they'll want to can me and sell me to the Russians."

"Stan," Julie gasped. "What the hell's gotten into you?"

He frowned; the question could have brought him pain. "Something cold." Then, in a heartbeat, he was happy again. "Do you want to dance?"

She was not given a chance to decline the invitation. Stan reached down, grabbed her ankles, and dragged her from the bathroom. A fit of kicking and screaming did nothing to slow him down. It was as if a five-gallon steroid bottle had been pumped into his veins that afternoon, he was so strong. Where were her neighbors? The music was on loud and someone should have at least called the police by now. I love L.A. —fuck. Passing her desk on the way to what looked like a bad end, she managed to grab the leg of the desk. But the furniture was old, the glue tired, and the wood brittle—the leg broke off in her hand just as Stan released her ankles and began to unzip his pants and reveal an erection the color of a slab of *E. coli* salami. Without four stable legs, her desk tilted and deposited a number of items on her face: paper clips, pens, stamps, a pair of sunglasses, and her letter opener, a Christmas gift from her father when times were tough. Nevertheless, the letter opener was a welcome addition because it was little different from a sharp-edged knife, although it was gold rather than silver and she had never used it to cut a slice of cheese. Julie grabbed the thing as Stan dropped his pants to his knees and leaned over to put his own version of an opener into whatever orifice happened to be available for forced entry. He grinned at her.

"I'm going to enjoy this," he said.

So am I, Julie thought.

Her right hand came up in a swinging arc. Stan either didn't see it or figured her puny blow could do him no harm. He must have failed to note the sharp instrument she held, though. Even a weightlifter on black acid would have thought twice about engaging in intercourse with a six-inch-long blade impaled in his neck. That was not safe sex, no way, no shit. Julie planted the letter opener approximately two inches below the line of his left jaw bone. His abnormal strength had not made his flesh any more elastic. The letter opener went in deep, and the blood that poured out was dark. Stan moaned and rolled to the side, and she scampered out from beneath him. His big dick waved at her as he went down just as Mick Jagger yelled for his brown sugar.

"Shit," Stan complained from flat on his back as he struggled to pull the knife from his jugular vein. To her great misery Julie realized that even with his blood pouring from his body, he was still in the mood to rape her, and other things. Another weapon, quick, what did she have? Her aquarium! Her fish! The glass case the fish came in! Stan was right below it. Reaching over him, she toppled the whole affair on his midsection. His still-smiling dirty penis took the brunt of the blow. As it shattered, the glass stripped the organ of skin. That hurt. Now she had his attention. Now he was pissed off. Now she needed to find something else. Her eyes darted over the apartment again. Why wasn't she into Samurai swords or Old West revolvers? Why didn't this fucker just quit?

Julie kicked at Stan as he reached to grab her leg. That was a mistake. He was too quick for her. He grabbed her foot and twisted it counterclockwise two hundred degrees, and she was back on the floor with the fish and the piss and the blood. The low-level perspective wasn't all bad, although as he hunkered to his knees behind her she had a hard time convincing herself of the fact. Until her eyes came to rest on the container of body powder under her bed. She remembered having put it there six months ago when she'd been dating Stan because the smell of it had driven him absolutely crazy. Just a whiff of it and his eyes would swell up like dinosaur eggs. Some kind of neurotic allergic reaction, she had thought at the time. Well, he seemed more fucked up than ever tonight, she thought. She reached out and grabbed the powder just as he put his paws on her legs again. The top didn't have to be unscrewed, simply yanked off. The cloud of powder she let loose enveloped him like a pink aura falling around a raging buffalo. He had a knife in his neck and a glass cutter around his balls but the perfumed body powder was the magic ticket. His hands flew to his eyes and he screamed as if he had been dropped into a vat of boiling Campbell's soup. Julie hurried back to her feet. All right, she thought, three good shots in a row. When was this guy going to drop?

She knew then he wasn't going to leave her alone until she killed him. And it was odd, in all the time they had wrestled, she had never considered for a moment that she actually had to end his life, not even when she had stabbed him in the neck. She had just been going on instinct. Now she had to use her head. She had maybe two seconds before his vision cleared and he'd have his revenge. What did she have in arm's reach to kill him? There was only one thing big and bad enough to cause irreparable physical damage. Her TV.

The set had a thirty-inch tube in it. The TV was so heavy she needed help carrying it into her apartment. Under normal circumstances she couldn't have lifted it on her own, certainly not above her head. But that night was a high-adrenaline-don't-you-mess-with-me-life-and-death situation. If Stan could kick in doors, she could lift her RCA world of color. Stan almost had the powder out of his eyes. It was now or never.

In two strides Julie crossed to the foot of her bed and picked up the TV. Try as she might, she couldn't bring it above her head, but she did manage to raise it chest high. Stan, still on his knees, turned to face her just as her jolt of Catwoman power ran out. She brought the set down on his head—or, more accurately, gravity brought it down. The picture tube imploded as it shattered, the glass flying at him rather than toward her. What it did to his face, his brain, she never knew for sure and didn't care to know. All that mattered was that as the set crushed his skull he went down and stayed there. His blood continued to soak the floor long after he stopped moving.

Julie stood there for a long time. Waiting.

The phone rang. She picked it up. Sara Morray was on the line.

"Julie," Sara said. "How are you?"

Julie sniffed. "I think I just killed my old boyfriend."

Sara sounded worried. "You can't be serious. What happened?"

"I don't know. But he's dead. How are you?"

"Don't worry about me. Look, if you've really killed someone then you'd better come here immediately. We need to talk."

Julie began to come back to reality, bit by bit. "Why should I talk to you?"

"Because I can help you." Sara added, "And because Peter is coming over here. In fact, he should be here soon. That's why I'm calling you. He wants to meet you here."

"What? Peter?"

"Just come, Julie. Come now. Everything will be all right."

"All right," Julie said, feeling *compelled* to say it. She set down the phone without saying good-bye and looked around her studio apartment. What a mess, she thought. She'd have to clean it up tomorrow, when her brain returned. Even though she knew intellectually she was in shock—she had memorized all the symptoms for an exam in her undergraduate years and she believed she was now suffering from each and every one of them—she could not talk herself out of the state. Nor could she understand why a woman who scored worse on the Rorschach than Charles Manson should call her twice in the same day—the second time to invite her back to her house to meet with a guy they both desired. Yes, Julie thought as she trudged to the door with her keys in hand, it was a strange day all around. But one thing was sure—if Peter's car wasn't sitting outside Sara's house, she wasn't getting out of her car. At the moment, she trusted Sara as much as she did the pusher who had sold Stan his last batch of steroids.

THIRTY

❀

P ETER JACOBS SAT in Dr. David Samuel's study and watched as
the doctor lit his pipe. Peter disliked the smell of tobacco and
had never been able to date a woman who smoked. On the
other hand, he loved fires and probably would have been a pyroma-
niac had he been unstable. When there was a major fire anywhere in
southern California, he'd drive to it on his motorcycle to see it, feel
the cinders settling on his hair, the blasts of superheated air. Sometimes he'd bring Matt, who loved fires as well. In his condo he had a
working fireplace, and if it was the least bit chilly he'd fire up the logs.
Therefore, Peter was delighted that Dr. Samuel had a small fire going
in the corner of his study and was only too happy to forgive the man's
pipe.

As Peter suspected, Dr. Samuel had been eager to see him in
exchange for information about Sandra Morray's child. The doctor
sounded shocked that Peter even knew of Sandra. Peter was determined to tell the doctor nothing until he knew what had really happened the night Sandra had gone into her coma. He told Dr. Samuel
as much, phrasing his condition tactfully. The doctor nodded.

"In exchange, I must have your word that you will not write
about what I am going to tell you," Dr. Samuel said. He was a burly
man, pounds of muscle gone to fat, but nevertheless still hard, still
someone who could throw his weight around. He tamed his silver
locks with a gold comb, which seemed something of a neurotic habit
with him. His brown sport coat matched his leather loafers; both

smelled of money and pipe smoke. The study was filled with more medical books than Peter thought there were parts of the body.

"Fair enough," Peter said.

The doctor shook his head. "You say that so easily. But you're a reporter. How am I to believe you?"

"Let's say my interest in Dr. Morray and Sandra is personal. I doubt I'm even going to write about them."

"Why personal?"

Peter shrugged. "I don't want to answer that, but I can assure you that nothing you say will go outside these walls."

"Before I begin, can you tell me if you've met Sandra Morray's child?"

Peter hesitated. "Yes. Have you?"

Dr. Samuel hesitated as well, then said, "No."

Peter smiled sadly. "We don't trust each other, do we?"

Dr. Samuel sighed and took a puff on his pipe. He stared at the fire. "I haven't spoken about Sandy or Larry in a long time—to anybody. Even my wife doesn't know the full story. To go back to those days stirs painful memories. Do you understand?"

Peter nodded. He had yet to recover from the shock of seeing Sara Morray in Ruth Randolph's yearbook. He had promised to tell Dr. Samuel everything he had uncovered, but he already decided to leave out the incest. He couldn't imagine that Dr. Morray knew who Sara was, just as he couldn't believe Sara *didn't* know. That was the part that hurt the most. What kind of person was he in love with?

Love? How could he love a woman he didn't know?

How could he care for a woman that drove others to insanity?

Of course, look how far she had driven him already. To Iowa, for God sakes.

"I understand," Peter said, pain in his voice. Dr. Samuel heard it, sensed it was sincere, even if nothing else he told him was. The doctor appeared to come to a decision. Peter sensed he was about to hear more than Dr. Samuel originally had intended to tell him. The man took another puff on his pipe and settled deeper into his leather chair.

"I met Larry my senior year at U.C.L.A. We were both in the pre-med program. We graduated with degrees in biology and were both accepted to the university's medical school. From the start I was drawn to Larry's intelligence, drive, and special intensity. Once class started, he dropped any sort of social life. He had to graduate at the top of his class, he told me. But he didn't tell me why, although it was easy to guess. Larry was one of those people who believed instinctively that he was destined for greatness. It permeated his being and made others believe it as well. I certainly did. Larry and I shared a small apartment, and many times I'd awaken in the middle of the night to find Larry studying. His teachers loved him. Many of his classmates feared him. We knew Larry would do anything to get ahead.

"It was in our final year of medical school that I met Sandy. I see your surprise, but, yes, I dated her first. She was finished with her studies. She worked as an artist for several small publishers on the West Coast, doing children's book illustrations, book covers. I thought she was brilliant. In those days, I thought about nothing but Sandy. I could hardly study. She was one of those special women who could light up a room, just by walking into it. It would be a cliché to say her charm was matched only by her inner beauty, but it would also be true. I realize in the short time I have spoken to you that I've used the word *special* to apply to two people already. I suppose it was inevitable that two such unique people, when they met, should fall in love. But when I introduced Sandy to Larry, the possibility hadn't entered my mind. Before I turned around, though, they were together. I can't express how hurt I was—especially by Larry. He was my friend, my roommate. I trusted him. You might wonder why I didn't blame Sandy. I couldn't because I loved her too much, still, and I could see Larry was the better man. I believed that then. Foolishly, I believed in his high destiny. I don't anymore.

"I can't remember how long they were together before they married. Not many months. Larry asked me to be his best man. I refused, until Sandy asked me. I was never able to say no to her. And I could see she was happy and that Larry was a changed man. He was still top in the class, but now he smiled occasionally. Sandy gave Larry a rare gift—true love. I know it sounds corny, but I mean it. She gave him everything she had and asked for nothing in return." Dr. Samuel's voice lowered. "She didn't even ask for him to sleep on his decision when she became pregnant during the second year of our residency."

"What decision was that?" Peter asked.

"We were both residents in cardiology at the time, at U.C.L.A. Medical Center. Larry's life had been enriched by Sandy, but he was still restless to get ahead. A child at that stage of his life was out of the question for him. It would divert too much energy from his ultimate goal of 'improving the human condition.' That was a favorite phrase of his. He told Sandy to have an abortion, which, at the time, you could do legally only in Mexico. She said fine, but she came to see me that night and I had to hold her to keep her from crying. She wanted the baby very much.

"Yet she did what her husband ordered and life went on. Both of us completed our residencies and were soon board-certified cardiologists. Larry began a practice in Los Angeles but I returned here, to Iowa, to start my own practice. We stayed in contact. It was mainly Sandy who maintained the link. She would write and make the odd Sunday evening call. I always loved to hear from her. I suppose I never stopped loving her, never stopped hoping that one day she'd leave Larry and come running to me. But I knew that would never happen.

"Then I received the call I'd never forget. I must have been thirty-three at the time—I know Sandy was three years younger than Larry and I, and that the nightmare started only a week after her thirtieth birthday. It was Larry, he was down in Baja, Mexico. There'd been an accident. Sandy had almost drowned. She was in a Mexican hospital, in bad shape, brain damaged. Larry sounded desperate. What was he supposed to do? he begged me. I told him I'd be on the next plane.

"When I reached the hospital I learned that Sandy was in worse shape than Larry had told me. She didn't just have brain damage—her EEG was as flat as a desktop. Do you understand what that means? I was a doctor, I did. She was alive. She was being respirated by mechanical means and her heart was still beating. But in reality, Sandy, the love of our lives, was dead. I went to see her. I sat beside her the entire night. I held her hand and stared at her still face. There was no one there. I told Larry to tell them to pull the plug. He said he couldn't. He wept and told me that if he let her die, then he would be a murderer. It was then he told me the truth of that night, and when he was done I almost killed him with my bare hands, I swear it.

"Larry had been working hard. What else was new? The guy always put in hundred-hour weeks. Sandy convinced him he needed a break. She knew friends in Baja. They could go stay with them for a weekend. The friends had a boat, a thirty-foot sailboat. Sandy said her friends might even let them take it out by themselves. Sandy had sailed regularly as a teenager. By this time both of Sandy's parents were dead, and she had no brothers or sisters. She had no family except Larry and me, if I could be called that.

"Anyway, Larry consented to the trip, and soon they were relaxing in the sun and playing in the surf. That was late May, maybe early

June. The third day there Sandy got her wish and her friends allowed her and her husband to take the boat out. Sandy was having the time of her life, Larry told me. There wasn't much wind but they were able to sail the boat several miles north of the friend's house. As the sun began to set, they felt as if they had the whole sea to themselves. Larry told me they made love on the forward deck as it began to get dark. It was shortly after that that Sandy dropped the bomb. She told him she thought she was pregnant.

"Larry didn't take the news well, and to this day I don't understand why. Here was a man who at the age of thirty-three had a thriving practice. I don't know what he was making, but it must have been a lot with all his Hollywood clients. Why couldn't his wife have a child? Why did she have to have another abortion, which is what Larry told her? The bastard—he was still in love with the notion of his grand destiny. He still believed a child would divert too much energy away from what he needed to accomplish. That was Larry—what *he* wanted. He loved his wife, I know he did. But he was still the center of the universe. It revolved around him. Get rid of it, he told Sandy. We can take care of it while we're down here.

"This time Sandy—God bless her soul—said no. It may have been the first time she ever said no to him. Certainly her refusal to have the abortion angered him. No, I chose too delicate a word. I believe from reading between the lines of his story that her refusal sent him into a rage. They fought on the forward deck on the very spot they had made love." Dr. Samuel paused. "Sandy fell and struck her head on the railing and slipped into the water."

Peter sat up. "Hold on a second. She *fell*? How did she fall? Did he push her? Did he strike her?"

Dr. Samuel was grim. "I asked him and he said no. But I knew him—I had known him for a long time. He was lying. I pressed him with the very questions you just put to me and he kept shaking his head. But he wept again, and Larry didn't weep easily. But he refused to elaborate so I guess I'll have to answer your questions. I believe the answer is yes. Sandy was extremely coordinated. She was a wonderful snow skier and wouldn't have fallen, even on a boat. He must have either shoved her or struck her. His guilt told me that as much as did his vagueness." Samuel shook his head. "Just because she wanted what most women want—a child. Can you understand when you first called why I told you I didn't want to talk about him?"

"Yes. But I don't understand why the situation turned so serious. The blow from striking the railing didn't cause her brain damage, did it?"

"No."

"Then why didn't he just pull her out of the water?"

"I asked him the same question. He said he couldn't swim."

"What? Everybody who grows up in southern California can swim."

"Larry couldn't."

"But didn't the sailboat have life preservers?"

"I asked him that, too. He said it did, but that he was afraid to put one on and jump in. He was terrified of deep water. All the while Sandy floated facedown in the water, he fought that terror. Finally, though, after several minutes, he drummed up the nerve and did put on a life preserver and leapt in and dragged her from the water."

Peter was shocked at how much the revelation upset him. He couldn't stop thinking of the shadow of the woman he had left behind at Kabriel Clinic—Patient 111.

"He shouldn't have waited," Peter complained. "He knew she couldn't survive without oxygen for more than a few minutes."

"I told him that. But what he should have done, what he shouldn't have done—it doesn't matter, not now and not then. That is what happened. By the time he got Sandy aboard, she had stopped breathing. Her heart was still beating, though. I never said he was an incompetent doctor. He was one of the best. Somehow he managed to keep her alive until she could be brought to the hospital. That's where I found them. That's where I cursed him. I told him that he was a murderer. That he had to tell the authorities exactly what had happened and let justice take its course. I told him I was going to the police. That got him—I was going to turn him in. He begged me to keep my mouth shut. How would it help Sandy, he asked me, if he went to jail? He was right, of course, it wouldn't help her at all. Still, I wanted Larry to own up to what he had done. I wanted the world to know exactly what kind of man he was. But in the end I did nothing to accuse him officially. I suppose Sandy's ghost haunted my conscience. No matter how guilty he was, she wouldn't have wanted her husband to suffer more than was necessary."

"What happened next?" Peter asked. "How did she end up in Iowa?"

"It was the deal I made with him for my silence. I'd take care of her. He was never to see her again. She would be mine now, as she had been mine to begin with. He never said yes to my proposal, but he never said no either. What was I taking from him anyway? Not Sandy. He had stolen Sandy from both of us when he'd hesitated to jump into the water." Dr. Samuel was bitter. "The coward."

"Was Sandy still pregnant when she was brought to the Kabriel Clinic?" Peter asked.

Dr. Samuel stared again at the fire. "Yes. But—it was not as I first believed."

"What do you mean?"

"You say you've been to the clinic and checked her records. You saw she had a cesarean. Did you notice when she had the operation?"

"No. The notes were scribbled. I could scarcely read half of them."

"Half those notes were in my handwriting."

"I meant no offense," Peter said. "What are you trying to tell me?"

"No offense taken. Had you been able to decipher the notes, you would have seen that she had the cesarean nine months to the day she entered her coma. Do you understand what I am saying?"

"Yes. She wasn't pregnant when she thought she was. She didn't get pregnant until that night."

Dr. Samuel chuckled without mirth. "Ironic, isn't it?"

"It's tragic. Does Dr. Morray know where Sandy is?"

"I never told him where I put her and he never asked. In fact, after that night, we never spoke again. He wanted me to hide his mistake, make it so that it never was. But he must believe Sandy's dead by now. It's a small miracle she isn't."

The questions popped out of Peter's mouth. "Why isn't she dead? Why haven't you given the instruction for her respirator to be turned off?"

"Legally, I can't give that instruction. Larry never transferred Sandy's guardianship over to me. She's at Kabriel Clinic because he didn't stop me from putting her there and because I continue to pay the bills for her care. Those are the only reasons."

"But it's been thirty years."

Samuel sighed. "I know. It may be a medical record. What keeps her alive? Perhaps, buried deep in her wasted mind, it's the thought of her children. Perhaps part of her wonders how they're doing and longs for them to visit her." Dr. Samuel eyed him through the hazy smoke of his pipe. "And now, young man, I've kept my end of the bargain. It's your turn to talk. How is Sandy's daughter doing?"

Peter was having difficulty responding. The maze never ended. The truth always emerged out of another level of deceit. "What do you mean, her *children*? For the love of God, she didn't have another after the girl, did she?"

"Lord, no. She had another the same time as the girl. I thought you knew—it was there in her medical record. But I suppose it was hard for you to read. Sandy had twins."

Peter felt cold. "A boy and a girl?"

Dr. Samuel scratched his head. "I believe so."

Cold as those who no longer breathed. "What happened to the boy?"

"I don't know. I was hoping you could tell me. All I know is they were turned over to Able Adoption." Dr. Samuel frowned. He was obviously still contemplating the matter of genders. "At least tell me what happened to the girl."

Peter closed his eyes and thought of Sara's eyes when they had last said good-bye. Those innocent mirrors on the soul, as artists would say. Peter thought of the Randolphs, especially Clyde, rotting in his own way in a hospital bed as Sandra Morray rotted.

"She's committed great sin," he whispered.

THIRTY-ONE

❀

G OVINDA SHARMA REALIZED he had reached the end of the road. He could follow Rak no farther. The realization had swept him before, true, but now simple facts spoke for the finality of the chase. He had no money left. What he had brought from India and managed to change at the airport had been spent on mad dashes into convenience stores, while Rak took an extra block lead on him. From now on there would be no food to give him strength to keep up with Rak. The blind man had mastered the sound of traffic. His stride was seldom interrupted now. He led Govinda to beaches in Malibu, doctors' offices in Westwood, apartments in Venice. Some places he entered, and did God knows what. Other places he just stood outside and stared, as if waiting for unseen acts to conclude.

Now Rak led Govinda right up to a cemetery.

It was dark, although the moon had grown since India. Govinda wanted to rush forward to stop him. Govinda had never cared for cemeteries, even though he had violated the rules of his childhood scriptures to bury his wife in one. But he knew those who followed the left hand of Tantra craved the burial grounds as a Catholic priest craved an anointed altar. Rak reached a tall wrought-iron gate that protected the entrance of the grounds, and it stopped him for perhaps five seconds. Govinda watched in amazement as he reached out with his large hands and methodically bent two of the bars far apart. As if they were made of thin aluminum and not two-inch iron. A miracle? Govinda asked himself. He'd known the man was powerful when he first laid eyes on him. The only miracle, Govinda thought, was the type of faith that required no miracles. And he didn't possess it. Rak smoothly slid between the bars and strode deep into the cemetery. Govinda followed him, the Master had said to follow him. But the Master had never said where the road would end. Yet as Govinda squeezed his body between the bars, he felt as if a part of him had come full circle, that the end was not far off.

He didn't know why.

A quarter of a mile into the cemetery, Rak sat down on the stone slab of a plainly marked plot. Govinda circled around and rested on a grass bluff a hundred yards above and behind him. Rak meditated on mantras long forgotten. Govinda wanted to sleep. But the night air was still warm with the fire of the day, and his head ached with the memories of Pandu's screams. In the dark, surrounded by corpses, he didn't want to think of the story of Rak's birth. But Keshava's tale seemed to have a life of its own in that place of the dead. Even as his eyes fell shut, Cira was there to remind him that sometimes even the faith of the devout was not enough.

4

Cira

THIRTY-TWO

✺

KESHAVA TOOK A sip of water and, at the Master's bidding, began the tale of Rak's mother and the birth of the strange soul. Govinda listened intently.

"Five thousand years ago, in ancient India, there lived a young female seer named Cira. She was Aryan, blond and blue eyed, and a virgin. She resided in the Shakti Pith of Kali Ma—one of the main seats of the Divine Mother's power on earth—in the foothills of the Himalayas. That center no longer exists today, but the spot is marked by a small statue of Kali that stands in an artificial cave constructed of gathered stones. I have been there. But when Cira lived the place was adorned with a large dormitory and temple. This was an ashram of women only. Although Cira was the most powerful seer at the pith, and the one most frequently consulted by visitors, she did not incur the jealousy of her fellow seers. She was but sixteen as this story begins, and her personality was charming and innocent as the Goddess Sati. Love surrounded her and left no room for petty attacks. Cira was liked by all and never had an unkind word to say about anybody.

"I call her and her associates seers. It was how they were described at the time, but to a realized yogi they were far from knowers of the supreme truth. A member of the New Age community in the West would have instantly recognized Cira for what she really was, which was a trance channeler. You know about channeling, Govinda? A person allows a spirit of some kind to speak through him or her. It is a waste of time and can be dangerous for a man or woman seeking liberation. But occasionally the process does produce interesting results. It all depends on the purity of the person channeling and what kind of spirit she attracts. The information given out is seldom enlightening, although it can be accurate. Cira was much in demand because her information often proved to be correct. Like trance channelers of today, she would sink into a relaxed state and allow whatever happened to be in the astral neighborhood to use her nervous system and vocal cords. The problem with this approach is that you don't know who's going to climb into your body. Cira never had any serious problems, probably because she was so sweet by nature. I don't think hostile spirits could be bothered with her.

"All the women at the pith had taken a vow of celibacy. Tradition had it that it would heighten their power and protect them from a variety of unspecified evils related to the use of their power. Now as fate would have it, a handsome young male doctor had the responsibility of overseeing the health of the women. His name was Charaka, and he was something of an oddity. He took the practical approach to health and illness. If someone slipped and broke an arm, he put the bone in a splint. If another person developed a lung infection, he would make them rest and give them fluids and prescribe herbs that were known for their antibiotic qualities. It was ironic that the seers at the pith were considered far more orthodox than Charaka, but such is the history we inherit. Nevertheless, he got results and the women trusted him, and he was kept on.

"Cira had a frail physical disposition and consequently saw Charaka more than the other women. And because she was so delightful, he soon fell hopelessly in love with her. Cira, too, was fond of Charaka, but not so infatuated that she was willing to break her vow and give up her life as a seer at the pith and run off with him into the night, which is what he frequently implored her to do. For all his progressive ways, Charaka was impulsive and emotional, and those qualities frightened Cira. His whole mood would sour if she failed to smile at him.

"One day the pith received word that the prince of all of northern India was to visit, specifically to see Cira. There was much excitement throughout the temple. But Charaka was not happy about the royal visit. He felt that if the prince liked Cira's reading, he would take her away with him to his palace. Not long before the reading was to take place, Charaka went to Cira's private quarters and begged her to leave with him immediately before it was too late. Cira laughed off his dire warnings. She was excited to meet the prince. The thought of living in a palace interested her, as it would any young girl. But out of pity for Charaka's heartfelt concerns, and to calm him down, she gave him a quick but warm kiss, the first kiss she had ever given any man in her life. That was her mistake.

"Charaka raped her. He didn't intend to. He honestly cared for her, but perhaps Cira allowed her kiss to linger a second too long. I am not trying to excuse his act, you understand, but am merely trying to make clear that he was not an evil person. He got carried away and that is the sad truth of the matter. Yet there was something else. In private Charaka would scoff at the women's trances, but he did recognize that Cira had a power that the others did not have. She was fairly accurate when it came to predicting things, although she made her share of mistakes. But Charaka thought that if she lost her virginity, she might lose her power as well and no longer be able to give supernatural advice so she could be his then. We see from this that Charaka was as superstitious as everyone else at the pith. He forced himself on her in a frenzy of passion. Yet a part of him knew what he was doing.

"Of course, when he was done, and Cira was lying half naked on her bed and weeping, he felt dreadful. He tried apologizing. He begged for her forgiveness. He offered to take a knife and fall on it. He had hurt her, you see, and she was bleeding. But she wouldn't even look at him. She wouldn't let him help her. She ordered him away and then, still bleeding, she put on her best robes and went out to greet her royal visitor.

"The prince was an important man and had many serious questions for her. Cira went into her trance, a very deep trance, deeper than she had ever gone before. Perhaps it was because she had lost so much blood and was so weak that she sank into that dark and cold place where she did not belong. The entity that came to her then was unlike anything she had ever attracted before. It was one of those rare beings that had never been in human incarnation before and was never supposed to be. It was immensely powerful. It entered Cira at the instant one of Charaka's sperm impregnated one of her eggs. It got stuck inside her, so to speak, at the moment of conception. Perhaps the being wished it so. Perhaps it was an accident. Who would know?

"Cira gave her reading, or rather, the entity inside her did. It knew a great deal, more than any passing spirit. It knew that the prince's best friend was having an affair with the prince's wife. Not surprisingly, the prince was angry about the reading. When Cira finally came out of her trance—with the greatest of difficulty—he almost ran her through with his own sword. Afterward, many righ-teous people wished he had killed her then and there, before the fetus had a chance to develop.

"The prince returned to his palace. Cira slowly began to regain her health. Yet she was no longer the same. She didn't feel herself— she didn't look the same. There was an aura about her that frightened the other women. Also, from that point on, whenever she gave a read-ing, she gave very specific information, of the past, present and future. She told people good things and bad but in a sense they were all bad because everything she foretold was true. Cira was never wrong about anything. Her reputation grew, and those whose lives she disturbed with her truth began to hate her.

"During this time her pregnancy progressed, until it became dif-ficult for her to hide her condition beneath her loose robes. Charaka took care of her. She had such a soft disposition, even with the entity inside her, that she hadn't the heart to report his wicked act, knowing that he would be executed for it. Plus, in a strange way, she began to care for him more than before. Finally, his idea of running off to the plains began to appeal to her. She could not stay at the pith, not as a seer, not with a child. She had no one to turn to but him.

"In the eighth month of her pregnancy, just when Cira was about to flee with Charaka to get away from the cruel gossip that had begun to circulate about her swollen belly, the prince returned unexpect-edly. He wanted another reading. It seemed Cira had been right about his best friend and his wife, and now the best friend was no more. Yet the prince still loved his wife, for the time being. He wanted Cira to tell him if the child she carried belonged to him.

"Cira went into her final trance. The entity spoke through her. It had a marvelous voice, as beautiful in many ways as the voice Rak would use in later years to hypnotize thousands. Yes, it said, the child belonged to the prince, and the child would be male. At that the prince smiled and was glad for he had been waiting many years for his wife to give him an heir. But then the entity added that the child would be born dead. The prince's anger in that moment was a terrible thing, more so because he had already seen a demonstration of her power and knew in his heart that Cira was never wrong. He drew his sword and started to run her through, even before she could emerge from her trance. But at the last moment something stayed his hand, and he turned the sword aside and only struck her a hard blow on the temple, knocking her over. The prince left the pith in a rush.

"Now, Charaka had been observing the reading from behind a curtain, and when the prince stormed from the room he ran to Cira's side. Her head had been cracked open and she was bleeding badly. She was not breathing, even though her heart continued to beat. Quickly he carried her back to his quarters and began to give her mouth-to-mouth resuscitation. He knew the technique from his teachers, who knew it from theirs. The technique is very old. Those in the West think everything they invent no one else has ever thought of before. Charaka breathed for her for a long time, hoping Cira would regain consciousness. But the doctor in him knew it was a vain hope. Her skull was split wide open. Nevertheless, he managed to keep her alive for three days, breathing her every breath. Finally, weak with exhaustion and despair, he took a knife and cut open her abdomen, delivered the child, and let Cira die. He left the pith in the middle of the night with the infant.

"That child was Rak. We know nothing of his early years, as I have said—except that, when he was still a boy, he murdered his father."

Keshava stopped speaking. Govinda sat silent, stunned. He had no questions. The sudden death of Cira had left him feeling empty, as if someone close to him had just passed away before his eyes. There was a power in the tale, he realized. But was it because it was true? None of these things were easy to believe. The Master nodded at Keshava.

"I would like to speak to Govinda alone," the Master said gently.

Keshava stood and bowed to the Master. He paused to touch Govinda's shoulder as he stepped toward the door. "May Shiva bless you on your journey," he said.

"May he bless you always," Govinda replied. "*Jai Guru Dev.*"

"*Jai Guru Dev,*" Keshava said and left.

The Master sat for several seconds staring at Govinda. There was such love in his eyes, such compassion, that Govinda knew in the days to come he would often reflect back to this moment. If the Master was not one with God, Govinda thought, then he carried something inside him as great as any God. The Master picked up a flower, a red rose, and caressed the soft petals. It had grown dark inside the kutir.

"I have something to tell you about the future," the Master said. "It's something not even Keshava knows, something no one but the Masters know." He nodded, thoughtful, if such a high being even had thoughts. "It will surprise you, Govinda."

THIRTY-THREE

❖

WHAT WOULD SURPRISE him now? Govinda thought. That for once Rak should not sit all night as if he were made of stone? That for once during the dark he should stir, as he seemed to be doing now? That he should begin to dig into the earth above a grave with his powerful hands? Dig as if he were hoping to find a corpse? Yes, all these acts surprised Govinda because they were too horrible to contemplate, even as they unfolded before his eyes. There was no horror without surprise, just as there was no death without life. The dead never feared each other, he thought, although the living often ran from their own kind. Govinda wanted to run but could not.

Rak dug rapidly. Govinda stood and backed into a man-size stump that seemed to possess invisible arms to hold him captive as Rak climbed into the hole he had created, and the black earth flew in the air about him. Rak — the five-thousand-year-old warrior, the master of Seedling, the omniscient entity that had once used his own mother to utter the words that had killed her. Soon Rak reached the bottom and lifted the coffin from the hole as if it weighed a few ounces rather than many pounds. He set it beside the grave, on the cemetery's manicured lawn, the grass the color of cloudy ice in the moonlight that stole through the leaves of the surrounding trees. After pulling himself from the hole with one powerful thrust and picking up his staff, Rak gave the coffin a swift kick as he walked away. The wood splintered as if from an *internal* blow. Wasn't that what this was all about? That what was inside was destined to come outside. To play, perhaps, with the foolish man who did not believe in Cira and her son, much less in Krishna and Shiva. Yet in that moment, finally, Govinda believed everything he had been told about Rak. He finally realized where he had been led and why the place looked familiar.

He was in Vani's cemetery.

He was staring at Vani's coffin. Watching it open.

The idea to flee came upon him just as the top of the coffin was shoved aside. Rak was gone. Govinda didn't know where to go. He ran in what he thought was the direction of the entrance, but since the coffin lay between him and the iron gate he ran in circles. He would not, he could not, look at the *thing* behind him climbing out of the box. He ran with the terror of someone who had only come to realize he had a soul the moment the devil reached to take it from him. He didn't need sight to feel the thing stretching its emaciated limbs and scanning the graveyard with its sunken eyes to find him. He could feel its purpose: to catch him, to show him what it had for him, what he had lost. He fled from the six-month-dead body of his beloved wife.

He ran in horror through a maze of madness and tombstones.

Somehow, he stumbled upon the iron gate.

But Rak had forbidden escape. The bars had been bent straight again.

"Help me!" Govinda screamed as he pounded upon the gate with his trembling fists. "Master!"

But his Master was not there, just as he had not been there the morning the cobra had come for Pandu. Shiva was not there. It was the devil who was omnipresent. It was the dead who squeezed the living between fragments of time, on both sides, the past and the future, making of humanity a ghoulish sandwich of doomed meat that had yet to learn to stop kicking. He heard movement at his back. He screamed and screamed, but only the tormented soul of his wife was there to listen. He heard footsteps behind him. He knew why she approached. She wanted him to take her torment from her. She wanted him to feel what it felt like to rot, even in a box overflowing with embalming fluid. A dry claw that had once been a lovely hand touched his shoulder. It bade him turn and meet his destiny. Moaning, he felt himself spun around into a dimension of madness.

Yet the worst that could be was really not so bad, after all.

She stood in shadow, a shadow of the night, and he could not see her clearly. He could only sense her outline, the creaking of her joints, the dry odor of her silent breath. She was clothed in the white sari he had buried her in. But white as well as black were lost in darkness, as hope as well as terror were consumed in awe. The void beyond death was as awesome as it was awful. His fear vanished as quickly as it had come. Her hand took his hand and placed it over her swollen belly. Life stirred in her dead womb. An unspoken sigh escaped her invisible lips and she lay down on the ground. He knelt beside her. He didn't know if he would not or could not let go of her hand. It didn't matter. They were going to have their baby, six months late and born dead as the prince's son had been destined to be born dead. They were going to have the child, he realized, because if they did not a part of him would always be dead. She parted her legs and movement rustled beneath the sari.

Cira, he thought. *Charaka.*

The child came out. Very small. He picked it up and held it in his hands. For a moment they held it together. It did not move, it did not cry. Its suffering had ended before its joy began. It was not so terrible a thing, Govinda thought. It was simply the way things were.

"Kubera," he whispered.

The dark outline, the memory of his wife, seemed to nod. Then she took the infant from him, clasped it to her chest, and lay back and was still. Govinda felt the hand let go of him. He was free, free to go. And now he did not want to.

Still, he had a lighter in his pocket, and he was, after all, a Hindu from birth. He was supposed to have cremated her. Here was his second chance—Rak's cruel gift to him. There was no need for oil and torches. What was left of her was dry as summer wood. Without consciously deciding, Govinda found the lighter in his hand, saw the spark grow into flames as it spread up her sari, over their child, over her invisible face. Yet he saw her expression clearly, for a moment, in the light of the fire, and she seemed at peace. All was well, he thought. Mother and child burned quickly and left little behind.

Govinda finally left the cemetery. He found a way out over a back wall. He had a job to do. Follow Rak. Follow him wherever he led. He would not quit until it was finished. He felt that would be soon.

THIRTY-FOUR

❀

J ULIE MOORE SELDOM thought of the day her little sister, Patricia, died. The squeal of the brakes, the sound of the bike crushing, the screams, the silence. She didn't blot out the experience, it was simply too brief to dwell on at length. It was not the trauma that was painful, she realized. It was the ramifications of it, the days afterward. Patricia was gone in a flash of lightning glimpsed in a rearview mirror. But her shadow was to stretch across the years.

Whom did Julie live with but her father. Whom was she given to suffer with but a man who never expressed a genuine emotion in his life. Yet even this scarecrow of a farmer would sit long hours in Patricia's empty bedroom late at night and stare at the stuffed dolls that he couldn't remember having bought. Sometimes in the early-morning hours Julie would awaken and find him holding Patricia's Pooh Bear and her Snoopy pillow case, clasping them as if they were injured. If he saw Julie, however, he would quickly stand and mutter something about his bladder. There was no helping him—they were of no help to each other. Patricia died when Julie was sixteen. The two years to her high school graduation and her escape to the West Coast were long for her. Yet she had few regrets about how seldom she returned to see her father, although she was curious as to how Patricia's grave site was being kept up. She hadn't been to her sister's cemetery in four years.

Julie thought of cemeteries as she drove toward Sara Morray's house.

She considered the two dead men in her apartment. The shock

was wearing off. She had to go to the police, she knew. They would listen to her; her acts had been in self-defense—the evidence was obvious. But she wanted to talk to Peter first, to get his advice. She wanted to get him away from Sara.

As she had that afternoon, Sara met her out front. She wore a midlength white dress and sandals. The evening was warm. Peter's car was nowhere in sight. Julie pulled into the driveway but didn't get out. Sara walked over.

"Where is he?" Julie demanded.

"He was here a moment ago," Sara said. "I told him you were coming. He said he would be down at the beach."

"Where's his car?"

"He drove it down to the beach. Why don't we walk there and join him?"

The beach was only a quarter of a mile away. Why would he bother driving? Julie didn't like the situation. She didn't like the woman. She studied the house. Every light was off. Had the socially isolated pathological personality been sitting alone in the dark? Julie wondered.

"I don't think so," Julie said. "When is Peter coming back?"

"He didn't say." Sara offered her hand. "Why don't we just go get him? We can be there in a few minutes."

Julie did not take the offered hand, but felt she would be safer outside the house than inside. What could happen to her at the beach anyway? For the first time she noticed her blouse was stained with blood from her battle with Stan. Why hadn't Sara commented on it? The red was visible in the silver light of the moon. The crescent hung over the ocean like an object tossed to fill in an incomplete sketch. Julie remembered that Sara often painted the sky. It seemed so haunting, so beautiful. Just like Sara.

"I don't want to walk far," Julie said, opening her car door.

"He couldn't have gone far," Sara said.

They strolled down to the beach. Sara didn't utter a word the whole way. She kicked off her sandals as she stepped to the edge of the surf. The waves were gentle surges of white foam and cool water. In southern California the water never got that warm. Julie didn't want to take off her shoes, didn't want to be bothered to put them back on. Sara turned to her, her long dark hair stirred by a gentle breeze. Peter was nowhere to be seen.

"Do you want to ask me something?" Sara said.

"Yes," Julie said impatiently. "Where's Peter?"

"I don't know. He said he was just going down the hill." Sara paused. "Did you want to ask me something else?"

"Yes. You're married. Why are you interested in my Peter?"

"Is he yours?"

"We're going out. He's more mine than yours. You have a husband—what do you want with him?"

"I want to have his baby," Sara said.

Julie snorted. "Is that all? Why just one baby? Why not have twins?"

Sara nodded, her face solemn, her eyes watching, always. "Twins are always a possibility." She paused. "How was your old boyfriend?"

Julie froze. She went as still as a wave that would never break. "You know," she whispered. "How do you know?"

Sara caught her eyes and slowly moved to one side. Julie had to turn to follow her. But it was as if she moved against heavy resistance. Something surged through the air, an invisible net of unspeakable will, and settled over her head. Julie suddenly felt as she had in the car that afternoon when the strange blind man had appeared, somehow drugged and focused at the same time. Only now there was a tightening in her chest as the space between Sara and her grew shorter. Julie sucked in a ragged breath and coughed.

"I was there before you," Sara said. "I danced with the boys. Dell tired swiftly. Stan was better. But not better than you, Julie. You're alive. I assume he's dead?"

Julie moved her head another two inches. Sara drew a slow circle in the moist sand, a tightening spiral. Tight inside as well as out. Julie had to work to draw in another breath, to get the one inside her lungs out.

"Yes," Julie said. "Why did Stan attack me?"

"Brain damage."

"I don't understand?"

"It does strange things to people," Sara said.

"How did he become brain damaged?"

"It doesn't matter."

"You know. Tell me."

"The same way Susan Darly and the others became that way."

Julie felt herself become more still, even as she turned her head to follow Sara, to stare into the woman's dark eyes, to see the black points of the reflected moon that held her transfixed. A numbing inertia came over her as her breathing stopped between an inhalation and an exhalation. Yet she did not feel as if she were smothering, not yet, more as if she were preparing her body for something it had never experienced before. She knew something unnatural was happening to her, but she didn't know how to stop it. It was hard to speak.

"You were there when Jerry's girlfriend almost drowned," Julie whispered.

"Yes. But she did drown. Do you know what it's like to drown, Julie?"

"No."

Sara stopped an arm's length away. She reached out and placed her right hand on Julie's left shoulder. Her touch was warm.

"It's not the worst thing," Sara said softly. "There are worse things."

Julie coughed again. It was the only way to shake life into her body, and the effect didn't last long. But the stir brought a wave of fear and a stab of recognition. A small hole was poked through the invisible net that had landed over her with Sara's initial piercing stare. This was not a normal situation. Sara was not a normal woman. She spoke about death and drowning as if they were tea and milk. Julie blinked and the twin moons in Sara's eyes were momentarily eclipsed. Julie didn't know what was happening, only that she had to get away from this creature. Yet when she tried to move, she couldn't. Sara's warm touch was very strong. Julie felt as if she were an unwilling post planted in the sand before an advancing surf. She realized Sara was not talking about drowning simply to make conversation.

"Who are you?" Julie gasped.

"I don't know," Sara said. "I have never been able to figure it out. All I know is I'm not human, and that terrible things happen to humans when they are alone with me." She leaned close as if to kiss her. Julie felt Sara's breath on her cheek, a faint gust from an endless field of white ice. "We're alone, Julie Moore," Sara whispered in her ear.

In that last instant a million years of self-preservation took over and Julie turned to bolt. But Sara Morray had been conditioned in the void, where a million years was nothing but a moment to forget. Julie got nowhere, and then Sara's hands were around her neck, over her mouth, and dragging her toward the water. Julie fought with every particle of strength in her but she could have been fighting a robot of steel. The water splashed around them. Julie thought of her shoes she had not removed. She thought of Peter she had loved only once. She thought of Claire who had died twice.

"There is, ultimately, no reason to be afraid. No matter what walks in this world, beyond it is the light of God. We will all go back to that one day."

Julie was afraid. She didn't want to go back today. She wept at what was happening to her. It was not fair! She was so young! It was not rational! This woman was a fucking monster! Sara's hand momentarily slipped from her mouth.

"Help!" Julie screamed as loud as she could.

The clamp was quickly replaced. Her cry died on the ocean surface as the water beneath her grew deeper. But it wasn't in the plan of the thing that held her to go deeper than two to three feet. Sara fixed her right hand on the back of Julie's neck and forced Julie's head under. Julie managed to suck in one last breath. But a last breath was flawed by nature. Eventually it ran out. The salt water stung Julie's eyes, the cold wounded her. Where was Claire? Where was the bright light? Julie felt her heart pound, her lungs burn. Her continuing struggle only fueled the fire of oxygen deprivation. Her pounding heart began to shriek, her chest to convulse as red lava poured into her mouth out of the cold water she would not let herself inhale. But like the fight-or-flight reflex, one last inhalation, even in the face of no air, was part of human conditioning. The inhuman beast that held her knew that, waited for that. Julie felt herself slipping down into a black hole from which no divine light could ever emerge. It was true, Sara knew the truth. There were worse things than drowning.

Julie opened her mouth and sucked in two lungfuls of salt water.

The pain of the terror. The psychological horror of the physical agony. Julie gagged upon her gags and still she was held under. Her heart threatened to rupture. The water hit the furnace in her chest, and it was like an explosion of steam. In her worst nightmares, Julie could not have imagined a torture so great. And because it transcended her imagination, it began to put her out. To kill her, yes, finally, from suddenly far away, she could feel herself begin to die. Where was the tunnel? Where was the grave? She would have accepted either gladly. Only that it should stop and be over with.

It was then Sara pulled her head up from the water.

Julie did not open her eyes, could not. Her lungs gave a shuddering gasp.

She heard a pleasant voice.

"That was the easy part," Sara said.

Julie felt the woman kiss her. The warm lips. The cold breath. Colder than a dead sun that had exploded in fury eons ago. Colder than the burned creatures it had left behind to freeze on ashen worlds. The space beyond the stars was vast. This breath said there was nothing there except death. Still, the breath contained within it a perverse doom that never perished. As it entered into Julie Moore, she felt herself topple into that abyss and die, even as she came to realize the truth of Sara Morray's last words.

She died but the pain kept getting worse.

THIRTY-FIVE

❖

THE COLD ONE noticed, as It walked up from the beach toward the house where It stayed, that Dr. Lawrence Morray was home. It could tell by the car parked out front because under normal circumstances the doctor put his car in the garage in the evening. The Cold One wondered if the doctor intended to go back out. Of course, the Cold One didn't mind being left alone, any more than It would have minded if the doctor stayed out all night and ended up dead in a car accident. It felt no more for the human It shared a house with than It did for the many humans It had killed—so It believed.

Between the house and the Cold One stood a tall, dark man in ill-fitting blue jeans and a light-gray sweatshirt. The man wore no shoes, but carried a wooden stick in his left hand. His long black hair was plaited in thick braids. He faced the Cold One as It approached. From the manner in which the man held his head and body, the Cold One thought the man was blind and wondered who he might be. He appeared to be waiting for It.

Farther down the road, a quarter of a mile away, was another man. He was from India—it was obvious—and he was anxiously watching the blind man—and It. The Cold One wondered if these two knew about It, and whether It would be killing them tonight. The thought did not disturb It. Even though the blind human was obviously physically strong, It knew It could destroy him with one hand.

The Cold One stopped in front of the man.

"Hello," It said. "Can I help you, sir?"

The man nodded. There was no question of his being blind now, even though he seemed to fix his eyes on the Cold One's face. It had never met a human who stood with such calm assurance.

"Are you waiting for someone?" the Cold One asked.

The man nodded.

"Who are you waiting for?"

"Friend."

His voice was soft, little more than a whisper. The emotion in it was difficult for the Cold One to define. Perhaps because there was none. The Cold One could not be sure if the man was telling the truth or not. But It had an idea.

"Are you waiting for Julie Moore?" It asked.

The man nodded.

"Are you by any chance Professor Adams? Her teacher?"

The man nodded. "I am teacher."

The man did not look like a college professor, the Cold One thought, but Julie had mentioned that the man was eccentric. The Cold One continued to have trouble analyzing the qualities in the man's voice. He clearly possessed a serene disposition, and peace was reflected in his speech. But there was something about his responses that made the Cold One believe he was not telling It the whole truth. Yet, at the same time, It detected no deceit in the words.

"I have been wanting to talk to you, Professor. My name is—"

"I know you," the man interrupted.

"Julie told you about me?"

"Yes."

"Good. She told me about you. I wanted to discuss an experience of mine with you, if that would be all right. Maybe we could go into my house and talk. It's right there. I'm sure Julie will be along soon. She told me she was coming over. Did she tell you to meet her here?"

"Yes."

The Cold One offered Its hand, actually touched the man's fingers. "Here, let me help you into my house. It's not far."

The man did not react to the touch. "No."

"You don't want to go inside?"

"No."

The Cold One withdrew Its hand. "All right. Fine. We can talk out here if you'd rather. It's such a lovely evening. Would you like to hear what I have to say?"

"I know you," the man repeated.

The Cold One paused, still trying to get a handle on what the human really meant since humans seldom accurately expressed what they wanted. The Cold One decided to exert Its *will* over the man's, something It was able to do without knowing exactly how. Usually focusing Its attention, narrowing Its gaze onto a human's face, was enough to force him to obey Its wishes. It had used this ability on Julie Moore only a few minutes earlier, although It had tried and failed to use the ability on Peter Jacobs. But that was to be expected.

"I want you to tell me what you know," the Cold One said softly. As It did so It fixed Its mind and vision fully on the man's unblinking eyes. It felt the movement of Its power through the air, a magnetic field that It perceived as shadow, from It to the man. Usually when It did this, the human winced or even collapsed. Yet the man continued to stand at ease. The Cold One perceived that Its magnetic field dissipated even before It reached the man. An interesting phenomenon, It thought. The man remained silent. The Cold One didn't know what to do next.

"Who are you?" It repeated.

"Tell me story."

"What story? My story? Why should I?"

"I explain. I know you."

"What will you explain? Me?"

The man gazed at It with his dark eyes. "Tell."

The Cold One felt something curious then, a compulsion to talk, to respond to the order. The sensation—it was physical as well as mental—was unlike anything It had ever experienced before. It was almost as if the human who stood before It was not a human at all, but like It, and had just used his will on It. Yet that was only an approximation of truth. The Cold One could sense that the man was not *cold* as It was cold. He was like something that had no temperature, no love but no destructive purpose either. It was as if the man did not exist, even though he possessed a body. The Cold One decided it might be interesting to hear what he had to say. It therefore made no effort to override the compulsion.

"When I was born into this body there were thoughts in my mind. They were not my thoughts. They belonged to someone else. There were feelings as well, images and memories. All these things were inside from the first day, from the first breath this body drew in. They were a part of me yet also apart from me. I never had the feelings of the Voice—that is the name I gave to this thing. The Voice, the thoughts, would come and go. I would watch them speak in my mind, and sometimes I would speak them out loud. But they were words written for me on a screen. I felt no attachment to the Voice, to anything, but physically I acted out the life that the Voice conceived. I painted; I came to live by the water; I married the doctor. I did all these things until the Voice stopped. Then I had nothing inside but a sense of what I had to do. I understood that I was not human. I understood that my nature was not compatible with humans. Therefore, I set out to destroy humanity. The task has occupied most of my time since the Voice stopped. I have run into a few difficulties but they will soon be resolved. But I don't care if they are or not. I feel nothing." The Cold One paused. "Am I nothing? Is there nothing? Explain this to me if you can."

"You are mother's child. Child's mother."

"I don't understand. Explain further."

The blind man bade It to come close. "Must whisper. Soft voice."

The Cold One was not concerned about being harmed by the man. It moved close as he suggested and allowed him to whisper in Its ear. The Cold One heard words then, but faintly, as if they came to It from far off. They were like the Voice. It doubted that the man even spoke the words aloud. He had little mastery of English.

Still, the Cold One listened closely.

"There is life, there is death. They are not opposites. They are complementary. One gives rise to the other. Without one, the other does not exist. There are no opposites. Opposites are illusions. No hero without villain. No health without disease. No savior without devil. No day without night. The last breath contains within it the first breath. The first holds the seed of the last. They are the same. It is a matter of expression. The first act of life is inhalation. The baby cries and everyone laughs. The final act of life is exhalation. A man closes his eyes and everyone cries. People often cry. Did the Voice cry in the beginning? In the end?"

"Yes," the Cold One said aloud.

"The breath belongs to the body. It resides inside the body, not outside the body. The breath is more than the air. The breath is close to prana. No prana without breath. But prana is more subtle than the breath. No life without prana. Prana and breath flow in rhythm, but they are also separate. Prana is a gift. Life is a gift. A gift can be given, a gift can be taken away. Your nature is to take, never to give. But the *nature can change. No gift is ever the same. No theft is ever forgotten. When you forget your nature, the thief will run. But in the hidden half the gift will remain to be given for a short time. Do you understand?"*

"No," the Cold One said aloud. "Explain further."

"All of life is there at the moment of death. It is seen; it is felt; it is understood. It happens. The mother has intercourse. Sometimes the seed travels fast. Sometimes slow. There is a fight. The mother dies at the moment of conception. The child is given life inside the dead mother. All that was seen by the mother, all that was felt, all that was understood — it is impressed on the child's psyche. The child becomes the mother. The mother becomes the Voice. But no living prana inside the mother's body at the instant of conception. No living breath to aid the undeveloped child. Breath is given from outside by the father, but it is forced inside and has no prana. Dead breath, dead baby. Replay of living Voice. A life without laughter. A death without tears. A night without day. No opposites to make complementary. Nothing there but you, Sara Morray, daughter of Sandra Morray — Cold Ruth. You are your mother, but your daughter is dead."

The blind man pulled his head back and stared down at her. He was very tall.

"Understand?" he said.

The Cold One did, finally. No wonder It had married Its father. Who else could It have married? "What about the brother?" It asked.

"Conceived a minute before the mother died," the man said. "Cool."

The Cold One nodded. "He is as I thought." It studied the man. "You're not Professor Adams. How do you know these things that no one knows?"

"I know that I do not know."

"What kind of answer is that?"

"I do not know."

The Cold One glanced around. Except for the Indian man down the street, the block was deserted. It could kill both of them and put the bodies in the backyard and take care of them later. The Indian man would run, of course, when he saw what happened to the blind man. But he would not get far. The Cold One began to circle the blind man. He did not turn as It moved.

"You know what I am," the Cold One said. "You must know what I can do."

The man nodded. "Control prana. Control all."

"You know too much. I have to kill you."

The man was unmoved. "Why you explain?"

The Cold One stood behind him. It started to put Its hands on the back of his neck, but paused. "I explain nothing to no one. I feel nothing when I kill. It's the way I am."

"Yes."

The Cold One swung around to stand in front of him. The calm had not left his face. "Why are you not afraid like the other humans?" It asked.

"I do not know."

"I will kill you if you don't answer my question."

The blind man remained unmoved. "Kill me."

The Cold One started to kill him. This time It felt no compulsion thwart Its will. No shadow of magnetism. No hesitation even. Yet It did nothing to him. It did not understand what was stopping It. Perhaps the Indian man down the street who followed this unusual man could explain. It moved to him. The blind man reached out and grabbed Its arm. His reflexes were not unusually fast and he did not hold the Cold One tightly. In fact, his touch was gentle.

"No," he said.

"No what?"

The blind man let It go. "No touch him."

The Cold One felt a stab of something. It didn't know what it was. Nothing physical. The object seemed to be composed of mental matter, the product of a mental state. Quickly It reviewed the experiences of the Voice. The mother had felt something akin to this when she had been told to have an abortion by the doctor. The Cold One understood. This was an emotion. It was anger. It had never been angry before.

"No one tells me what to do," the Cold One said.

"I tell you." The man lifted his staff and pointed in the direction of Its house. "I tell father. He waits."

The emotion continued to exist inside the Cold One. It did not know how to act on the emotion so It did nothing. "He's not my father," It said. "He's my husband."

The blind man found the remark amusing. A faint smile touched his lips before he nodded and turned away. He walked in the direction of the beach. The Cold One did not go after him, or even after the other man who continued to wait at the end of the block. It wanted to know why Dr. Lawrence Morray was waiting. The father.

The Cold One went inside Its house.

Morray sat on the living room couch staring at two bottles on the coffee table. One was a bottle of Scotch whiskey; the other a large medical beaker. The whiskey bottle was half empty, or half full. A complementary state, the Cold One thought. The medical beaker was mostly full. A three-month-old aborted fetus flopped around in the fluid inside it. The fetus was alive in the sense that the Cold One was alive. The Cold One understood. The fetus was from Its miscarriage. But naturally the fetus had been doomed from the instant of conception because the living sperm was incompatible with Its dead eggs. Also, Sandra had had an abortion at the same age It had had a miscarriage.

"You are your mother, but your daughter is dead."

The pattern could not be changed.

Not for thirty years, the years of the mother.

The father had been drinking. The odor filled the air.

"Hello," the Cold One said. "How was your day?"

Dr. Morray glanced at It. He was drunk, clearly, but there was horror in his eyes as well as intoxication. He looked, as humans were fond of saying, like he had just seen a ghost. His expression was bitter as he gestured to the swimming fetus.

"Don't you have a question about this?" he asked.

"No."

"It's still alive, dammit! I've experimented on it for years and it refuses to die!"

"No." The Cold One sat on the couch beside him. "It's not the way you think."

Dr. Morray lowered his head and reached for the whiskey bottle. "You don't know what I think. You know nothing about me."

The Cold One studied him. He had never acted this way with It before. The blind man must have gotten to him. The man had said as much. The Cold One reached over to touch the doctor. He jumped and brushed Its hand aside.

"Ah," the Cold One said. "What do you know about me?"

The doctor took a slug from the bottle, then stared at the brown liquid as it slowly settled. The fetus moved like a tadpole. The doctor stared through the whiskey at the unborn child.

"Sara, Sara," he mumbled, as if trying to make the sound something it was not. "My Sara."

"Yes?"

He whipped his head around. "Where did you come from? You never really told me."

"You never really asked."

Dr. Morray flashed a sick smile. "Yeah, that's right, *Sara*. Because I didn't want to know. Because if I did know who I was sleeping next to I would go stark raving mad. Am I right?"

The Cold One considered. It could reveal what It wished. If It felt threatened, then It could always kill the doctor. It would have to find the blind man later and destroy him as well, after it understood why It had not destroyed him already. The Cold One nodded.

"Perhaps you would have gone mad," It said.

Dr. Morray's sick smile retreated deeper into his face. His expression was a painful wound from an old disease. He had known but not really known until now, the Cold One realized. Still, he couldn't face the truth.

"Who are you?" he asked.

"You know. You have always known."

"Answer me!"

The Cold One shrugged. "One name is the same to me as another. Humans call me Ruth or Leslie or Sara." It added quietly, "I remember being called Sandy."

Dr. Morray coughed. Or did he gag? He had never choked around It before. It had never placed Its black breath inside him before, and he had never reacted to Its day-to-day breath, not as Clyde Randolph and the others had. Dr. Morray's face was white.

"Who called you that?" he whispered.

"You. David. Esther."

Dr. Morray closed his eyes and sucked in a breath. The veins on his skull bulged through the skin. For a moment he froze in place. Then suddenly he lifted the bottle he held and broke it on the corner of the table. A shard of glass flew off and struck the Cold One next to Its eye. It blinked it away. The beaker toppled to the floor and the lid popped off. The bloody fetus rolled out, squirming on the white carpet. Dr. Morray stared down at it.

"I was going to name him after David," he said miserably.

"The first time or the second time?" It was curious.

He paled beyond white. "The first time or the—" He could not finish repeating Its remark. His mind was trapped in a past moment. "What do you mean *humans*?"

"You know, Dr. Larry." It was curious why It had the sudden

urge to taunt him. Sandra, It knew from the tape of the Voice, had called him that nickname. It was curious why It had urges at all. Another emotion, to add to the anger. The anger had yet to leave It. In fact, watching Dr. Morray, It found Its anger increasing. Dr. Larry—the man who had stood and watched the mother floating facedown in the sea water. It reached over and grabbed his right arm. "The answer was floating right in front of you," It said.

Dr. Morray tried to shake It off but was unable. Thwarted, he instead raised his right knee and brought down the heel of his shoe on the upper half of the flopping fetus. He ground it into the floor. Blood and tissue squirted over the carpet. The bottom half of the fetus, the legs that were little more than a tail, continued to kick. Morray let out a strangled grunt of revulsion and covered his eyes. For some reason that made the Cold One smile. It released the doctor.

"You never wanted to be a father," It said. "Did you, Dad?"

The comment struck deep. Dr. Morray leapt to his feet off the couch and moved away from It and the crushed fetus. He stared down at It as if It were an alien crawling out of the womb of the sofa fabric. He was now completely sober. His eyes were as wide as they could be and still be in their sockets.

"*What* are you?" he swore.

The Cold One slowly stood. "I now know where I came from. The blind man explained the process to me. What did he tell you?"

He shook his head in rigid centimeters. "Nothing."

The Cold One took a step toward him. Now, as It placed Its bare foot on top of the fetus and crushed the lower portion, It remembered the crab on the beach in Baja. The creature that had bitten Its toe. The broken beaker glass cut into the bottom of Its foot and It felt blood flow. It remembered many things, especially about the doctor.

"He told you something," the Cold One said. "You will tell me."

Dr. Morray backed up a step. "No."

"You will tell me or I will take you into the backyard." The Cold One took another step forward. "I will throw you in the pool. I will watch you try to swim. I will see if you drown." It added, "Dr. Larry."

This time the nickname failed to demoralize him. He straightened, his fear diminishing. His normal state of control returned. The Cold One understood. He never tolerated ridicule. Even in the face of death, it annoyed him. There were some emotions stronger than the fear of termination, It realized.

"He told me about a boy who drowned in a cold lake," he said. "But he was not talking about me."

The Cold One paused. "Who was he talking about?"

"You."

"I cannot be drowned. I do not need to breathe."

Dr. Morray nodded. He spoke his next words as if stating a scientific fact. "Then you are not human," he said. "I have answered your question, now answer mine. Tell me what you are."

The Cold One considered. It had taken to pausing before responding because It believed It was enjoying the confrontation and, of course, It had never enjoyed anything before and wanted to prolong the experience. A portion of the pleasure was related to the anger It felt, the fear It invoked. Yet there were other things happening inside It as well that It didn't fully understand. The blind man's explanation had affected It deeply, It realized. Somehow, It had always suspected that the truth would. That must be why It sought out the truth. The blind man had connected the memory of the Voice inside It with a real person, and thereby made the feelings personal. A revelation, humans called unique insights. The blind man had given It that. It had wasted Its time having oral sex with the preacher and ripping his ribs out. Yet It now contemplated doing the same to the doctor. It felt the act might heighten Its pleasure—for a few minutes.

On the other hand, even though emotions were present and they were interesting, It was still cold. The movie continued to play on the distant screen. It didn't care whether the doctor lived or died. All that mattered was that Peter Jacobs would return soon. Humanity would be exterminated. Such an end was inevitable, the presence of the blind man notwithstanding. He was but one, and soon the Cold One would be many.

"I don't know what I am," It said. "And now I don't suppose it matters, Dad."

He was ready to resist It. He had mastered his fear, at least for the moment. Yet once again the remark hit a nerve and he winced as if struck. "Why do you call me that?" he whispered.

The Cold One stepped within arm's reach and stuck out Its hands. But It did not strike him, It did not harm him in any way. It merely straightened the doctor's tie in the way It had done so for the past several years. It wasn't aware that the gesture was the same one the mother had used years before. Its simple act filled the doctor with disgust. The Cold One smiled again.

"What were you and Sandy going to call the baby if it was a girl?" It asked.

He swiped Its hand away. "We didn't discuss names!"

"You didn't give her a chance. But she always liked the name Sara. Her mother wanted to call her that. Did you know that?" The Cold One paused. How did *It* know that? The information was not sequenced in the memory of the Voice. Well, It thought, what did it matter? Nothing ever mattered and nothing ever would, even if It did feel a few emotions while It stood close to the father. He continued to stare at It with eyes not so different from Its own. They looked like a pair, the two of them. The Cold One smiled at the irony. But the doctor had had enough and shoved It away. Once more It stepped on the squirming fetus. Dr. Larry's voice came out strong and defiant.

"You're a *witch!* You'll be stopped—this has got to stop. I know what to do."

The Cold One threw Its head back and laughed. "What will you do, Larry?"

He pointed a finger at It. "You drowned once, Sandy. You will drown again."

He left the house, the Cold One let him leave. He posed no threat to Its plan, It thought, not in his unstable state. In the suddenly empty house, It felt Its emotions vanish as if they had been nothing but ripples on water. It took cleaning supplies from the closet in the kitchen, wiped up what was left of the fetus and put it down the garbage disposal. The thing wouldn't stop kicking. Best to have the mess out of the way. The Cold One didn't want to scare Peter Jacobs when he finally came home to It.

THIRTY-SIX

GOVINDA SHARMA DIDN'T know if he should try to kill Rak or if he should thank him. There was no standard emotion that he could allow himself to experience because what he had just gone through had no parallel in human history—not that he was aware of. Although, for all he knew, people had brought corpses back to life all the time five thousand years ago. Maybe it was how they spent their Saturday evenings, Rak and his followers. Govinda had no doubt now that the blind man had been alive when Krishna had walked the earth. He had no doubts about anything, Krishna or Shiva. The devil had showed him a miracle. A devilish marvel at that, but one that nevertheless gave him faith in God. Wasn't that the temptation of priests in the Middle Ages? Searching for the devil in people accused of witchcraft in the hope of proving to themselves there was a God in there as well? Govinda didn't know if he'd succumbed to sin when he took the dead child his dead wife had offered. He only knew that, finally, he understood what the Master had tried to tell him the first night they talked together.

"All who are born die. All who die are reborn. Don't grieve over the inevitable."

Govinda suspected the Master had sent him to follow Rak knowing Rak would show him something miraculous. The vision of Vani, glimpsed in shadow, in death, had filled Govinda with horror, and the memory of the meeting stayed with him even as he followed Rak down to the beach, down the hill from the home Rak returned to again and again. Yet his grief for his dead wife was gone. The heartache that had plagued him for the last six months had been replaced by an absence of sensation that was somehow a welcome relief. Perhaps, Govinda thought, he should thank Rak before he killed him.

But how could anyone destroy such a man?

When even Lord Krishna had been unable.

Govinda followed Rak to the beach. The crescent moon hung a short distance above the horizon, its silver light casting long shadows over the dark sand. Rak was perhaps a hundred yards in front of him, heading in the direction of a woman who was lying half in the water. A wave disturbed her clothed body and tossed it helplessly in the foam. Seeing her, Govinda felt sick at heart and wondered what could have happened to her. Rak knelt when he reached the woman. Govinda also halted, and watched, but his long days of watching and following had come to an end. When Rak leaned over and pressed his mouth to the woman's mouth, Govinda felt as if he could be a silent witness no longer. He let out a loud cry and raced in their direction. He didn't exactly know what Rak was doing—at the back of his mind he considered it possible that Rak was giving her mouth-to-mouth resuscitation—but anyone who woke dead people in the middle of the night could be trusted only so far. Rak raised his head a moment before Govinda crashed into him and sent the two of them sprawling in the foam.

"Shiva!" Govinda cried as he found his feet. He leapt up expecting to wrestle Rak and have his back quickly broken in two. But Rak only sat next to the poor woman, his head raised up to Govinda, the moon in his eyes. In that moment, even fraught with uncertainty, Govinda couldn't help but marvel at the beauty of Rak's eyes. A wave came and the woman's head gently rolled from side to side, her long blond hair at the mercy of the currents. She was now lying facedown; she must have been knocked over in the collision, Govinda thought. He moved to turn her onto her back, but Rak stuck out a hand for him to stay back. The woman was still breathing. Govinda could hear the action of her laboring lungs on the quiet beach. Yet it sounded like no set of inhalations and exhalations he had encountered before. She was fighting for breath, all right, but it was as if she struggled against an animal that had crawled inside her chest cavity. The noise frightened Govinda. It wasn't a sound a human should be able to make. Still, he had to help her.

"She's smothering," Govinda said.

"Yes."

"You have to let me save her!"

"No."

"Why not? Don't let her die."

"No."

"Get out of my way." Govinda strode forward. The splash of the salt water stung his eyes. Rak dropped his arm; he didn't try to stop him. Govinda rolled the woman onto her back. There was a break in the waves; he was able to clear her stringy hair from her face. Her strange breathing continued; it sounded as if she were sucking in mouthfuls of insects that exploded inside as they came into contact with the delicate membranes of her lungs. The weird sound didn't support his diagnosis, but he could only assume her lungs were filled with salt water. He tried to remember the technique of mouth-to-mouth resuscitation. First, he had to clear the air passage, then tilt the head back. Carefully, he forced her mouth open and peered inside, checking for obstructions. He didn't see anything but reached in her mouth with his index finger to be doubly sure. It was then she opened her eyes and stared up at him. Her eyes were not so beautiful as Rak's were. They were downright scary.

She closed her mouth hard and bit off the top of his finger.

"Jesus!" he cried as he jumped back. When he was afraid, Shiva was his asylum. But when he was hurt or outraged the Christian Jesus always sprang to his lips. The woman, blood dripping from the side of her mouth, sat up and glared at him. In the soft white light of the moon, she appeared to swallow his finger. Her right hand came up faster than he could see, bent into a claw, and reached out to grab him by the throat. But Rak had excellent reflexes of his own. Before Govinda could comprehend what was happening, Rak had placed his hand over her heart and settled her down. She closed her eyes and let out a sigh and lay back on the sand. Her wicked breathing continued, however, although it was more gentle now—the scraping of moss-covered stones against one another. Govinda glanced down at his hand and couldn't believe he was missing the top half of his right index finger. He had never suffered a serious injury in his life. He tried to calm his breathing. He couldn't allow himself to go into shock. He realized he should have listened to Rak. The blind man sat and stared in his direction, undisturbed.

"What's wrong with her?" Govinda asked.

Rak gestured to his chest. "Cold inside."

"She's like an animal."

"Yes."

"Can you help her?" Govinda could not stop staring at him, even to take care of his hand. Surprisingly, the finger was not painful, although he imagined it would be later.

"Yes."

"Then help her." Rak didn't move. Govinda gestured to the woman lying on her back, eyes closed. Another wave was coming; it could wash over her face. For the first time Govinda realized she was the woman Rak had spoken to in the car the other day. She was very attractive, even with his blood on her face. "Let's at least move her. She'll inhale water."

Rak shook his head as if it didn't matter. "Talk," he said.

Govinda moved close to his right side and knelt beside him. The remains of the wave came and soaked his pants. The water splashed the woman's face but did not submerge her mouth. Her long hair was once more dragged spokelike through the sand. But on the whole the tide appeared to be moving out. Soon, perhaps, it would leave them in peace. Rak's blind eyes appeared to be focused out over the ocean.

"I've been following you," Govinda said in Hindi. From his observations at the airport, he suspected that Rak spoke little English.

Rak nodded, his expression inscrutable. He was like something carved from stone, yet alive in a way few humans were. The moonlight glimmered on his skin as if it radiated from his pores. Yet his serenity was not like the Master's. Rak did not exude love or compassion. Indeed, he gave off no positive or negative aura, except perhaps one of profound mystery.

"Are you truly blind?" Govinda asked, continuing in the language of his birth.

"Yes," Rak answered in Hindi.

"Krishna blinded you?"

Rak blinked and lowered his head. "Yes."

"I was told he used Pasupata on you." Govinda added, "My Master told me."

"Master taught you secret of Sudarshan. You breathe in circular rhythms. Sudarshan is also Krishna's weapon. The flaming discus. The burning circle." Rak raised his head back up and touched his brow. "Eyes are gone."

Rak spoke of Krishna's weapon in the present tense. The discus was in fact called Sudarshan, Govinda remembered, the same name the Master had given to the kriya. He found the relationship interesting, as he did Rak's voice, so soft, simple really, devoid of strain or desire. There was not a hint of manipulation in it.

"My Master told me about Cira," Govinda said.

Rak momentarily closed his eyes. "Cira gone," he whispered. "Ma."

"She was gone before you were born."

Rak turned his head in his direction. "Never born. Never die."

"Who are you?"

"No you. No me." Rak shook his head. "No one."

"Why did you come out of the Himalayas?"

He nodded in the woman's direction. "Kali Ma."

"I don't understand. Are you saying this woman is an incarnation of Mother Kali?"

"Child inside. Kali Ma. Kalika."

Govinda took a moment to absorb what he was saying. The Vedas spoke of the sacred trine: Brahma the creator, Vishnu the maintainer, Shiva the destroyer. Lord Krishna was supposed to have been an incarnation of Vishnu. He took human form to preserve the creation. To destroy the wicked and protect the righteous, as he told Arjuna in the Bhagavad Gita. At the same time, the three aspects of Brahman or God were often mentioned in conjunction with their shaktis, or consorts. Kali was Shiva's wife. Kali was dark as Krishna, naked as space. It was she who gave Shiva the power to destroy the creation when the time of the dissolution approached. Kali was usually portrayed as living in the cremation grounds, sitting in meditation atop a funeral pyre. Kali was supposed to be wonderful beyond words, horrible beyond imagination. Her worshippers sometimes called her Kalika.

"Kali is inside this woman?" Govinda asked, stunned.

Rak nodded. "Now."

"Oh, God. But why? Why inside this woman?"

Once more Rak touched his hand to his chest. "Prana. Tamasic."

The prana was the subtle life energy in the breath. The three modes of nature, which corresponded loosely with the three manifestations of the supreme Brahman, were *sattva*, *rajas*, and *tamas*. Sattva was purity, alertness, goodness. Rajas was action, restlessness, bondage. Tamas was dullness, inertia, evil. Manifest, Kali was tamasic—if she could be called evil when she was in reality supposed to be beyond all pairs of opposites. Yet of all the manifestations of God that could come to earth, of all the avatars, Govinda could not imagine a form he would less like to meet than Kali. Even Shiva, it said in the Vedas, feared Kali.

The Master, just before Govinda had bade him good-bye, had touched upon the fact that a great avatar would soon come to earth. But the Master had indicated the incarnation would be wonderful. Rak appeared to be saying the opposite.

"Why is she coming to earth?" Govinda asked.

"To play." Rak paused and turned his head toward the woman. "Wait."

Govinda watched as Rak returned to what he had been doing when Govinda had interrupted him. Rak did not kiss the woman; he drew in a full breath and, putting his mouth to hers, exhaled deeply into her lungs, turning his head slightly to the side while she exhaled on her own, listening, it seemed, to what beat unseen inside her body. Rak did this seven times and when he was done the woman lay quietly. The repulsive sound ceased inside her chest and her face was at peace. It was as if, with his powerful breath, Rak had removed something unsavory from inside the woman. Govinda felt the air lighten. Rak stood suddenly, his wooden staff in hand, and Govinda scampered to his feet.

"Go now," Rak said in Hindi. He turned away.

"Wait!" Govinda cried. He hurried in front of Rak; it seemed the only way to stop the blind man. "What am I supposed to do now?" he asked.

Rak stopped. "Kali wears garland of severed arms. Symbolic. No doership. Do nothing. Kalika comes."

There were tears on Govinda's face. He was just a human being, he thought. He had hopes and fears; he could not grasp such cosmic matters in such a short time. Nor could he simply return to his day-to-day life with the knowledge of their existence. He feared Rak as much as he would have feared Kali herself, but he feared more that Rak should simply abandon him, as he had Cira.

"But I have to do something," Govinda pleaded. "I've followed you halfway around the world and I still don't understand. Pandu, my friend, is dead. Did you kill him? Vani, my wife, was dead. Did you bring her back to life? Why did you do these things?"

Rak stared at him one last time, and as he did so, the moon, which shone with clear reflection in his lustrous eyes, began to set beneath the curve of the dark ocean. A faint smile touched Rak's lips then, but it may have only been an illusion of the failing light. Govinda was never to know for sure.

"There is no why," Rak said.

Then he turned and walked away. Govinda did not have the energy to stop him a second time. It seemed Rak had stolen his last drop of strength. Of course, where there was no doership, there was no need to struggle. Behind him, Govinda heard the woman stir. As he turned, she opened her eyes and looked up at him. Once more he thought how attractive she looked, not unlike Vani when she would awaken from a deep sleep in the middle of the night. During her pregnancy, Vani had often had bad dreams, as this woman seemed to be having this evening. Govinda was surprised at his reaction to her. She had, after all, just bitten off his finger. It was probably still in her stomach. Yet he could not blame her for what had happened; the black cloud that had surrounded her was gone. Rak had blown it away. Clearly, the darkness had been something thrust upon the woman from the outside and was not a part of her nature. Govinda withdrew the handkerchief from his pocket and wrapped his wounded finger. The pain had arrived full force.

"Is she gone?" the woman asked.

Govinda knelt by her side. He would take her to the hospital, he knew. He would care for her, whether because of the child she carried or despite it. He took her hand in his uninjured hand. He would never tell her how he had been wounded. He could see already from her innocent expression that she did not know. Yet she was so cold to touch.

"Who?" he asked gently.

She trembled; pain pinched her face. But she was growing stronger with each passing second. "The evil woman," she whispered. "*Kali Ma. Kalika.*"

"Yes. She's gone." Govinda paused. He had no idea what had been done to this woman, and frankly, after all he'd been through, he did not want to know. Nevertheless, he stroked the woman's brow. He had a feeling that in the days to come he would be spending a lot of time with her. He wondered what her name was and, especially, who the father of her child was. "Don't worry," he said. "She won't be coming back."

THIRTY-SEVEN

❀

U NITED AIRLINES DID not have a nonstop flight from Cedar Rapids to Los Angeles. The route went through Denver, one of the airline's hubs, and it was there that Peter got stranded for three hours because of mechanical difficulties. He passed the time reading a *People* magazine and trying not to think, mutually inclusive activities to be sure. His emotions were mixed. The previous night, when Dr. Samuel had finished his story of the bad-luck Morrays, Peter had been anxious to fly home and confront Sara, but the last plane to the West Coast had long gone. He'd had to wait for the following morning. Now he was still anxious to see her, but the thought of the meeting filled him with dread. He realized, for the first time, that part of the reason Sara so intrigued him was because she scared him. That she had from the initial hello. Fear was supposed to be the most potent aphrodisiac of all. As long as it was kept at arm's distance, he thought cynically. There was nothing sexy about having a vacuum cleaner welded to one's lips. He would just have to keep his hands off her, certainly her mouth off his.

Yet he had never had trouble breathing around her.

"What happened to the boy?"

"I don't know. I was hoping you could tell me."

A vain hope. Peter had told Dr. Samuel nothing of what he had uncovered. The doctor had kicked him out of his home. Peter hadn't cared one bit. As if he had anything to say that the man would have believed. Also, he couldn't have told him about the boy if he'd wanted to.

Not a thing.

Peter didn't know why he couldn't stop thinking about Lisa Cantrell, his last girlfriend. Her miscarriage, her haunted stare in the car as she sat in the puddle of her own blood. The silent accusation: *What did you put in me?* It had been so unfair, the way she had left him. He hadn't done anything to her. Not that he knew of. Why couldn't he stop thinking about her? Was the magazine failing to perform its mind-numbing job? Was he holding an exceptional issue? Or was he holding on to the last thread of a crumbling illusion? The real-life fantasy of Peter Jacobs. Cool handsome successful *Los Angeles Times* reporter. Lover of beautiful women, caretaker of the less fortunate. Master sleuth.

So cool, under pressure. Like Sara Morray.

Fifteen minutes before his flight was scheduled to depart, Peter found a phone and dialed Lisa Cantrell. It was nine in the morning in Denver, only eight in Los Angeles. By chance he remembered her number, which he found out right after she had left him. He hoped he woke her; her voice always sounded so nice in the morning.

She answered on the first ring. Didn't sound sleepy.

"Hello?"

"Hi, Lisa, this is Peter Jacobs. Remember me?"

Long pause. Plenty of memory in the silence. Quite a few regrets, on both ends of the line. "How are you, Peter?" she asked finally.

"Fine. How are you?"

"Good." She took a breath. "This is unexpected. Why are you calling?"

"No reason. Just wanted to say hi. See how you were doing."

"I'm fine. How did you get my number?"

Ed Foley had got it for him. "I can't remember. Look, I didn't call to bother you. I was thinking of you and I had your number. How are you really?"

"OK. One of my patients is suing me for malpractice and it looks as if I'm about to lose the lease on my office. Other than that I can't complain. How's Matt?"

"Oh, you know Matt. He's a happy camper. He just hasn't realized he's not in the woods. He mentions you every now and then."

"Tell him I said hi."

"I will."

"You sound like you're in an airport."

"Yeah, I am. I have a flight leaving in a few minutes. I'm researching a big story. I don't have a lot of time to talk. But I did want to ask you something." He paused. "If that would be all right, Lisa?"

She hesitated. "Is it about us? If it is, maybe you shouldn't ask."

"It's not a big deal. It's just something that's confused me for a while. It will only take a moment of your time to clear up my confusion."

"Peter, please."

"Why did you get so spooked when you had that miscarriage?"

Dead silence. But she didn't hang up. That was something, at least. Her voice came out weak and wary. "Why do you want to know?" she asked. She didn't deny the fear.

"Because I have a right to know. You were my girlfriend. We lived together. We were happy together. Then you had a miscarriage and left without saying good-bye. Tell me what really happened that night, Lisa. You were scared. Why were you scared?"

"It's natural to be scared when you're having a miscarriage. Ask any woman."

"Yes. But you weren't just scared of losing the baby. You were scared of *me*. You kept looking at me as if you'd just found out that I had leprosy. What did you *feel* that night?"

"Peter."

"Tell me, dammit!"

"Scared! What else can I tell you?"

"But why? Why of me?"

Another long pause. Static on the line. "Because it was *cold*."

Peter stopped. He spoke softly. "What do you mean?"

Lisa wept. "What was inside me. What came out of me. It was cold." She drew a shuddering breath. "That's why I ran away. I was afraid if I stayed with you, it would come back."

"What would come back? You're not making any sense."

"Whatever the thing was, Peter. It wasn't natural. There's no explaining it. But even before that night, I knew there was something different about you. You're not a normal guy."

"Sure I am."

"No, you're not. There's only one Peter Jacobs. You're not made of the same stuff as other people. You're like something that was constructed in a crystal cave on another planet. I'm sorry if that makes no sense, but that's the truth of it. Now I've answered your questions, and I've got to go. Best of luck, Peter. I cared about you, I really did. But please don't call me again."

Lisa Cantrell hung up. Peter stared at the phone in his hand.

"Thank you for sharing that with me," he muttered.

He dialed Sara Morray's number. He didn't give a shit who answered.

"Hello?" Soft voice. Sweet with drowsiness. His Sara.

"Hi, this is Peter Jacobs. How are you?"

"Very well. How are you, Peter?"

"Splendid. Can I see you today?"

She sounded pleased. "Yes. When would you like to see me?"

"In three hours."

"At my house? My husband will be out."

"Your house is OK with me if it's OK with you."

"It is. I'll be waiting for you, Peter."

Dr. Lawrence Morray drove Interstate 80 out of Chicago across the state of Illinois toward Iowa. He'd taken an early-morning flight out of Los Angeles and had arrived in Chicago at eleven in the morning. He'd spent the previous night pacing LAX waiting impatiently for his flight into the past. He knew where his old friend David had stashed Sandra, and he knew that she was still alive. He would have been notified if she'd died. The Kabriel Clinic knew who her real guardian was, though they were only too happy to take David's money. There were many things Dr. Morray knew that David had tried to keep from him. Like the cesarean Sandra had had nine months after she slipped into her coma. Like the boy and girl she'd delivered. Dr. Morray knew he was a father twice over, even though he had no idea what had become of the children once they'd been turned over to the adoption agency—until yesterday evening.

"I remember being called Sandy."

"Who called you that?"

"You. David. Esther."

His wife had said these things to him. Thirty-year-old Sara Morray, who had never met Sandra Morray. Dear Sara, who in fact had never spoken to a single person who had known his first wife. Sara had talked as if she knew his wife intimately. Worse, much worse, she had acted as if she were Sandra.

"You know, Dr. Larry. The answer was floating right in front of you."

But "much worse" was not as bad as truly awful.

Sara had acted as if she were his daughter as well as his wife.

"You never wanted to be a father. Did you, Dad?"

And beyond truly awful there lurked horror. The kind humans imagined they experienced when they had a close brush with death but that usually showed up only when the real thing was at hand. Sinking all alone in a pit of quicksand. Bleeding in a barrio gutter from a deep knife wound. Smothering from a heart attack in a hospital emergency room. Why had he spent so many years researching near-death experiences? He hadn't been looking for the soul as the medical community thought. He'd just been trying to ascertain that there was no hell. Why had he stopped his research? A more significant question, with a shallower answer. Because he had begun to feel that the answer to his quest was a barren "no." But no hell, that was only a relief as long as you didn't realize that probably meant there was no heaven either. Which meant there was nothing left of Sandy. Nothing but a sack of decaying tissue pumped up and down ten thousand times a day by a plastic tube attached to an electric motor.

But people lost their loved ones every day. It was a cruel world.

Back to real horror.

Sara had touched upon such a creature with her other strange remarks.

"One name is the same to me as another. Humans call me Ruth or Leslie or Sara . . . I cannot be drowned. I do not need to breathe."

What did her comments mean? What did it mean that he had been unable to shake free of her grip, even though he had always assumed that he had twice her strength? What did it mean when she had sneaked up on him at that museum one day and had, with little more than a smile, fastened his mind onto a memory that he had striven to forget? She looked familiar, sure, he had known that from the start. A ghost from the past—he had tried not to think about that the day he proposed. He should have thought about it. But not just any ghost, not his new and improved Sara Morray, or Sandra Morray, or whatever the hell her name was. But one with a womb capable of producing imperishable fetal tissue.

But back to real horror.

She was an incestuous spirit.

"And now I don't suppose it matters, Dad."

And she knew what maybe only David and himself knew.

"You will tell me or I will take you into the backyard. I will throw you in the pool. I will watch you try to swim. I will see if you drown."

That he had struck her mother in the face before she had fallen in the water.

And told the whole world it had been an accident.

That is why her ghost had come back to haunt him. He knew.

He knew other things as well. The blind man had told him.

"You drowned once, Sandy. You will drown again."

As he entered the State of Iowa, he crossed into a thunderstorm. Raindrops as large as golfballs pelted his car. Lightning flashed on the black horizon, the dangerous kind of bolts that were capable of disabling power plants, not to mention light bulbs and electrical motors. He flipped on his wipers and glanced at the map Hertz Rent-A-Car had provided. He'd be there soon, he thought.

The whole world would know when he got there.

THIRTY-EIGHT

❀

THE DOOR WAS open. The house was silent. Peter rang the bell. No one answered. He stepped inside. He didn't call out. It wasn't in *her* script that he should be so obvious. It was a setup, he realized. Had been from Chuck's first call. Their meeting at the museum had not been accidental. Blank had said it all from the start:

"*I think he was smothered and didn't resist. None of these* non-bleeder cases *shows a single sign of struggle.*"

Her adopted brother had shown no signs until he went insane.

Peter stepped into her studio. The paintings were everywhere: warm oceans, cold stars. And only the one work that combined both themes—Sandra's view of the nighttime sky as seen through a coral reef. A daughter who had lived her mother's life. Married her own father. A daughter who had somehow split and perverted the whole that was her mother. A daughter who scared people.

Peter found Sara in the backyard in the Jacuzzi.

Naked, she floated on her back in the bubbling steam.

"Hello, Peter," she said, not opening her eyes.

"Hello, Ruth."

She smiled. "You've been researching me. That's a shame."

He crouched beside her. Her long dark hair played in the hot currents. Her full breasts played with his mind. Despite all that he knew, he still wanted to touch her. He was as sick as she was. That was what bothered him the most, that he knew that. But he kept his hands to himself.

"Why is that?" he asked.

She opened her eyes and seemed to let the bubbles turn her until she was sitting on the top step of the Jacuzzi, close to him. Her hand touched the tip of his right shoe. She stared up at him with her delicious smile, her hair now plastered over her naked back all the way to the top of her butt.

"Because it could have been fun for you," she said. "Now I'm afraid it'll be hard for you."

"What will be hard?"

Her hand moved to his calf. "For you to make love to me."

"I'm not going to make love to you."

She squeezed his leg gently. "Yes, Peter Jacobs. You will."

"Why would I want to make love to a witch like you?"

"I didn't say that you would want to. I said that you will."

Peter glanced down at the hand on his calf. She had tightened her grip some. "You told Chuck to call me," he said.

"Yes."

"You're the one behind the murders."

"Yes."

He had to take a breath. He had only suspected. He hadn't known. But now that he did know, she didn't look any less beautiful to him.

"How can you do these terrible things?" he whispered.

"It's the way I am."

"How did you find me?"

"I could sense you. Your special qualities. It was easy."

"What do you want with me?"

"I told you." She moved closer. He could feel the heat radiating from her skin, the coolness of her breath on his face. "Make love to me, Peter. Make it easy on yourself." Her grip went from a firm hold to something close to painful. He was not surprised. To accomplish what she had, she would have to have been very strong. He wondered if that meant he was going to be killed. She added, "I'm ovulating today."

"What?"

She caressed his cheek with her free hand. "Won't you?"

"They come to me automatically."

"Why is that?"

"Because I'm their mother. Won't you?"

"Won't I what?" he asked although he knew she hadn't changed the topic. He'd had the same thought in his nightmare. The girl on the boat on the dead lake. The cold fish—Chuck and however many other cronies he had. Sara was their mother. Her hand moved from his cheek to his zipper. She tugged on it; he let her for a moment or two—it felt kind of nice, her touch—then pushed her hand away. But her fingers moved right back. "Stop that," he said.

"Won't you?" she asked.

"No! Goddammit, you're my fucking sister!"

She nodded. "That's why it has to be you. Yours is the only seed that can survive inside me. Yours is the only seed that will make the perfect child." Her hand stroked his crotch, and he seemed unable or unwilling to stop her. "The perfect cold one."

His voice was soft, strained. "You seem pretty fucking cold yourself."

Again, she nodded. "But I had a living father. That is why I can't make others like myself. But you are like me. Our child will be able to do what it wishes."

Again he tried to shove her hand away, but as he did so she clasped his fingers in hers, gently this time. Her vicelike grip on his leg relaxed. She held her mouth up to be kissed, although her eyes never left his. Never blinked. He could feel her power then, trying to work its dark magic on him. His erection made him feel dirty. He drew his head back.

"I am not like you," he whispered.

"Yes. We are the same."

"No! I could never hurt anyone."

She regarded him with amusement, her mouth did, although her dark eyes never changed. "Really? Pain is relative to a human. When you played the part of a man, you did what you wished. That's what I do. That's the way I am."

"I don't understand."

"You will," she said.

Both her hands suddenly came up and grabbed the back of his skull. He was pulled face first into the bubbling water. Pain exploded in his head as every nerve in his brain registered the fact that the Jacuzzi was scorchingly hot. His legs flew over his head, and he toppled through a somersault. As he splashed down and before he could sit up again, she had shifted one of her hands to the top of his head. There she gripped his hair and forced his face down onto the blue-white cement floor of the Jacuzzi. He squeezed his eyes shut; the boiling water felt as if it were melting away his pupils. His mouth was closed as well, but how long was that last breath going to last him? He struggled against her grip but found it up there with Superman's. He was *not* like her. He could hold his breath a long time, but not until the pool cleaning people showed up.

Still, he fought her. The pain in his chest grew like a chain reaction in a plutonium reactor. His oxygen debt swelled like a molten coal inside his heart. Never had he realized how much he loved life. He knew that he fought her in vain, but he didn't want to give her the satisfaction that he was as dead as she was.

She held him down until his bursting lungs forced him to inhale chlorinated water.

Then she yanked him up, gasping.

He couldn't believe that her expression hadn't changed.

"Wouldn't you rather be having sex?" she asked.

He coughed. "Fuck you."

"Yes. Please, Peter."

He shook his head. "Witch."

She forced him back under. Another hard lesson in cooperation, or the lack thereof. What a fucked family, he thought. Darling daughter doing it with Daddy Larry and brother Peter. It was just as well he'd never been told about his real parents while growing up. He would have drowned himself in the bathtub when he was two. A part of him hoped she didn't pull him up again. He didn't know if he had the strength left to spit in her face.

But she did pull him back up, and this time she was not staring calmly into his wrecked face. Her eyes were turned toward the wide glass door that led from the house into the backyard. Seeing through a pink haze of scalded eye capillaries, Peter followed her gaze. Matt stood dumbfounded with a pink slip and a newspaper in his hands.

"Zeus!" he said. "Is she hurting you, Pete?"

Peter knew in a flash what had brought Matt to the Morray residence. When Peter had initially called Sara, he had jotted down her address on the back of one of Matt's new-customer slips. Because he had memorized the address immediately he had left the paper on the table. Sara had not just given him a street number, but directions as well, and it had been a habit of Peter's in the past to write down directions for Matt on the back of the slips so that he would have an easy time finding a new house. Matt must have noticed the slip that morning and thought that Sara Morray needed a paper. Never mind that her house was located ten miles off Matt's usual route.

"Matt," Peter said softly. "Run."

"Matt," Sara said sweetly. She released Peter and stood from the Jacuzzi. Naked, she strode toward Matt, who stared at her with a mixture of amazement and fear. Peter tried to stand but ended up collapsing back into the water. The pain in the center of his chest weighed on him like a black hole. He believed one or both of his lungs had collapsed. And he was supposed to have sex now? She sure didn't know shit about how to warm up a guy, even if the flesh on his face did feel like it was about to peel off and go down the drain. He could only watch as Sara reached out and took both Matt's paper and his hand and led him toward the Jacuzzi. She added, "Of course I'm not hurting your friend, Matt. Why would I want to hurt Peter?"

"I don't know," Matt said uneasily, staring down at him. "He sure looks hurt. Maybe we should call a doctor. Nine-one-one. Emergency operator."

Sara patted Matt on the back. "My husband's a doctor. He'll be home soon."

Matt's eyes momentarily left Peter to glance at Sara's chest. "You have nice titties," he said shyly.

Sara smiled. "You like them?"

Matt nodded. "More than Julie's."

Sara laughed. "Peter, what have you been teaching this boy?" Then she stopped laughing, as if she had simply thrown an inside switch on an expression control board. She put her arm around Matt's shoulder and stared down at Peter, her face cold. "I told you, it can be easy or it can be hard. Understand clearly how hard it can be."

Peter could not stop choking. "Run, Matt." He gasped. "Run."

Matt frowned. His eyes shot back and forth between them, finally settling on Sara. "I think you're wrong. I think Peter's hurt. He looks blue. I want to call nine-one-one." He turned. "I'll do it if you don't want to do it."

Sara grabbed his arm. "Do you know how to swim, Matt?"

Matt tried to shake free but was unable. "No," he said nervously.

"That's too bad," she said.

There was no mercy in her. Her right hand went to the back of Matt's neck, and it was a second before the two of them were in the Jacuzzi with Peter. She held Matt's head down firmly and was not bothered in the slightest by his violent kicks. Peter reached out and tried to stop her, but he was a crippled ant arguing with a boot. She shot out her free hand and clamped her fingers around his throat, not tight enough to smother him, but firmly enough to keep him in place. Peter felt as if he slapped a tree trunk as he whaled on her arm with his oxygen-starved hands. Matt's thrashing body heaved and shuddered but his head never rose above the water line.

"Stop it!" he cried.

"After we've made love," she said.

"You're killing him!"

"Yes."

"OK! OK! We can make love. Just stop."

She glanced at him. "Are you just saying that to make me think you're interested in me?"

"Yes! No! Stop it, damn you!"

She spoke conversationally. "I knew this preacher once. He was in love with me. At least that's what he said. But after the first time we had sex, he lost all interest. By the time I was done with him, I think he believed I was already dammed."

Matt's kicks faltered. His lower back convulsed up out of the water, before flopping down again into the melting pot. Matt continued to fight her grip but his strength was dwindling quickly. Peter realized Matt must not have had a deep breath in his lungs when she forced his head down. Only a couple of minutes had gone by since she had grabbed him and already it looked as if he were going to die.

"I have said yes," Peter pleaded. "What else can I tell you?"

"You know," she said, a bit puzzled, "I find myself enjoying this. Before yesterday I never enjoyed anything. I met this blind man outside my house. He gave me a lesson on life and death and the breath, in a few sentences. He said that the last breath contains the first breath within it. The first holds the seed of the last. They are the same. It is a matter of expression. The first act of life is inhalation. The baby cries and everyone laughs. The final act of life is exhalation. A man closes his eyes and everyone cries. What do you think about that, Peter?" She paused. "Are you about to cry?"

Peter lowered his head and wept. "Yes. Please let him go."

"The word *please* holds no special meaning for me."

Matt stopped struggling.

She removed her hand from Matt. "What have we here?" she asked the air.

The water in the Jacuzzi was turning red.

"Oh, sweet Jesus," Peter whispered.

Matt's face bobbed to the surface.

"I never met anyone like this blind man before," she said.

Blood poured from Matt's twisted mouth. His eyes lay open and staring.

"Perhaps someday you will meet him," she continued, turning her attention back to Peter. "Now, where were we? Oh, yes, I do things quickly. I do not explain myself. I act and then the action is done. I want your sperm. If you do not give it to me soon, I will take it by force. I have a packet of syringes in the house. I can remove your sperm from you when you're dead. I can rip off your testicles and artificially inseminate myself. I can save the seed I don't use in a special solution in the freezer. I have planned this all out. I can attempt to inseminate myself for many months to come, until I am successful. I can even rip off your testicles while you're still alive." She leaned close. "So how is it to be, Peter Jacobs?"

He couldn't stop staring at Matt. His good boy. This thing that sat beside him was a liar as well as evil. Peter Jacobs may not have led the most noble life, but he had always cared for his children.

"What will our child do to the world?" he asked.

"Eventually it will destroy all living beings on earth," she said.

Peter chuckled bitterly. "He sounds dysfunctional."

"It could turn out to be a she."

"Somehow that wouldn't surprise me one bit." He looked at her. She didn't seem beautiful anymore. He didn't know what he had ever seen in her. "I'm afraid, Ruth, I'm just not in the mood this afternoon. You're going to have to do it the hard way. And maybe it won't work. Maybe, you'll go to your grave barren. I do hope that's soon, by the way. But a word of warning. I have powerful friends who will come looking for me."

She smiled. "No one who meets me ever sees me. No human power can ever match my own." She reached out her hand, her claw. "This is going to hurt, Peter."

Then the fates shuffled the deck. She stopped abruptly. Her hand fell into the water. Her head whirled in the direction of the house. "Larry," she whispered.

"What is it?" He was curious.

She stared at him as if stunned. She blinked twice.

"Our mother," she whispered.

* * *

His entrance was formal and polite. Dr. Lawrence Morray asked the nurse at the front desk of Kabriel Clinic if he could please see Sandra Morray, his wife. He presented identification and the woman checked her files and then he was led to the south wing of the facility, where ten beds and nine patients lined a single wall. Sandra was in the fourth bed. Patient 111. He tried not to look at her. The thing lying on the bed could not possibly match his memories. He understood too well what thirty years of coma could do to the human body. He was a doctor, after all. Had she married someone other than a doctor, he thought, he wouldn't have possessed the skill to keep her alive until she'd reached the hospital. She wouldn't be where she was now. Also, another man would not have struck her in the face when she refused to have an abortion.

"Could I please be alone with her for a few minutes?" he asked.

"Of course," the nurse said.

A physical therapist worked on a patient three beds away. Dr. Morray paid her no attention. Still avoiding his wife's face, he moved closer to the bed and removed the portable surgical kit from his back pocket. Even though he was a well-known cardiologist, he'd had trouble bringing the kit onto the plane. The airlines had made him check it as if it were a piece of baggage and pick it up at the other end, in Chicago. Maybe the haunted look in his eyes had worried them. Yet he did not feel haunted now, for perhaps the first time in the last thirty years. He felt his old self, the ambitious youth, very much in love with the incredible woman his best friend was dating. Tears sprang to his eyes. He couldn't remember when he had last cried. Had it been in Mexico?

Finally he did look. If only to say good-bye.

Dr. Morray did not see the pile of shriveled flesh and brittle bones that Peter Jacobs and Penny Hampton saw as Patient 111. His love for Sandra was always more than skin deep, and time had not erased the strength of his devotion to her. As his eyes settled on the bed, he was not repulsed or ashamed, but illumined. Why had he spent years interviewing people who had just come back from the dead? Why hadn't he flown to Iowa to sit beside Sandra and listen to what she could have told him? Honestly, for the first time since he had entered medicine, he felt as if he sat beside an angel. There was no accusation on her face. Somehow, before her brain had been destroyed, he knew that she had forgiven him for what he had done to her. He knew it in his heart.

Dr. Morray withdrew the scalpel from his surgical kit.

"That was his special skill, his secret knowledge. Others tried to imitate him but were never successful. They either almost drowned or else grew too fearful. As boys and girls do, they grew jealous of this young man. One day, while he held on to his longest pole and probed the lake's deepest floor, they yanked his pole away. They stole his air. They believed, of course, that he would hurry to the surface gasping for breath. But he never did and they never saw him again. They assumed he died. But it was they who died, in their time. He never did, even though he never took another breath. But what they did to him, it destroyed him in a sense. Never again was he to be part of the world. Always, for the rest of time, was he to wander in places far from humanity."

He owed a debt to that blind man, whoever he was. He believed the whole world did. He understood why the man had come to him the same day Carbone had died. Only on such a day could he have understood a lesson on immortality. He did not understand what Sara was up to, but he knew it could be no good. She had to be stopped. This was the way, what the blind man had said. But better to cut the air tube, he thought, than simply pull it away. That way the nurses on duty could not easily replace it, should they try to overpower him. He grabbed the tube in his left hand and pressed the tip of the scalpel blade onto the clear plastic. Beneath him, Sandra did not stir. But there was someone behind him.

"Hey," a woman said. "What are you doing?"

"Mind your own business," he said. He sliced into the tube; the forced air gushed out. But he had only nipped at the airway, he hadn't severed it. He raised his scalpel to finish the cut. It was then the woman grabbed him from behind.

"You mustn't do that!" she screamed. "Help! People! Help! There's a crazy man here with a knife!"

The woman was valiant, Dr. Morray thought, even if she was a pain in the ass. He had no trouble throwing her off. Unfortunately, her cries brought a herd of nurses. He thought quickly. Now chances were they'd be able to stop him and keep Sandra alive. Well, desperate solutions called for desperate acts. Even as he shoved the physical therapist aside, he reached out once more and pulled her back. He put the scalpel to her throat. She struggled for a moment, saw the silver blade, then went very still. She sounded as if she suffered from a medical condition herself, possibly asthma. He thought he could examine her afterward and be sure of the diagnosis, but then realized he was not going to be examining anyone for a long time to come. He was going to jail, as he should have done thirty years ago. But at least now his conscience would be clear and that *thing* living in his house in California would be dead.

Dr. Morray knew why Sara had said she didn't have to breathe.

He knew whose breath kept her alive.

"Stay back, all of you," he shouted. "Or I will cut this woman's throat."

The white-uniformed herd paused.

"This woman lying here is my wife," he said. "I'm going to finish cutting her air tube. I'm going to kill her, and even though she is already comatose, I will be responsible for her death. When I am done, and she is dead, I will release this woman that I hold, unharmed. Then you can call the police, I don't care. Do you understand?"

The nurses nodded. But not the physical therapist in his hands. Dr. Morray was surprised to see tears run over her cheeks. Because they were tears of sorrow, not of fear.

"If she dies, will I die?" she whispered.

"No," Dr. Morray reassured her. "You will be relieved, as I will be."

He reached out with his knife and severed the plastic tube. The end attached to the electric pump fell to the floor and sprayed the dust beneath the bed, stirring that which had been hidden away. His prisoner began to cough, to choke, as the monitors sounded their high-pitched alarms. Dr. Morray stroked the physical therapist's cheek with his free hand as he continued to hold the scalpel to her throat and stare down at his wife's lovely face.

"Don't worry," he said. "It'll soon be over."

"What is it?" Peter repeated.

Sara drew in a deep shuddering breath and sighed. She looked at Matt floating dead in the Jacuzzi, at Peter, and down at her own hands. She coughed weakly.

"I have only a few minutes," she whispered.

Something had changed. Something had *left*. Even with his

dead friend only a few feet away, the air had changed, as if a storm had come and gone. A storm that had torn at the heart as much as at the throat. Sara's eyes appeared dazed but there was a person behind them now. She blinked at Peter as if seeing him for the first time.

"I'm sorry," she said.

"What has happened?" Peter asked, staring at her, spellbound by the transformation. Outwardly, she looked the same, but it was as if he were seeing her for the first time as well. At least since they had come out of the womb together. She crossed her arms over her naked breasts and lowered her head.

"I'm dying," she said. "Larry has cut the cord. Cut off the air." She nodded to herself. "The blind man must have told him."

"Told him what? What blind man?"

"I don't know his name. He came, he said a few words to both of us. And now everything has been changed because of him."

"Are you saying Dr. Morray is with Sandra Morray?"

"Yes. He's with me." She strove to show him a real smile but her facial muscles were not used to such an expression. Plus she was obviously failing fast. She slumped forward in the hot water and he put out a hand to support her. His gesture seemed to touch her deeply. It saddened her and at the same time brought a smile to her lips. "Oh, Peter," she said softly.

"He's with me."

She spoke as if she was his mother, not his sister.

"Are you dying?" he asked.

"Yes."

He felt such pain. Why? Over a tormentor? He was not reacting as he should, but as he felt. He trusted his feelings. The change in her had been total. She still looked like Sara Morray, but she wasn't.

"But why?" he asked. "Just because she's dying?"

Sara put a hand to her head as if it hurt. "This body was never alive. Only the mother's body gave life to it. Now that the mother's body is going I have to go, too." She raised a limp arm and tried to pat his arm. "I knew her well, Peter. Better than you can imagine. She would have been proud of you."

The words blurted out of his mouth. "She would have been proud of you."

Sara shook her head sadly and gestured to Matt. "No. I cannot be proud. Look what I've done. How could I have done this?"

"But it wasn't you. It was what was inside you that did it." He paused; he had to say it. After all, she had been choking him to death a moment ago. "What was that thing? Where has it gone?"

She was thoughtful, but still sinking, growing weaker. "I don't know if there's a word for it. I don't know if there's a name for the place it came from. This body was conceived in a dead womb. It came out of a dead woman. But while that woman still breathed—was forced to breathe, I should say—that *thing* was able to walk in the world. Somehow it came into the world through that unnatural portal, through that hole between what had died and what was not allowed to die." She nodded. "I think it kept my body alive as much as my body kept it alive."

"*Your* body? Who are you, Sara? Who are you now?"

A tear rolled over her cheek. "Now that it's gone, I don't know. I'm a memory replayed over thirty empty years." She sniffed. "But I must tell you, there was much that was beautiful in Sandy's life. All that was missing was a little boy for her to play with. A little girl." She squeezed Peter's hand and shook her head. "You never had a sister, Peter. I'm sorry, really, I'm no one. That is the truth."

He did not want to believe her because he didn't believe he could suddenly care so strongly for someone who did not exist. But perhaps he had met a part of her already, under different circumstances, in the Kabriel Clinic in Iowa. His affection for her was not so mysterious if she was indeed so connected to his mother. He didn't understand everything she was saying, but at least now he felt he knew why he had kissed Sandra Morray good-bye.

"You're someone to me," he said.

She continued to shake her head sadly. "Something awful. Look, your friend is dead. So many are dead because of what this body did. What can I do to change what has happened?" She sighed again and her sorrow tore at his insides. "I was given life again, but I never got to have a life."

He moved closer to her and put his arm around her. The water was no longer painfully hot. It was as if it had absorbed a portion of the coldness of the thing that had fled her body. She trembled under his touch.

"If I'm like you, then we'll die together," he said. "I don't mind. It's good that we should be together."

She shook her head. "No. You have a life. You came first, while there was still life in my body." Her voice faltered. "I don't want you to die."

There was a mysterious note in her tone. A message. "What is it?"

She touched his cheek, with great effort, then her hand fell back down with a pitiful splash. "I can't tell you," she said, her words barely audible, her breathing strained. It was as if she smothered even with the whole sky above her to breathe. Her back arched in pain and briefly she squeezed her eyes shut. "Don't ask me."

But Peter understood already, partly. It was as if they were connected once more, as in the womb, and communicated with each other without words. "My life is my own," he muttered to himself, repeating her comment, seeking for hidden meaning. "Is it my own to do with what I wish?" He had only an intuitive feeling that what he said was true.

She shook her head, rocking in pain now, crying. "Don't do it."

"Do what, Sara? You must give me the choice." He added, "Tell me, Sandy."

She gasped at the mention of her *other* name, but then managed to speak. "It was something the blind man told me. I didn't know what he meant until now. He said, 'Life is a gift. A gift can be given, a gift can be taken away. Your nature is to take, never to give. But the nature can change. No gift is ever the same. No theft is ever forgotten. When you forget your nature, the thief will run. But in the hidden half the gift will remain to be given for a short time.' " She paused. "Do you understand?"

"I'm not sure," Peter said. *The hidden half? Him?*

"Good. I don't want you to do it." A shudder racked her body. Her skin took on a blue tinge. "Oh, God, this is hard."

He hugged her tighter. "Can I do anything for you?"

"Hold me. Love me." The words seemed to inspire her and she was able to relax a bit. "It's so good to be able to say that to you, Peter."

"I love you. I have always loved you. That's why I kept looking for you all these years. I did it without even knowing what I was looking for."

Even with her pain, she chuckled. "I guess I'm not what you expected."

He smiled. "All's well that ends well." He spoke seriously. "Can I give my life to another?"

She stared at him. He couldn't fully comprehend what memories she saw him through, but he was beginning to get an idea. "I would have been proud," she said.

"You have to tell me."

She nodded reluctantly. "Yes."

"I can give it to Matt?"

"Yes." A fit of coughing caught her. When it was through she slumped exhausted into his arms. He cuddled her as if she were his child. Her voice came out weary but nevertheless passionate. "But don't, please don't. For your mother's sake. Live and be happy. Sandy was happy, I tell you, even if I could not follow her example."

He spoke with feeling. "It's not right that you should go alone."

She looked up at him. Sandra Morray's brain cells must have been on their last gasp. The brain may take five minutes to die, without oxygen, but he realized it must steal consciousness before then. Sara's eyes clouded over, her expression becoming dreamlike.

"Will I be alone when I get there?" she asked. "Maybe my mom will be there. Maybe yours will be there." Her voice sunk lower. "Will I find myself there?"

"You've found yourself already." He took his arm away from her. "Give me a moment."

She managed to reach out and touch him. "Are you sure, Peter?"

"Yes."

"You're young. You're beautiful. This can be a beautiful world."

Peter glanced at Matt. "It has to be this way. We don't belong here."

She nodded weakly. "Perhaps you're right. Do it quickly then. You won't have much time."

He paused. They were skipping an important point. "What do I do?"

Sara's eyes fell shut. "You will know if you know you don't know."

"Sara?" He paused. "Sandy?"

Silence, although she continued to breathe, very softly. She could not help him.

Peter moved to Matt and lifted his friend onto the side of the deck. He closed Matt's eyes and wiped away the blood. For a moment he stared at his friend's face. Even in death Matt's comical expression had not been destroyed.

"Because you're not dead," Peter said to him. "You're only sleeping." He looked up at the sky. "Help me with this one, whoever's up there. I need some help."

As if in response, Sara said something. He whirled but found her still sitting silently with her eyes closed. Yet he could have sworn he heard her speak. Or were their memories once more connected in that strange womb, that mysterious portal, through which a blind man now peered? It came to him, then, what he had to do.

"The breath belongs to the body. It resides inside the body, not outside the body. The breath is more than the air. The breath is close to prana. No prana without breath. But prana is more subtle than the breath. No life without prana. Prana and breath flow in rhythm, but they are also separate. Prana is a gift. Life is a gift."

"A gift can be given," he whispered, repeating the secret phrase. "A gift can be taken away.

Peter drew in a deep breath of the fresh ocean air that blew in from the west. There was a fragrance in the air, a coolness—he thought that perhaps the long heat wave was finally over. The inhalation was invigorating; he felt the strength of it flow through his limbs, past his heart and into his head. Quickly he leaned over, opened Matt's mouth, and exhaled deeply into his friend's lungs. Matt's diaphragm rose once sharply. Peter drew back a bit, feeling a wave of dizziness, and watched as Matt's rib cage rose again and then again. It was a miracle, he thought, it was a right. Soon Matt breathed on his own. Soon he would awaken and learn to live on his own. Peter knew the memory of today would fade for him, in time, and that he would be all right. He patted Matt's hand.

"My boy," he whispered, for now it was all he could manage. "My good boy."

Then Peter returned to Sara's side, his mother's side, and put his arm around her once more. He held her so close that he knew that it was not possible that he would lose her a second time. He closed his eyes and listened as her breathing grew quieter, shallower, and softer, as his own breathing did. Their breathing was like two distant sighs lost in a breeze that had once again crossed the path of the world, the course of this living planet as it made its endless journey through space. Had the wind really come before, thirty years earlier? He couldn't be sure. It was a cold breeze, it was true, like that of winter, yet it carried on its tail a faint stirring of the spring that was to come. Feeling the mysterious current, swimming on it away from his body and down a long dark tunnel, Peter sensed that the time of mankind was soon to change.

It was to be the last thought Peter Jacobs was to have in this world.

EPILOGUE

❋

GOVINDA SHARMA WALKED along the path in the park toward the blond woman who sat alone on a bench watching a group of children playing nearby. Govinda had only just returned to California from India, after a three-year absence. The hydroelectric project at the foot of the Himalayas was finally complete and his company had granted him a special two-month vacation. He had not seen Julie Moore in all that time, although they had talked occasionally on the phone. As always the sight of her stirred deep feelings in him, and he realized, though he tried to pretend otherwise, that he was a little in love with her. He wondered how she felt about him. He had spent several months with her, before her daughter was born, and some time afterward. But their relationship had been platonic, which was fine with him, in those days. And with the coming of Cira, Julie had had so much love to give, and to receive, that he felt they were happy and didn't need him. So he had taken up his old job. But he'd missed Julie and the little girl as well. Cira was such a lovely name, he thought. Perfect for such a lovely child.

Yet he had not forgotten where the name had come from.

Kali Ma. Kalika.

Govinda had also returned to India to be with the Master. But the Master had gone into silence the day Rak left India, in a secret cave back in the mountains. Even Keshava had not spoken to him since. Still, Govinda reassured himself, the Master had promised to come out into the world, into the West even.

The Master had just not said when.

During the time they spent together, Julie had never discussed Peter Jacobs, Cira's father, and Govinda had never pressed her for information on him. The topic had obviously been too painful for her. Govinda still did not understand how Peter had died. He doubted Julie understood.

Govinda raised his hand and waved. "Julie!" he called.

She seemed happy to see him. She kissed him as they hugged.

It had been too long, Govinda thought.

They sat and talked of many things. She was doing well; she looked great. Her therapy practice was growing each month, even though she continued to test children for the state. She had an apartment by the beach, a new car. She wasn't seeing anyone. Between her daughter and her work, she said, she was too busy. But her lack of a social life didn't seem to disturb her. Govinda could only nod and smile. Of course he was relieved she was still available.

Finally he had to ask.

"How is Cira?" he said.

Julie beamed. "Wonderful." She turned her head and raised her voice. "Cira! Come, see your uncle. Come on, baby doll, leave the boys alone."

A tiny dark-haired girl emerged from the tangle of children. She wore a red dress and a red ribbon in her hair. Her eyes were big and dark. She walked straight toward her mother, her expression serious. Julie embraced her with great affection.

"Cira," she said, "this is Govinda Sharma, Mummy's good friend. You don't remember, but Govinda was there the day you were born. Say hello to him."

The tiny girl turned in his direction. He was surprised when she stuck out her hand. There was no fear in this child, he thought. She regarded him curiously with her huge eyes. He offered his own hand.

"Hello, Cira," he said. "It's good to see you again."

"It's good to see you." She glanced at her mother. "I remember him."

Julie laughed. "Sure you do, honey. You can play some more if you want. Or would you like a drink first? It's pretty hot today. I have some lemonade in my bag."

Cira let go of Govinda's hand and shook her head. "I'm not hot," she said.

Julie paused. "That's fine. Play until you get tired. I'll wait for you here."

Cira nodded and, with a final glance at Govinda, hurried back to join the other kids. Govinda rubbed his hand on his pants' leg. The little girl's fingers had been strangely cool; they had left a tingling sensation in his palm. Julie seemed to notice his rubbing and he stopped it.

"She's growing up beautifully," he said.

"Isn't she?"

"You must be proud."

"I am." Julie nodded. "Very proud."

Govinda fanned his face with his hand. "It's funny, I just came from India, and I feel hotter here than I did there." He nodded toward Cira, who was already climbing the ladder of the tall slide, ahead of all the boys and girls. "I wish I had Cira's physiology."

Julie nodded, thoughtful. "Yes. She never gets tired or hot." Julie paused. Or did she shiver as well? Govinda couldn't be sure. But a shadow did seem to cross Julie's face as she added, "It's the way she is."

The story of Rak, Julie's Child, and the Master will continue in:

The Cold One II
Seedling